Strai

Michaelbrent Collings

Written Insomnia Press
WrittenInsomnia.com
"Stories That Keep You Up All Night"

Sign up for Michaelbrent's Minions
And get FREE books.

Sign up for the no-spam newsletter
(affectionately known as Michaelbrent's Minions)
and **you'll get several books FREE**.
Details are at the end of this book.

DEDICATION

To...

Dr. Hoopes, for helping me stay sane(ish),

All my friends at Idaho Pizza (especially since they finally got wifi there),

And to Laura, FTAAE.

Prelude

The man has died twice. He does not know what will happen if he dies a third time.

He suspects he will not like it. Not at all. But he does not know for sure. There are many things he does not know, now, because so much has changed.

He was One.

He now is just one.

"… one?"

The man – the one man, the *lone* man – blinks. "Sorry?"

The woman on the other side of the counter frowns as though the man has committed some vile act. Her name tag says *Jayn,* and the man wonders if Jayn's parents hated her at birth, to spell her name like that.

Jayn sighs, puts her hands on her hips, and says, "Are you at pump number one?"

The man nods, though he is not at all sure if he is. He does not remember where he parked his van, or much of the past few days. He remembers pain.

He remembers seeing himself die, then seeing himself die again.

And if I die a third *time? What happens to me then?*

"You tryin' to hypnotize me?" says Jayn.

"What?" says the man.

"You're staring."

"Oh," says the man. He does not say he is sorry. He did not know he was staring, and if he does a thing in ignorance it cannot be a sin. He does not merit punishment for such an act.

Jayn nods over his shoulder. "There's other people waiting."

Jayn cannot be more than twenty, which the man thinks is too young to have piercings in her nose, lip, and tongue, and he wonders if he should take her to task for this. Then he decides not to as concern spreads itself over her expression. "You need help, mister? You okay?"

The man smiles lopsidedly. He has always smiled this way, even when he was One instead of just *one*. "We all need help, Jayn. That's what we're put here to do: help each other."

He turns away, intending to head back outside to his van. As he does so, he almost smashes into the "other people waiting" to which the sadly-named Jayn referred. A man and a woman crowd close to each other, and close to him. Too close, and they should have stepped back when the man turned toward them.

But apparently it was a shock to them, because the woman snarls, "Watch what you're –"

Her companion puts a hand on her arm. The man notes this, and notes how the hand jitters, even on its short trip to wrap around her bicep. The man notices how the woman's companion squeezes so hard the knuckles brighten and the fingers go pink.

The woman's mouth shuts so quickly there is an audible click in her jaw. She nods. Her nod is just as jittery as her companion's hand.

"Move along, dude," says the woman's companion.

"Move along," she mirrors.

The man nods. He has no desire to stay here.

He turns away, barely noticing as Jayn says, "Gas?" and the woman shakes her head – jittery again – and says, "Pack of Kools."

The man goes out the door to the gas station. A bell over the door *ting-a-ling*s as he exits to face an unfamiliar landscape. He wonders where he is, and wonders if it matters.

When he arrives at the van, he starts pumping gas – he was at pump number one, after all – and tries to ignore the fact that he is already waiting at the pump when he arrives.

No. That is not me. I have always matched, and neither of the mes *waiting at the pump look alike.*

That is true enough. He has always looked like Himself. He has always looked like One, but now – after that last job – he looks Different.

Before the last job, he had had brown eyes, brown hair that receded a bit at the temples. Pale skin. He had been of medium build, but stronger – much stronger – than he looked.

Now… he still has thinning brown hair and brown eyes. He still has the pale skin and he is still strong. But while *he* looks the same as *he* always did, the other Hims do not.

One of Him has bloated, purpling skin, bulging eyes, and a tongue that lolls out of his mouth when he is not speaking. *That* Him still has brown hair and brown eyes, but the hair is permanently wet, plastered down over his brow and dripping down his equally-sopping clothes. When he speaks, water rolls out of his mouth.

The third and last Him has no hair, no skin, and eyes that are simply coal-sparks in the charred remnants of his face. His clothes have been burned away, and soot-stained bone shows through much of what remains of his flesh.

"You'll have to speak to me, you know," says the version of Him that was burned to death in the house where everything changed.

"It makes no sense *not* to speak to me," agrees the one of Him who drowned in the pool behind that same house.

Both the burned Him and the drowned Him have voices almost exactly like his. It is the only thing about all the Hims that still matches – and even then not perfectly, because the drowned corpse's voice bubbles and froths from a throat permanently full of water, and the burned thing's tones rasp and rake through a throat burned to bone and char.

"I can't talk to me. Can't talk to me, because I'm dead," murmurs the man, the lone man, the *one* man who survived.

"Yes. And maybe no," says the burned One. Then, seemingly at random, the burned once-version of Him says, "Do you remember before we were One?"

"Do you remember?" echoes the drowned Him. "When we were *three*?"

The man – the whole man, the right man, the *living* man – shakes his head and bunches his shoulders. He puts the gas pump in the side of his van and squeezes the handle. The gas starts to flow, whooshing through the tube and into his van. It sounds like blood in a vein, like blood pumping out of a slit neck.

"We aren't three," says the man. "We're One. We've always been One."

"We *weren't* always, though," insists the burned Him. "We were born as three."

The man doesn't like this. He puts his free hand over one ear and starts humming the song "Bizarre Love Triangle" by the band New Order. Even as he does so, something inside him screams that this is different, strange, wrong. There has always been something in his head that has kept him from admitting how much he likes music. How much *more* he likes it than his other Selves.

Whatever the reason for his song choice, it does not work. It does not drown the burned man's voice – what was once His voice – which sounds in the living man's head just as loudly as before. "Born as three, but Father never wanted three. So he made us, didn't he? Made us One."

"Made us One," agrees the drowned Him.

"Made us One," echoes the man who still lives. He whimpers. He hates the noise; he cannot remember the last time he made such a sound.

I made it in the Dark Place. The place where Father put us to convince us we were all the same. All One. Not three, not triplets… just a single child, a single boy, a single man.

"But I *like* being One!" he almost wails.

"But we cannot be One. If we ever even were," says the burned man.

The living man throws up. It happens fast and hard – one moment he is pumping gas, the next he is leaning on the front of his van, vomiting on the ground.

He feels a hand on his shoulder. Feels the crackle of scorched flesh as it shatters and flakes apart when it touches him. No blood, though. Whatever blood the charred one once had was boiled away by the fires that killed him.

The man looks at the charred once-Him. The burned and still-burning man looks back "I'm dead," says the burned man. "It's better if you accept that."

Another hand touches the man's shoulder. The flesh *squishes* like it is an over-saturated sponge. "So am I," says the drowned being. "You have to believe it."

"But *I'm* not dead," whispers the man. "And I want to be."

The charred once-Him stares into the living man's eyes. "We are separate now," says the burned man. "We don't match." He licks his teeth before he continues speaking. The teeth are blackened by smoke, the tongue a twisted, scorched twig in his mouth. There are no lips. "We don't match, so we have to be three again."

"How can that be?" whispers the man. "I've been One so long…"

"We'll still be here with you," says the drowned version of himself –

(No, not myself, not me, not me but how can that be how can I NOT BE ME?)

– and the man almost sobs when he hears those words.

"You will be here?" he chokes out. "Forever? For always?"

The drowned man nods. Water runs down his face in a neverending river, like the greatest tears ever shed. "Forever," he says.

"For always," says the burned man.

"But you're…" The man, the one man, the true man, the *living* man struggles to finish the thought. "You're dead."

"Yes," says the burned man.

"But that doesn't mean we won't be with you," says the drowned man. He laughs. Water bubbles out of his mouth in sharp bursts as he does. "In fact, being dead means we'll be closer than ever."

"But not One," says the living man.

"Not One," agrees the burned man. "Just three."

The living man rolls that around in his thoughts. He hasn't been three since… he can't remember how long. He vaguely remembers struggling to be three when he was very young, vaguely remembers himself –

(No, not myself, it was one of the others, one of my brothers, one of the two who died.)

– arguing with Father, telling him there were *three,* there were *three,* he had *three* sons. But even that memory is dark. Veiled by time, shrouded by pain.

Still, he thinks he may be able to remember more. If he tries to. If he wants to.

"You will try," says the burned man.

"You do want to," says the drowned one.

The man looks at the drowned one, who smiles. Water gushes out of his mouth and over his chin as he says, "You should give us names."

The charred man laughs. The lips are gone, but the laugh comes out lively and strong. "Yes, do."

"Names?" says the living man, unsure. The concept is alien.

But is it bad? Is it… wrong*?*

He thinks perhaps it is neither of those things.

"You should call us what we are," says the burned man.

"What is that?" asks the living man.

"You know already," says the drowned man. "We are the two halves. The two parts that you will carry with you. The soft and the hard, the light and the dark."

"Then name yourselves," says the living man.

The burned one nods. "Fine. I am Fire."

"And I," says the drowned one, "am Water."

"And what should I call myself?" says the living one.

Both Fire and Water smile their ruined smiles. Flesh crackles, lungs burble. "What would you *like* to call yourself?"

The man thinks on this. He remembers Father calling him a name. Calling him something as he rained down beatings, as he threw the One –

(the three*)*

– into his room, into his bed. But he cannot remember what the name was.

"Then choose a new one," says the drowned man. Says *Water*.

"You can choose one all for yourself," says the burned man. *Fire*.

That is going too far. The living man is not ready for anything "all for yourself." He may not be One, but he cannot divide himself so readily. Perhaps it is easier for Fire and Water. They are dead, after all, and it is possible that the dead can change with less pain or terror than the living must endure.

But the man – the *one* man – *is* alive. He cannot change so easily. "I don't want to be alone."

"Don't be," says Fire.

"You won't be," says Water.

"I don't want my own name," says the one man.

"Then…" Fire seems unsure what to do with this.

"Then don't have your own name," says Water. He snaps his fingers as though in the middle of some great revelation, and wetness flicks off them into the darkness. "Have many names!"

The living man thinks on this. He nods and, for the first time since two-thirds of him died, he smiles a wide, sincere smile. No water bubbles out. No flakes of charred flesh drift downward. He is alive. And he has his name. "I am Legion," he says.

Hands clap down on his shoulders, his brothers embracing him tightly. The wet hands and arms leave no moisture on his skin or clothes, though, just as the burnt ones leave no stains of soot.

Neither is real. They're both dead, and I…

Am I crazy? Am I insane?

Legion does not know the answers to these questions. He realizes he does not much care about them, either. All that matters here, now, is that he is not alone. His not-selves – his *brothers* – are dead. But they are still with him. They are together now, and together they will forever remain.

"That is true," says Fire.

"That is right," says Water.

"We…" Legion begins to speak, but his voice catches on that oh-so-unfamiliar word. He swallows dryly, then tries again. "We should get moving."

"That's true," says Water. He still has his arm over Legion's shoulder. That wet arm squeezes Legion and again leaves no moisture behind. "We may be three, but we still have things to do!"

"Do we?" says Legion. He wonders, abruptly, if he *does* have anything to do. He used to – he traveled from place to place, finding people who needed correction and teaching them, refining them, purging them of their imperfections.

But wasn't that a job he did as One?

"Yes," says Fire matter-of-factly. He is angry, even in death, and his coal-eyes blaze with fervor. "You did it when we were One, but the job still needs doing. The guilty still need teaching. The unrepentant still need instruction." He nods over Legion's shoulder. "And unless I miss my guess, we have work to do right now."

Legion looks in the direction Fire has indicated. He knows what he will see, because he heard the scream even as Fire spoke the words.

He sees the gas station convenience store. The poorly-spelled Jayn standing at her previous spot, only her hands are not on her hips and her expression is no longer one of bored derision. Now the hands are held high, her expression manifests only terror.

The man and woman who crowded behind Legion are both pointing guns at Jayn. Even at this distance Legion can see that Jayn is now biting her lip to keep from screaming again. He wonders, even as he runs toward the gas station, if biting your lip hurts when you have a lip ring. It isn't important, he knows, but life is full of these delightful mysteries.

He moves quickly. He does not know if he was *born* fast, but he certainly had to become that way. He was born as one of three, he is starting to understand, and had to be

One under the insane urging of his father. Three who become One must be quick of necessity.

He is quick now. Quicker than he looks, stronger than he looks. Borne on the wings of righteous need, and at the burned/drowned urging of the dead.

"Faster," whispers Fire, his breath hot and dry.

"Faster," whispers Water, his voice frothing and wet.

Legion reaches the front door to the gas station store at the same time that the twitchy woman apparently remembers they might not be alone. She turns her gun and shouts in surprise and fear when she sees Legion open the door to the merry tinkling of the bell over its frame.

Legion wonders if now, in the final moments of her life, she is also seeing the dead. If she sees not just him, but Fire and Water.

"She sees," hisses Fire.

"She knows," bubbles Water.

Legion is fast. He is strong. He is also *smart*. So he takes in the geography of the moment. He sees Jayn, terrified. He sees the robbers, and notes the trembling in their limbs that he knows in his core means they are not just robbing the place, but robbing it to supply a pair of serious drug habits.

All this in an instant. All this in the time it takes for the woman to swing toward him. He sees it all, and sees her finger whiten against the trigger. He sees, he knows –

("You know what to do," both Fire and Water say at the same time.)

– just as he sees where she is standing, and how in spite of her trembling she has the gun pointed right at his head. And he sees also how to make all those things work for him.

Legion sidesteps. He hunches slightly as he does, knowing that the woman will continue following the path of his head. Knowing that she will not be able to stop herself from pulling the trigger.

She tracks his head.

She fires the gun.

The bullet does not hit Legion's head. He knew it wouldn't, because he knew when he slid to the side that the woman was standing on the far side of her companion, and Legion knew that his movements would line up precisely at the right time. He knew she would fire, and that her drug-addled mind will not be able to stop the trigger from pulling even as she realizes that there is something between her and Legion.

The something is her fellow-robber's head.

The bullet ricochets through brain and bone which deflects the projectile away from Legion, just as he knew it would.

Jayn drops behind the counter, using the moment to take shelter. The surviving robber screams as her partner sags onto her.

The robber who has been shot in the head does not scream. Nor does he appear to stand with Fire and Water. He is dead, but not a ghost. He has learned his lesson, so perhaps there is no need for him to exist as a spirit, or to do anything else but cough up a great gout of blood through what remains of his head and sag bonelessly back into his shrieking partner.

Legion keeps moving, turning his sidestepping slide into a quick forward lunge that has him standing in front of the remaining robber. Her gun arm got pinned against her chest when her partner fell. But she has it free now, free and she is still screaming as she brings the gun around in a short arc, bringing it quickly to bear on Legion once again.

Legion drops to one knee as the gun goes off. He feels the air heat in a line along his back. He does not think the bullet hit him, or even grazed him. But it was close.

The woman fires again as Legion continues his motion. He pushes off his back leg, rolling forward. The second bullet passes above him again, a bit wide as well as panic creates a strange warping of gravity. The bullet whines a high-pitched ricochet off the cement floor behind him.

Legion completes his roll. And something clicks in his head. He knows what to do. Because Fire is the angry one. Water is the kind one. And Legion… he is – and always has been – the one who knows how to *fight*.

He catches the woman's gun hand above the wrist. He strips the gun away from her in a single, swift motion. The woman shrieks as three of her fingers break, bent so far that the nails scrape against the back of her hand.

The fourth finger does not just break. It is caught in the trigger guard of the gun, and it tears most of the way from her hand, dangling by a thin twist of skin and tendon.

The woman screams, and clutches her ruined hand to her breast for a moment. Then, still screaming, she tries to push the fingers back into place. She grinds the mostly-disembodied finger against the stump it came from, like a child trying to jam a broken toy together.

The finger, unhappy at this final insult, gives up its tenuous hold to the rest of the hand. The woman drops it and it rolls away, disappearing under a display that holds Hostess snack cakes.

The woman looks from her hand to the dead man on the floor in front of her, to the blood and brains that have spattered her clothing and skin. She screams and Legion sees in that instant that her finger is not the only thing she has lost. Whatever small grip she had on sanity before coming in this place has let go. Her scream rises in volume and pitch. She leans away, and Legion does not know if she is going to fall, or flee, or is simply rearing back as preparation to attack.

"It doesn't matter," shouts Fire. "She tried to kill that woman! She tried to kill *you!*"

"She's suffering," says Water, his voice low and burbling like a stream in a peaceful glade.

Neither person asks a question. Legion has an answer for their observations, all the same.

He reaches out and stops the woman's screaming. He does not think, just *does*. Perhaps it is because her mouth is where the noise is coming from. Perhaps it is just an easy target, open so very wide as it is.

Whatever the reason, Legion's hand darts forward. He gets three fingers hooked over her bottom teeth and he jerks down as hard as he can.

Legion is of normal build. He is of *ab*normal strength.

The woman's front teeth collapse inward under the sudden downward force. Legion feels a wash of warmth that may be spittle or blood. In the next moment he feels twin pops as the would-be robber's jaw unhinges on both sides.

The woman tries to keep screaming, which he can respect. But it is hard for her given that her lower jaw – to which he still holds tightly – now drags against her breastbone. Her tongue waggles over Legion's hand. He finds it obscene, so he puts the gun which he still holds in his other hand against her open left eye and pulls the trigger.

The woman stops screaming.

"There," whispers Fire. "Now don't you feel better?"

"I do," says Legion.

"I knew you would," says Water brightly.

Legion puts the gun in his pocket – waste not, want not! – and leaves the small store. He goes to his van, noting the twin rectangles on the front bumper as he approaches. They mark where twin bumperstickers used to ride the chrome. One said, "Honk if you love Jesus;" the other, "Honk if you love Satan." He bought them when he was One, all of then-Him amused at the irony of announcing numerous forms of divine reckoning as he drove – and more amused that even though he put them in front, so anyone could see him coming, no one would. Because people so very rarely looked back to see if their sins still followed them.

Now the bumper stickers are gone, leaving behind bright spots on the front bumper surrounded by flecks of road-dust and bits of rust. He ripped the stickers off after his last work went awry. The people he intended to punish *did* suffer – some died, and some survived, which is sometimes an even greater punishment than dying – but his Oneness ended.

Legion had begun that job – that *lesson*, for so he had been taught to think of his work – as One. The three of Himselves had found a family steeped in sin and hypocrisy, and had trapped them in their home and shown to them the nature and result of their secrets and their sins. It was something he had done many times before, but this time the family turned out to be more than Legion or his then-Selves had expected. The family had proved resourceful, and had burned the One who is now Fire, and drowned the One who now calls himself Water.

Of all the One, only Legion remains, alive and alone.

"Not alone," says Water. His eyes, wet and bloated, glance over Legion's shoulders. "Better take care of that."

Legion knows what Water is talking about. He is not done here. He walks back to the gas station convenience store. He enters. The bell *ting-a-ling*s.

Jayn is still curled on the floor behind the counter where she earlier threw herself. She screams as she hears the counter creak as Legion leans over to look at her.

"It's all right," he says. "They're gone."

"Gone?" she whisper-whimpers.

"Gone. Good and gone and never again will they bother you or anyone." He laughs a bit at that, though he is not sure why.

"Because you're happy," says Water. "And there is no sin in that."

"True," says Legion. Then to Jayn he says, "Do you have a security camera?"

She nods automatically. He sees something flash in her eyes and wonders if she debated lying to him. Just as well she didn't. He would have known. He can always spot a lie.

"I need you to show me where the recording security devices are."

"Why? You saved me. You're a hero."

"Maybe, but I'd rather not be involved."

Jayn nods. She starts to get up, but Legion holds out a hand. "You might want to face away when you stand up," he says.

She doesn't answer for a moment. Again he sees a flash. There is rebellion in this girl. He would have seen that now, even if he hadn't already spotted it in her piercings or her attitude earlier.

He considers that rebellion. Worthy of punishment?

No.

Jayn nods at last. She stands, turning away from the store as she does. She does not see what lays in broken bits on the floor beyond her counter.

"It's over here," she whispers, pointing at a door a few feet away.

Legion gestures at the door. "After you."

Again, Jayn considers saying something. Again, she thinks better of it. Again, this probably saves her life.

She opens the door with a key from her pocket. She goes into a small office that holds little more than a desk, a small computer, and an air of suffocating desperation.

A monitor also sits on the desk. Jayn gasps as she sees the video feed from the store. The monitor is small and black and white, but it is enough to show clearly the figures of the robbers, broken in pieces and floating in blood on the floor of the convenience store.

"Why…" She does not finish whatever she was going to say. Just as well.

Legion looks at the monitor. He doesn't know it specifically, but he does know a lot about electronics and communications equipment. He learned it for his work, for his lessons. He knows, therefore, that this monitor is hooked not to a video recorder or a DVD burner, but to a solid state device that digitally records the surveillance video feed in case it is needed later.

Jayn stares dumbly at the monitor as Legion follows a small wire from the side of the monitor to a much smaller box on the floor beside the desk. He yanks the box away, pocketing it. He will destroy it – and the video evidence of his presence – later.

He turns to Jayn. He smiles, hoping she will see the smile for what it is: friendly, hopeful, and honest. Honest above all.

"Jayn, I stopped two people from killing you, and was glad to do it. They deserved it, I think. In return, I'm taking this." He patted the pocket with the recording device. "I'd also like you to sit in here and wait a few minutes before calling anyone. Not long." Legion gestures at the monitor. It may not be recording anything, but it still shows the store, and a timestamp still displays in the corner. Legion points at that timestamp. "I would like you to wait ten minutes. Longer if you can, but I'll understand if that's all you can manage. Can you do that for me?"

He waits, but Jayn is staring at the violent tableau on the monitor. Two dead people, variously maimed.

"Jayn?" Legion says softly. When she still does not respond, he reaches out and places a hand against her cheek. He pushes gently, guiding her gaze to his eyes.

"Be kind," says Water.

"But firm," says Fire.

"Of course," Legion says to both.

"What?" says Jayn. She looks confused.

Legion debates for a moment. He thinks about telling her of his once-Oneness, his new separation. He decides to stay on point.

"Jayn, apart from the piercings, you haven't done anything really wrong that I can see. So I'm going to leave you alone. I'm going to drive away, and I'm going to let you call the police. But I'd like ten minutes before you call. You can tell the police you were in shock if they ask – or, even better, the truth."

"What truth?" Jayn asks in a querulous voice.

"That the man who saved you said he would take you away if he thought you would call before ten minutes were up. That he would know, and would carry you away, and would punish you for trying to keep a secret from him." He leans in close. Jayn smells like spearmint and sweat. "Tell them that if you didn't wait, you'd be dead, too. Only it wouldn't be quick or easy, like it was for the two who tried to rob you."

Jayn's eyes flicker to the display. To the bodies. He can see the thought in her eyes: *That's quick and easy?*

Legion waits until her gaze returns to his, then says, "All right?"

She nods.

He waits.

She nods again.

"She's telling the truth," says Water.

"I think so, too," says Fire. He sounds a bit disappointed, like he hoped Jayn would try to lie.

"I think she is," agrees Legion. He leans toward Jayn. She flinches, but he is not trying to hurt her. He kisses her forehead instead. "Please remember that it was your own good choices that saved you tonight."

He leaves. Or starts to. At the last moment he turns and says, "You should think about taking out all the piercings. You're prettier without them, and they don't send a very wholesome message."

As he turns away, Jayn is already fumbling at the stud on her nose. Legion smiles.

He goes to his van. When he gets in, Fire and Water are both already inside.

Legion turns the key in the ignition. The van roars to life but he does not begin to drive. He sits a moment, then says, "It's all changing."

"How so?" says Fire. Though Legion suspects that the burned man knows the answer already.

"Our Oneness," says Water. He lays a cold, clammy arm across his brother's shoulder.

"That," nods Legion. "But more. We – *I* – never punished someone so quickly before. I looked for sins, but also for secrets. Only those with both were ever the focus of my studies."

"Different now," agrees Fire. "And is that a bad thing?"

"You saved the girl, you helped two wayward people learn the error of their ways," says Water contemplatively. "And you also encouraged her to take out those ghastly piercings."

"I'd say it was a good day," says Fire.

Legion nods. "A good day," he muses. "A different day."

"But," begins Fire.

"… different…" continues Water.

"… is good," finishes Legion.

He puts the car into drive.

He pulls away from the gas station, out into the street. Ten minutes is more than enough to get away from here, to lose himself in whatever place he has come to.

He begins to sing "No I In Threesome" by the band Interpol. A moment later, Fire and Water begin singing as well, and they harmonize their way into the rest of the night.

1

Danielle had always hated her last name. She loved it now, because now she had a new one. Still, it was jarring to hear herself referred to as "Mrs. Anton" – particularly only three days into her new life – a new life as a married woman and, more importantly, a life that signaled she had started a family. Not babies – her husband had thought they would benefit by time alone, time spent devoted to one another without the pressure of one more human in the relationship – but a unit far removed from the one which she had first known.

For a moment, she saw her mother's eyes. Then she saw her brother's.

She never could tell which was worse.

"Mrs. Anton? Earth to Mrs. Anton? The Office of the Public Defender and the Great State of California calling Ms. Aaaaantonnnnnn?"

"Would you *please* stop calling me that, Leroy?"

She could almost hear her paralegal's good-natured smirk through the phone. "Sorry, but the proper papers have been filed, the courts have been notified. It now says 'Danielle Anton, Office of the State Public Defender' on the office letterhead. You're officially screwed." His aural smirk deepened. "How *is* that going, by the way?"

"None of your business."

Leroy sighed. "You know it's jealousy speaking. Of the two of us, I deserve to be the 'Mrs. Anton.' But alas, I, a lowly, gay, stunningly gorgeous paralegal, could never exhibit the irresistable sex appeal of a public defender on the fast track."

Danielle tried to stifle the laugh that came, but only managed to turn it into a weird cross between an elephant trumpet and a shotgun blast. "Well," she said, "of the two of us you're definitely the better-groomed one. So there's that going for you."

"I *knew* it," crowed Leroy. "I *knew* you'd go see Pierre. He's magic, isn't he? Best wax-and-lash guy I've ever met. I bet you look gorgeous."

Danielle laughed as he pronounced "gorgeous" as "*goah*-jus."

"I have the eyebrows of a supermodel," she agreed.

"Welcome to the club, dear. Now if only you had my fashion sense." Leroy sighed dramatically. *Everything* about Leroy was dramatic, from the way he spoke to the pictures on his desk – he'd been to every Disney theme park in the world, and he had the pictures with Mickey (most of which featured a man in a Mickey suit who was hopefully blissfully unaware of the borderline obscene facial expressions that Leroy inevitably wore when posing) to prove it. "At any rate, what do you want me to do about McDonnel?"

Danielle sighed. "Shoot him?"

A matching sigh from Leroy. "Alas, a mild tasing is all we lowly public defender paralegals can afford."

"Then do that."

"Body part preference?"

"Anything below the belt." They both laughed again, then Danielle frowned. The expression felt sadly at home, and she hoped she wouldn't end up with frown lines only a year or two into her new marriage. "Go ahead and ready the papers I prepared for filing. Were they accurate?"

"One hundred percent." Leroy's smirk-sound turned into an equally audible frown. McDonnel was the counsel from the prosecutor's office who was dealing with the case currently eating up Danielle's time, and he was a misogynist, homophobic, ageist, racist jackass who managed to be constantly patronizing and demeaning without doing anything *quite* worthy of dismissal or even reprimand from the D.A. "The guy filed exactly the evidence you suspected he'd been pocketing, and waited *way* too long to do it. I know you'll want to read the letters McDonnel sat on before filing, but I doubt you'll have to change a word of your brief." A hopeful note: "Think we can get him into trouble for unethical practices?"

"Doubtful. You know how hard that is." Another sigh. "Email me the letters, okay?"

"Already winging their way to your inbox." Leroy paused, then said, hopefully, "I *could* ask someone else in the office to verify before filing; have them file the papers under your signature so as not to bother you during your extravagant five day bang-fest."

Danielle stifled another laugh, then subbed in another sigh. "I don't want to put anyone else in McDonnel's cross-hairs."

"Will *Mr.* Anton be okay with you reviewing evidence and case files on day three of the honeymoon?"

"He knew what he was getting into."

And that was true enough. That was one of the things that seemed so perfect about her new husband. Danielle had never thought of herself as a swept-off-her-feet kind of girl, but the minute Alex showed up everything seemed so *perfect.* He had loved that she defended people, he had loved her job. Her job seemed to love *her* more with him in it. She had had her nose to the grindstone for years, doing everything to see that her clients got a fair shake in a sometimes unfair system. She had spent hundreds of hours in prisons interviewing the accused on everything from purse snatching charges to grand larceny, learning as much about what they were accused of and how to combat the charges as she could. She had been at the office on nights when the rest of the nine-to-fivers were long gone, and on weekends and holidays.

It hadn't seemed to matter. No matter what she did, no matter how hard she worked on understanding law and crime to the point some of the other young attorneys joked that she was probably on police "person of interest" lists as someone with the technical know-how to commit any crime large or small… none of her legal and factual expertise seemed to make a difference in a bureacracy that sometimes seemed like "stagnation" was its motto, vision statement, and ultimate end.

Then Alex arrived. No fanfare announced him in her life. He was just another office worker stopping at the same Starbucks day in and day out. When he approached her she geared up for the usual. She was driven –

(Thanks to Jakey, thanks to my brother and thanks to my mother.)

– she was smart. But men didn't approach her for that. They approached her because she was *beautiful*. Danielle knew better than anyone how little beauty mattered, and anyone who approached her on that basis got little consideration and even less patience from her.

But Alex didn't cast any of the usual lines. He just handed her a cup of coffee.

"I already have one."

"You look like you needed an extra one today," he said, then winked and walked out without another word.

They were married two months later.

Leroy laughed, bringing her back to the present. "If you're sure lover-boy won't be jealous of your job I'll send the papers over," he said. Then, in an unusually restrained voice, he added, "What do you think is going to happen?"

Danielle shook her head. "I think that our client is black, has been in and out of jail, and definitely does *not* have the magical Monsieur Pierre grooming him. He's going to get five years, easy."

"Even though this time he actually didn't do it," said Leroy.

"And he didn't try to escape, either – the dumbshit officer failed to properly secure one illegally arrested black man, then added attempted escape to his 'crimes' when he found him sitting there with the cuffs on his lap in the back of the police cruiser."

"I know," said Leroy dryly. "I'm on the case with you, remember."

Danielle sighed. "I know, it just… it bugs me. How does the prosecutor sleep at night?"

"Alone."

She shook her head. "That's unfair, I guess. I know prosecutors are supposed to be the enemy, but some of them are okay people."

"Uh-uh," Leroy disagreed. "*No* lawyers – other than you, oh companion of my soul – are actually people. And opposing counsel on this one is an ass of the lowest kind."

Danielle had to agree. Her client, Antoine Lewis, had been discovered in the back of the police cruiser wearing only boxers, which made sense given how he had been yanked out of bed in the middle of the night and dragged off for a robbery he didn't commit. Danielle had pointed out this fact to the prosecutors office, knowing full well that escaping police cuffs without a key or at least some kind of wire was impossible. "And since Mr. Lewis didn't have any such thing on him, and no such thing was found during a top to bottom search of the cruiser, it was clearly the fault of our esteemed police officer."

Assistant District Attorney Rudy McDonnell's response: "He ate it or shoved it up his ass or –"

"You know that's not possible, McD –"

"My job isn't about what's *possible*, princess, or even what's *true*. It's about what I can get a jury to *believe*. And I can get them to believe this guy scammed Eskimos into buying ice." Then he hung up and that was that.

Danielle had graduated in the top one percent of her law class at UCLA, which meant she could have worked pretty much anywhere. Three dozen or so private firms actively courted her during and after her schooling. She turned them down, opting to work for the California public defender's office, making maybe a quarter of what she could have been pulling in anywhere else.

That was fine. Criminal defense was the area of law she focused on, and the *only* field she'd ever wanted to work in. But unlike a lot of new public defenders, she was hardly a zealot or an idealist. She knew and accepted that a lot of her clients *were* guilty, and though she represented them to the best of her ability, she did not lose sleep when they got put away for exactly what they'd done.

This one, though… he was one of the good ones. So many people made bad choices because they wanted a permanent life on Easy Street, and so many more tried to get back there again even when they'd found that Easy Street was usually a straight line to prison.

Antoine Lewis had tried to get to Easy Street. But he'd wised up inside a cell. He had spent half his life in a gang, but once he got out he cut ties with them, he did his best to start over and play by the rules and do it *right*.

But he still had a past. He had done in his teen years exactly what he was now accused of once more, and the fact was that he belonged to the wrong socioeconomic level to get a truly fair shake regardless of his criminal history. It burned her, to see the injustice, and that was why she had told Leroy to call her regularly with updates. She was on her honeymoon, sure… but an innocent man's freedom was at stake. She couldn't just put that aside for a week.

Alex had understood when she told him there was a good chance it would be a working honeymoon. He had seemed a little irritated for a moment, but that was understandable. Still, that night at dinner – takeout, since neither of them cooked much – he put down his chopsticks, stared hard at her, and said, "I've been thinking."

"Never a good thing in a fiancé, and an even worse thing in a husband."

He smiled. He wasn't snarky like Leroy, but he had a quick, dry, sarcastic wit she loved even more. "I'm stopping soon, I assure you. Turning over all my thinking to those who are better qualified."

She batted her eyes. "Whoever might that be?"

"The shareholders of Alex Anton, Inc., have spoken: the new CEO, CFO, COO, and the entire Board is to be composed of the unique, intelligent, kind, and eminently gorgeous Ms. Danielle Smith."

She smiled and almost laughed, but something about his expression quieted her. Internally, though, she was screaming.

This is it. He's breaking it off. He's too good for me. Always was. He –

"I think there's enough of you to share for a few minutes on the honeymoon. Since I'm going to be turning over the paying of the bills, the handling of the investments, and pretty much everything else that doesn't involve me basking in the sun and sipping expensive drinks to you, well… I guess you can have this one." He grinned, and his eyes said "it's fine" and she smiled back and her eyes said "I love you."

"In fact," he continued. "If we need to put off the wedding a few days… I know the case is heating up, and we're just doing a civil ceremony, so I can always just work late for a few extra days to bury my sorrow and –"

"No," she said. "There'll always be a case I don't want to miss. There'll always be people who need help." She smiled at him, and put every moment of her life into that smile. She tried to tell him, in an instant, how much she needed him to face every moment that came next. "But if I don't get married to you – soon – I won't be able to help them as well as I want to or as well as I deserve."

"You saying I complete you?" he asked. He asked that a lot, ever since their third date when he discovered (to his dismay) that she abhorred the similar line in the movie *Jerry Maguire.*

She shook her head. "No. I'd never say something so ridiculously trite. But I *will* say that I don't want to wait a single second past ten a.m. on Tuesday morning to be your wife."

Alex hesitated. Looked like he was going to disagree. Then he nodded. "Can you keep up with what's happening while we're on the honeymoon?"

Danielle smiled lopsidedly. This was what she had been planning on telling him before he jumped the gun on her. "I had asked Leroy…"

"To email you as things happen in the case?" Off her nod, Alex said, "Good. That's the right thing to do."

"I love you, you know."

"As you should. You are a woman of great taste." He pointed at her plate. "Even if you *do* like China Wall's sesame chicken."

She kissed him, sesame chicken breath and all.

And now he was her husband and she was his wife.

"Okay, I'll look for your email," said Leroy, drawing her back to the present.

"If there are any changes –"

"I know, I know. You'll email them to me and messenger a signature page. But there won't be changes, because you are brilliant and almost as good a lawyer as Pierre is a waxer."

Danielle laughed. "Let's hope so. I'm not sure I can even find someone who could get a signature page over that fast."

"How *is* the ass-end of the universe?"

"It's not the ass-end of the universe."

"No, by my calculation you should only be about halfway there. Have you reached Salt Lake City? Are you a Mormon yet?"

"No, but I'm considering it. Utah is cleaner than L.A., at least."

A final, overblown sigh of exasperation from the cell. "You should have gone to Disneyland. Could have stayed at the hotel and been close enough to commute to work during the honeymoon."

"Alex loves Yellowstone. Besides, we stopped at Vegas. You like Vegas, Leroy."

"Tacky. And I bet you didn't see a single show worth seeing." He snickered. "At least, no show that anyone could get tickets for. Just you and –"

"Gotta-go-email-me-the-papers-bye!" She shouted the sentence all as one word, and as she ended the call she could still hear Leroy laughing.

"Do I have to be jealous?" asked Alex.

Danielle jumped, giving a small scream. She hadn't heard him walk up. She turned and saw another new thing. She had known she would be Mrs. Anton, but had not known that came with a husband who loved to down Dr. Pepper on road trips, and as a result also had to stop off at pretty much every gas station or convenience store they saw from the freeway. The plan had been to get married Tuesday, go to Vegas, then travel to Yellowstone and spend a few days there before traveling back home on the same path. Now Danielle wasn't sure if that was a doable plan given how often they had to stop for pee breaks – which she had started referring to as "Empty out your cup for a refill" stops.

Sure enough, Alex was holding a transparent plastic cup with "EXTREME EXTRA EXTRA LARGE" written in blue across the side of it, the dark liquid inside already a third gone.

"I think *I'm* the one who should be jealous," said Danielle. "Is Dr. Pepper a woman?"

Alex shook his head. "He is a large man with nose and ear hair you could braid."

"How large?"

"Three hundred pounds. Which is a hundred pounds outside my acceptable range for men, even given the added bonus of the ear-and-nose-hair thing."

"Yuck!" Danielle laughed.

"Beauty is in the eye of the beholder," said Alex.

"And I'm glad of that," Danielle said, and kissed him.

"Besides," said Alex when they came up for air, "I know my wife is a criminal mastermind masquerading as a defense attorney, so I've taken extra care to hide all my mistresses."

"Yuck!" she shouted, wrinkling her nose before kissing him again.

They separated, Alex leaving one more small kiss on the tip of her nose before he said, "Besides, you can hardly complain about my dalliances with Dr. P. when you yourself hold a large place in your heart for..." He produced something from behind his back.

She gaped at the Cadbury egg in his hand. "Where did you get that?"

He shrugged and actually blushed. "Well, you love them, so –"

"But they're only out around Easter. It's *June*, Alex."

The blush deepened. "I bought a couple of them off the internet. For the road trip. And to soften the blow of your inescapable competition with Dr. P. –

"And the mistresses!"

"– yes, and the mistresses – for the deepest, most profound depths of my heart."

She laughed. She kissed him. He kissed her back. They headed to the car, laughing still – then laughing harder as she tore the foil wrapping off the chocolate egg and put the whole thing in her mouth and ate it with such ferocity and glee that her eyes watered.

That was what she told Alex: her eyes watered. But she knew it wasn't that she had put the entire treat in her mouth at once. She could tell that Alex knew it, too.

He didn't say anything. He just got in the car with her, then held her hand so tightly it ached and let her cry until she was done.

She needed to cry. She needed to shed those tears over the life she had had – not tears of sadness that they were gone, but tears of joy that they were over, finally and fully and forever.

He held her hand. They drove.

And neither she nor Alex noticed the nondescript gray car that had been parked several spaces over from them at the convenience store, or the fact that it pulled out shortly after they did, and followed them as they drove up the I-15 toward the hotel they would never see.

2

Sheldon Steward loved his work. Always. But sometimes he did not like the *timing* of his work.

Take yesterday, for example. He had reached a particularly beautiful moment in the trimming of his bonsai tree, and wished only to enjoy that moment, to savor it. He had been watching the new growth on the tiny tree for days, waiting to truly see its shape, and so also to truly see whether that shape would mar or further perfect the miracle of the tree. After three days, he decided in favor of pruning the new growth. He had pinched off the leaves with his thumb and forefinger, crushing them carefully to train the plant in the way it should go then putting a wire around the miniscule trunk to bind it and train it further.

He followed the crushing and binding with several tiny cuts with equally tiny shears. Then he leaned back in the creaky office chair he used whenever engaging in the near-ritualistic pruning and training of the tree. The chair shrieked as it always did, and as always Sheldon thought that he should oil the chair – knowing all the while that he never would.

His life was perfect. The chair was part of his life. Therefore, the chair was perfect.

The tree sat, a tiny miracle of beauty in the bright sunlight that streamed in through the nearby window. Sheldon reflected on the first time he had seen such a thing. He had been at Zhang Yong's home in New York, watching the man carefully move leaves, twist wire, cut shoots. Watching as he created a living thing that was somehow more alive for the cutting and twisting and tying. Sheldon almost wept to see it.

That was why he spent extra time torturing Zhang. The man was capable of such beauty, and did not he also deserve to be bound and wired and cut and trained to a state of exquisite, bloody perfection? And when he finally cut the man's throat at the end of two very enjoyable days, Sheldon let him slump over the very tree he had been working with. The red blood flowed across the greenery of the tree and somehow managed to make it more beautiful still.

Sheldon *did* have instructions to torture Zhang before killing him, but the orders had explicitly required he break the man's bones and use fire as much as possible. Sheldon had never refused a job, and never before had he fudged the orders. But this time – this one time – he did.

Zhang was already dead, and as Sheldon staged a pre-death scene involving blunt force trauma and third-degree burns, he was surprised to find that torturing a man was much *harder* with a dead body. Not just making sure there were livid bruises around the bones of the hands, wrists, and arms as Sheldon broke them one at a time with the claw hammer he had brought for the purpose. Not just the burning with small propane torches that seared off the man's fingers and toes, then his nose, lips, tongue, and genitalia.

No, the hardest thing was just the fact that he *was* doing it after the man had already died. Because Sheldon *loved his job.* Not just the money it provided, or the knowledge that he had the power of life and death in his hands, but the way his targets' eyes glistened with tears as he removed everything they had thought of as their most intimate secrets. The way they wept, the particular pattern of snot under each one's nose – the ones whose noses remained that far into the process – the unique trails of blood each one left as a testament to Sheldon's care and attention.

Breaking and burning a dead man… it just wasn't the same. The *soul* of the event wasn't near-mystical, it was just butchery.

Even so, Sheldon had done it. He had suffered the indignity of faking a murder/torture scene, and the greater indignity of lying about a job that he knew full well he could have done better than anyone else. He had abased himself by taking money he really hadn't earned – though he did salve this last by giving the money to several preachers on the television and giving five dollars of it to a homeless person he saw later that same day.

He had done it. He had suffered and given his all for Zhang, because how could he do less for the man who had changed his life?

Now, Sheldon looked at the tree – the first one he had completed since taking the online course on bonsai pruning – and said a small prayer to Zhang. He did not believe in God, not really, but he thought it only appropriate. Then, proper respect paid, he cracked his back and sat back to look at the rest of his office.

Like everything else around and about Sheldon, it was perfect. It was the office of an intelligent, discerning, and thoroughly manly man. Brown leather books sat on mahogany shelves, bracketed by dark marble bookends. The books were written by real men – men likeEarnest Hemingway and Lord Byron and Hunter S. Thompson, who were all people recognized by online sources as being very masculine literary figures. Sheldon had not read any of the books yet, but he knew he did not have to. He had seen some of the movies made from their works, and had watched trailers of many more of them on YouTube, and that was enough to understand the works themselves.

Sheldon was insightful like that.

Other than the books, pictures of nudes adorned the walls. Nothing trashy – Sheldon wasn't a pervert – these were tasteful things he had bought from high-end galleries. His favorite was the woman who hung upside down from a pair of hooks inserted through her bloody feet. Titled "Cristus Invertus," it was just the kind of image that Sheldon liked best.

Second-best.

The tree was first. Now it was perfect, so it was first in Sheldon's heart. He would muse upon it, he thought, and perhaps even write a poem. He had never written a poem, but he knew that he would be good at it should he decide to try one. He was good at everything he tried. Talent was a fact of his life.

Properly relaxed and in tune with his surroundings, he turned back to the tree, wondering if he would keep it as it was or burn it, perhaps breaking it to pieces first. Probably the latter. Perfection was never quite so beautiful as it was in the final instant before being destroyed.

Sheldon's phone rang. His *special* phone. The other one was one he used for normal events – booking theater tickets to the hottest shows; purchasing tickets for wine-tasting retreats; or the occasional reservation to Per Se, which Sheldon favored because tripsavvy.com had assured him it was one of New York City's finest dining establishments.

But his special phone had one purpose, and one purpose only. He picked it up and waited. He never said anything. That was not how it worked.

The man on the other end of the phone spoke. That was unusual, because usually the voice on this line was a computer-simulation that sounded a lot like Stephen Hawking's voice, which Sheldon had heard once on an episode of *The Simpsons*. But this time it was the voice of one of two actual people with whom Sheldon had created enough of a relationship to entrust him with the number. One was his beloved, thoroughly angelic and sometimes bloodthirsty mother. The other was the man speaking to him now.

"One. Three. Zero. One. Four…" The man reeled off another dozen digits. Sheldon hung up the phone. He turned on his computer and went to Portobello Road, the dark web site where he booked his jobs. The digits he had been provided were an access code which, when combined with his own password, allowed him to see the details of the assignment. A double-blind technique that kept anyone from either overhearing details of the job or being able to crack one or the other of the men planning it.

Well, involved *in it.* I'm *the only one* planning *it.*

True enough. The man on the phone had many talents, which was no surprise given his background, but he was not nearly as skilled at the sister arts of kidnapping and torture as Sheldon was. It was one of the man's real flaws.

This job looked simple enough. Names, photos. A set of work and home addresses. And, of course (and most important) a verification that his price had been paid. Good relationship or not, Sheldon insisted on payment for every job he did. "If you're good at something, get paid for it," Mother always said. And she would know.

Indeed, Sheldon took care not only to get paid, but *how* he got paid. That was why he turned to a second computer, opened a very special browser that went to a secured server in Asia, which in turn encrypted all web access. Anyone trying to hack into Sheldon's web history would see only gibberish.

Sheldon accessed the Cayman Islands bank that received transfers of this type. The funds were there. The extra charge for delivery was also there.

Sheldon disliked delivery jobs. He liked to do what had to be done in solitude. But he would bring dead bodies as proof, or live bodies so that his clients could enjoy watching Sheldon work on them. It cost extra, though.

After logging off the second computer, Sheldon returned to the Portobello Road site and entered a single word on the dialogue screen that waited for him. "Time?"

The screen blinked. A date and time appeared. Sheldon had two days. That was less than he liked to prepare, but he had been paid extra for that, too.

Sheldon logged off. He did not assure his special client that he would get the job done. That man knew Sheldon well, but even if he hadn't, anyone who called Sheldon knew that about him: he took every job, and (with the exception of the blessed bonsai master Zhang) he delivered results on time and in the exact way requested.

Sheldon looked at the bonsai tree for one more moment. Then, with sudden inspiration, he knew what he should do with it. He would bring the tree with him. He would explain the fine art of bonsai to the man and woman he had just been paid to torture and murder. He would show them how the tree's beauty bloomed only after it had been crushed, snipped, wired, and broken.

He would do that to them.

He would make them trees. He would make them beautiful, just as Zhang had been beautiful. And as his targets died in small bits and pieces, he would paint the tree with their blood and she would shine anew before he burned his targets alive and cast the tree into the flame as well.

This meant he could not keep referring to it as "the tree." He would call it by its name, because he did not kill nameless things. He knew his targets, his *prey*, as only a talented, wise, insightful hunter could know a thing. He knew their names, and he would give this tree a name to die with.

But what name? What name could represent this beauty?

Of course, there is only one name for something this perfect. Other than Sheldon, there is only one name so wonderful.

"Lucy," he breathed. He would tell his mother about the tree next time he visited her, and tell her he had named it after her and then killed it and she would be so pleased.

This decided, Sheldon stood and began his preparations for the trip. He packed light, as usual – everything went in a single bag. Two changes of clothes. A few rain ponchos that made cleanup easier. The taxidermy tools he planned to use on the couple. A few healthy snacks. His gun would travel under his arm. He did not have to worry about any of his tools being confiscated on the flight he booked: the benefit of flying out of a small, private airfield on a private jet.

Then he packed Lucy. He put the tree in a bucket, the bucket in a box, and the box in a duffel.

Sheldon was not just attractive, smart, and talented, he was also careful.

He went to the Teterboro Airfield, where the jet was waiting for him. That was part of his deal, too – the client paid for travel expenses. Sheldon was a fair man, so he rarely ate expensive food or stayed at five-star hotels while on a job, but he did insist on traveling in style.

He reviewed more information he received during the flight, and made several calls to arrange things properly. Other than that, the flight was uneventful, as was the renting of a gray Hyundai under the name Chris Downey. Chris Downey had a credit history, a job, a home address – all of which would stand up to everything but the highest scrutiny, even though Chris Downey was just one of a dozen wholly fictional creations Sheldon had made for use on his jobs.

Chris Downey was a totally blah, middle-class kinda guy, so he was fine with a Hyundai. Chris Downey worked from home as a web designer and consultant. Chris Downey sounded like someone whom Sheldon would gladly have murdered for free, not least for the sin of being all right with an economy vehicle.

But it was necessary for the job. Sheldon would have preferred a Maserati or a Bentley, perhaps a Ferrari if he was feeling frisky. But he intended to tail his targets for some of the trip, and did not want to risk being spotted. A gray Hyundai four-door was as close to invisible as you could get without actually having the Cloak of Invisibility like the one Sheldon had seen in a Harry Potter movie he watched while waiting in a closet for one of his targets to go to sleep.

He had not liked that movie – it was very complicated and boring – but he had totally grooved on the Cloak of Invisibility.

Sheldon drove the Chris-Downey-appropriate Hyundai for an hour, then picked up his targets' trail right outside Las Vegas. He followed them into Utah, and even parked a mere twenty feet away from them when they stopped at a small convenience store. He cracked the window and pretended to be texting, while in fact he listened to the woman talk on the phone to someone named Leroy. The man came out and he found out that the woman liked Cadbury Eggs.

That would make her even more fun to torture and kill. Sheldon had tried one of those eggs once and found it unbearably sticky and cloying. Online reviews by gourmet websites also derided them, which sealed his opinion of this woman as a slob and a degenerate and totally kill-worthy.

The man who came out of the convenience store mentioned he had bought a number of the crappy chocolates, though, and that perked Sheldon up. If his very special client approved, Sheldon would shove a few chocolate eggs up each of his targets' asses. It would degrade the targets, break their spirits, and also show proper lack of respect for the sticky, nasty treats the woman evidently liked.

Sheldon determined, however, that he had no opinion for or against the man's Dr. Pepper obsession. Interesting. He would analyze the question with his full faculties, and would no doubt provide an epic conclusion *in re* the merits of Dr. Pepper and might even seek publication in a medical journal or something.

Sheldon rolled out of the convenience store parking lot twenty seconds after the man and woman. There had been several other vehicles in the parking lot, and that was a concern, if only a minor one. If any of the vehicles followed, they might be too close for him to instigate his plan in the exact way and at the exact location he had determined.

No one did. The other shoppers were no doubt stocking up on jerky and potato chips and other things designed to sully one's body. Sheldon himself knew his body was excellent – attractive and well-muscled – and he had no wish to destroy it with Pringles and Slim Jims.

He followed the couple for ten miles, then pulled ahead. Not too fast – just a few miles an hour above the speed limit. He glanced at the couple's car as he did so, and saw them talking with energy and animation. Sheldon approved of this. Lively people lasted longer, and that made them more fun.

The stretch of freeway he had chosen to make his move was in the middle of nowhere, between several of the towns in Utah that, so far as Sheldon could tell during his quick research on the plane, existed only to highlight the truth of Sheldon's opinion that everything between New York City and Los Angeles was essentially an uninhabited wasteland.

He pulled to the side of the freeway. There were no on- or off-ramps between him and the point he had passed up his targets. That was important, because he did not want others coming up on him first. There was a risk of a state trooper coming by, he supposed, but in that event it would be easy enough to kill him and dump him on the side of the road. No one stopped to take a close look at cop cars, so in all likelihood Sheldon would be well out of range of reprisal by the time the trooper's body was discovered.

Luck smiled on Sheldon: no trooper came by. This was no surprise, because Sheldon suspected that Lady Luck probably had orgasms just thinking about him.

By the time the black sedan his targets were driving had appeared, Sheldon had already popped the hood and trunk of his car. He stepped into the road as soon as he saw their car, and started waving his hands.

Sheldon knew that the world was a bad place. It was full of cruel, mean-spirited people with no beauty in their souls. But he also knew that even the rudest, nastiest, basest person would sense in Sheldon a creature of beauty and light. If there *was* a God, Sheldon knew he was close to being Him, and knew also that people – even rotten, scummy, uneducated people who traveled through rotten, scummy, uneducated places like Utah – would respond to this.

Sure enough, his targets' car slowed as they approached. They passed him, but only by the hundred yards or so it took to safely pull off to the side of the road. The car's reverse lights flickered on, and they drove backwards along the shoulder until they reached him.

Sheldon had started running toward them as soon as they were on the shoulder. He wore what he knew would be a thoroughly convincing expression of relief on his face – he was, among other things, an excellent actor – and when they reached him he went around to the side of the car. The woman cracked her window.

"Are you o –"

Sheldon punched her in the face. He moved quickly, the punch precise and so fast it was a blur even to someone with perfect eyesight like his. The woman's face rocked to the side and she slumped.

The man's eyes widened, and he fumbled at his seatbelt. Sheldon had time for amusement at that: what did the man think he was going to do?

Whatever it was, he stopped moving as Sheldon pointed one of his guns at him. The gun's name was Thompson, and he was an expensive Beretta M9 which had been modified to allow for the suppressor screwed onto its end.

The man did not look afraid. More resigned. But he had steel in his voice when he said, "You don't want to do this. It will turn out badly for –"

"Alex Anton," said Sheldon. "I'm so glad to meet you."

Alex didn't bat an eye. He just said. "You should walk away before you get –"

Sheldon didn't hear the rest. He shot the man with Wolfe, who was named after a woman because it was not a gun but a mere taser. Still, tasers, like women, could be beautiful and useful in their own ways.

Wolfe chittered and chattered as the two flechettes flew out, hit Alex Anton in the neck, and he jerked in place before slumping.

Time to work fast.

Sheldon jogged back to his car. He grabbed his overnight bag and the second bag holding his bonsai tree from the trunk. He wiped down all the surfaces of the car he had touched, using baby wipes he had soaked in a combination of cleaning fluids that would remove all DNA traces from the Hyundai. He even vacuumed the car with a handheld vacuum cleaner he had bought for the purpose, and which he would toss out the window somewhere on his route.

He put a sign on the rear window – which he held by the corner, using a corner of his shirt to hold onto it and avoid leaving fingerprints – that said, "Gone for gas. Back in twenty minutes." Any passing traveler would ignore the car, and any passing state trooper would stop, run the plates, find them clean, maybe leave a ticket, and would go – no doubt not bothering to do anything else unless he or she saw the car was still there several hours later.

Chris Downey would be flagged. But that was fine; Sheldon had planned to retire Mr. Downey after this job anyway. There were enough Hyundai-loving douche bags in the world.

Satisfied with his work, Sheldon took his overnight bag and the second bag with his precious Lucy to the targets' sedan. The man was moaning a bit, the woman still slumped. Sheldon spritzed their faces with a chloroform derivative of his own creation, which he had created using his excellent chemistry skills and also getting the recipe by torturing a CSI lab tech. Both his targets slumped still further, and he moved them into the back seat.

They had some luggage, which was irritating, but he would deal. Sheldon was mentally and emotionally strong, so he could handle such irritations.

Besides, he had known they were traveling, and the luggage was actually useful. Opening it, he found a variety of garments – the woman had some very fun lingerie, he noted, and would probably want to model it for him at some point – and Sheldon wadded up a coat and a sweater which he propped beside each of his targets' heads. A passer-by would see two people on a long stretch of highway, snoozing in the backseat while their unlucky travel buddy drove.

It was an excellent hide-in-plain sight technique which, coupled with his baseball cap and his boring clothes, would render him impervious to identification.

Sheldon put his luggage in the passenger side foot space, and his bonsai tree in its protective layers on the front passenger seat. A moment later he removed Lucy from the bag, because he suspected she was hot and dusty in there and he did not like to cause her pain. He left the tree in the box, but popped open the top so she could get good air and sunlight. Then Sheldon got into the drivers seat – the car was still running – and buckled up with a murmured, "Safety first!"

He almost pulled out, then thought better of it and took one more moment to buckle up the tree as well, knowing Lucy would be appreciative of his intense kindness.

Sheldon glanced at his targets. The woman's face was turning a lovely shade of purple. The woman was beautiful, but the exquisite coloring he had given her made her even more beautiful, because now she was a bit of a Sheldon Steward Original. The coloring would fade, and that was a pity. But he would paint her with new colors soon, so she would return to that height of loveliness once more.

Neither she nor the man moved. The drug he had given them would keep them under for at least an hour – more than enough time for him to get to the next phase of the job.

He smiled. He patted the tree. He signaled left, then pulled onto the highway.

He whistled as he drove. The client had interrupted his pruning, but he *did* love his job. This was a day that would end on a high note overall, and Sheldon counted himself as both an optimist and someone who showed appropriate gratitude to the universe for gifting him with so much.

He smiled broadly. He even tipped his baseball cap when a highway patrol vehicle passed by. The officer inside threw an offhanded wave without even looking, which meant that he had passed the now-dead Chris Downey's car and had either stopped and not found anything amiss or, more likely, had dismissed it completely and gone in search of sleepy or speeding travelers.

Sheldon was neither. He was always attentive – amazingly so, he had to admit in spite of his above-average modesty – and though he did break the speed limit when a job required, right now he was driving at exactly one mile below the speed limit.

Yes, a good day. Sheldon tipped his hat again, this time to no one in particular, and his whistling grew in volume. The sleepers behind him remained asleep, which was good for the job but sad for them, as they would have enjoyed his whistling. Sheldon was an excellent whistler.

3

Marcos thought preppers were a crazy bunch. Absolutely nutso, bonkers, coo-coo-for-Cocoa-Puffs.

And he thanked God for them every day. Because the two biggest logistical problems any meth lab of serious size faced were ventilation and seclusion, and preppers had handed him the answer to both.

The production of meth required seriously dangerous chemicals, and ventilation was necessary to avoid poisoning or explosion. That meant that "superlabs" – labs capable of producing more than the tiny bits cooked up in homes and trunks of one-man operations throughout the United States – needed ventilation measures that would be a red flag for anyone seeing them.

The obvious answer would be to house the lab in a factory somewhere, with heightened security to keep out trespassers. But that kind of thing gave itself away as often as not. No matter how good the security, a pair of binoculars and a little curiosity could blow the lid off most serious productions. And people tended to notice the smells the superlabs gave off, and the dead plants and vegetation that marked where meth producers dumped the byproducts of their production.

Enter preppers.

People who believed "the end is nigh," as the old sandwich-board loonies so loudly proclaimed, varied in their seriousness. Some just hoarded a week or two of food in their garages, some owned gunsafes with a few over-accessorized rifles.

Others went whole-hog and created underground bunkers designed to keep them safe in any eventuality ranging from biological attack to nuclear holocaust.

Similar to the preppers themselves, the bunkers ranged in seriousness and style: from simple boxes with pallets of military rations and drinking water to elaborate underground complexes complete with water and air filtration systems capable of handling just about any kind of bioweapon attack known to man, home theaters, and multi-lane bowling alleys.

The kind of person that went in for the latter was, obviously, paranoid. And that paranoia extended not only to the need for a place to run in the case of zombie apocalypse (which Marcos had found a surprising number of people actually believed to be a possibility), but to the fear that others would find the bunker and steal it away before the rightful owners could get inside and seal themselves away from a worldwide episode of *The Walking Dead*.

As a result, the most serious preppers had not only elaborate networks of tunnels that could keep a dozen people alive for a generation, but equally elaborate methods of concealment. The entryways, radiation-proof hatches that could weigh a ton or more, were cleverly concealed as rocks or patches of vegetation, or housed in shacks made to look like cannibal hillbillies squatted there.

Even better – and critical for a meth superlab like the one Marcos now ran – the bunkers tended to have ventilation systems that wound through unpopulated areas until they ended at the surface as far as five or six miles away from the bunkers themselves.

Ventilation was necessary. Ventilation was also a giveaway. So having the lab in one place and military-grade ventilation and filtration sending the fumes somewhere far away was a perfect solution.

An underground meth lab was unheard of, but when Marcos first heard of the extremes to which some doomsday preppers went to prepare underground facilities and to conceal their preparations, he knew that he had stumbled onto something wonderful.

Of course he told Demyan – that was Marcos' job, as Demyan's right-hand man. And of course Demyan recognized the genius of it and immediately sent Marcos to make the arrangements necessary to put the plan to work.

And – also of course – that was what Marcos had been waiting for. It was time for a change in the organization. Demyan was old, and his heart was failing. Everyone knew that, just as everyone knew that when he did die there would be a coup and, likely as not, that coup would be followed by a purge. That was the way of things in the Odessa family.

Marcos had no desire to wait around in hopes that whoever succeeded Demyan would be someone who was a fan of Marcos. So the logical solution was to be the one who seized power himself.

He had been a good little soldier. He had been recruited by Demyan himself, though that brought little cache in Odessa. Demyan was a Russian immigrant to the

United States who had come with nothing but pocket lint and who had eventually become a leader in the manufacture and distribution of illicit drugs. His lineage gave him an "in" with a family that had its roots in Mother Russia or the Ukraine.

Marcos, as the son of a Cuban prostitute and a Polish ne'er-do-well, was seen as little more than a mutt. A trained monkey that Demyan had taught to do amusing tricks, but little else. Russian mafia families – even those that were strictly U.S.-based – were still steeped in tradition, and the idea of anyone without the right national background rising high in the organization was unheard of. Even though Marcos had severed ties with his family as much as possible, they still hung over him as a stain.

But times, they were a-changing. Faster, with the advent of Marcos' brain child.

It took some work, to find exactly what he wanted, but eventually he was successful. He always was, and that was another reason he knew he was bound for glory in Odessa.

Marcos found the perfect bunker, owned by the perfect mark. The old man who built the thing was rich but had no heirs and was more than a little hostile toward government institutions; everyone expected him to die intestate. But when Reggie Browning ended up dying a few years earlier than expected, an examination of his home found a will drafted in his own clear handwriting, signed by him, that left all his property – liquid and real – to a charitable organization called Teeny Tikes.

Teeny Tikes was a charitable corporation, a 501(c)3 business entity registered in strict accordance with state and federal laws. It had a website that declared its mission "to end worldwide illiteracy." It had a bank account. It had letterhead and office space in a small strip mall outside of Brooklyn.

All of these were legitimate, and scrupulously legal, though the office was empty save a cleaning service that stopped by once a week.

Teeny Tikes also had a board of directors. It had additional offices in Paraguay, the Dominican Republic, and Nicaragua. Unlike the website, bank account, and office, these were all fictitious. But Marcos knew that so long as the money left to Teeny Tikes stayed in the bank and even showed a bit of growth from time to time, there was little chance of government scrutiny. Watchdogs were primed to look for money *loss* in non-profits, not money *stagnation*. Occasional outflows and intermittent purchases of books – donated to inner city children in quantities of several hundred per annum – maintained the fiction of Teeny Tikes as a legitimate charity.

So Reggie Browning's money stayed in the bank accounts, to the tune of about five million dollars. That was the price of doing business, and it was a price Marcos convinced Demyan was worth paying. A drop in the bucket. It wasn't the liquid funds he wanted. It was Browning's real estate.

The real estate was left to Teeny Tikes, just like Browning's money. Teeny Tikes sold the modest house Browning had owned as soon as the probate process ended. The money went into Teeny Tikes' account. Another three hundred thou.

The big question Teeny Tikes – meaning Marcos – had to answer was what to do with several thousand acres of seemingly undeveloped land?

Answer: nothing. It went into a trust, with the land to be sold "at some later date, when said land proves to be of use and value to Teeny Tikes and to the community at large." This, as with everything else, was in accordance with good business practices and totally legal. The land had no real use, no interested buyers, so putting it on indefinite hold was something that, again, would draw no attention.

That was good, because Marcos' plan relied on the proposition that no one would ever pay attention to that land. Development was unlikely – it was too remote for any business to be interested in building malls or parking lots there, and there were no mineral or oil deposits that would interest energy or mining conglomerates. There was just six thousand square acres – a bit over eight square miles – of woodland in northwest Idaho, a hundred miles from the Montana border.

And hidden right in the middle of that land: Browning's real reason for buying it all, and Marcos' real reason for his interest in the unfortunate Reggie Browning.

Browning had been careful. He had hidden everything. No one but the contractors and suppliers he hired knew of the existence of his underground bomb shelter/doomsday retreat. The thing was a system of interconnected bunkers; an underground complex big enough to have housed two dozen people for a hundred years. Marcos suspected the old man had had plans to bring in a harem of women from the surrounding area, promising them safety during the *Dawn of the Dead* scenario in return for helping him repopulate the human race in his underground sex-lair.

Whatever his ultimate plans, though, Marcos had tracked down the bunker by hiring a hacker to ply open the customer lists of one of the biggest manufacturers and installers of the metal boxes that served as underground shelters. After winnowing through the list, Marcos had decided on Reggie Browning as the man he wanted to talk to.

It had been a simple matter after that to meet Browning as he came home one night, and systematically break the man's toes, knees, and one femur. Marcos knew the job was crude – someone like that nutbag Sheldon would have done it far better – but they were sufficient to "convince" old Reggie Browning to write the will Marcos wanted. Then it was simple to arrange a scene where it appeared the old man slid off a canyon road while driving drunk, with the resultant carefully created crash serious enough to pulp most of his bones and hide the pre-crash injuries from the cursory autopsy that followed. After that it was an equally simple process to move the people and equipment Marcos needed onsite to Reggie's ultimate panic room.

Et voilà! In a matter of weeks, Marcos had become the man who doubled the meth output of one of the largest support groups of the Odessa mafia.

And a few weeks after that, Marcos had put his plans into motion. Not the ones to get the meth lab running and distribution flowing properly. No, his *real* plans. The ones that involved getting Demyan "demoted."

Demotions in the Odessa mafia only came in one form. Odessa was the largest Russian mafia organization in the United States, and it maintained its position through a combination of shrewd business moves and ruthless "personnel" decisions.

Marcos' plan had several parts: the first, which was establishing the meth lab, was done. The second had been to reach out to Nikolai Chernov. Chernov was a *pakhan* in the organization: a boss-figure who oversaw numerous of the support groups in charge of various aspects of the syndicate's criminal activities; as well as overseeing the security groups that provided physical and operational security, which included infiltrating spies into each of the support groups. Chernov was the boss of Marcos' boss – the man Demyan reported to.

It was common practice for *pakhans* to have at least one or two spies in each of the support groups they ran, but that didn't change the fact that Demyan would have cut off the spy's balls and fed them to him had he found out his identity.

Marcos had ferreted out one of Chernov's spies four years ago; had actually caught the man in the act of making a report to the intermediary who would pass on information about Demyan's drug production and smuggling operation to Chernov. That day, when Marcos found the man making a call to his real superior when he should have been running numbers for Demyan, was the day he began to plan Demyan's overthrow.

It took careful preparation and patience. Marcos had both. He had grown up on the street, part of a "family" that even the kindest person would view as cruel and even horrific. He had left that family behind as soon as he could, opting first for street life, then being recruited to a crime family where he knew anyone who wasn't Russian would be drummed out over time. But Marcos had resisted the bullying, the beatings, the tauntings. He was a planner, and he knew from the time he was a child that his time would come.

By the time the underground meth lab was in place, Marcos had his plan moving. He called in his long-overdue favor, and had Chernov's spy reach out to his boss with a proposition: Marcos would more than triple production of meth in Demyan's support group, as well as maintaining all other levels of production. In return, Marcos wanted to be promoted to head of the support group.

He wanted Demyan gone, and he wanted himself to ascend to Demyan's position.

At first, Chernov resisted. Money was money, and he wanted more of it. But there were appearances to be maintained, and he wouldn't move on Demyan without the proper pretense. Marcos supplied that pretense with one word: "Sasha."

After that it was a no-brainer. Chernov had been worried about Demyan's rising power in the syndicate, so it followed that Chernov would jump at the chance to depose Demyan and put a younger – and, theoretically, more pliable – person in control of the support group. There was a final twist, though: Chernov said Demyan had to die, supposedly for the huge breach that "Sasha" represented… but he wanted Marcos to see to it personally. Chernov wanted video of Demyan dying – painfully – that he would take to his own Odessa superiors along with the information about Sasha as reasons to put Marcos in charge of the meth lab.

Marcos understood the man's reasoning. He even applauded it, though it made his takeover of Demyan's group a damn sight tougher. Saying Demyan would be hard to kill was about as accurate as saying Marcos' mother was a little promiscuous. Marcos' mother was a whore who gave it up to anyone with a nickel, and Demyan lived in a home with security measures that would have been the envy of a Saudi prince. Killing him at home was impossible, and when he traveled, it was in a bulletproof limo modeled after the vehicles used by the President of the United States. Besides that, Demyan never allowed anyone to know his itinerary in advance. Ambushes were impossible.

So Marcos had to make the man come to him.

How? That was the question – the one on which everything hung.

And the answer had presented itself almost by accident: Sasha. A few relatively small payments made out of Demyan's personal funds. So small that they passed by unnoticed… by everyone but Marcos, who had access to Demyan's records in order to properly cook them in case of IRS audit.

Marcos found evidence of a few odd plane tickets. Several trips to New York. A payment to someone skilled in the creation of new identities.

Marcos kept digging, and *there it was*. The way he was going to kill Demyan, take over as head of the support arm and – eventually – would become a *pakhan* himself. Maybe even the first non-Russian head of Odessa.

He made a call, placed some money in an account. A day later he went to the lab for a "surprise inspection" and asked for the three men who ran the place to meet with him.

They showed up quickly. Mongrel or not, he *was* Demyan's number two, and to slight him would be seen as an insult to Demyan. So the men Marcos thought of as Heckle, Jeckle, and Beaker practically ran to him as soon as he had gone to his desk in the small room of the bunker that served as his private office.

Heckle and Jeckle were the two men who oversaw day-to-day production of the lab, watching the dozen workers who stayed there for two weeks at a time before being shuffled out and replaced by the next shift. Demyan had picked them without Marcos' input, even though this whole place was Marcos' child. Rude to pick a babysitter without asking the father what he *thought*, at least, so it was easy to hate the guys.

As for Beaker… he was a disgraced chemical engineer who had worked for a major pharmaceutical company before getting fired for showing up high as a kite one too many times. Beaker watched over the actual production and refining operations to provide maximum output with minimum waste or risk to Odessa's onsite assets.

When the three arrived at the office, Marcos was waiting. He smiled, beckoned them into the office, then beckoned a second time for Jeckle to close the heavy submarine hatch-style door that hung between every room in the bunker. There were no locks on any of the doors, but that was fine: Marcos wouldn't need locks.

While Jeckle had his back turned, Marcos put a bullet in Heckle's forehead. One shot from his favorite gun – a CZ 75 B 9mm pistol he had named Gandalf, after his favorite character in his favorite fantasy series – and one of the two men he thought of as babysitters just… *ended.*

He wasn't worried about the sound carrying – the steel door to this place was so thick there was no way the sound of gunshots *or* screams would make it out as more than muffled hums, and even if they did the production room was too loud for anyone to notice extra noise there. He had planned this perfectly.

Jeckle, still turning back to Marcos when his coworker's brains went from innies to outies, went for his own gun. "Nope," said Marcos. Then, in a fit of uncharacteristic wit, he added, "You shall not pass."

As he expected, Jeckle didn't understand the *Lord of the Rings* reference. Jeckle was an idiot who had no taste for the fantasy literature Marcos secretly adored. The man just nodded and moved his hand – very, very slowly – away from the gun tucked in a shoulder holster under his arm.

As for Beaker: as Marcos had expected, the man simply sank to the ground and began babbling. Marcos spared a single glance at the man. "Shut up. You play this right and you live through the day. Maybe even get a raise."

Beaker shut up. He was in his fifties, doughy and soft with the pallid complexion of someone who spends the majority of his time out of the sun. There were UV lamps in the living quarters of the staff that worked here, because Marcos had read a number of studies that showed such things provided a mood-stabilizing effect as well as healthier overall constitution for people who worked underground. But rumor had it that Beaker *liked* his pale, pasty skin, and avoided the lamps. He gave Marcos the creeps. But he was useful, and Marcos meant what he said: the man would live, and even prosper… so long as he did exactly what Marcos told him to do.

During the two seconds when Marcos was telling Beaker to shut up, Jeckle had tensed. Again, Marcos expected that. He had hidden his love for fantasy literature – Odessa higher-ups wouldn't like such a genre leaning, and would probably label him a queer and so not to be trusted if they found out about it. That meant that one of his life-long dreams to be a world-class Dungeon Master in Dungeons & Dragons games would likely go forever unrequited. But he loved to plan campaigns in his head, and that meant becoming a master of strategy and scenarios. So Jeckle going for his gun again was expected, even planned for.

Jeckle was the smaller of the two minions Demyan had left in charge of day-to-day operations, but he still weighed in at a good two-twenty, and had tattoos all over his body attesting to the men he had killed and his loyalty to Odessa. He edged forward and at exactly the moment Marcos expected, Jeckle lunged at him. Marcos took that opportunity to swing the lead pipe he had been holding out of sight, just behind his leg and hip. Jeckle flew forward, then reeled to the side as the pipe took him in the shoulder.

In movies, fighters took blows like this, shouted in pain, and continued the fight. In reality, the blow shattered the man's upper arm, turned his clavicle into a line of ragged sticks, and cracked his scapula in three places. Jeckle was tough, but no amount of tough could make his arm work again.

Marcos waited, again giving an opening. And again, the other man acted exactly as the script Marcos had written in his head demanded. Marcos waited for the man's arm to dart inside his jacket, groping for his gun. It was on the wrong side, though, and the man ended up with his good hand scrabbling ineffectually inside his jacket.

Marcos whipped the pipe around again, imagining it was Andúril, the once-broken sword of Aragorn. Now both Jeckle's arms and shoulders were a pulp. Still the guy stood, even looked rebellious, so Marcos added the *coup de grâce*: he dropped the pipe and slapped the guy.

It was just an open-handed smack to the other man's cheek. But such a slap, Marcos knew, could be more demeaning and demoralizing than a closed fist. A fist meant you were fighting a man who feared you, or at least viewed you as a potential threat. A slap, on the other hand – that was the kind of thing a man did in response to a mosquito. Marcos' palm told Jeckle he was less than a man. He was a bug. He was a *nothing*, and Marcos could squash him at any time.

The slap did its job. Jeckle fell at last. And here, finally, was a divergence from Marcos' script. Marcos expected Jeckle to pass out, but the man hit his right shoulder on the floor and *that* pain was enough to jolt him to full consciousness, not to mention making him piss his pants.

Marcos hauled him upright. He reached into the man's jacket – not for the gun, which he ignored since Jeckle could not even touch it, let alone fire it – and pulled out the cell phone he knew had a direct line to Demyan.

"He won't do it," said Jeckle. He had a thick Moldovan accent. Another thing that burned Marcos about the glorified babysitter: even a goddam *Moldovan* thought he was better than Marcos.

But that would change. Marcos would be a *pakhan*, and he would force the men who had looked down on him and spoken ill of him to eat their own tongues.

"Whatever you want of Demyan, he won't do it," Jeckle repeated. But Marcos saw fear in the man's eyes.

"I think he might," said Marcos. That was when he pointed his gun at Jeckle's right eye. The pistol felt heavy and sure in his hand, and the bore would be the size of a cave in the sight of the wounded man who knelt before him. "Not yet – you're right about that. But soon."

Jeckle's lip curled. "Not yet? You think Demyan will ever –"

Marcos pistol-whipped the man, enjoying the way three of Jeckle's front teeth flew out and hit Beaker on the forehead. Beaker, still cringing nearby, cried out. "Shut up. Be a man," Marcos spat at him. The guy's panic-sounds were starting to annoy him.

Beaker nodded so fast it was a wonder he didn't give himself whiplash. He jammed a hand against his mouth, stifling the scream that still wanted to come, though he couldn't quite halt his whimpering. Marcos sighed.

You do what you can do with the tools you have to work with, Marcos. If a hobbit dealt with dwarves trashing his place, you can deal with this wimp's whimpering.

Marcos turned to Jeckle, who was now flat on the floor, groaning around a mouth full of mushy gums and splintered teeth. "It's so hard to find good help, don't you think?"

Jeckle groaned. Marcos thought he was just making pain sounds, but realized a moment later that the man was trying to say something.

"Wone 'all 'im," Jeckle said.

Marcos frowned, working the sounds over in his mind. "You won't call him? Demyan?" He shrugged. "I don't care. I don't need your phone to *call him*. I just want him to hear me answer when he calls you in a panic to verify that everything has gone to hell. I just have to wait for one thing to –"

As if on cue, another phone rang. It was Marcos' personal cell, sitting on the desk at the back of the room. Cell phones didn't usually work twenty feet underground in a room in the middle of Nowhere, Idaho, but Marcos had had a cell transmitter installed and wired into this room so that he and the once-babysitters could make and receive calls.

He kept his gun leveled at Jeckle, though he doubted even a tough guy like him would make much trouble at this point. He walked backward, feeling for the phone, then brought it to his ear.

"Yes?" he said.

"I got the package," came Sheldon's voice. As always, something about the cheeriness of his tones, the brightness of them, creeped Marcos out. The man was closer to Marcos than just about anyone, but he was bugnuts crazy.

Is that *really a surprise?*

Out loud, Marcos said, "When will you be here?"

"Tomorrow. It's a bit of a drive, but I'll pop a few Ritalin if I get tired and I'll be aces for the fun parts." Sheldon sighed, the kind of noise an amused parent might give while watching his child perform at a recital. "Lucy won't like all the travel, but –"

"Wait, *she's* with you? I don't want that old bi –"

"Be respectful," said Sheldon, his voice suddenly low and dangerous. "That's my mother you're talking about." The brightness returned. "It's not her anyway. Lucy is my bonsai tree. I just named her that, and it's a splendid name, don't you think?"

Marcos shook his head and gave a "what are you gonna do" shrug to Beaker, who whimpered again. In spite of the major creeps Sheldon always brought with him, Marcos forced his voice to sound strong and firm – a sound suitable to the man who was about to ascend to a position of power inside the Odessa organization, not to mention the kind of Dungeon Master who would make players climb over each other to participate in one of his campaigns. "Great. Whatever. What's your ETA?"

Sheldon hummed and made clicking sounds, as though unsure whether to sing a little ditty or act like a calculator. Finally he said, "Twenty hours. A little less if I hurry. But I don't like to do that. I'm an excellent driver, of course, but speeding increases the chances of being pulled over, and killing police officers can be a pain." He sighed. "I always have to do it so fast."

Marcos grinned at Jeckle, who had managed to get to his knees again. "That timeline works fine," he said. "I'm sure I'll find a way to pass the time until you get here."

"Coolio. See you then. Toodles," said the other man brightly, and hung up.

Marcos put the phone down on his desk. He looked at Beaker, who had finally stopped whimpering. "How are we doing on the day's production?" he asked.

The business question had the effect Marcos intended. Beaker visibly relaxed, as though being asked such questions allowed him to hang onto a pretense that everything, if not precisely *normal*, would work out all right in the end. "We're good. We already finished the shift quota, and might even make an additional twenty percent by end of the day."

"Good." Marcos nodded. "I have every intention of keeping you on."

"I'm…" Beaker gulped, his eyes flitting nervously between Marcos, the maimed Jeckle, and the very dead Heckle. "I'm glad my work is satisfactory."

"Me, too," said Marcos, noting that the man had very adroitly managed to avoid saying anything for or against either Demyan or Marcos. That was fine. Self-preservation was a good thing, so long as the scientist remembered that the first and only rule of self-preservation from here on out was simply Do Not Cross Marcos.

He turned to Jeckle, who made no sound but could not help the paleness that had crept across his face even as he said, "Demyan isn't going to do whatever it is you want. He'll kill you and then –"

"Actually, he *will* do what I want. He'll call me at my convenience, and then he'll come here and eat a bullet if I ask him to." He grinned, a leer that made his cheeks ache. "And I *will* ask him to, don't you worry." He looked at his watch. "But first I have to wait for a friend to get here."

"You have no friends."

Marcos grinned. "Why would you say that? Don't you think I'm a likable guy?"

Marcos had put down his lead pipe. Now he picked it up again. He holstered his gun and tapped his open palm lightly with the pipe. He grinned again – even wider this time, if that were possible – and said, "Well, Jeckle, I have twenty hours to kill. However will we pass the time?"

A few seconds later, Jeckle began to scream. Beaker did, too, but Marcos didn't hear that sound. He was too deep in the particular joy he felt bludgeoning a Moldovan cocksucker who had never thought of Marcos as anything but a dog.

Now, though, the man was realizing that dog or no, Marcos had a bite to be feared.

When he was finished, he stepped over Jeckle's jellied corpse and walked to Beaker. "I want you to do two things. You hear me?"

"Y-yes, sir."

"First, I want you to tell the production staff to clear out. No one stays but the security already onsite."

Marcos could see clearly the questions Beaker wanted to ask: *Why? What will I tell them? When do I tell them to come back?* Do *I tell them to come back?*

But even more clearly, he saw the final and most important thought: *Just do it or Marcos will kill you.*

"Security might not like it," he managed. "What should I tell them?"

"Tell them I said *it's time*. They won't bother you while you clear everyone out."

Beaker nodded, digesting both the instruction and the implication that Marcos wasn't the only one in on the coup. "And… and the second thing?

Marcos looked at his now-bloodstained clothes. "Find someone who has clothes that will fit me and bring them."

Again, more questions flitted almost visibly through Beaker's mind: *What kind of clothes? What if I bring you the wrong size? What if I bring you something you don't like?*

Surprisingly, the man managed to not only *not* say that, but he actually contributed something worthwhile to the moment.

Beaker gestured at himself. "We're about the same size. And I have changes of clothing in my room. Would you like me to bring something of mine?"

Marcos nodded. "Good idea. But tell production to head out first."

Apparently emboldened by his small victory, Beaker said, "And when should I tell them to come back?"

Marcos decided to answer him. "Tell them a week. But they should stay in town until then."

"Are you worried they might raise suspicion, all checking into a hotel or motel at the same time?"

This time Marcos *did* get a bit irritated, and contemplated using Gandalf again. *Pow-pow-pow* and Beaker would stop his questions.

But he didn't do that. He could replace Beaker, sure, but it would be a hassle, and he wanted to start production up right away. Besides, Beaker again added something helpful. "I have a small house outside town."

Marcos glanced sharply at him. He hadn't known that, and he didn't like not knowing things. "You do?"

Beaker visibly shied away. "It wasn't a secret. Everyone knew –"

"I didn't."

"It never came up. You never asked. But it was common knowledge, you can ask –" Beaker stopped speaking, looking silently at the remains of Heckle and Jeckle. "Well, you can ask a lot of the production staff. They knew as well."

"Fair enough," said Marcos. "Yeah, tell them that. But they should leave in shifts. Half hour apart, no more than five at a time."

"Usual protocols after that?"

Marcos nodded. The usual protocol was for people coming in to work one of the two-week shifts at the bunker to pose as hikers just looking for a new place to explore. They would get rides into the area – Uber had made it easy to do without much in the way of records – then walk long enough to be sure they weren't followed, and only then would they go to one of the hidden entrances to the bunker.

The process was the same in reverse. Only this time they wouldn't be going to a city hours away, they'd be staying at Beaker's new-to-Marcos house.

And that would work. Because Heckle and Jeckle weren't the only ones Marcos had planned to change out for his own, loyal people. The production staff, too, was going to be "retired." He had arranged for each of them to get picked off in various places, but if they were all staying together in a single confined location…

He smiled and clapped Beaker on the shoulder. "Tell them to stay close, though. Tell them there's new equipment coming in and it's dangerous to install, so that's why they're leaving. But their shifts aren't over, so they're to stay in your house – do you have enough supplies for that?"

"Yes, yes, of course, I –" Beaker did his whiplash-nod again. The guy was terrified of pissing Marcos off, and that was just right. Just how it should be.

"Great. Good. Tell them to stay put, to stay out of sight, until I send someone for them."

"And whom should I say will come for them?"

"You shouldn't." Marcos put a smile on his face that would have been the envy of Smaug the dragon as he toyed with the doomed souls who came for his treasure. "Believe me, they'll know him when they see him."

Beaker got the message. Marcos saw it all fall into place behind his eyes: they would stay in his house until Marcos sent someone to kill them. Or did it himself.

"I'll get right on it," said Beaker.

"Do that."

"And then the clothes."

"And then the clothes."

"And after that? After they leave?"

"Find something to do. But I'd stay in your room to do it."

Beaker hesitated, and again Marcos saw the question in the man's eyes: *But if he's gathering the production staff to kill them easier, does that mean he's going to kill me in* my *room as well?*

This time, Marcos answered the man's unspoken question. "Relax, man. If I'd wanted you dead, I'd have killed you like I did them."

Beaker nodded. He turned to leave, but Marcos had one more thing to say. "You know what my nickname for you is?"

Beaker looked confused. "Uh… what?"

"Beaker. It's what you'll answer to from now on. Because you remind me of that geeky Muppet with the perma-frown."

It was a last test. Beaker *would* be harder to replace than the production staff, and Marcos preferred not to have to do that. But he would, if necessary. So he was going to see how Beaker reacted to this insulting statement, and to the imposition of what amounted to a new identity under Marcos' rule.

The guy passed the test. Marcos was good at judging people's thoughts – he had to be, to get even this high in a group as offhandedly devoted to racism as the Odessa family, not to mention a potential Dungeon Master capable of creating the most complex mental worlds – and he saw not a single trace of fight or even simmering resentment in Beaker's eyes. Just resignation and the desire to survive the day.

"Yes, sir."

"Good job, Beaker." Marcos clapped the man on the shoulder. "Now get going."

The man got going.

Marcos was alone with the dead. He looked upon them with the same haughty glance as Aragorn no doubt looked upon the vanquished Orcs and Uruk-hai after the Battle of Helm's Deep. And, like Aragorn eventually did, Marcos understood this truth: he was born to be king, even if it meant destroying all those who came against him.

Beaker came back a while later. He had a change of clothes for Marcos. Marcos changed into them, transferring Gandalf's shoulder holster. Halfway finished, he blew Beaker away. It would be an inconvenience to replace him, but the guy had brought him a *track suit.* Some insults just couldn't be ignored.

4

Danielle had a sense of movement and of time passing. But she didn't feel either as concrete things. They slid around and under her the way a river might if she were floating lazily down it, dozing on a raft or an inner tube while a hot summer sun beat down on her.

The heat grew, and the sun became less a pleasantly-calming thing than a stifling force. She breathed in, and the air felt like a convection oven had taken up residence in her mouth. She tried to move, slowly coming out of the floating dream, and felt something binding her ankles and knees. Her wrists and arms were pulled behind her back, tied as well at the wrists and elbows.

She had been blinking as all this happened. At first she thought she wasn't opening her eyes after all, because there was no light. Then she realized her eyes were both open, both working. It was just dark.

Not completely, though. She saw a red glow, so dim it was almost as dark as the greater blackness around her. But even the nearly invisible glow was welcome as she tried to free herself. She gave up after a few moments. The ties, whatever they were, were too strong. More than that, she found that she was pressed up against something hard and hot in front, something soft and slightly-less-hot behind.

Metal. My cheek's pressing against something metal. And my legs and back –

She realized what was pressing against her on both sides in that moment, the same moment she realized what the red light was.

She was in the trunk of a car. Her face was pressed against the back of the chassis, her eye staring right at a crack where light had filtered in around the housing of the rear brake lights. Her back was pressed against…

Alex.

The name sounded in her mind, even as she tried to shout it. But now she realized that part of the reason her breath was so hot was the thick layer of cloth in her mouth. A gag.

She murmured. Wondered what was happening. She was nobody. Just a public defender in an overworked office.

Oddly, she thought of McDonnel in that moment, and even more oddly the thought ran through her mind: *Is he kidnapping me?*

That was ridiculous, of course. McDonnel was a tool, and he would play dirty to get a conviction, but he wasn't going to mastermind a kidnapping and –

In that moment she remembered the man, running toward her and Alex's car. The look on his face: benign to the point of vacancy. The flash as something shot out and the pain that bloomed – then nothing.

She felt that pain still, pounding through her chin and mouth. She groaned, this time louder than before.

She realized something else, too: the car, which had been humming almost subliminally as the tires passed over what sounded like asphalt, was slowing. The peculiar crackle of rubber on loose dirt or gravel – the shoulder on a highway? – sounded. A moment later, nothing, followed by the rattle-click-thud of a car door opening and closing. The rasp of shoes over that same gravel.

Light speared into Danielle's eyes as the trunk popped, so bright that it disoriented her anew. She blinked, tears streaming down her face. Hands grabbed her by the shoulders and with surprising gentleness levered her up and out of the trunk.

"Easy," said a voice that belonged to a blur in the brightness. "The drugs and the knock on the noggin probably have you a bit hazy."

Danielle kept blinking, and the blur turned into the man she had seen running toward her. He smiled a genuinely concerned smile. "You okay?"

She tried to tell him what she felt, but it came out through the gag only as a muffled, "Ug oo."

The man's smile shifted to an expression of consternation. "Sorry. I should have taken off the gag before asking." His hands moved toward her face.

Danielle flinched. She couldn't help it. She wanted to stand up to this man, whoever he was, but her body shrank away from his touch.

The man sighed. "I just want to take off the gag, okay?" His hands moved forward again, then stopped as he apparently had a thought. "You might want to scream. But there's no one to hear you." He gestured, and for the first time Danielle was able to take in her surroundings.

They were on a highway. Small – two lanes to a side – and on either side were long stretches of gray scrub, some undefined mountains looming in the distance to her right. The light that had so hurt her eyes was actually quite low – the sun was setting, dipping slowly into the waiting bosom of one of the mountains.

She saw no cars, no houses, no trace of anyone but her and this man who was still looking at her expectantly.

The man waited until Danielle's eyes returned to his face, then said, "No screaming. Any of that nonsense will just get you another noggin knock and back in the trunk you go. Okay?"

She nodded, and this time only flinched a little as the man reached behind her head. The gag fell away from her mouth. Danielle worked her jaw a bit, and turned to look behind her and verify what she already knew: she was standing in front of the open trunk of some car – a Crown Vic or some other car made with so much trunk space it could only be pure-bred USA – in which her new husband lay, trussed and gagged in the same manner she had been.

"He's all right," said the man. "I've done this a lot, so I'm good at transporting my packages safely. He'll wake up in a few hours and be none the worse for wear. More or less."

Danielle swung back to look at the man again. "Why are you doing this?" she said.

The man either intentionally misunderstood her or was just plain crazy. He shrugged and said, "The drive is boring and I wanted company." Then Danielle decided it was definitely the "plain crazy" option when he added, "And Lucy, while beautiful and with just the right number of leaves, is a lousy conversationalist."

Danielle stared, open-mouthed and stunned not merely from a blow to the face but from the madness of the moment.

The man smiled and bowed. He said, "My name is Sheldon Steward. Not Stewar*t* – a lot of people get that wrong – but Stewar*d*." He gave a little jig, as though to emphasize his joy at a name that ended with "d."

A sense of panic shoved the weirdness of the moment aside.

He told me his name.

Danielle knew a lot about crime – more than enough to know that this was a bad sign. Whatever this man's endgame might be, he didn't care if she could i.d. him by name or face. Which meant he wasn't planning on letting her live.

She considered lunging at him. But with arms tied behind her and her legs bound together with what she now saw were tight layers of duct tape, what was she going to do? Headbutt the guy? Even if she managed by some miracle to connect, she wasn't a Navy Seal or closet MMA fighter and would likely just knock herself out instead of hurting Sheldon Steward-not-Stewart. She had learned a lot about robbery, theft, mayhem, and murder. But that was different than actually doing them.

Again, the guy spoke in a friendly tone. Again, the weirdness of the moment made her reel internally. "I'm going to free your arms. I'd loose your legs as well, but I'd rather not have to chase you down." He produced a short, razor-edged knife from somewhere under the sweater he wore. "Don't move, 'kay?"

He waited until Danielle nodded, then leaned around her and she felt a distant tugging. A moment later her elbows swung wide as they were released, and then her wrists came free as well. Fire burned as her arms – kept in unnatural positions, crammed behind her in a trunk – moved in front of her and blood screamed its way through veins that had been compressed beyond relief.

Sheldon leaned into the trunk and Danielle had to stifle a cry as he aimed a cheap spray bottle – the kind you could get for a buck at any hardware store – at Alex. He spritzed something against her husband's face, then turned and smiled at her. "He's fine," he said.

"Okay," she answered. It was the only word that she could manage.

Sheldon laughed as though she'd just told a clever joke, then turned toward the front of the car and motioned for Danielle to follow. She did, hopping around the passenger side of the car. She looked around, hoping to see a car – preferably a cop car – somewhere nearby. The road was empty for as far as she could see. There was a curve probably a half-mile behind her, so maybe –

She was looking behind her, so didn't see Sheldon stop suddenly. She hopped into his back, then bounced back and, most of her mobility robbed by the tape around knees and ankles, fell on her butt in the dirt. She was wearing blue jeans, but still felt pain as the rocks and grit of the shoulder dug into her backside.

She gritted her teeth as Sheldon smirked. "You should watch where you're going, Danielle."

Another wash of cold. *He knows my name.*

Sheldon didn't offer to help her up. He opened the passenger door and said, "Hey, Lucy. You okay to ride in the back for a while?"

Apparently "Lucy" answered in the affirmative, but no one got out of the car. Instead, Sheldon withdrew a tiny tree in a pot.

Bonzai tree? No, bonsai. That's it.

And who cares? Focus, *Danielle. Find some way out of this.*

Sheldon moved to the rear passenger door. He opened it and, still holding the tree, leaned into the backseat. The *click* of a seatbelt followed. Then Sheldon leaned back out *sans* tree and shut the rear door.

He turned to Danielle. Held out a hand and helped her up. The dreamlike sensation returned as he escorted her into the front passenger seat of the car –

(It is *a Crown Vic! Nailed it.*

Woohoo! It's important to know what car is taking you to your death.)

– and then shut the door. He ambled around the front of the car. Danielle's eyes flew to the steering column of the car, hoping that there would be keys there. If so, maybe she could –

No. Nothing there.

Tears steamed again, this time not because of bright light stabbing at her eyes but due instead to the dark despair stabbing at her heart.

Sheldon slid into the driver's seat. He reached into a pocket of the sweater he was wearing, which proclaimed "I drove down Route 66 and All I Got Was This Dumb Sweater!" on its front, and pulled out the car keys. He turned the key in the ignition and the car hummed to life, but instead of pulling onto the highway Sheldon turned to her. "Hands on the dash, please."

Almost in a trance, she did as he said. Sheldon reached under his seat and pulled out a roll of duct tape, which he used to once more bind her wrists. As he did so, the motions deft and well-practiced, he said, "You may be tempted to try and hit me, maybe take control of the car. I can assure you, it wouldn't work. And," he added with a wide grin, "I'd break all the little bones in your right hand for trying it. I'm supposed to bring you in one piece, but no one said I can't *encourage* you to be a good little girl. Okay?"

She nodded. Sheldon put the duct tape under the seat, rummaged around for a moment, and brought out a foil package which he held out to her. "Chickpea?" he said.

"No."

"Suit yourself." He popped a few in his mouth and, finally, pulled onto the road.

The sun dipped lower. It was still day, technically, but the low sun and the high mountains conspired to create an early gloaming.

Sheldon looked at her. "So what do you do?"

"Lawyer."

He glanced at her. "I like it."

"That I'm a lawyer?" she said, the surreal feeling still riding her, making her answer this madman's questions instead of trying to resist.

"No, not *that*. Lawyers are a bunch of bloodsuckers, mostly. But I *do* like that you said 'lawyer' instead of 'attorney.' Shows a bit of humility." He sighed deeply. "Not that that'll last long."

He could have been saying her humility wouldn't last long. But she doubted it. "What… what are you going to do with us?"

He smiled, but the only answer he gave was to pop a few more chickpeas in his mouth. After swallowing them he said, "So what do you think of the Marvel movies? I myself don't favor popular cinema. I like art house movies. I'm deep like that."

She didn't answer. Her attention had been arrested by something she saw in her side mirror.

A car had appeared in the distance. It was far behind, but coming up fast. Sheldon was driving at exactly the speed limit, but the car – a small SUV – was moving so fast it drew almost even in only a minute or so.

"Don't try anything," Sheldon said, still speaking in the same happy, easy-going tone he had used since the first moment.

"I won't," she said.

The SUV passed by. Sheldon didn't look at her, and she didn't look at the SUV. She shifted as it passed, though. She raised her hands slightly, hoping that whoever was in the SUV would see down into the car and notice her duct-taped hands.

Sheldon sighed. "Really?"

Everything happened very quickly after that.

Sheldon whipped the wheel to the side, veering the car suddenly toward the SUV, which had been passing on the left. The SUV swerved and braked to avoid slamming into him, but Sheldon had no intention of collision. He swerved away then jammed the accelerator to the floor. The Crown Vic surged forward, lurching ahead of the SUV.

Another spin of the wheel, and suddenly the car was sideways, blocking both lanes of the freeway. There was a median wall in this part of the freeway, and a metal crash-wall just outside the shoulder on the other side, so the car effectively blocked traffic.

Sheldon had spun the car so that he was closest to the SUV, which had jammed its own brakes and come to a stop not twenty feet away. Now Sheldon threw the door open and jumped out of the car in the same instant it stopped moving. A few quick strides and he was at the SUV.

Danielle heard herself screaming. She leaned to the side, trying to see what was happening, but saw only a series of bright flashes. Then Sheldon opened the SUV's driver side door and pushed something. He got in and the SUV edged slowly past the Crown Vic. He drove it to the side of the road. A moment later the hood popped, then the liftgate.

Then Sheldon was back, smiling as he got into the car. He put something in her lap, and Danielle stared at it, barely hearing him as he said, "Let's not do that again, Danielle? Okay?"

Danielle stared at the bloodstained plush toy in her lap. A unicorn.

"Okay," she whispered.

Sheldon drove for a few minutes. He ate a few more chickpeas. Then he slowed suddenly. As though Danielle had asked what was happening – which she certainly had not, given she had bent her will entirely to not throwing up – he said, "I don't know. Just give me a sec."

The car slowed still further. Stopped right in the middle of the road. A moment later Sheldon shrugged and started driving again. "Thought I saw something is all," he said. He smiled at her. "You sure you don't want a chickpea?"

5

Legion feels as though he is being led.

He knows that is not likely. He is not religious. He was brought up in a religious home –

*(*We *were brought up in a religious* place. *Not a home. A* place.*)*

– but he has never believed in God particularly. He believes in good, and believes in evil, but questions of things more powerful and holy have always disquieted him. Still, the feeling persists as he drives along, moment after moment, mile after mile.

"Maybe you *are* being led. Maybe there *is* a God," says Water. Legion does not have to turn to look at him to know that it is his drowned brother who spoke. Not just because of the wet sound of his voice, but because he suddenly realizes that Water has always been like this. He has always believed in God – or at least believed in the possibility of a God to believe in.

"Stupid. There's just us, Water."

Again, Legion knows without looking that it is Fire who speaks. And again, it is less because of the whispery, flickering sounds of syllables spoken through blackened teeth and charred flesh than it is because Fire has *always* felt this way.

Water has always believed.

Fire has always refused.

And what about me? Do *I believe in God? Do I believe in* anything, *or nothing at all?*

"That's for you to find out, isn't it?" says Water.

Legion looks at his brother. Water and Fire are both in the back of the van, moving around the many supplies they have carried with them wherever they go, and as he looks back he sees Fire staring at him. Water is picking through electronics, peering at monitors. He often did this before jobs, before *lessons* in which they taught evildoers to rue their sins. Legion knows it is not real, but he still sees his brother going through jamming equipment, checking radio ranges, counting and sorting the blasting caps and wires and leads they have so often used.

I'm insane.

"Not insane," says Water, his voice calm and soothing. "You're seeing what you have to see."

"If I'm not insane, then how come you hear me when I think?" says Legion.

Fire snorts, a dry whip-crack of a laugh following. Something clinks as he rifles through the surveillance equipment and electronics and everything else that lives in the back of the van.

Only that's not really happening. I'm not hearing those things, they're not doing those things. It's just an imagining. Like Fire and Water. Just memories made flesh in my mind.

"Awww, that hurts, L," says Fire. "Calling me an imagining. I thought of myself as more of a feeling. Vengeance made flesh."

"Stop taunting him, Fire," says Water.

"Make me, Water. Legion likes it when I push his buttons. Always did." The sounds – real or imagined – of things being moved around stop now, and a moment later Legion feels Fire's breath, hot as the flames that baked his skin and flesh away, on his neck. "You like it, right, L?"

"Call him Legion," says Water. "He likes that name."

"Does he?" says Fire. "Well, he looks more like an 'L' to me." To Legion, he adds, "Right? An *L* is just a straight line that got all bent at the end. That's you, right?"

"I don't like this conversation," says Legion.

Everyone falls silent.

Legion feels as though he is being led, but he does not know by whom, or for what purpose. Most of all, he does not know if he *likes* feeling as though he is being led.

"It's all right. Just let it happen," counsels Water. A wet hand touches Legion's cheek, an almost-caress that reminds him of all the kind touches he never felt as a child.

"Yeah, Dad was a prick," says Fire, as though hearing Legion's thoughts, though in fact he simply *was* part of Legion's thoughts.

I am *insane. Just like he was. Just like Father. Perhaps it would be better for me to die like he did.*

"He did his best," says Water, but even kind Water sounds subdued as he says it.

"He was a prick," insists Fire. Then the hot breath returns to Legion's cheek as his dead brother whispers, "Right, L?"

For a long moment there is no sound other than the hum of asphalt under tires. Legion likes that sound; always has. He has always liked being on the open road between lessons.

"Yeah," insists Fire. "You like being on the road because stopping too long reminds you of where we grew up, and that reminds you of Dad. And Dad," he crows, with a pointed look at Water, *"was a prick."*

"Fire," says Water, a trace of warning in his voice. "Don't bother Legion."

"I think we're way past bothered, bro," says Fire. "I'd say we're halfway to *crazy*."

"Only halfway?" says Legion.

The words bring a mix of emotion. Half terror, half relief. The terror at wondering if he really is insane, and what he can possibly do about it. The relief at the idea that if he *is* insane, he doesn't *need* to do anything at all.

"That's the spirit, L. The greatest gift of madness is the ability to live a life without consequences."

"That's not true," says Water. "We all have to live with the consequences of our actions. That's what we believe, right? It's why we've done what we've done for so long?"

Legion nods. He remembers the last job. Remembers cutting the throat of one person, beating another to death and then impaling them with branches over and over. He remembers hanging a third, watching the feet twitch in the last moments of death.

And before that… so many other people. So many other *students* he has punished and – when necessary – killed to teach them the error of their ways.

"Good times," whispers Fire.

"*Necessary* times," says Water. "We aren't here to enjoy it, we're here to help people rise above themselves."

"Bullshit," says Fire. "We kill the people we think are worthy, that's it."

Silence again.

Legion feels less now as though he is driving over a road, and more like the world is unspooling behind him. Like the only thing that is real is the past. The only thing *tangible* is all that he has left behind.

Neither of his brothers speak for a long while. That's a mercy. Legion knows now that they are and always have been three, not One. But the idea of One was so real for so long, and coping with the reality of the break in his mind is hard. Tiring.

Not to mention the driving itself. That's tiring, too. How come it never seemed so hard before?

"Because we took turns," says Water, voice wet and flat. He sounds like he is crying. "We were always three."

"Never One," agrees Fire. He does *not* sound like he is crying; something so burnt away cannot cry, surely. But he does sound like the pain of his death is here again, new and bright.

We are suffering. We are. We. We…

The tires hum. The world unspools below them, leaving a past that is real and understood behind, every turn of the wheels drawing them toward a future that moves ahead as they do and so never will be quite real.

The future, Legion realizes, is just a hope. A faith.

We put our feet down because we believe we will be able to stand.

We walk because we believe that we will carry ourselves to something good.

We live *because we believe that our lives will matter.*

He knows then that he does believe in something. He believes that his work is not over. There are still people to help, to *teach*. Some he will help like he helped Jayn the gas station attendant: by saving their lives, by showing them that mercy and grace are real, and miracles exist. Some he will teach in the way that he taught the two junkies: by showing them the error of their ways in a final manner; by taking their evils and snuffing them out and grinding them to dust below his heel.

"We do believe," says someone. Legion does not know if it is him, with his real lips and lungs and tongue and mouth, or if it is the voice of one of the brothers he still imagines. He does not know if it matters, either. In this, he knows, they are still – and always will remain – truly One.

"We believe." Legion speaks the words, and as he does they become true.

A hand falls on his right shoulder. Wet, cold. "We believe," Water agrees.

Another hand rests on Legion's left shoulder, hot and far too light with so much of its flesh burned away. "We believe," says Fire.

"We are being led," says Legion.

"We are," says Water.

"We are," says Fire.

He drives. The world unspools. The van moves toward the future.

Legion drives for hours. He takes interchanges at random. Sometimes he leaves the freeways and goes to highways. Sometimes he drives over surface streets and for a long while he drives over dirt roads.

He is being led.

He sleeps. Curls up in the back of the van among the equipment he used when he was One, to bring sinners to a knowledge of their sins, and to purge the sins or extinguish the sinners themselves.

He dreams. It is a long dream, a dark dream. He dreams of Father. Father stares at him, and Legion knows that in the dream he is a child again.

"Commies could kill us all," says Father.

"Yessir," says Legion – though at the time of his memory, he did not have that or any other name. Father called him *Son,* and beyond that Legion knew only of Himself, the three of the One.

In his memory, the two other brothers sit silently nearby. They have learned that over the years: only one of them should speak at a time. If more do, then Father will at best ignore the others. At worst, he will throw them into the Dark Place. He will put them in there and turn off all the lights.

No light penetrates that room. No light penetrates *any* room in here. When Father turns off the lamps, the darkness is so complete it becomes a thing alive. Legion does not like this. Neither do his brothers.

Father only wanted one child. So one child is all he sees.

From time to time they go outside. They leave the place they live and go where Legion can hunt, or learn woodcraft and survival skills, or just to "enjoy the world before it ends," as Father puts it.

Now, staring down at him, Father says, "Commies could kill us all, and we're all we've got. Just you and me, son."

"I know," says Legion. His brothers – the other two thirds of the One that Father has created – stand silent. They look down at the floor. That is safer, too. Father does not like six eyes looking at him when he expects only two.

"What will you do if they come?"

"Survive," says Legion.

Father nods as though Legion has said something wise. Legion does not know how wise a thing it is. It is just his life: he survives. Father hunts and brings back food. Sometimes it is enough to feed all three of the One. Sometimes it is enough only for one part of the One.

Legion is always hungry. He leaves the house and hunts on his own whenever he can, because that is the only way to beat back some of the hunger. But Father gets angry when he leaves like that.

Father gets angry a lot.

"You'll survive, Son," says Father. "It'll be hard. You gotta know how to do anything and everything. But knowing how to survive is the measure of a person's worth."

Legion knows what Father is about to do: a test is coming. Father is always teaching and then testing the One. "You gotta know how to do anything and everything," he always says.

Father shows Legion the gun in his hands. It is a good gun, but hard for Legion to shoot well. His hands are still small enough that pulling a trigger and aiming is hard. He is better with the small .22 rifle he uses when he hunts alone.

"Disassemble, clean, and reassemble it," says Father. He holds up a stopwatch, then clicks one of the buttons. The timer starts.

Legion does not ask anything further. He drops to the floor and starts taking the gun apart. One of the other brothers – other parts of the One – brings him tools as he needs them. Father does not seem to mind this. Legion is glad. Perhaps someday he will be better with the weapon, but for now he needs help to meet Father's demands.

The gun is stripped, cleaned, and put back together. The button is clicked. Father stares at the stopwatch. "Acceptable," he says.

Legion exhales sharply. He has passed the test. The One has been found worthy, if only for the moment.

"Get your books. We're going to learn about communications equipment and disruption today," Father says.

Legion nods. He leaves the room. He goes to the room where his single bed rests. He takes turns with Himselves, one of the One sleeping in the bed, then spending two nights on the floor, then another night on the bed.

Beside the bed are piles of books. Father has said that everything he might need to know to survive are in those books. They have internet access as well, and occasionally Father uses that to teach Legion. But mostly it is books.

He grabs one of the books Father has focused on lately: *Telecommunications – Standards and Planning of Radio and Satellite Infrastructure*. Legion does not like the book. But one of the others of the One loves it. And so he hands the book to the other of Himself, and that One takes the book in hand. That One will take the lesson, and will learn the things that Father wants the One to know.

Father teaches the One.

The One learns.

That is the way of things.

Because of that, because today he has satisfied Father, there will be no time in the darkest part of this place. Not today. Father is pleased.

Father eats. Father defecates in the bucket that they use for these purposes. He tousles the hair of one of the One. He even kisses that boy. "Your mother would be proud," he says. Then he slaps that One. "Too bad you killed her."

In Legion's dream, Father sleeps, and in the dream Legion watches over him with the other parts of the One.

At that, he wakes in reality. He stares up at the ceiling of the van. It is hot – too hot, uncomfortably hot.

Something shifts and he looks over. Water sits nearby. "You always liked the tech stuff," says Legion to his drowned, dead brother.

"I did," agrees Water. He smiles a sad smile.

Legion turns his head to the other side. Fire is sitting nearby on that side. "You always liked the guns."

"Yup," says Fire. His charred thumb and first finger make a circle, the blackened sticks of the other three fingers splayed as he makes an "OK" symbol. "I was good at it, too."

"And me?" says Legion. "What was I best at?"

"You were the fighter," says Water.

"Come on, L. Just say it," says Fire. He looks at Legion with his two coal-fire eyes. "You were the one who finally figured out how to kill the old man."

"That was a good day," says Water with a sigh.

"A *great* day," says Fire.

Legion does not reply. He gets up, stretching the kinks out of his back. He was laying on the floor in the narrow aisle between racks and rows of equipment and weaponry that take up space in the van. Not a lot of room. But more than there used to be.

Because it used to be three of us sleeping in here, even if we had forgotten that fact. Even if Father's mad insistence that there was just one of us had finally rubbed off and we believed it, there were still three people in this tiny space.

For some reason, the thought makes Legion happy. He thinks it is because the simple act of recognizing how very crowded a single life can be when three people are living it at once means that he is going to have room to stretch out a bit now. He can spread his wings and perhaps he will fly.

He gets out of the van. He had parked on the side of a small road in an area that looks fairly rural. No one stopped to check on him, no police officer woke him to tell him to move along. He is alone.

He voids his bladder beside the road. He does not need to defecate, so he gets back into the van and starts driving again.

He drives for more hours. Eventually he finds himself in another convenience store. He waits behind a man who fills a cup the size of a bathtub with Dr. Pepper, then Legion gets his own soda. He ambles through the aisles of the convenience store. Water and Fire are there, of course, but neither is in a talkative mood, it seems, for they do nothing but watch.

The man who bought the Dr. Pepper pays for it and leaves. Legion sees him go outside and talk to a beautiful woman. They laugh together, and Legion smiles. The world is full of lovely moments, and he is glad to be seeing this one.

They get in the car and leave. Legion wishes them well.

A moment later, another car pulls out of the gas station. Legion does not see who is driving it, but he feels strange. Something is tickling his instincts. Something is *wrong*.

He frowns.

"Something about the driver was weird," says Fire.

"But is it a sin? Is it evil?" asks Water quietly. "To be weird?"

"No, but it could be the sign of someone with… *issues*," says Fire. His black-stick tongue wanders over his sooty teeth as he ruminates. "Should we…"

Water sighs. Froth bubbles out of his mouth and splashes down his neck and is soaked up by his already-sodden shirt. "I guess we can follow him, since you've obviously got a burr in your bonnet about it."

"It's burr in your *saddle*. *Bees* go in your bonnet," says Legion.

"What was that, pal?" says the man behind the convenience store counter. Legion turns toward him. The other man is obviously worried about the lone man who is standing still and watching cars leave and (apparently) talking to himself. The man is in his sixties, probably someone who recently discovered that his social security payments and meager life savings would not support him, so had to take a job like this as the only one that would hire someone his age.

Legion feels bad for him.

"Maybe you should kill him," says Fire. He clicks his tongue, *tsk tsk tsk.* "Sad case like this one –"

"No, he doesn't need killing," says Water. "He needs a bit of compassion is all."

"You're too soft," says Fire. "Soft and wet and bloated with feelings."

"You're too hard," responds Water loftily. "And your feelings have burned away and look what's left behind?"

"Shhh!" hisses Legion. He does not want an argument right now.

"I… didn't say anything," says the man behind the counter. He starts edging toward a nearby phone.

"Sorry," says Legion. He looks at the man, wondering whether he should kill him or give him some other sign of kindness. In the end he opts to give the man a twenty-dollar bill for his snacks and tells him to keep the change.

"Shoulda killed him," says Fire as they leave the store.

"You did the right thing," says Water. "He needed a kindness."

"Sometimes killing *is* a kindness," says Fire.

"True, but if we'd killed him it would have slowed us and we might not have been able to follow the person who felt weird," says Legion.

Both Fire and Water agree that this is sound logic. Legion gets in the van. By the time he has opened the door and gotten inside, Water and Fire have appeared in the van as well. They are riding in the back again, but Legion can hear them talking to each other.

The dead are loud in this place.

Legion pulls out of the convenience store parking lot. He goes the direction of the car driven by the man who felt *off*.

It isn't long before something makes him slow down. The road goes on in a straight line for miles, and he sees nothing but empty road ahead. He has not caught up with the weird person, but something *is* there. Something…

"What am I looking at?" says Legion.

Fire sighs behind him. "We only know what you do, L." He chuckles. "Maybe it's just gas. You gotta fart?"

Legion turns to look at his burnt brother. "When did you get so crass?" he asks.

Fire chuckles again. "I've always been this way. Just you always thought it was *you*, so you noticed it less. People never notice annoying things when they're the ones doing it."

Beside Fire, Water is pointing at something in the back of the van. "You should trust your instincts, Legion," he says.

Legion pulls to the side of the road. Once parked, he goes into the back of the van. He picks up the binoculars his drowned brother had been pointing at, then goes back to the front seat and looks out over the long stretch of road.

At the extreme end of the binoculars' vision, he sees movement. "Can't make it out," he says.

"Swap the binoculars for –" begins Fire, but before he finishes the sentence Legion has already grabbed the larger, more powerful binoculars from the drawer below a rack of automatic weapons.

He looks through the front windshield. Focuses the binoculars, and sees two cars. One belongs to the strange man, the other to the man who bought the Dr. Pepper and the woman that was with him.

The other belongs to a man Legion has not seen before. Just a normal-looking guy with a baseball cap. But he definitely *is* weird. Only a weird person would drag unconscious people out of the front seats of a car, then shove them into the back seat and drive away, leaving the car he arrived in alone and unused on the side of the road.

Legion puts down the binoculars. He is surprised to find he is smiling.

"Why're you grinning like that, L?" asks Fire.

"You know why," burbles Water.

"Says who?" says Fire. His blackened teeth grit together.

"Says me," says Water. He's always been the kindest of them, but he can sound steely when he wants to. He sounds steely now. "Legion knows why he's smiling, which means you and I know as well."

Fire chuckles. "You got me there, Water."

Legion looks at his brothers. "Something bad is happening."

"Obviously," says Fire.

"And we should stop that bad thing," says Legion.

"Indubitably," says Water.

"Do we kill him?" says Legion.

"I'd wait," says Fire. "Let's find out what's going on first."

"Is that because you want to properly teach a sinner, or because you're curious about what made you feel weird?" asks Water. His eyes, always bulging, frozen in an eternal moment of drowning, now narrow a bit.

Fire shrugs. Ash puffs from his joints. "Hey, don't blame me. If I'm curious it's because L is curious."

Legion nods, smiling a bit in embarrassment. "I admit, I *am* curious."

"Then go with it," says Fire. "Follow your gut. Right, Water?"

Water shrugs. Legion notices for the first time that when the water falls from his brother's body and clothes, it puddles below him – but the puddle never gets any bigger. "I did say you should trust your instincts," says Water.

"Then we follow them," says Legion.

He puts the van in gear and heads after the car. They follow for hours – always staying so far back that Legion has to use the binoculars as often as not. He almost loses them at one point when the mysterious driver pulls off the freeway and into a series of hilly roads. Legion spends half an hour wandering aimlessly through the hills before finally returning to the highway…

And that is where luck smiles on him.

Legion sees a large black car in the distance. It is a Crown Victoria, which he knows because Father knew that an understanding of vehicles might come in useful, just like understanding telecom equipment and hunting and explosives might be useful.

"And they *did* turn out to be useful, didn't they?" whispers Fire. "Because knowing those things has let us teach so many bad people, right? So many sinners? Making the world a safe place, so no more kids have to live in houses like ours, hiding from the bad things."

"Do we have to do this now?" asks Water. "Why don't we just –"

"Shut up, both of you," says Legion. He leans far over the steering wheel, pushing his face toward the windshield as though the few extra inches will grant him some divine understanding.

He reaches for the binoculars, which rest on the floor beside him. He keeps driving, but glances through the binoculars long enough to see –

"It's him. It's the guy!"

He is surprised how excited he sounds.

"What about the other two?" asks Water.

"I don't see them."

"Did he drop them somewhere?" asks Water. "Think we should go back and look for them?"

Legion shakes his head.

He follows the Crown Vic, staying back far enough that he is confident the car's driver cannot see him.

The sun starts to set. The Crown Vic slows. Legion does, too. He pulls to the side of the road and watches the man in the baseball cap stop the car, then go to the back.

The man opens the trunk of the car and pulls out the woman from the convenience store parking lot.

"Think Dr. Pepper guy is in the trunk, too?" asks Fire.

"Shut up," bubbles Water.

Legion says nothing. He's watching the man with the cap talk to the woman. He can't hear what they're saying, but he sees the man loose her wrists and arms from behind her back. He watches the man move to the side of the car, take out a potted plant –

"Yeah, he's weird," says Fire.

– from the front seat, put it in the back seat, and then gesture for the woman to sit up front. He sees the woman fall because she's got silvery tape wrapped around her legs. Then the woman gets into the front seat, and the kidnapper closes her door. Legion watches the kidnapper get in the car, talk to the woman for a moment, rewrapping her wrists with tape as he does.

Then they drive.

"This is getting good," says Fire.

Legion follows them. Before long an SUV comes up behind him. Legion pulls to the side to allow the faster-moving vehicle to pass. He is still using the binoculars to track the car at an extreme distance, so he knows he isn't seen by the people he is following. They think they are alone on the road.

No doubt that's why the kidnapper, whoever he is, feels so content nearly running the SUV off the road, then shooting all the passengers and returning to his own car with a bloody toy in his hand.

"Definitely getting good," says Fire in a near-reverent voice.

The kidnapper drives away. Legion follows.

He felt like he was being led. He does not know by what force, but he now knows what he is being led *to*.

Legion will follow this man. He will watch. That is what he does. He follows the wicked and the fallen, he watches their sins and misdeeds and, when he feels he knows enough, he *teaches* them.

This man is in need of teaching.

Legion begins to sing a song, the best song crooned by the lovely and talented 1980s pop star, Tiffany: "I Think We're Alone Now."

A moment later, Water begins whistling wetly as well. Fire cannot whistle – he has no lips – so he hums along. The three of them harmonize well, and that is no surprise at all.

6

Sheldon Steward knew that he was good at a great many things, so when the woman beside him did not speak when spoken to, he knew it was not because of him. He was a fantastic conversationalist – he had read a Twitter thread about the art of conversation – and knew that he was good at it. So it must be Danielle.

That was sad, and he tried to pity her. What would it be like, to go through life unskilled at something as important as the art of conversation? Sad, sad, sad.

Even so, the pity waned after an hour of silence. He had brought her up here to *talk* to him, hadn't he? If he had wanted to do a monologue, he could have just kept Lucy up in the front seat with him.

Finally, Danielle's continuing refusal to speak surpassed even his superhuman patience. He had not hit her again. He had been witty and charming. He had offered her snacks – not junky ones, either, but healthy ones because he thought she should have the option to treat her body as a temple just like he did.

The day started off well. The job had gone to plan.

Still, he was irritated.

"You should really speak when spoken to," he said. Danielle said nothing. Just continued staring straight ahead or out the side window. She did not make eye contact, which was also rude. She *did* occasionally look at the bloodstained toy he had given her earlier, but not him.

Sheldon brought out his trump card. "Would you like some freeze-dried seedless grape slices? I bought them at Trader Joe's – they have the best ones, I think – and wasn't planning on sharing them, but…" He held out the bag and shook it. The wrapping crinkled. It reminded him of the time he found a baby bird as a teen and crushed it in his hand. The baby bird had crinkled like that, all squeaks and then tiny pops and cracks as tiny bones became powder, and even after he ground the thing to goo in his fingers he could still hear those sounds.

But even the power of pleasant memory had not the power to keep his hurt feelings at bay when Danielle refused his kindness. He had offered to share his favorite snack, and she had not even given him the basic courtesy of a "no thank you."

Now he was not just irritated. He was *angry*.

He had to admit, too, that part of his negative feelings were brought on by the vague sense that he was… *missing* something. He had the sense that he was being watched, and that feeling had persisted for hours now. He had no reason to believe it was the case. Sure, he'd seen other cars from time to time, but he was very good at noticing patterns. None of the cars had been following him, or was even part of a group trying to surveil him. He would have known if they were.

But still the feeling persisted. He could not pinpoint why he felt that way, though, and that also made him angry.

He withdrew the snack bag, folded it one-handed so nothing would spill, then slid it under the seat. He glanced at the clock in the car's dashboard. Calculated weight to dosage.

Should be pretty soon.

As with everything else, Sheldon Steward's knowledge of pharmacology approached the stupendous, so it was satisfying but not surprising when the expected thud came not five minutes later.

Sheldon looked around. He was on a stretch of freeway that had a number of off-ramps leading only to vast tracts of empty land used for farming or humping cows or whatever people did in boring places like this. He used one of the off-ramps, pulling off the freeway less than a minute after he heard the first thump in the back of the car.

Beside him, Danielle was clenching and unclenching her hands. He wasn't worried that she would try and attack him. She knew that would be a bad idea – she was definitely rude, but he didn't get a *dumb* vibe off her. No, her hands were doing that because she had heard the sound, too. She knew what was happening behind her, just as Sheldon did.

He drove a quarter mile up the road. Stopped on a soft shoulder that crinkled and crackled like baby bird bones. He put the car in park, then turned off the engine and pocketed the keys.

He smiled at Danielle. "Rudeness is its own punishment. I read that on a billboard once. I thought it was pretty darn wise. But I also think sometimes it's not *enough* of a punishment."

Danielle's eyes widened. Sheldon doubted she knew exactly what was coming, but he could tell that none of the possible scenarios she was imagining were happy ones.

Good.

"Wait, don't –" She began the sentence, but Sheldon was already out of the car and walking toward the back. She started screaming wordlessly, terror and perhaps a bit of anger in her voice. The scream grew words, however, when he touched the button on his key fob that popped the trunk of the car.

"No, please, whatever you're doing please don't don't *don't do it –"*

The screams went on, but Sheldon was not listening to them. Part of being great at things was helping others, and he thought that Danielle really needed this lesson. So he would ignore her cries, though it went against his kind nature to do so.

The trunk showed Sheldon exactly what he had expected to see. There was Alex Anton, new husband and VIP: Very Important Package. Trussed and gagged just as Danielle had been, but where she had looked at Sheldon with fear and pain, Alex just glared at him.

"Please don't, please please please *please please PLEASE –"* Inside the car, Danielle's cries had become stupendously loud. Still, Sheldon knew she would be able to hear what came next.

He ungagged Alex. The man tried to *bite* Sheldon, which was a surprise. But Sheldon enjoyed very fast reflexes, so he avoided the tooth-based amputation of his fingers.

"You sonofa –"

Alex Anton did not finish whatever empty threat he had started. Sheldon did not permit it. In the middle of the second word, he slammed his fist into Alex's groin. He did not use all his power – he was under specific orders about Alex's well-being, and those orders did not include jellying his testicles. Yet. But the blow was enough to kill the man's voice, replacing it with a strangled retching.

Danielle was still screaming, but the screaming had quieted, as though even panic had given way to a need to hear what was happening – which, Sheldon knew (as permitted by his highly developed intuition), was exactly what had occurred.

He waited. Waited. The trunk was open, and the lid blocked his view of Danielle, but he knew what would happen next.

There it was. The *click* of Danielle's door unlocking. The *k-chunk* of it opening. He waited, knowing she was now thinking of whether she could do anything if she got out; wondering if to do so would help or hurt the situation.

Sheldon took the choice away. "If you get out of that car, I will kill him right here. It will hurt, and it will be messy. When I am done I will throw you back in the trunk for the rest of the trip. You will have pieces of your husband all over you when you get out."

A long moment of silence stretched out between them, broken only by Alex's ragged coughing as he struggled to get his spasming body under control.

A moment later, the door creaked as it started to shut.

"Danielle?" Silence greeted him, but he knew the door was still open. He had supernal hearing. "You're going to hear something in a moment. You can scream if you need to, but if you open the door again, your husband becomes a smear in the trunk."

He heard retching – this time from the front of the car – and wondered if she was actually going to puke. He waited a moment, because that was the polite thing to do. When he was confident she would not spew in his car, which would make very bad smells and might even catch Lucy in the Jiffy Super Chunk-style crossfire, he said, "Close the door, Danielle. Now."

Squeak.

Clunk.

Click.

The door shut just as Alex Anton regained control of his voice. It was ragged and breathy, but the fire was still there as he said, "You have no idea what a shitstorm you're walking – *what the hell are you doing*?"

Alex tried to writhe away, but bound and shoved in a trunk there was really nowhere to go, and he did not even slow Sheldon down for a single moment. It was the work of only a second to get the guy's pants undone and then slide them down his hips. Alex kept bucking, kept shouting, "What are you doing?" over and over.

Sheldon looked at the man's boxers. They were comedic – bright blue with red kissy lips all over them. Sheldon approved. A good sense of humor was important, he knew.

He yanked them down as well. Alex got halfway through his tenth, "What are you doing?" and then Sheldon flicked him.

It was light. Just a fraction of the punch Sheldon had sent at his groin earlier. But he aimed it well, and his fingernails struck the tip of Alex's penis. A quick bark of pain exploded from Alex's lips. Sheldon repeated the motion. Another cry, louder. Sheldon did it again, and again, and a fifth time.

By the third slap, Alex was screaming. By the fifth, he was shrieking. When Sheldon flicked the man a sixth time, the shrieking became a chorus as Danielle added her own voice to the mix.

"Such a little thing," said Sheldon. He was referring to how easy it was to break a person. Just a bit of pressure in the right place… Then he realized that his "little thing" comment could be taken another way, given where he had focused his attention. He laughed. Wonderful to enjoy a sense of humor as profound and clever as his.

Mother had always liked his sense of humor. She still did, even if other people – one he was thinking of in particular – did not.

Don't think about that. Just enjoy the moment, Sheldon.

He flicked Alex again, and laughed as Alex and Danielle shrieked. He had been lying about killing Alex, and that just made this even funnier. He was not going to kill Alex – that was strictly against orders. And he had been ordered to bring him in unmaimed and in good health. A knock or two on the head was expected in this kind of work, but Sheldon's most special client had been explicit about not harming anyone beyond that.

But Sheldon also knew that, though the man's testicles and penis might be bruised, he could easily pawn it off as something that had happened in transit. He would still be paid, and he had to admit that the fun of this moment had brought his mood right up.

He removed the spray bottle from his sweater pocket and spritzed Alex's face. The man went to sleep, and Sheldon repeated the spritzing several more times, then sprayed the inside of the trunk. He wanted Alex asleep for a good long time. He didn't want to be interrupted. He wanted to have a good conversation, and that was impossible when someone was thumping around like a spastic fish in the trunk.

He made sure to pull Alex's pants up – he was a kind and thoughtful person, so did not want the man to wake up trussed and fearful *and* naked – then closed the trunk and walked around the side of the car. *Crunch crunch crunch* went the rocks. Sheldon imagined thousands of baby birds on the ground, and imagined that he was stomping them all to paste. It lightened his mood still further, and he was positively beaming when he got back into the car. He would have to bring Mother to a road like this, and they could dance on the shoulder into the small hours of the night.

Once in the car, Sheldon looked over at Danielle. She was no longer screaming. She had bitten the back of her hand to stop, apparently, and blood streamed down her wrist and arm. Sheldon sighed. He reached across her. She recoiled, but he had no interest in touching her.

The car was not his. It was stolen, prepared in advance for his use by contacts he had called on the plane ride over here. But stolen or not, Sheldon liked to be prepared, so he had asked for a small first aid kit to be included in the car when it was left for him to find. He fished out the kit and pulled out a Band-Aid. Acting carefully so as not to touch the sterile pad, he tore off the wrapping and removed the plastic strips that covered the adhesive. He held out the Band-Aid.

Danielle did not say thank you. She didn't even hold out her hand.

Another sigh. "Danielle, I just want to stop that bleeding. It looks painful and I don't like blood on my things. Well, the car isn't mine, really, but even so…"

He gestured with the Band-Aid. Reluctantly, still looking as though she might spew, Danielle held out her hand. Sheldon put the Band-Aid on. It fit over her wound perfectly. In another life, he reflected, he might have been a famous doctor or world-renowned surgeon. He was very good at things like that.

He put the car in drive but did not pull onto the road. Not yet. He stared at Danielle, waiting. He knew the question that must come next.

"Is he…" Danielle could not finish the sentence.

Sheldon smiled his most winning grin. He practiced this grin twenty-five times in the mirror every day, so he knew it was a very sincere, calming smile. "Alex is alive and well. He's just sleeping." Now he let his smile tilt downward, into a perfectly-crafted expression of loving remonstration. "But I will kill him if you keep ignoring me."

Again, a lie. Under the parameters of the job, Sheldon wouldn't be allowed to kill Alex for quite some time. He was going to do *other* things to the man – and to Danielle, as well – as part of the job. But he wouldn't be allowed to kill either of them and wash Lucy's branches in their blood until they had suffered as long as his skill and medical science would allow.

But Danielle didn't know that.

She nodded.

"So you'll talk back?" She nodded. He waited. She looked blank. He cocked an exquisitely groomed eyebrow.

She shrank back, but said, "Yes, I'll talk back."

"Good."

Now he *did* pull the car into the road. He performed a three-point-turn that was almost artistic in the perfection of its execution, and headed back to the freeway. He grinned that practiced grin again as they took the on-ramp. "It's a road trip, Danielle. Try and have some fun with it, okay?"

"O… okay."

They merged onto the freeway. The sun had gone down, and the sky was dark. Headlights could be seen ahead, not many but enough to remind Sheldon that the world was full of people and full of the possibility that they brought. Behind him, other headlights trailed in the distance. That was nice, too. Even in the dark he would notice a tail. He noticed things like that.

"So… what do you like to do?"

"Do?"

Sheldon activated his turn signal and slid into the leftmost lane. He would stay there unless someone came up on him fast and hard, then he would yield. Many people who drove the speed limit stayed in the far right lane, but Sheldon knew that, statistically, the right lane in the freeway was where most accidents occurred. He had read that in a BuzzFeed article. So he always drove at least one lane over when possible.

Secure in the safest lane, he said again, "What do you like to do, Danielle? I know that you're a lawyer, but that sounds dreadful and I don't want to talk about it. So how about it? What are your hobbies? Do you like to dance? Sew? Do you do macrame? I like growing bonsai trees. I'm new to it as a hobby, but I can already tell I'm very good."

Danielle blinked. For a moment Sheldon worried she had blown a mental fuse. If that was the case he would have to dope her and toss her in the trunk with Alex-the-genitally-bruised. What a drag.

Thankfully, something flickered in her eyes and Danielle sat up a bit straighter as she said, "I like to play video games."

"Really?" Sheldon laughed. *That* was a delightful surprise. "What kind?"

"Uh… I like *Fortnite*. And *Call of Duty*."

"Yuck." Sheldon shivered. "I don't like the shooting games." He waited. When Danielle said nothing he added, "Danielle, I really need you to commit to this conversation. There has to be give-and-take, and if you just leave me hanging too often I'll get bored and visit your husband."

"No! Don't –" Danielle forced herself to silence, visibly trying to get herself under control. "I… I would have thought someone like you would –"

She cut herself off again, as though suddenly realizing what she was saying and what a dreadful mistake it surely was to intimate that your stellar conversation partner is a violent person.

Sheldon waved carelessly. "Don't worry, Danielle, I'm not going to be offended. That's a good question. I read an article called 'Fifteen Things Every Good Conversation Should Have,' and asking good questions was number three. So good job!" He gave her a thumbs up that he knew would drive home how proud he was of her.

She was silent a moment, but not too long. She was learning. "So… I would have thought someone in your line of work would like that kind of game."

He glanced slyly at her. "What do you think my line of work *is*, Danielle?"

Silent a bit longer this time, but again Danielle answered quickly enough that he deemed it acceptable. "I don't know. You know my name. You know Alex's name. So this wasn't an accident."

"No, indeed it was not, Danielle. Full marks for that deduction!" He sent another thumbs-up her way, because Number Eight of "Fifteen Things Every Good Conversation Should Have" was *affirmative listening*.

"You're good at the job, whatever it is."

"Thank you, Danielle. That's truly kind, and I appreciate it. But may I ask how you came to that conclusion?" (Number Twelve: Ask good follow-up questions!)

"You nabbed us on a public stretch of highway, but at a time when there was no one around. You were waiting for us and we had no chance to respond. You obviously have supplies – from cars to whatever it was you knocked us out with. You have done this before." Her voice, trembling as she began, smoothed and was close to normal in tone and steadiness by the end of her little speech. It returned to a quaver for a moment, though, when she added, "And you know our names. You know we're married." She took a deep breath. "Can I ask…"

She petered out. Sheldon gave her a shot of Number Nine: a frank and open environment. "You can ask anything, Danielle. If I feel like I can answer, I will. But unless your question is intentionally obtuse or irritating, you and Alex will continue just fine."

For the moment.

"Why?" she said. "What did we ever do –"

"Ahhhh, Danielle. I'm afraid I can't answer that. Suffice it to say that we're going to have a chat with someone who wants very badly to meet you. And it's because they're stupid."

Danielle blinked. "Uh… what?"

"*Fortnite* and *Call of Duty*. They're stupid, that's why I don't like them. I try not to engage in violent video games. Facebook and Twitter have articles showing that they're addictive and waste time, and several influencers on Instagram think the same thing. Stupid. I prefer to spend time with Lucy."

"Who's Lucy?" Danielle asked. Sheldon suspected she was asking more because she was afraid to be silent than because of actual interest. But she was trying, so he decided not to mind her lack of enthusiasm.

He jerked a thumb over his shoulder. "Lucy is my bonsai tree."

Danielle looked behind her. Any sane person with an ounce of class and a matching ounce of intelligence would have marveled at the beauty of the living art riding in the backseat.

Apparently Danielle was lacking in sanity, class, and/or intelligence. She said, "The tree?" and sounded supremely unimpressed.

"Not just the tree. The *bonsai* tree. They're an art form very few practice, and even fewer with any skill."

He waited.

"It's… very lovely."

"Thank you, Danielle." He smiled his practiced-to-perfection grin. "See? Isn't this nicer now that we're having a real conversation?"

She smiled back at him. "Thank you. Yes. It is."

He reached under his seat. "Freeze-dried seedless grape slices?" he asked. This time when he extended the bag, she took it. Her hands were still bound, but she managed to get the bag open and pour a few of the snacks into her hand and then toss them in her mouth without spilling any of them on herself or the car. Sheldon approved.

"You're a neat person. That's good."

"Neat?"

"You obviously take care of yourself. Though I have to admit that liking Cadbury Eggs is not something that will serve you well over time." He wrinkled his nose. "Yucky."

"I'll have to do something about that. Wouldn't want anything yucky around me."

Sheldon's grin disappeared as his eyes snapped to the side. Danielle tried to mask the expression on her face before he saw it, but moved too slow – or (more likely) it was better said that he moved too fast. He was very fast. So he saw the derision on her face before she managed to cover it with a vacant stare.

"We were having such a pleasant conversation, Danielle." He shook his head. Reached under the seat again, but this time he did not bring out chickpeas or some other healthy snack. He pulled a pair of pliers out and laid it on the leg closest to Danielle. "I'd like you to have some manners. If you can't..." He worked the jaws of the pliers, opening and closing them so they snapped *snick snick* and looked like the claw of an angry crab.

"I'm sorry. Please. Don't…" Danielle stopped talking. She took a long, shuddering breath, then seemed to gather herself mentally. She looked at him with a smile that, if not as good as his own super-sincere smile, was still pretty good. Excellent, even, considering the circumstances. Not many people could put a smile on following what Danielle had been through in the past few hours.

When she spoke again, her voice sounded utterly normal. Calm, relaxed. Like she was talking to a friend about some life-enriching Insta photo. "I'll be better. But I would like to ask you something." Her smile widened. Kind and inviting and so very sincere that Sheldon knew in that moment she wanted to have sex with him. That wasn't a surprise. Most women wanted to have sex with him. He was very attractive.

"What would you like to ask me?" said Sheldon.

"Could we stop? I have to go to the bathroom."

Sheldon frowned. "You aren't trying to put something over on me, are you?"

"No, I just have to pee. Pretty badly, actually."

Sheldon thought about this. He nodded. "All right."

Again he pulled off the freeway, and after a quarter mile of driving he pointed to a field, scrubby and empty. "You can go there."

He got out of the car and helped her out of her side. She was still tied hand and foot, and she gestured at her legs. "Can I…"

"What?"

She sighed, obviously trying not to be rude but failing more than a little. "I can't do it all tied up."

"Sure you can. Just go."

"But it'll get all over me. That means it'll be all over your car as well. I don't want to mess up your car."

Sheldon frowned, but nodded. He himself was possessed of a bladder of preternatural capacity, and rarely had to go more than once or twice or sometimes three times a day. But some people were less gifted in this respect – nearly everyone, in fact – so it made sense that she might want to pee.

But she had been right: he was good at what he did. And that meant he was not about to cut her binds. Not without some ground rules.

He pulled out his favorite knife, which was named Hemingway. Nearly as sharp as Sheldon's wit, it would easily cut through the wraps of tape on her legs. He leaned toward her and was pleased that she did not flinch. Not even when he said, "I'm going to cut the tape off your knees, but not your ankles. You can hop over there," he added, gesturing to a small spot fifty feet away that was clearer of scrub and brush, "and do what you have to do. But the second I think you're up to something, or spot you trying to loose your bindings any more than I've already done, and I will open the trunk of my car. I will lay Alex's head across the edge of the trunk and I will slam it until it looks like his neck is attached to a bag full of country-style soup. Understood?"

Danielle nodded. She even smiled again. He cut the tape on her knees and then she hopped toward the tiny clearing. He watched her carefully. He had no desire to invade her private space – not right now, at least – but that didn't mean he wasn't going to watch her like a hawk.

She did her business. She didn't whine or complain about the lack of toilet paper, and that was a good thing, too. Sheldon was really going to enjoy scraping her toughness away, one layer of skin at a time. Maybe he'd even let her have sex with him at some point in the process. That would be nice of him.

She finished and returned. Sheldon had already grabbed another roll of duct tape. He waggled it in her direction. "You're going to lie down on your tummy and not move while I re-tape your legs. Okay?

"Sure. Do you want to keep talking after?"

"Well, of course, I –" His voice died suddenly and he stood up a little taller. He felt like a red-hot iron spike had just been inserted into his spine. Something was wrong, his instincts were shouting. But he couldn't tell what it was. There was something in the night, something he couldn't see.

That feeling of being watched was back.

"Come on," he said gruffly, and gestured for Danielle to lie down. She did, and he tied her knees again. Then he helped her up – far more roughly than he had originally planned – and all but shoved her into the car.

"Do you –" she began.

"Shut up."

She did. Sheldon swung around, looking to all four points of the compass. He saw nothing, no one. They were alone. No need to bloody his hands on some inconvenient traveler. No reason to feel antsy.

Yet he did.

Sheldon closed Danielle's door. He hurried around the back of the car, stopping at the driver's side and looking around again.

It was night.

They were alone.

But he didn't feel alone. Sheldon Steward had great eyesight, even better hearing. He knew his senses were telling him to enjoy this solitude. But something inside him was screaming. And unlike when he was making screams happen in others, the screams in his own mind were something he did not enjoy at all.

7

Danielle was struggling to keep up.

First getting knocked out, then waking up in the trunk of her car with Alex, then getting pulled out by the psychotic Sheldon Steward-with-a-*d*. Trying to escape – abortively after the madman now riding beside her murdered an SUV full of people –

(A family*!*

Don't think about it. Later. Not now.)

– then trying to maintain the pretense of a calm, happy outlook that Sheldon seemed to require.

He was trying to be charming, erudite, kind. But everything he said was terrifying, shallow, and laced with threat.

She had meant what she said when she asked to relieve herself: she didn't have any intention of running away. She had no idea where she was, it was dark out, and – most of all – she wasn't going to let Alex be taken away by this madman.

So she squatted in the scrub and did her business. She wasn't exactly thrilled about the situation, but it was something she could handle. She could handle anything, if it meant getting her and Alex out of whatever this was.

She plastered on her best smile when she returned to the car, then felt again like she had to run to keep up with whatever turn of events fate was tossing her way, because Sheldon went from friendly-murderous to just crazy-murderous. He kept looking at the rearview mirror, sometimes spinning suddenly in his seat as though he might catch someone hiding in the backseat.

He was obviously worried about being followed. Danielle didn't know whether she hoped someone was actually following them or not. Of course she *hoped* it was a SWAT team bristling with automatic weapons and maybe a few rabid dogs.

But what if it was another car holding nothing but innocent bystanders?

Danielle risked a glance at the mirror on her side of the car. She saw nothing but darkness behind them. On a long stretch of unlit freeway, she would have been able to see headlights following them a mile away.

There was nothing.

Again, that mix of emotions: despair, because there was no one following, and that meant no one coming to help. Elation, because she didn't want anyone else getting hurt trying to help her.

That thought led to Alex. He had been out for longer than her. What if Sheldon was wrong about whatever drug he had used on them? What if Alex was back there right now, convulsing silently or drowning on his own vomit?

She shook her head, as though by doing so she might shake loose the dark thoughts that threatened to overwhelm her. Sheldon saw the movement and looked at her sharply. "What is it? Do you see someone?"

Danielle had to struggle to keep from laughing at the absurdity of her captor asking her to act as assistant lookout. She hid the emotion – one she knew instinctively that Sheldon would not like or respond well to – by casting her eyes down. "No, sir."

The "sir" seemed to shake some of the paranoia loose in a way that Danielle shaking her own head had failed to do. He smiled widely and said, "No *sir*s here, Danielle. The only sir I ever knew was my dad, and we stopped talking a long time ago."

"I'm sorry," said Danielle. Another "has the world gone insane?" moment – the madness of offering condolences to her enemy. But it was automatic, an ingrained response to the grief of another human, even, apparently, when the human was a loon.

"Don't be." Sheldon's eyes got dreamy. "He left when I was little. Ditched his little family." He winked at her, a slow open and close of his eye that seemed somehow obscene. "I found him though." He inhaled and smiled, as though savoring the smell of cookies in the oven. "And sometimes he screams for me."

This time Danielle didn't manage to mask her expression, and she could tell that Sheldon clearly saw the horror there. Surprisingly, though, he did not react with anger or even irritation. He laughed.

"I haven't *killed* him, Danielle." He shook his head and grinned ruefully, like a parent might at a child who had made a foolish but adorable mistake. "I wouldn't kill my own dad, that's crazy. What kind of son would that make me?" Another deep breath of air, another blissful smile. "No, he's still alive. Sometimes I visit him." His smile tilted down at the edges. "Poor Mom," he said. "She was never the same after he left. But she's happy now. I take care of her." Shaking his head disapprovingly, he added, "Because I *love* my mom." Then he glanced slyly at Danielle. "What about you?"

"What… what about me?"

"Do you love your mom?"

Danielle opened her mouth to answer. She didn't know what she was going to say, but knew she had to say something.

Before she could, Sheldon spoke again. "I have a file on you, Danielle. I got a lot of information to prep for this job, so I know a *lot* about you." He waited, but she didn't answer; didn't know if she was *supposed* to answer. Sheldon sighed and repeated that disapproving shake of his head. "Don't lie to me, Danielle. That's all I'm saying. *Liar, liar, pants on fire*. Remember that saying?"

"Yes."

"Good." A predatory smile curled his features, illuminated by the dashboard lights so that he looked ghoulish and all the more frightening. "Because lie to me, and it's not just a saying. It's what happens to you." She nodded. The ghoulish smile disappeared, replaced by one she knew was meant to be calm and sincere but which instead conveyed barely-contained madness. "So: do you love your mother?"

Danielle turned forward. She stared out the front window, seeing nothing of the road ahead. "No," she said.

"And why is that?"

"Because she was a vicious bitch who killed my –"

A sharp pain exploded in her already-bruised face as Sheldon slapped her. "Don't say words like that. Ladies shouldn't curse."

Danielle blinked back tears. "I'm… I'm sorry." She tried not to add a sob to the end and succeeded, if only barely.

"It's all right. Not everyone is as cultured as I am. I get that. In fact, *few* people are as cultured as I am." Sheldon shrugged. "But if we aren't punished, we never learn." He flicked a glance in the rearview mirror, but apparently still saw nothing. His body relaxed a bit. "So you were saying? She was a vicious bitch who killed your…"

"My brother," said Danielle.

"Interesting," said Sheldon. "Tell me more."

"What do you want to know?"

"How she did it. And remember –"

"No lying." Sheldon got that irritated look again when she interrupted him, so Danielle hurried forward with the story. She didn't want to tell it, but she wanted Sheldon angry with her even less.

"I was twelve. Jakey was fifteen. He was a good kid, but he fell into a bad crowd. Nothing too bad, actually, but they smoked pot and drank and it drove our mother nuts."

"So she was crazy?"

Danielle sighed, still staring straight ahead. "I honestly don't know. But she certainly was controlling –"

Danielle flinched, worried that the insult aimed at a mother would earn her another slap. Sheldon just nodded that she should continue. "It didn't even bother her really that he was smoking pot or later doing some harder drugs. What bothered her was that she had told him not to, and he did it anyway."

"So he defied her? That was the worst of it for her?"

Danielle nodded. The road ahead was still utterly dark, the black fought back only a few dozen feet by the car's headlights. But she saw something in the nothing that preceded them all the same: her brother's eyes the last time she saw him. Haunted. Terrified. In pain.

"She called in the cops. Showed them his stash, and he got sent to juvie."

"That doesn't sound all that bad. He was a user, he got turned in." Sheldon sniffed. "Drugs are terrible for you. Look at this body." He gestured at himself. "You think I got this way by being an addict? No sir. The body's a temple. I think Kim Kardashian said that, and she would know. A *temple*. So it was good that she – your mom, not Kim Kardashian – turned your brother in. He could get clean that way."

Danielle strangled another laugh, this time one of despair. "He didn't get clean, he got killed."

"Tell me more. Spare no detail," said Sheldon. That wolf-grin returned. "No detail at all."

Danielle waited for a moment to see if her brother's eyes would fade from her memory, from the darkness in front of her. They didn't. They never did, completely.

"He was in a fight in the detention center. Two older kids got him."

"What exactly did they do to him?"

"They pulled the leg off one of the bunks, cornered Jakey, and took turns beating him to death with it."

"Did you see him after that? His body? What did it look like?"

"No, I didn't see it."

"Not even at the funeral? *Was* there a funeral?"

"Yes. There was a funeral. But it was a closed casket. I can remember the funeral director telling us that would be better."

Danielle had no wish to reveal things to the smiling madman beside her, but she felt herself falling into the memory nonetheless. She saw the funeral director's office. She smelled the cinnamon from the lit candles on a bookshelf. She also smelled other things, sharp and rotten, that played at the edges of the intentionally thick odor of the candles.

She saw her mother.

"Mr. Schmidt was his name. I remember him. He was nice. He had a blue bow tie and –"

"Boooo-ring," intoned Sheldon. "Who cares what he looked like. What did he say about your brother?"

"Just that he was… that a closed casket would be best."

"Oh, come now, Danielle. I bet he said more than that. You haven't lied, yet – not exactly – but I know you're leaving things out. *Liar, liar, pants on fire,* but it might also be *leave things out, I cut things off.*" He glared at her. The madness flickered brightly in his eyes, a bonfire in his skull that had burnt sanity to ash. "What did Mr. Schmidt say?"

"He –" Danielle's voice caught in her throat. She swallowed. "He said he'd never seen a body so disfigured."

"To you? To a little girl?"

"No. Not to me. To my mother."

"But you were there."

"She insisted."

"Ahhhh…" Sheldon laughed, then licked his lips sensuously. "How kind of her."

"She wanted me to know what happens to people who cross her. Who *disobey* her will."

"But he *was* doing drugs. She *was* right to put him in jail."

Danielle turned to look at Sheldon, wondering if she should say what was in her heart. She glanced out the window. There was Jakey, the way his eyes had looked, so hurt, so afraid. That decided her.

"Jakey was a good kid. No record. He would have – should have – gotten a slap on the wrist. Maybe probation, maybe even a few weeks in a low-security juvenile detention to scare him a bit."

"Evidently the court disagreed." Sheldon shrugged. "They would be the ones who knew best, wouldn't they?"

"No. Because what really happened was my mom got the public defender helping my brother kicked off the case. She hired the best attorney she could buy –"

"And even with high-quality legal aid your brother was still found guilty. He must have really been *awful*."

"I didn't say high-quality."

"You said he was the best money could buy."

"I said he was the best my *mother* could buy. For herself." Danielle was staring out the front window again. Staring at Jakey's eyes. She couldn't see *him*, just those eyes. Keeping pace with the car, moving ahead at exactly the same rate of speed she herself was, so he was always just barely in sight, always just barely out of reach. "She got a guy who not only pleaded guilty, but managed to convince the prosecutor that there was enough evidence to convict him of possession with intent to distribute."

"But that's illegal."

"Not if you have money like my mom did." She closed her eyes. She couldn't look at Jakey's eyes – not even the memory of them, cloaked in the darkest of nights. "She got him tossed in a detention facility for the hardest, most high-risk kids."

"And you said when you saw him last… when was that?"

"Please," she whispered. "Please don't do this."

She didn't know if she was talking about the situation in general, asking for the man to release her and Alex, or if she was talking about his insistence on her revealing these deepest, most sacred, most awful parts of her mind.

"I'm afraid we have to, Danielle." He glanced in the back seat. "Lucy looks even more beautiful in the night, I think. So she agrees, too." He tapped the pliers. "Talk, Danielle."

"It was a week before he died. He knew it was coming. I went to the detention center – alone. Mom refused to go, and refused to take me. I took a bus. They weren't supposed to let me in – I was a minor. But a few of the guys who ran the place knew that Jakey didn't belong there. A few more had met Mom, and that was enough to convince them to take pity. To let me see him."

"So you met with him and…"

"And he cried. He hadn't cried in front of me, not even at the trial. He was crying now, and he said that these guys were after him. They were going to kill him."

"What did you say?"

"I said they weren't. That he'd be fine."

"But you knew different, didn't you." It wasn't a question.

Danielle nodded. She gasped a ragged breath that felt like the air was full of broken glass. "Yeah. I did. He didn't lie. Not to me." Whispering now, she said again, "He didn't lie."

"And did he say why these boys wanted to kill him?"

"Because Jakey touched one of them."

"Oh, I see." Sheldon's hand drifted to his crotch. Danielle looked out the side window now, worried that she might vomit if she kept looking at him.

"Not like that. He just sat next to one of them at lunch and jogged his elbow. That was all it took to earn him a death sentence."

Sheldon let out a strange, wheezing sigh. Danielle kept looking away, afraid of what she would see him doing – or about to do – if she turned back to him. It was hard to do, though. Her neck and back and the shoulder closest to Sheldon kept prickling. Her body knew – perhaps even better than her mind – how much danger she was in. It ached to turn, to see how close to her doom she might be.

She told her body to shut up. Told her mind to close its eyes and focus on the now of it all. To turn from the sight of her brother – he already had a black eye the day she saw him, that last day – and face the danger that sat close to her in this moment.

"They killed him. You got a closed casket." Sheldon sniffed and in a cartoonishly mournful voice said, "That is a truly sad story, Danielle."

She flinched as something touched her, whirling in her seat to see Sheldon reaching out to her. Then, to her utter shock and amazement, he knuckled a tear from his eye. "Sorry," he said. "I'm very empathetic, you know. More so than most, if I'm being truthful. So this is hard for me to hear. Going through life with a mother who doesn't adore everything about your mind, soul, and body." He shuddered. "I can't imagine."

Danielle could. Not her own past – she didn't have to imagine that, or the ugly realities it had brought – but the way the man said, *and body* made her realize that he hadn't just been born evil, he had been born *to* evil.

Danielle had become a public defender. It didn't take a shrink to figure out that was in large measure because of what had happened to Jakey. But the fact that she wanted to save kids and others from corrupt people – both in and out of the court – didn't change the fact that she genuinely believed people deserved a fair trial, and second chances. She had met a lot of bad people, a lot of people who had done evil things. But most of the people she met and defended had been warped by circumstance, led on paths they didn't really understand until it was too late.

If these people were wayward souls, though, then Sheldon was the devil. Somehow she knew that. She knew he was born into a rotten home, and the rot of it had already been in his heart when he came into the world.

She was sitting next to someone she suspected to be truly, wholly, *purely* evil.

And isn't that what you wanted to fight against? Not just people who would take a buck to warp a case, but against those rare people who truly destroyed others? Isn't he *exactly what you wanted to protect others against?*

The thought seemed to set off a firecracker in her mind. Everything was illuminated in a bright *pop*. She saw the past, she saw the present. She saw Jakey's eyes – but she also saw her mother's. So cold, so distant, buried behind layer after layer of sociopathic desire and a pathological need to be worshiped, obeyed.

Mother was evil. Not like Sheldon, but evil. Strangely, it was the first time Danielle had ever thought of her that way, and the idea of it made her sit up a bit taller.

Danielle had spent her career fighting corruption, pettiness, and chances lost. She had been preparing all that time. Preparing to fight evil things, which had been her path since Jakey's death. Danielle's mother had been evil, but Danielle had been too young to do anything about it.

She wasn't so young anymore.

This man was evil.

She sat up straighter still. She would escape. She would save Alex. She would stop this.

Sheldon looked at her. One eyebrow cocked. "You don't look like you're thinking about anything good."

"Good?" She laughed. A titter of real merriment. "No, I'm thinking of something *great*."

Sheldon frowned. He took out his spray bottle. Danielle turned her head, but it was too late. She felt wetness on her face, smelled something oddly reminiscent of Mr. Schmidt's cinnamon-scented office.

Darkness clouded her vision. It closed until she saw only Jakey's eyes gazing out of the black, looking into her soul. Then those eyes disappeared as well. Another set of eyes appeared, cold and haughty. Danielle's mother stared at her from the blackness, and when the darkness closed over her gaze completely, still those eyes followed her.

So did one other thing. A rapid-fire series of thoughts:

I will stop this.

I will save Alex.

I will save myself.

I will stop this evil.

8

Alex Anton was used to being in tight spots. He thought of himself as a pretty mild-mannered guy, and had taken great pains to make sure other people knew that. That had been his *modus operandi* his whole life – or at least ever since the day he found out what happened if he got upset, or lost his temper.

But mild-mannered guy or not, he knew two things in this moment. The first was that he and Danielle were in serious trouble. The second was that trouble was familiar territory, and he had no doubt he would figure out a way out of it.

Danielle didn't know about his ability to massage whatever situation in which he found himself, to get out of tight spaces and into the clear. He had hoped she would never *need* to know, and even now, bouncing around in a dark trunk traveling to some unknown place, he wondered if there was any way to keep that part of his life as an unknown to her.

No way to know. Not until they stop the car.

He tried to figure out where he was by the sound of the tires and the hum of the engine. He didn't hear any gear changes, and the thrum of the tires over the road was a consistent rasp that spoke of a highway in good condition. At one point he felt the car bump over something. Not so high that it bounced him off the trunk above his head, but hard enough that he definitely noticed it. The monotonous buzz of tires over asphalt changed to something rough and rasping.

A surface street somewhere? Were we on a freeway and now –

The car shuddered, dampening thought. The vibrations transmitted to Alex's body and made his head – already aching from whatever he'd been doped with – throb furiously. His groin felt like someone had dripped molten lead across it. His hands and arms sang their own choruses of pain as well, as did his feet and legs. All his limbs had been blessedly numb when he fought out of a drugged stupor, but as the road roughened they started screaming.

Alex thought about passing out. It would be simple and welcome in a way – his body and mind hurt, there was nothing in this tiny space that he could see, other than a muted red glow that was sensed more than seen, and which lent no definition or detail to his cage. He saw red, he felt red, and it would be so easy just to slip from red to black and *sleep*.

He resisted. He didn't know what was happening, but he knew that his survival would depend on his staying awake and aware of any possibility of escape.

The car hit something again. Another thud and the pavement must have evened out, because the softer hum – and the blessedly diminished vibrations – returned. That tickled at Alex's brain. He fought through fog and pain to concentrate on it, and finally remembered: there were several long stretches of construction on the road between the area they'd been taken and Yellowstone. He knew that because he'd mapped out possible alternate routes they could take just in case traffic got jammed.

One such road was just past St. George, Utah. He didn't think that could be what he now felt – he had vague recollections of being doped once, maybe twice. So he figured he had to have been out long enough to pass that area, and that left the stretch of grading that was being done on the freeway up by Blackfoot, Idaho. That meant –

Stupid.

He would have hit himself in the forehead if his arms and wrists hadn't been tied. Dramatic, yes; but it was also an apropos move for someone who'd just engaged in such a dunderheaded series of thoughts.

The truth was, he didn't know anything that had happened while he was out. He could be anywhere. The car could have been attached to the underbelly of a helicopter and flown to Mexico for all he knew.

No. It's too cool for that.

That was true. The trunk was stiflingly hot, but it wasn't the kind of hot he would have expected in the desert or even the valleys and lowlands to the south, east, and west of those spaces. No, they had to be north of the desert areas they had been traveling through in the last few hours he remembered. But that still left a lot of possibilities. A whole country – a whole *world* of –

He nearly groaned as he realized one more thing: he didn't even know where Danielle was or if anything had happened to her. He didn't know if Danielle was in another part of this same car, or somewhere else. He didn't know if she was alive or dead. He knew *nothing*.

That thought was too much, and he allowed himself to fade mentally. He fell into the nothing that he had resisted; the nothing that now defined his world. Black edges appeared at the boundaries of the red glow in which he floated. They wavered, disappeared, then returned. They circled lazily, each rotation consuming a bit more of his sight and a bit more of his mind.

He drifted in the dark. The part of his mind that had struggled to figure out where he was and anything else that might aid him slept, but the lower parts of his mind curled and twisted in helpless rage. There was something reptilian there, something he put away for months and sometimes even years at a time, but which had awakened again. The thing blinked, and started crawling out of its cell inside Alex's mind.

When he woke again, the car was silent. It had stopped. He thought he was facing toward the front of the car, but he couldn't be sure. Not in this ill-defined space. He twisted in place, trying to roll over to face behind him, to see if the light was brighter there and if he could find anything useful. It didn't work. His bindings were too tight, and he almost cried out as he pinned his arms painfully below him for a moment before returning to his original position.

He choked back the sound. He couldn't afford to let his captor know he was awake. He didn't know what was going on, exactly, but knew that chances of survival would go down if he didn't take advantage of every opportunity – including any surprise he might gain.

The car started moving again. A momentary stop for a change of road, a stoplight, a traffic jam.

Could be anything.

In the next moment, he realized something that had evaded him before: sometime during the ride he had soiled himself. That was uncomfortable, but ultimately a blessing in some ways. Anyone opening the trunk would get hit by a truly unpleasant odor. Maybe they would back away. Maybe they wouldn't examine him too closely, or would loosen his bindings to clean him.

Any of those scenarios would improve his situation. Any of them might be used to stop what was happening.

Alex rode in silence. He listened carefully, and at one point he thought he heard murmured voices. A woman?

He contemplated yelling. Calling out that he was okay in case the voice belonged to Danielle, in case she could help once she knew he was safe. She had to be going crazy with fear, but if she knew he was all right it might help. Again he nixed the idea – whoever else was there with her, if it was indeed her, would either ignore him or stop the car long enough to come around and dose him or beat him unconscious or worse.

No. Silence was the best course. For now.

Alex started to move his arms, shifting them minutely up and down. At the same time, he twisted his wrists, seeing if there was any give on the bindings. Again hot agony rushed through his limbs, but this time he was ready for it. He clenched down on the gag that kept him silent, and channeled the pain.

He twisted, he shifted.

Was there any play in the tape?

Maybe.

There has *to be.*

He kept moving, focusing on finding an escape.

And then, after? He smiled at that. Because when Alex was hurt, or angered… bad things happened. He didn't want them to, and occasionally tried to convince himself that he wasn't the cause of those bad things. There was truth to that: it wasn't like he *asked* for them to happen.

But somehow they always did.

He buried that thought in motion. Kept up the near-microscopic movements of hand and wrist and arm that he hoped would lead to freedom. Constant, repetitive. Every bit of motion made his arms hurt, even as it numbed his mind. Over and over he felt himself drifting into the red glow of the trunk, the redder glow of his pain.

A few times he fell into darkness complete – either because he had fallen asleep in the rhythm of his hands and the ebb and flow of pain that accompanied it, or because his overwrought body just decided to check out here and there.

He felt the car leave whatever road or highway it had been on. His gut swung sideways as it turned tightly – what Alex guessed was a curving off-ramp. The car continued along a paved road – though the hum was now lower in tone, the car traveling along at a greatly decreased rate of speed.

After what felt like an eternity, he felt a needle of hope. It hurt – everything hurt now – but he welcomed the pain. His hand had slipped. He thought he might be able to get free soon.

Soon, soon…

Each time he repeated the word in his mind, he rubbed his arms, twisted his wrists. He felt wetness on them and could not tell if it was sweat or blood. Either way, the wetness was good: it would help him slip free that much faster. Losing a bit of water or a bit of blood was well worth it, if that was the price of escape.

Soon, soon, soon…

The blood-sweat flowed faster. His wrists started to feel like there was more play. A quarter inch more was all, but that was something. Enough?

He strained to free himself, but to no avail.

No worries. I'm used to tight spots.

He kept moving. Another forever, another *un*time where he existed only to escape, and the reptile crawled higher in his mind.

One wrist popped loose.

The sudden freedom was agonizing. Blood that hadn't enjoyed unfettered access to his hands suddenly rushed in, and he felt like they would explode. He groaned – he couldn't help it this time – and did his best to rub his hands together, both to free them of pain and to get them working properly again.

The pain didn't go away completely, but it eased. He waited. Patient. His body wanted to thrash around like a fish frantically trying to escape a hook. But he told his body to simmer down. He'd get to it.

The pain stopped – or at least became manageable.

Alex's upper arms were still bound, so he shifted the effort he'd placed in twisting his wrists every which way to moving his arms around, trying either to part the tape or to feel something sharp he could cut it with.

He found nothing that would cut the tape. Just his body; his sweat and blood and will.

After the third or fourth eternity he had experienced since being shoved in this trunk, he felt something snap. For a horrible moment he thought his bones had broken, just shattered under the continual pressure he had put them to. Then he realized that it was the tape. Continuous movement had sheered some of it away.

He stopped moving. An insane thing to do, so close to freedom. He couldn't help it. Exhaustion got the better of him, at least for a moment.

Then he saw Danielle in his mind. She was beautiful in face and form; that was what he had first noticed about her. But she was lovely inside as well – smart and kind and so very different from everything he had known growing up, and those things were what made him not just notice her, but *need* her.

It was also what made him hide so much of himself from her. Not for him, of course, but for her. Knowing too much would only hurt her, and he couldn't bear to do that.

He strained. Pulled. Yanked. Once. Twice. Three times…

The bindings snapped. He was free. Well, no, that was definitely an overstatement. His legs were still bound, and he was still stuck in a car, huddled in his own offal and likely getting to the end of the road – figuratively and literally. But his hands were free.

His started to remove his gag, then thought better of it and left it on. Not only would it keep him from screaming should he find more pain in this place, but it would allow him to pretend he was still bound when the trunk inevitably opened again.

He lay in the red-dark, shivering and shaking like a leaf waiting for one more winter gust to tear it free from life. Gradually, though, the shakes slowed. He flexed his fingers. They hurt – everything hurt – but they felt like they had their strength.

The car sounded like it was slowing. He could hear the telltale sound of gravel and dirt under the tires, and the car bounced up and down as it passed over a rough path or backwoods dirt road. There was no way that was good news. Not like the kidnapper planned to take him and Danielle for a field trip in the woods or a sightseeing jaunt in America's heartland. No, the car was getting to wherever it was the kidnapper intended to finish the journey. Alex had to get ready for action.

Do I though? What about my angel?

He knew in his heart that the creature that watched over him always, that had given him freedom and money and beauty, would help him. The angel always did, and Alex always loved to see that creature's work.

But the angel had not yet appeared. Perhaps the angel was testing Alex, to see if he was willing to work things out on his own. Alex had no doubt the angel *would* appear eventually, but for now… for now there was only him and the lessening sound of tires spinning over dirt.

When the pain again ebbed, Alex decided to go ahead and remove the gag that had been wrapped around his mouth and the back of his head. He would have a bit of warning before the trunk opened, and he was grabbed. That would give him time to replace the gag – at least enough to give his kidnapper the impression that Alex Anton was still bound and trussed.

Removing the gag hurt – of course it did; *everything* hurt in this place. It had been tied so tightly that it tore out hair and even a bit of skin as he teased it free.

He opened his mouth wide and gasped in a great draft of air – air that had never tasted so sweet before, fecal stink notwithstanding. He gave himself only a moment's rest, a moment's unrestricted breathing, then started inching his exhausted hands over his legs to find the tape that bound his knees and ankles. His fingers searched for the seam where the tape ended.

It took forever, and every moment he lost searching for the tape's edges was a moment closer to the end of this path.

The car slowed, slowed, stopped.

Alex had finished with the tape around his knees, not his ankles. He froze, growing tense. He was far from full strength, but he still intended to leap out of the trunk –

or as close as he could come to that – when it opened. He would tackle his kidnapper, then would –

The car started moving again. Maybe the driver had stopped to look at a map. Maybe he just needed to howl at the moon. Whatever the reason, Alex had a few more moments.

He scrabbled and scraped at the tape. The pads of his fingers were bleeding now as well, making everything slippery.

Almost there. Almost…

He finally found purchase against a tiny nub of tape that he was then able to tease up enough to grip between thumb and forefinger. Despair for a moment as he lost his tiny fingerhold. Then he found it again and pulled.

The tape tore away from itself with a *rrrrrip* that sounded far too loud in his ears, here in the close confines of the trunk. He waited a moment, his whole body tuned to the sole purpose of discerning whether the noise had given him away.

The car kept driving. The crackle-crunch of tires over unpaved road continued unabated.

Finally free, Alex dared to try rolling over again. The fit was tight, and every move he made brought pain and the certainty that he had been heard and would soon be captured once more. But at last he had swung around and now rested on his left side, where before he had lain on his right. He still saw nothing more than a red glow.

The road the car drove on had gotten bumpier, and now it hit something. Not like a crash, more like it slammed down a sudden rut, then up the opposite lip. For an instant Alex felt nothing but air around him, his body weightless as the car dropped out from under him. Then it slammed upward and Alex's hip and head bounced off the floor of the trunk. The car dropped again, but Alex was still flying up, up, up, and now he bounced his head off the *top* of the trunk. There was a deep, solid *thud* as bone and flesh met plastic and metal, and by the time he had fallen, he was again asleep.

The darkness had taken him again, but this time it was a different kind of darkness. The last unconsciousness had been the dark of oblivion – frightening, but welcoming in its own way. This darkness was the far blacker and more terrifying darkness of memory.

Perhaps it was called up by the reptile awaking in his mind. Perhaps it was just an overburdened brain that had suffered one too many shocks, jolts, and concussions.

Whatever the reason, Alex found himself back in his youth. Back in the Home.

That was what everyone who stayed there called it: the Home. Even though it was nothing of the sort; the furthest thing possible from the love and belonging that such a name connoted. But it was what the people who ran the place called it, and they liked the kids there to call it that as well. So the kids did just that, because the punishments for refusing to follow orders could be severe.

Alex Anton – though of course that had not been his name back then – had been there only three days when he found out what happened to those who refused to do what they were told.

Orphans were bouncier than raquetballs, so by the tender age of ten Alex had already lived in a dozen different places. A few had been okay, but those tended to be the ones that got shut down or lost funding first. So life had been a series of orphanages, a few foster homes, and more than a day or two on the streets as he tried to run away from one place or another.

Now, three days into his time in the Home, he stared at Mr. Haskell and tried to keep his face blank. That was usually the best course. Blank faces told nothing, and that meant that those trying to read him would be taken by surprise.

Haskell's face was *not* blank. It tried to be, but Alex saw something in there. Something a bit like anger, but dirtier around the edges. Frayed.

He knew the word *insane*. He had never used it – not seriously, at least – but that was the word that came to mind right now.

"You didn't want to wash dishes?" said Haskell. He was old – at least fifty, Alex guessed – and he had a pair of huge, thick glasses hanging precariously from the tip of an upturned, piggish nose. Alex thought the guy probably had his glasses like that on purpose, because it allowed him to look down on everyone, no matter what.

He looked down on Alex now. Waiting.

Alex shrugged. "I didn't know where they were."

"They were in the sink, dear boy."

Alex bristled internally. He wasn't *anyone's* "dear boy." If he was, he wouldn't be in a place like this, would he?

"I didn't know where the sink was."

Haskell smiled, and Alex's heart skittered. Mr. Haskell's smile was genuine, and that was terrifying, because for a man like this to smile a sincere, wide smile meant something bad was coming.

Alex braced for a slap, for some quick savaging. One home he had stayed at liked its "lost souls" to pray when they were disobedient – kneeling on rock salt that became agonizing after only a few seconds. Surely Haskell would have something like that up his sleeve.

Alex cursed himself for being a pain. That wasn't the way to get along, to *survive.* But he had been tired, reeling at the fact that the last place – one of the *good* places – had been closed and the children there tossed out practically overnight. So when the cook at the Home – a woman who was short enough and fat enough that Alex figured she was the same height whether standing up or lying down – told him to do dishes, he just went to bed.

And now... Haskell was smiling.

"Well," said the man gently. Then again: "Well..." He stepped out from around his desk. He reached for Alex, who cringed in spite of his best attempts to the contrary. But there was no slap, no punch, no angry grappling. Instead, a soft hand fell on his shoulder, guiding him to stand and then moving him gently – *lovingly?* – to the office door. "I guess you should ask one of the older boys to help you find the dishes next time, okay?" said Haskell, his voice velvety soft.

Alex nodded, shocked. He was usually good at reading people. This time, he'd missed the mark completely. The Home, as he already knew it was to be called, had seemed *off* since he got here. But maybe he was wrong. Maybe it was one of the good places.

With a final, friendly squeeze to his shoulder, Haskell propelled Alex out of the room. Alex turned as he went, wanting suddenly to ask Haskell what was happening, was this a good place, was it really a *good place*?

But the door to Haskell's office was already shut. Alex stared at the cheap wood. There were weird stains on it, blotches here and there that he hadn't noticed when first ushered in. He fixated on them, his confusion trying to latch onto some concrete detail so that it could recalibrate and start over.

Something grabbed his head from behind. Fingers twisted into his hair, and a strong hand shoved as hard as it could and Alex's face bounced off the door and now he knew what the stains were as he stared at a bright new patch of blood on the door.

The hand in his hair yanked, twisted. Alex screamed and pushed against it, but the hand was strong. It powered him forward again, and another blotch joined the Rorschach nightmare of the door.

Alex felt something crack. He thought he might have lost a tooth. His legs quivered, then his knees went out from under him. His scalp screamed as the hand in his hair tightened and for a moment his entire body weight hung from his hair alone.

The hand let go. Alex tumbled to the floor like a broken doll. He looked up and saw Randall Jones. Jones was twelve but already had the physical constitution of an

NFL linebacker and the mental abilities of an NFL linebacker who refused to use a helmet.

"You gonna do dishes?" said Jones.

Alex didn't move. He wanted to nod, to plead for his life, to cry. But his body was still in shock. He managed only to turn over and throw up a bit of breakfast and – there it was! – a single tooth in the middle of the remains of cold oatmeal.

Jones flinched and scooted back out of the splash zone. When he was sure Alex was done, he reached down and grabbed the smaller boy by his hair again. Alex tried to fight. A small fist rocketed out. It took Jones in the shoulder, and all that happened was that the monster with a pituitary imbalance grinned and slammed Alex into Haskell's door again.

The door clicked as Alex hit it, so fast that he knew instinctively that this was a rehearsed routine. He could picture Haskell saying, "Knock three times and I'll open the door," to which Jones probably said, "Knock with what?" and Haskell, irritated, responded, "With his *face,* dummy."

So Alex's face went *clunk,* blood went *splat,* the lock went *click,* and the door opened to show Haskell. The director's mouth opened in a comic-book "O" to show how surprised he was. "Yes?" he said, looking at Jones. "What's going on here?"

"Uh…" Jones frowned, obviously trying to remember what he was supposed to say.

"The kitchen?" prompted Haskell.

Jones snapped his fingers. "Oh. Yeah." He shook Alex by the hair. Pointed down the hall. "Kitchen's that way."

"And the dishes…" Haskell led the boy in a weird play where only one of the three characters knew all the lines.

"Dishes are there. Do 'em when you're told," Jones said, and beamed at Haskell. Haskell smiled and tousled the boy's hair (he had to reach *up* to do that), then handed him a Hershey bar.

"I am so glad to have your help, m'boy," he said. Then looked at Alex. "Well. Well…" He stepped back. The door closed.

Jones dropped Alex, who crumpled again. Peeling open the wrapper to the Hershey bar, Jones prodded Alex with his toe and took a huge bite of chocolate. "Go clean up. Lunch is soon." He leaned close and grinned a smile coated with bits of chocolate that looked a lot like the blood now congealing on Haskell's door. "You're on dish duty."

Alex nodded. He stood, shaky, and wobbled toward the bathrooms. Jones, his part of the play over, chuckled and lumbered away in the opposite direction.

Alex didn't go to the bathroom. He knew he should have, but he didn't.

Don't rock the boat. Just do what they say. Survive. You know how to do that.

He ignored the inner voice. He knew it would cost him, but right now he needed air. He passed by the door to the bathrooms and kept going. There was a window at the far end of the hall that opened up to the yard. Alex wasn't thinking of escape – not yet. He just needed to breathe.

The window opened when he pulled on it. Not far – certainly not enough to allow even most kids at the Home to use it as a passage outside. But Alex was thin and desperate, and that combination, along with a willingness to sacrifice a bit of skin from his back, let him wiggle through.

He fell out on the other side, plopping through the space between window sash and window frame and dropping like a baby who had been forgotten right at the end of the birth process.

Not far from true.

Alex lay on the ground a long moment. He half expected Jones to smash through the wall beside him like an oversized version of the Hulk. It didn't happen. Probably because Jones had already forgotten about Alex and was getting felt up or whatever it was Haskell did for him beyond giving the bastard Hershey bars.

"Hey."

Alex heard a soft voice. He turned his head, painfully, in the direction of it.

Ten yards away, across a stretch of asphalt cursorily bordered by a scrubby "lawn," the outer fence of the Home stood. Beyond it was a city street, but it was a bad part of town and Alex suspected not many people walked around here. Good citizens would be afraid, and bad citizens would know there was nothing worth boosting, buying, or selling near the Home.

But someone was on the sidewalk. A man dressed all in black: black suit, black shirt, black tie. He wore a dark trenchcoat over all of it, and the whole outfit together gave the impression that this man was draped in a shadow.

The man wasn't old like Haskell, but he was definitely old. Maybe his late forties. He had blonde hair, graying at the edges, and a neatly-trimmed beard that stood out sharply from the dark delineation of the black collar and tie at his neck. His eyes were even bluer than Alex's own. "You okay, kid?" he asked. He had a strange accent.

"Who's asking?" muttered Alex. Blood had pooled in his mouth, and another tooth fell out when he spit.

"Come here, kid," said the man. Alex ignored him. The soft voice grew a bit harder as the man repeated, "Come here."

"Why should I?" asked Alex.

"*Now*." The steel in the man's voice was unmistakable. There was a coldness to it that terrified Alex, even though the dark-suited man was on the other side of a wrought-iron fence topped by spires designed to impale anyone trying to climb over.

Alex found himself going to the man. He managed to stop, but only when he was less than three feet away from the fence. "What do you –" began Alex.

The man wore a frown that had deepened with every step toward him that Alex took. "Who did that to you?" he asked, pointing at Alex's mashed-up face.

"What's it to you?" Alex asked.

Behind him, a door slammed open. Apparently Jones was done eating his Hershey bar and/or getting diddled by Haskell, because he was rushing out, running toward Alex.

"Hey, get away from there!" shouted Jones, and Alex couldn't be sure if he was talking to him or to the strange man at the fence.

Neither of them moved. Alex didn't know why the man didn't, but something in that dark figure's bright eyes told him to stay put as well.

Jones' huge hand fell on his shoulder. "What the hell are –"

The man at the fence cut in. "Did you do that to him?" he asked. His tone was quiet, almost a whisper, but for some reason Alex felt himself grow cold – colder even than when he had talked to Haskell.

Jones' mouth moved up and down like it was a pump trying to prime his brain into some useful action. "Uhhh…"

That was enough for the stranger. He looked carefully at Jones, then back at Alex. "Take care," he said quietly, then turned and began walking away.

Jones watched until the guy turned a corner and disappeared, then dragged Alex to the cafeteria. Alex tried to peel away, but the big boy yanked him toward the kitchen. "No lunch for you," he said. He grinned. Still chocolatey. "Mr. H. wants you to start on the dishes."

He took Alex into the kitchen and watched as Alex did the dishes. But he took the time to relieve Alex of another tooth before that.

Alex did the dishes. He burned with shame and hatred and pain and the knowledge that he could do nothing about any of it.

Turned out he didn't have to.

The next morning, Alex woke to the sound of sirens. Two men rushed into the dormitory, hurrying to a bed where one of the kids – a nearly deaf little boy named Lenny – was screaming hysterically.

The men, whom Alex finally recognized as paramedics, ran to the bed beside Lenny. They started moving over something, and a moment later another paramedic ran in with a gurney and the three of them grunted and strained as they hoisted something. They ran out of the room, pushing the gurney and calling out orders to each other as they frantically tried to get their patient out of the Home.

Still, as fast as they moved, as confused as he was, Alex caught a glimpse of who lay on the gurney. Of the blood. The head that had indented in several odd places.

Later, when Haskell appeared at the cafeteria during dinner, shaken and almost crying as he delivered the news, Alex was not surprised.

"Many of you know Randall Jones. He's a good boy. He needs your prayers." Then he added, wringing his hands, "Well… well…" He turned on his heel and left then.

Haskell wasn't the only person who worked here, and all the orderlies and janitors and other employees were cut from similar angry, abusive cloth. There were a half-dozen beatings that night. Alex avoided them, but he was close enough to several that he heard them talking: someone had come in. Someone had crept into the Home. Someone had broken in expertly, done what he came to do, and left again without a trace.

Alex knew then. He *knew* who had come in. And the next day, when it was announced by a fully-weeping Haskell that "our friend and one of the best boys in the Home, Randall Jones," as Haskell put it, was dead, Alex *knew* who had done it.

It was the first time.

It would not be the last.

Alex Anton had been marked. The mark followed him. He suddenly found himself protected. Like a guardian angel stood by, ready to aid him at any time. Only he had never heard of a guardian angel that broke bones and twisted fingers out of their sockets and one time even put a plastic bag over a man's head and waited until the man was a vegetable then left – as always – without a trace.

No one ever caught the man. No one ever *knew*.

But Alex knew. Young Alex knew, and teen Alex both knew and reveled in the knowledge.

He kept moving. He bounced like all orphans bounced. He lived in places that were each a bit nicer overall than the last, and whenever he met a bully or an administrator with a warped sense of discipline or morality… the guardian angel would appear. Alex would see him at a gate or a fence. The man would ask him a question or two. The next day the problem would be gone.

And now, bouncing in the trunk of a car, in and out of a twilight half-consciousness, Alex remembered the angel. He remembered the men and women who had done wrong by him and who then showed up to work with broken bones or burnt flesh or simply disappeared.

Most of them were because the guardian angel stepped in. But not all.

And yet, even then the guardian angel came to him. Alex had not been born Alex, but had had another name. Yet one day it all became too much for him, the day he lost it just a little – just a teeny, tiny bit – and the guardian angel showed up again. His hair was grayer, his eyes a bit faded. But he still had a strong body, and his hands did not tremble as he handed over the identification. "Your name is Alex Anton," he said. "Do be careful with this name."

Alex Anton had a degree, a good work history. He had a bank account with enough money to be comfortable. Alex Anton was happy, and Alex Anton continued in a life where those who helped him and those he loved – usually the same thing – were given his favor and somehow found themselves with promotions and business opportunities they had never had before.

And the ones who got in his way just disappeared.

Like Brenda.

He had met her soon at a bar. She had been perfect: beautiful, sexy, willing to do almost anything in bed, and (best of all) utterly devoted to him. She seemed happy at first, but when she found out she was not the only woman he spent time with, she had overreacted. "I'm your wife!" she kept shouting, no matter how much he explained the realities of life to her.

He felt trapped. He felt unhappy. He hadn't planned to actually *kill* her, but the day they were driving through the mountains, it somehow happened. She was yelling at him – like *always* – and said she wanted out of the car. He stopped at a turnaround, and when he saw her at the edge of the road, leaning on the fence that marked the sharp demarcation between asphalt and a hundred feet of nothing at all, he was pushing her before he even thought about it.

She was gone. He was happy. And when the guardian angel showed up, told tell him that he had taken care of his *own* problem. He had done it himself, and he was a man.

The angel nodded. Still more gray in his beard and in his skin, he was getting older. Still an angel of some kind, but Alex could not figure out the rules he operated by, or how he always seemed to *know*. Just like he knew now, nodding and saying in his strange accent, "Yes, I know. Her body was… found."

Alex felt a thrill of fear. The angel saw it and waved it away. "By no one you have to worry about. The problem is taken care of. You didn't do it all yourself, boy, and it is good that you know that." The guardian angel squinted. "It is good that you know you cannot do this alone." Then he smiled. "But I am here. The body is gone, so you file a missing persons report in a day or two, mourn for a month or two, then I would perhaps move from here."

"But… I *like* it here."

The guardian angel shrugged as though he was unconcerned, but Alex saw darkness in his eyes. He felt a thrill of fear, wondering if the angel would ever turn on *him*. "If you like it here, that is fine. But you are more likely to run into people concerned about you, and about what happened to Brenda."

Alex moved. He found – surprise, surprise – an even better job waiting for him. And though he was sad for a while, soon he found a routine that pleased him. Wake up, get dressed. Coffee on the way to work. The job itself bored him, and he suspected he would leave it sooner or later, but it was what the guardian angel had gotten for him and he wanted to show his gratitude.

After work: a bar, a strip club. He was handsome and he drove a nice car and had a good job, and that was more than enough to keep him busy and satisfied – happy, even. Or so he thought.

Then he saw Danielle, and knew he would never be happy again until he had her in his arms, in his bed. Until she fell for him and doted on him the way Brenda had never quite managed to do.

He knew she would require a different kind of attention than the strippers or the barhoppers he usually hit on, so he watched her carefully. He still satisfied his urges most nights, but each morning he only had eyes for her.

He finally asked her out, and she said yes. Her life improved the way lives always did when they lived in the shadow of his favor. They were married.

In truth, he did have concerns. He wondered if she was quite as devoted to him as he would have liked, but chalked that up to a charming, childlike enthusiasm she had for her job. That would wane, he was confident. And he loved her and he was patient, so he would put up with the demands of a life with her. He rolled with it, which was why he was upset when she told him she might have to work on their honeymoon, but after some thought made it work. He suggested putting off the wedding so she could focus on her work – there was a girl passing through town on those days that would provide more than enough entertainment, so he could certainly let Danielle have her space and still keep himself happily occupied – but she had said no.

He *was* irritated again. But she made it clear that she couldn't wait to be Mrs. Alex Anton, and that made him happy enough that he forgave her. She would learn soon enough.

Alex floated through all of this. He floated in memory. He floated in safety. He had a guardian angel, and that angel would make this all right. He floated, then floated up out of the river of yesterdays as the car slowed around him. The car stopped. The *clunk* of a door opening nearby brought him to the sound he heard when his face hit the door of a foster home and Alex first found out what kind of power he wielded.

The trunk flipped open. Daylight streamed in. Alex blinked as needles of light seared his eyes. He saw a figure haloed by tears, and for a moment he knew who it was. It was *him*. It was his guardian angel.

Then the halo disappeared. The angel became a devil.

"You untied yourself!" shouted the man who had kidnapped Alex and Danielle. "Good for you, that's quite an accomplishment."

He sounded genuinely cheerful, and that alone would have kept Alex in a state of shock that did not permit speech, even without the pain and the disorientation caused by so long in the trunk and the even more disorienting realization that the kidnapper held a gun in one hand and a tiny tree in a pot in the other.

The kidnapper leaned in, then stopped short. His lip curled. "Ew," he said. "You pooped yourself." He turned slightly, as though hiding the tree from the sight or odor of the man in the trunk. He sighed. "I know that not everyone is possessed of my intestinal control – I have excellent control of my bowels at all times, and have never pooped myself in my life – but I still thought you would have managed better than this."

Alex lunged at him, his hands reaching for something, anything, that would let him put a stop to whatever was happening. He halted when he saw a form crumpled on the dirt beside the kidnapper.

"Danielle," whispered Alex. Hands still outstretched, he said, "Is she –"

He didn't say it, but he thought it: *Dead? Is she dead?*

How can she be dead if I love her? How would the angel let it happen?

The kidnapper giggled. He waggled his finger and, moving so fast it was a blur, he pocketed his gun and pulled out a spray bottle.

"Wait!" shouted Alex.

In the next moment he felt wetness on his skin, and in the moment after that he fell into darkness again. No floating this time, there was only a hard plummet into oblivion. No guardian angels, no questions about what was to happen next. Just a black even darker than dark suits and even more penetrating than blue eyes that grew hard and flashed before someone turned up hurt or dead.

He felt something rear up inside him. Pain, yes, but also rage and a smug satisfaction that reminded him of the simple fact that everyone who had done this to him would die.

But what if the angel can't help? What if that asshole who used my dick as a nail polisher is too tough even for an angel?

Alex had felt satisfaction at the thought of the suffering of those who had done this to him. Now that same part of him quivered, not with fear so much as anger. *It's not fair!* he shouted to himself. *Everything bad always happens to me.*

9

Danielle slept, and did not have any dreams until one where she felt like it was raining. Something wet on cheeks and brow and eyes. It rained in her dream, and a tiny, tiny part of her knew that Sheldon was dosing her with his spray bottle. And then there was no dream – or anything else – at all.

The oblivion left her, though after how long she could not say. She raised her head, realizing at once that she was no longer in the car. Now she lay on her back on a cold concrete floor. Sitting up, she moaned and felt her head, which felt like it was on the verge of falling off – and she suspected that would be a huge improvement.

She sat up and looked around. The first thing she saw was that she was in a room, about twenty feet square. The walls looked metallic, but were painted a light blue that seemed strangely at odds with the otherwise Spartan space. A few lights hung overhead: flickering fluorescent bars that hung in cages on the ceiling. They made the rooms blue walls glow coldly.

She tried to turn to the side, but something yanked at her arm. She looked at it and realized a few things very quickly: the first was that her right wrist was handcuffed to a ring set into the wall. That chilled her, because the fact that this room was empty, save the means to secure someone to the wall, meant that it was a room with only one purpose in mind: this was a cell, plain and simple – and surely not one with any kind of good outcome.

The next thing she saw only bolstered her first impression: the walls and floor had stains on them. Dark blotches here and there, in patches and lines that she had seen in post-mortem crime scene photos.

She shuddered, turning away from one of the largest stains, only inches away from her head. And that was when she noticed the final thing: Alex.

He was on his back, one arm lifted a bit in the air, hanging from a cuff the twin of the one that secured Danielle to the wall. She realized now that she had awoken in the same position, and that her wrist ached at being suspended that way.

"Alex!" she shouted, and lunged toward her husband. He didn't move, not even so much as a twitch. Even when her handcuff jerked her forward motion to a stop so hard that she cried out in pain, he did not move. She leaned back, cradling her hurt arm, blinking away tears.

Don't cry. Look around. There has to be a way out of this.

The only problem was that she didn't even know what *this* was. She had no idea why she was here, or what came next.

She reached for Alex again, a bit more carefully, but again came up well short of being able to touch him. She thought about calling out for him, but didn't know if that would be a wise choice. She saw now that one of the walls had a door that reminded her of something one might see separating rooms in a submarine. No little porthole like in the movies, though, just solid metal with a red lever in the middle that she guessed would swing to the side to allow people to unlatch and open or close the door.

No window was good in a way – no one was watching, and she saw no cameras in evidence that would allow someone to do so remotely.

But no windows also meant there was no way to see what was beyond this small cell; no way of determining exactly what manner of nightmare she had fallen into.

Is this what Jakey saw in his last moments? Just an empty room, no help around, no help coming, no one to –

She slapped herself. It was a sudden motion, and it surprised her. It felt like someone had taken over her hand, and attacked her with it. But she knew in almost the same instant that the possession was a benevolent one. The smack jarred her, shocked her. It knocked the creeping defeatism out of her. It made her angry, and angry was better than scared.

She took a breath. Held it. Let it out, willing the negative thoughts out along with it. She repeated the motion, and again, forcing herself to be calm, to remain in control.

In times of deep stress, Danielle tended to see Jakey's eyes. When things were even worse, she was more likely to see her mother staring at her, as she did now. She wasn't insane; she knew it wasn't real. But knowing it for a form of PTSD did not take away its power over her. Her mother manipulated her life and emotions, it seemed, even in death.

Helena Smith had been a marble statue of a woman: lovely, cold. Something carved by a master who had a perfect eye for beauty, but who also hated his creation on some deep level. Always in Danielle's mind Mother looked the way she had on the day of Jakey's funeral. She had worn black, but Danielle knew the choice was not one of mourning. The wardrobe choice was because black made her mother's porcelain skin look almost translucent, and made her red lips stand out like a single bright star in a moonless sky.

Her mother had cried at the funeral, because that was expected. But before and after, she had worn different expressions: amusement and irritation. Amusement at how this had all turned out. Irritation that Jakey had defied her in the first place, irritation at the fact that she had to take Danielle along to the funeral for the sake of appearances, and irritation (most of all) at the mere fact that part of her day was stolen by the event.

She had missed a facial. "And for nothing more than *that*," she told Danielle later that day – and the way she said that last word held so much dismissive bitterness regarding the burial of her son that Danielle knew she would devote her life to seeing that things like this did not happen again.

The sight of her mother's eyes in her mind, cold and cruel and dismissive as they had been that day, galvanized Danielle to action. She had defied her mother. She had escaped *that* prison. She would escape this one, too.

She slid her legs around until they were pointing at Alex. Then she sat flat on her bottom and slid her hips forward until she was extended as far as her handcuffed wrist would permit. It gave her just enough play that she could reach out and touch Alex with the toe of her shoes. Not much – she couldn't have pulled him over to her, even if he hadn't been chained to the wall as she was. But she was close enough she could tap his cheek with the toe of her shoe.

Part of her advised against even that. She didn't know what had happened to him while she slept. He could have internal injuries, his spine could be on the verge of breaking. But then, it wasn't likely that paramedics were on their way, and chances were better if both of them were awake and aware and looking for a way out of this madness. So she continued tapping Alex's face with her shoe.

"Alex," she whispered, glancing at the doorway as she did. "Alex," she repeated, a bit louder this time.

He rewarded her with a moan. She called his name again, her voice almost sobbing with relief that he wasn't dead. "Sweetie, get up. Get up, we need –"

Clank.

Danielle turned to the large red lever in the middle of the metal door slide in an arc from left to right. There was another metallic sound, then the thud of something sliding home. A final noise, and the door swung heavily open.

She tried to scoot back to her place by the wall. She wasn't sure why she tried, but in that moment it seemed important that whoever came through that door not think that she was trying to escape.

It didn't work. Before she had gotten her legs under her again, a familiar – and hated – voice said, "No, please. No need to get up. I appreciate the courtesy, but it's only me, Danielle."

Sheldon Steward had poked his head around the side of the metal door, like a friend looking in on her. Now he stepped all the way through. Turning, he slid the bar shut behind him, allowing Danielle to see that he was holding Lucy under his arm.

He turned back to her and stepped forward a few feet before setting the tree on the concrete floor. He patted it, then said, "Stay," like now Lucy was possessed by the spirit of a cocker spaniel. He grinned at Danielle. "I'm not crazy, you know."

"I… I didn't think so," said Danielle. A total lie, but telling the truth – "You're crazier than a guy who's been eating lead since birth" – seemed like a bad idea.

"No, it's okay. I know you do. You're undoubtedly attracted to me, which you shouldn't feel bad about since women do tend to be attracted to me. Even so, many people think I'm crazy at some point." He grinned that wolf-grin of his. "I don't mind. The ones who hire me still pay, and the ones who *don't* hire me scream all the louder for it. I'd call that a win-win, wouldn't you?"

"I don't know."

"I do. Trust me." He patted the tree again. "Lucy, my sweet, perfect friend… I know you're going to love this."

"Love what?" asked Danielle. She was terrified what the reply might be, but more terrified of not knowing.

"What comes next."

"What's that?"

Sheldon's grin widened. He waggled a finger back and forth. "Oh, no. No telling. It's got to be a surprise."

Behind him, the door clanked and again the red lever swung to the side, this time releasing the latch. In walked a shortish man with dark hair and eyes that reminded Danielle of anthracite, dead and dark. He stared at her, and she was disconcerted to realize that he seemed not to blink.

He was just as crazy as Sheldon, she could tell. Maybe a different *kind* of crazy, but there would be no help from him.

He wore a track suit, which she thought odd. He didn't look like he belonged in such a thing. He looked like a dark suit kind of guy, though she couldn't be sure why she thought that.

"You the girl?" he said, then turned to Sheldon. "She the girl?"

"Evidently," said Sheldon, and sniggered.

The man glared at Sheldon, and Danielle felt a ray of hope. There was clearly no love lost there – at least not on the side of the newcomer. Maybe she could use that.

"Sir, I don't know what this man," she began, nodding at Sheldon, "is do –"

"Shut up," said the man. He reached for a shoulder holster, drawing out the gun he held there. He stared at it lovingly for a moment, then held it up for her to see. "Beauty, ain't it?"

"It's really nice," said Sheldon, in a voice that sounded utterly sincere. He sounded like he appreciated the gun almost as much as he revered Lucy and organic snacks from Trader Joe's. "But," he added, and suddenly snickered, "he *names* it."

"Shut up!" shouted the man.

"Don't feel bad," said Sheldon. "I started naming mine, too."

The other man looked apoplectic. "Oh, shit, Shel, don't tell me *that*! And you don't get to make fun of my guns if you name yours as well!"

Sheldon sniffed. "I name mine after great poets and wise men. You name yours crazy, nonsense names."

"I told you that stuff in confidence, Sheldon! And the names aren't nonsense, they're from *Lord of the* damn *Rings*, you cretin!"

Sheldon sniffed again and folded his arms. "I heard that movie was terrible."

The man in the track suit had a face so red Danielle would have worried about him having a heart attack in any other situation. "It's a *book*, you –" He cut himself off, breathing deeply and visibly struggling to get himself under control before saying, "I'm not having this conversation with you again."

The man in the track suit turned to face Danielle. He stepped toward her, holding his gun close to her eyes, as though daring her to make a grab for it. She didn't. She had no illusions about her ability to wrestle the weapon away, or what she would do with it even if she got it.

"You like my gun?" he said.

"No," said Danielle. "I don't like it or you."

Those last words came out before she could stop them. She knew instantly it was a mistake, even before the man raised the gun over her head and then hammered the butt down at her. But the impact never came. She looked at the gun, hovering an inch away from her brow. Then at the man who had narrowly kept himself from pistol-whipping her.

The man was glaring at Alex's still-unconscious form. "Not yet," he murmured. "But soon."

"Why are we here?" she whispered. "We haven't done anything to you."

The man in the track suit actually chuckled at that. "Sometimes existence is reason enough for punishment. That's the attitude the universe takes toward us." He spread his arms wide. "I'm just an instrument in the universe's hands." He leaned in then, whispering, "Plus, you're going to be very useful." He turned to Sheldon. "Right, Sheldon?"

"I think so, Marcos," answered Sheldon, absently caressing the leaves of his tree while a dreamy grin graced his face.

"Why –" began Danielle, her stomach clenching at Sheldon's words.

"Because I'm done being the red-headed stepchild," interrupted the man, Marcos. "It's *my time*."

"Your mother didn't have red hair, Marcos," said Sheldon. "And you know it." He got a dreamy look on his face. "We should always respect our mothers, don't you think, Alex?"

Danielle spun to see Alex sitting up. "Alex!" she shouted.

"Oh, good. The prodigal son returns to us," said Marcos. Abandoning his place in front of Danielle, he squatted in front of Alex. "I have *so* been looking forward to meeting you."

Alex sat up, wincing. "You shouldn't do this," he said. He jerked a few times on his handcuff. The metal clinked uselessly.

"I don't think you're in a position to tell me what to do or not to do," said Marcos dangerously.

"He's been saying nonsense like this every time I've spoken to him," said Sheldon. He whirled his finger around his ears and stage-whispered to Danielle, "I think your husband is crazy."

Marcos laughed uproariously at that. "No surprise, there, given who he is!"

Sheldon laughed, too. Alex just looked lazily at them. His eyes were cloudy, unfocused. Even so, he smiled. "You *really* shouldn't do this."

Marcos responded to that by bringing his gun down on Alex's head, and this time he *did* connect. Alex slumped, unconscious again. Blood ran down his temple.

For the first time, Danielle noticed how dirty Alex's clothes were. And there was a stench coming off him that said clearly he had voided his bowels and bladder into his clothing. For some reason that raised her ire in a way that nothing else had done.

Because they don't care. They've stolen us away, and they want to steal our dignity from us as well. Just like she *did.*

"You assholes," she said. "What do you want from us? Huh? Or are you afraid to say?"

Marcos turned back to her. Anger flared in his gaze, and was just as quickly dampened. "What do I want from you? Not much. Just your pain, sweetie."

He might have said more; looked like he *would* say more, in fact, but the light in the room suddenly dimmed. As it did, a red light flashed from a bulb set in one corner of the ceiling. It flashed, on-off, on-off.

"What is this, Christmas?" asked Sheldon. He frowned. "I'm not sure what I feel about Christmas. J Lo – I think it was her – posted on Insta once to warn us about letting the holiday get too commercial."

Marcos spared a moment to glance at Sheldon, his face clearly showing that he didn't know what to think of the other man, but *definitely* didn't like him.

The red lights flashed again. "I know Mariah Carey likes Christmas," began Sheldon. "She did a Christmas album that –"

"Shut up. The light means there's someone here," said Marcos.

"There are always people here, aren't there?" said Sheldon, looking genuinely confused.

"Someone who's not *supposed* to be here." He glared at Sheldon. "Were you followed?"

Sheldon shook his head. "Of course not. I'm very good at what I do."

"Then why you look like someone crammed a lemon up your ass?" demanded Marcos.

He was right: Sheldon looked suddenly disconcerted, his mouth twisted like he had tasted something sour or rotten. Somehow Danielle knew that Sheldon was thinking about whatever it was that had made him pull over several times, had made him jerk in his seat and stare into the rearview mirror.

Then he shrugged and said, "It doesn't matter. I wasn't followed. No one's ever done that, no one ever will."

Marcos muttered something under his breath. Then, louder, he said, "Come on."

He left the room. Sheldon followed, but turned back after only a single step. He went to Alex's still form, then touched the place where Marcos had struck Danielle's husband. Sheldon pulled his fingers back, and she saw the tips were stained red with blood.

Sheldon noticed her attention. He smiled at her, then went to Lucy and carefully wiped Alex's blood on a few of the leaves on the small tree. "Even better," he said in a near-whisper. He looked at Danielle. "Don't you think so? Doesn't the red look nice against the green?"

She shook her head. She couldn't think of anything to say.

Sheldon sighed. "So few people can see what I see." He shrugged. "But you will. You'll paint the tree, and you'll see how beautiful it can be."

He left without another word. Danielle held her breath as he went. She didn't know where they were, or what was happening, but she held onto the only hope she had: Marcos seemed to think Sheldon had been followed. And she knew Sheldon was worried about that as well, no matter how casually he tried to deny the possibility.

Had someone followed them? Could there be someone nearby, maybe even a cop?

No. Don't hope for that. Just look around. Pretend this all depends on you, because it does.

"Alex," she called. Her husband remained where he was, motionless and bleeding.

For the thousandth time, Danielle tamped down the urge to panic. She felt at her pockets, wondering if there was anything in them she could use. No go. She remembered having some cash in one of them, her cell phone in the other. Now all of it was gone, the pockets empty.

"Dammit," she said.

She looked around the room again and saw exactly what she had seen before: nothing at all.

Tendrils of genuine hopelessness curled into her. She didn't have any tools, she didn't have any way out of this mess. Worst of all, Alex was caught up in it as well.

Why are we here?

Could it be one of my cases?

She had heard the same stories as any other public defender, of course: tales spun about lawyers who suddenly found that they "knew too much" and so were disposed of. Had those stories, which she had always viewed as a lawyerly version of campfire tales, turned out to have a basis in fact? Had she discovered something that someone powerful didn't want her to know about? Maybe something about the Antoine Lewis case?

She dismissed that almost immediately. Nothing in the file of a once-burglar wrongly accused of robbery and attempted escape would justify the risk and cost associated with everything now happening.

But they *had* come for her and Alex. She spared another glance at her husband. He was breathing, and that was good, even if blood still streamed from the cut Marcos had opened up on his forehead.

Could this be because of Alex?

She didn't see how that could be so. He did actuarial studies. His job was dull, his life uneventful. He thought so as well, and it was part of his charm: that he was so upbeat doing things that would make most people seriously consider eating a bullet to avoid the boredom. Lots of late nights at the office – he often came home well after Danielle herself had gone to bed – but no matter how hard he worked or how much he had to do, he was always smiling.

So no, it couldn't be Alex.

Which means it's me.

But why? *What did I find out? What do I know?*

She searched her mind and memories, trying to ferret out whatever information had landed her and Alex in this place. She came up with nothing, and that failure made her deflate even further.

She and Alex *were* together, and she had seen plenty of movies and books where couples drew comfort from knowing that their loved ones were near. In her case, though, Alex's presence just made her feel worse. She had brought him to this misery somehow. She had –

She sat up suddenly, three words ringing in her mind.

The prodigal son.

Marcos had called Alex that, and the sudden remembrance shifted Danielle's view once again. What did Marcos mean?

She stared at Alex. Beautiful, dear, charming, wonderful Alex.

And did he have something to hide?

He couldn't be an *actual* son, Danielle knew that. He had told her that he was orphaned soon after birth. So if Marcos was speaking figuratively, then that must mean that Alex had left some job or activity, and Marcos had pulled him back in. It sounded very *Godfather*-y, and Danielle had trouble reconciling it to what she knew of Alex. Alex mostly refused to talk about his childhood, other than mentioning he had grown up in orphanages and foster homes, and that much of the experience had been painful. After that, she knew he'd led a charmed life by most standards. A full-ride scholarship to a good school, followed by a series of jobs that were each better than the last. He was in demand, and brought plenty of money to the relationship. A career, a life – one he had chosen to share with her.

It was all on the up-and-up, so there was no way Alex was involved in any of what was happening – at least not knowingly.

Then what did Marcos mean when he said that?

A long time went by. She jumped as the door lever swung to the side with a loud clank. Marcos entered the room, followed by Sheldon. "False alarm," said Sheldon.

"Shhh!" hissed Marcos. He was holding a phone to his ear. "I really think you should think hard about this," he said into the phone.

Danielle couldn't hear the words, but she heard the tone as whoever was on the other end of the line started shrieking in rage. Marcos winced and held the phone away from his ear. When the screams petered out, he said, "You done?"

That was enough to kickstart another bout of screaming. "Shut up!" Marcos screamed. The words were a shotgun blast in the room's confined space, and Danielle let out a small yelp of her own.

Sheldon smiled at that. He winked at her, then put a finger to his lips.

The person on the phone with Marcos – a man, judging by his deep voice – said something quieter.

"Because I have something you want," said Marcos. He waited, and a small frown played across the corners of his mouth. "One word: Sasha."

He nodded as he said it, and Sheldon walked toward Danielle. She forced herself not to shrink away, though the panic she felt redoubled as she realized the madman wasn't actually moving toward her, but toward Alex.

"Don't do anything to him," she pleaded.

"Quiet," said Sheldon. "It's not your turn yet."

At the same time, Marcos said into the phone, "I'm going to send you something. Stand by." He hung up and nodded at Sheldon again.

Sheldon hunched beside Alex and slapped his cheeks several times. "Wakey, wakey, eggs and bakey," he said.

Alex moaned. He started to sit, but Sheldon pushed him down gently. "No, don't move. You'll only make your head hurt worse. It's not time for that, either."

He pulled something from a pocket. Danielle gasped as she saw what it was, and realized also that Marcos was pointing his phone at Alex. "I'm recording," Marcos said.

Sheldon nodded. He leaned in close to Alex and whispered into his ear. Danielle started shaking her head, panic and terror piercing her heart as she heard Sheldon say, "Now I need you to scream nice and loud for me, okay?"

Alex was barely out of his stupor, the concussion he had suffered obviously still doing a number on him. "Wha… what are you…"

Sheldon took Alex's hand – the hand that had held the ring out to her when he went down on one knee to propose, the hand now bound by a handcuff to a very different kind of ring – and splayed it out against the wall. Alex struggled weakly, but Sheldon shoved his other arm down and then knelt on it. "Move too much and your elbow will break," he said.

Then he brought down the hammer he had taken from his pocket. There was a strange sound, a mix of wet *thunk* and dry *crack* as the hammer slammed sideways on Alex's little finger.

Alex shrieked, and the shriek rose in pitch and volume as Sheldon methodically broke each of the fingers of his right hand.

Danielle was shrieking as well, wordless cries that mingled with those of her husband as his beautiful hand was destroyed. On the fourth finger, Sheldon paused long enough to point the hammer at her. "You're messing up the scene," he said simply.

Danielle choked back the rest of her screams. She didn't know if he was threatening to do the same to her, or to do worse to Alex. But there *was* threat in his voice, and either way she somehow found the strength to bite back the next scream, and the one after that.

Alex wasn't screaming anymore, either. He was sobbing. He hitched words between the cries. Even through her terror and panic and despair, the words surprised Danielle. She would have expected him to beg for his safety, for hers. She would have expected him to plead for Sheldon to stop this cruel torture.

But he did neither. Instead, he gasped, "You… assholes… are dead… *Dead,* you… hear me? You're –"

Thock. The hammer crushed Alex's thumb, wringing fresh screams from him.

Sheldon turned to Marcos. "Should I do the other hand?" he asked. He almost sounded high, like hurting Alex had put him into a state of euphoria. That terrified Danielle even more – almost as much as the fact that she could see Sheldon was physically aroused.

She looked away from that part of him – which turned out to be a mistake since raising her eyes allowed Sheldon to catch her gaze with his own. "Don't worry," he said. "I know you want me, and you'll get your wish soon enough."

"Want you?" She choked out the words.

"Don't be ashamed. Most people do. Even men," said Sheldon. He frowned a bit, his eyes growing cold as he said, "Homosexuality is okay. Lots of celebrities say so, and they would know, even though I myself prefer women." He looked down at Alex, seemed to realize suddenly that he was still on the man's arm. "Sorry," he said, sounding genuinely abashed as he pulled his knee away and stood.

Alex curled around his mangled hand, sobbing. "You… assholes," he said again.

"Shut up," said Marcos. He was looking at his phone, his thumbs moving as he texted. He stopped and waited a moment. He glanced at Alex, then at Danielle. "It's nothing personal with you," he said. "Just business."

Danielle looked at her husband. He was no longer speaking, no longer voicing threats. "Sweetie," she began, but had no idea how to finish the thought. What was she going to say? *"It'll all be okay"*?

No. Nothing was okay.

Marcos dialed a number, then lifted the phone to his ear again. He waited, and again screams emerged. "I guess you got the video," said Marcos once they died down.

Again, the voice on the line grew quiet. A plaintive sound to it now.

Marcos grinned and shot a thumbs up at Sheldon, though his voice remained cold as he said, "You know what comes next." He waited, listening. "You have three hours." The voice started to say something, but Marcos cut him off. "Bullshit. I know where you are right now, and I know you can get here in that time. Three hours, or I break ten bones for every ten minutes you're late. If I run out of bones I start removing things." He grinned at Sheldon. "I've got a guy who's very good with pain, and I guarantee it lasts *days*." Another pause, and he said, "And come *alone*." The voice on the phone started to say something, but Marcos said, "You don't wanna call Chernov. It'll just get worse for you here. And you've gone to too much trouble to see it end the way I can *make* it end."

With that he flipped the phone shut and jerked his chin at Sheldon. "Let's go," he said.

He left, Sheldon close behind, leaving Danielle alone with her maimed husband and with a question that rang over and over in her head:

What happens in three hours?

10

Legion follows the kidnapper as he drives. He pulls off the freeway when the other car does, which is regularly to fill up the gas tank. Legion always feels a bit of stress when this happens, because he cannot follow too closely, but he also has to gas up his own van. So he waits until the man finishes, always parked a quarter mile away, invisible to the kidnapper's eye in the darkness though Legion can see him well enough, aided by bright gas station lights, by binoculars and – since it is fully dark and Legion does not wish to risk headlights – by a pair of night vision goggles with a zoom feature. He tries to time his tank fill-ups with that of the other man. He waits until the other man is done, then he pulls in, gases up the van as quickly as possible, and follows again.

That means there is a gap between them that occasionally takes the other car completely out of sight. They could lose him.

This is why, on one of the stops, Legion risks driving up while the man is in the convenience store for his gas. He parks on the other side of the island that contains the gas pump used by his prey. He glances inside and sees the kidnapper talking to the night clerk.

Legion knows his face is hidden from the woman in the kidnapper's car; he purposefully parked so one of the gas pumps is between him and her. Even so, he must be quick. He must be stealthy.

"You can do it," whispers Water. His fingers squish as he claps his hand on Legion's shoulder, though Legion feels none of the wetness.

"'Course he can," says Fire, and swipes his brother's arm away. There is a flash and a crackle, and both brothers withdraw from one another. Legion finds this interesting, but has no time to think about it.

He darts out of the van, still keeping the pump between him and his quarry. For a moment he considers freeing the woman. He dismisses the thought. She has been kidnapped. The man she was with is in the trunk. They are at a disadvantage, to be sure. But that does not mean they are clean.

He will wait. He will follow. He will see, and so seeing, will teach the right lessons and mete out the right punishments.

For now, he bends down, well below the line of her sight as he almost crawls around the pump island. He glances over when he gets to the back. The kidnapper is still talking to the night clerk.

Legion darts over, withdrawing from his pocket the tracker he prepared before pulling in. A moment to slap it under the back wheel well of the car, where it is unlikely to be discovered without a serious inspection. He glances over. The kidnapper is finishing up in the store. Handing over money.

Legion rushes back to his van. Gets inside quickly. Pulls away.

A quarter mile down the road, he pulls off a tiny side street. He waits. The only light in or on the van comes from the tracker he holds. He holds it to the side, so Fire and Water can see. He knows he does not need to do this, but feels compelled to do so nonetheless. Led as before. Guided as he has been since this strange trip began.

He does not believe in God, so what could this be? Where does this odd feeling come from?

"Maybe it *is* Father," says Water.

Fire's voice crackles. "Not him. If he's anywhere, it ain't here. If he's anywhere, he's burning in Hell." He grins his lipless, soot-toothed smile, and his coal ember eyes flare with sudden heat. "Which is ironic coming from me."

"Whatever it is," Legion says, "I am glad it is helping us."

"Not if it's Father," says Fire sharply.

"It isn't," says Legion. "You're right: he's not here. But it feels like *something* is helping us."

"What?" says Fire.

"Does it matter, really?" asks Water. "Isn't it enough to be glad we haven't lost this guy?"

"I suppose," says Fire.

The tracker beeps. The device has built-in GPS that shows streets and other geographical features of interest. The dot that represents the tracker Legion placed on the kidnapper's car is moving closer. He waits until the kidnapper is well past, then pulls his van onto the road. He turns on the lights. He will not need to drive in darkness. He follows his prey now with confidence.

They drive for a long time. No more stops.

"Hey, you see that?" says Fire.

"Yes," says Legion. He had noted the car pulling off the freeway. There is nothing here but long stretches of forest and mountain. He wonders where the man is going.

"There's no services for fifty miles," says Water. "So what's he pulling off here for?"

Fire shrugs, and the bones of his shoulders crack and split like burning logs. "Who cares? We should just catch up and kill him."

Legion does not answer. But he knows he will not do that. He will follow the car, and he will find out where it is going. Only then will he decide on a course of action. Lessons must be learned, but before he knows what those lessons should be, how will he teach them?

The kidnapper's car pulls away from the freeway, and Legion follows nearly a minute later. The freeway off-ramp feeds him onto a two-lane road. In one direction a few faraway farmhouses dot the land. In the other, he sees only thick trees and a single thin road between them.

His quarry, his prey, his *students* have proceeded into the trees.

Legion risks closing the distance between his vehicle and the other. He has the tracker, but he worries that the small streets here have not yet been mapped completely by Google, which powers the map feature of his tracker. That would make things more difficult. He judges it unlikely that his prey will see him through the trees. Worth the risk.

He follows. Never *too* close, but never too far, either. Legion has done this before, many times. He knows he is good at it, but still has to concentrate to keep from losing the connection between him and the other car. Sure enough, it eventually turns away from the road shown on the GPS and starts moving to the side, though there is no corresponding road shown.

Legion follows. It is difficult, given that he must now watch the tracker and try to make sure he remains on the same unknown road as the kidnapper he follows.

"And the woman," says Water, once more speaking to Legion's thoughts, rather than anything Legion actually said.

"And the dude in the trunk," Fire adds.

"Yes," says Legion. "And them, too."

A few minutes later he slows and then stops. A gate looms before him, cutting off the small road he has followed. Day has arrived in the last hours, so the sign is easy to read. Thick, blocky, white letters on an angry red background shout, "**NO TRESPASSING. VIOLATORS WILL BE PROSECUTED AND RISK DEATH OR INJURY BY OWNER.**"

Legion has followed his students into the Gem State of Idaho. He knows that is a firmly red state, largely agrarian, and with a broad view of Second Amendment rights. Even so, the warning on the gate seems extreme – and that makes the situation even more interesting.

He looks again at the gate. It is tall and heavy but barely wide enough to span the small road that Legion has followed here. Wire fencing ten feet high borders the gate on either side. Barbed wire spins tight coils along the top, and when Legion gets out of the van for a closer look, he hears a hum that tells him instantly that the fence is electrified.

He purses his lips. The fence can be shorted or circumvented easily enough – Father taught him to do that, along with so many other things – but he does not know if the fence also has alarms. Again, he can deal with such measures, but not until finding out exactly how this property is protected.

"Wonder what the guy's doing here," murmurs Fire. The voice is still angry, smoldering, but the fires in it have banked as the shade's curiosity takes hold.

"Let's look around a bit," suggests Water.

Fire's gaze snaps to his drowned brother. "What if he gets away?" he says, nodding toward the forest into which the other car has disappeared.

Water shrugs. "Not likely. This is probably the only way in or out." He looks at Legion, obviously dismissing Fire's concerns.

"Hey, don't ignore me, you –" Fire's burnt finger-nubs snap together as he reaches for Water. But he stops short of touching him.

Interesting.

Legion does not know why his imaginations cannot touch each other. But in the next moment he decides that it is a question for another time.

"We'll watch the tracker for a minute and make sure the car isn't going to move again," he says. "If it isn't, we'll look around."

"Solid plan," says Water.

"Fine," says Fire. He sounds like he is sulking, though it is hard to tell when his face is burnt to a point that most expressions are impossible.

Legion goes back to the van. He looks at the tracker. The red dot representing his students' car does not move. After twenty minutes he nods, then turns around and drives back the way he came. He goes a quarter mile, then pulls off the small road and continues into the forest until he is sure that no one will see the van from the road.

He parks, turns off the engine, and moves to the back of the van. He grabs a small messenger bag full of highly useful – and, in many cases, highly illegal – tools, and slings it over his shoulder. Items for circumventing security systems, a favored knife or two, a few small blocks of plastique and enough blasting caps to face anything short of a platoon of tanks: the usual. Legion is a very good teacher, flexible when it comes to the needs of each particular student. Even so, it is better to be overprepared than not prepared enough.

"You can say that again, brother," says Fire. He grits his sooty teeth together and grimaces as he relives his final pain.

"I'm sorry about that. About both of you," says Legion.

Water shrugs. "We always knew it might happen. It's the price we pay for making the world a better place."

Legion nods. He puts the binocular leash around his neck and is good to go.

Thus armed, he goes back to the gate and follows the fence into the forest to the east of the road. He walks for a hundred yards or so. The fence hums beside him. Signs – all of them just as hostile as the first one he saw – hang from the fence every dozen yards.

"A lot of signs," says Fire.

"They're hiding something," says Water.

Legion says nothing. He is looking at the tracker, which is small and has a battery that allows him to bring it with him. The dot sits motionless, he estimates about a quarter to a half mile away.

He looks at the trees beyond the fence. Something about this place, about the setup of it all, is familiar. "I wonder…"

He lifts the binoculars. Fortune smiles on him, for there are enough spaces between the trees that he is able to see between them. He is also able to see the cameras that hang from some of them.

"This whole area is under surveillance," he says. The tickling of familiarity grows stronger.

Water whistles a bubbly up and down tone. "I don't like this."

"But it's what we have to do," says Fire. For the first time he sounds neither angry nor standoffish. He can feel what Legion feels, and knows that they are standing on the threshold of a dangerous decision.

Legion shrugs. He walks a few more yards along the fence, being careful to stay out of range of the cameras beyond the fenceline. At last he comes to a box on the fence: part of the power system, and also the most likely place to find indications of alarms.

He opens the box with tools from his bag.

"Easy," says Water. "Don't move it fast, just in case there's a motion sensor."

"You were always better at this part," says Legion.

"I know. But you watched. You know nearly as well."

"I hope so."

He opens the box. Sure enough, there are several alarms built into it. Using alligator clips and a special circuit router of his own creation, he fools the alarm into not noticing what he will do next.

He removes a number of objects from his bag. The first are a set of rubber gloves. The second is a set of wire cutters with rubberized handles. He puts on the gloves, then approaches the fence and begins snipping wires.

The average electrified fence supplies approximately one joule of energy per six miles of fence. Father told him this, a long time ago. Between the rubber gloves and the wire cutters, he figures he will feel a bit of a shock, but nothing too severe. Certainly nothing that will stop him from cutting enough of the fence wires to either step through without touching them or, more likely, to short the fence completely.

He is surprised when he touches the fence with the cutters. There is a bright spark and instead of the tingle he expects, a bolt of pain surges through his fingers and up his arm. The power running through this fence is set at a level that probably would be fatal if he were not wearing gloves and holding the rubber handles of the pliers.

As it is, the very high level of electricity works to his advantage in a way. The surge causes all his muscles to clench, including those of his arm and hand. His fist clenches around the handles of the wire cutters, snipping through the very line supplying the electricity.

Another spark, and then Legion falls back, gasping, as the circuit is broken and the surge dissipates from his body.

"That was close," says Water.

"Be more careful," Fire almost shouts, though Legion knows it is worry more than anger that motivates him. "You don't wanna end up looking like me."

"Should be all right," says Legion.

"You hope," Fire says glumly.

"I hope," he agrees.

Legion steps to the fence again. He is about to touch one of the unbroken wires with the wire cutters, then thinks better of it and positions himself with the jaws of the cutters wide, one on either side of the wire.

"Going to do the shocky-cutty trick again, eh?" says Fire. He grimaces. "How many times you think you can do that before your heart stops?"

"I don't know," says Legion.

"Let's not find out." Fire shakes his head. "You die, I die. Again."

"What choice do we have?" asks Legion. He waits to see if either of his brothers comes up with a better idea.

Neither does.

He grits his teeth, then cuts.

There is no pain. The first cut must have caused a surge that blew out the fence.

Moving quickly, he makes cuts to five more lines – enough for him to step through the fence.

He walks deeper into the forest. Every step brings him more strange sensations. More the feeling of…

He stops. He stands rigid.

He looks at the surveillance cameras that hang from the trees. He has spotted all of them – easily. Almost…

"Instinctively," says Fire.

"Oh, no," says Water.

"Oh yes," says Legion.

He backs off again. He looks at his tracker. The car has not moved. The people in it – his students – are no doubt not just sitting there, but Legion suspects they will not have gone far.

"So what do we do now?" asks Fire.

"We teach," says Legion.

"But first we prepare," says Water.

"Yes," they all say at once.

Legion hikes for a long time. The area is unfamiliar, but he knows where to look for what he hopes to find. And when he does find it, he knows what to do with it. He puts down some of his supplies.

"How long you want?" says Water

"Maybe an hour?" says Fire.

"At least four," says Legion. He sets a timer for that long, then walks away. He is not done with recon, so he continues in a meandering circuit that brings him deeper into the forest. The cameras are thicker here, much harder to avoid. But he has done this many times, and has a unique preparation for doing such. The cameras are different than those his father employed once upon a time, but they have the same purpose, and Legion suspects that they monitor the area around a place similar to the one where he grew up.

He walks for another hour. He has not been in woods like this for many years, but he remembers all he has been taught, and makes excellent time. After a few miles, he notices something: the trees here are starting to look sickly. Beside him, Fire sniffs. "Smells like burning plastic."

Water mimics the sound. "You sure? Smells more like nail polish remover to me."

Fire bristles. "Who do you think might know what burning stuff smells like?" he indicates his charred frame. "If we want to know what chlorine smells like, you're our go-to guy. But burning… that's my thing."

Legion smells the air. "You're both right. There's kind of an eggy smell, too."

"What does that mean?" says Fire.

Legion gestures at the trees. Beneath them, many of the bushes and bits of brush that would otherwise be here seem to be absent. Even the dirt seems sick somehow.

Another idea circulates. He starts looking around, and spots what he expected. The filtration systems are excellent, well camouflaged, but he knows what to look for and spots the intakes hidden in real-seeming boulders.

"So *that's* what they're up to here," says Water. He shakes his head. "Clever. Awful, evil… but clever."

"How long this time?" says Fire as Legion again unlimbers his bag. "Same time," says Legion. He sets another timer, then straightens and begins walking. Recon is done and it is time to enter the belly of the beast. His newest classroom, where his students wait in dire need of education and correction.

"What are you doing?" asks Water.

Legion turns to see that his brothers, for the first time, have not followed him. "Our job," he says.

"But we'd have to go back to a place we swore never to return to," answers Water.

Fire bristles. "Not the exact place. That place is gone."

"A place like it, then," says Water. He shrinks away from Fire, as though his dead brother's heat might melt him.

Both brothers look at Legion. They wait for him to join his voice to one or the other.

"We don't know what's there. Not yet. So there's no need to plan for the best – or the worst."

Both his brothers nod.

"No need to panic," says Water.

Legion wonders what would happen if Water *did* panic. Nothing good, he suspects. Again he remembers the bright flash when his brothers touched one another.

Legion ignores that. He is discovering that having his brothers around – even if dead, and imaginary – is good for him. They allow him to talk out questions he has. But the flip side is that he has to put up with *their* questions. They also interrupt him from time to time, which never happened before. Father would not have liked it, so it was to be avoided at all costs.

Apparently the dead imaginings of his mind were no longer operating by those rules. A good thing, overall. But also a bit of a pain.

"Let's go," he says. He walks to the cameras, and hears Water and Fire following behind. He stands in plain view now, not bothering to hide from the surveillance cameras and even waving at a few.

He only has to wait a few minutes before he hears a rumble. A moment later, a trio of four-wheel all-terrain vehicles come into view. Two are driven by stone-faced men, the last by a woman who reminds Legion of a cobra.

"*She* got hit by the gorgeous stick," murmurs Fire.

"Rude," says Water. He whispers as well. "But true."

"And the guys are straight-up ugly," Fire continues.

"That one's *just* true," Water whispers back. "Maybe even a bit charitable."

Legion doesn't know why his mind bothers having these imaginary people whisper, or why he himself then murmurs, "Shut up," to both of them.

The ATVs encircle him, the drivers making no attempt to appear casual about that fact or to hide the fact that each is armed.

All three level weapons at him as soon as they come to a stop. The woman, evidently in charge of the crew, says, "You made a bad mistake."

Legion cocks his head. "Interesting accent."

One of the men – the bigger of the two, a neckless creature that Legion can instantly tell is *not* the brains of the operation – cocks his gun. "We kill?" he says. Like the woman, the man has an accent. Russian.

The woman nods. "Sure. I haven't killed anyone today."

This is not good. Legion doesn't want to die yet. Who would imagine him back alive? "Aren't you wondering if I came alone? Or what's in my bag?"

The woman's eyes, beautiful but utterly devoid of anything but efficient cruelty, narrow. "We can take bag off your body," she says, but Legion can tell she's worried. Perhaps they were just trying to scare him earlier and were always going to ask him if he came here alone. Either way, she's definitely contemplating the question now.

"Sure you can," he says easily. He knows from experience that speaking calmly in the face of overwhelming danger can be extremely disconcerting. And it's working: both the men are fingering the triggers of their guns as though worried Legion will transform into a monster at any moment.

"What's in the bag?" asks the woman.

Legion shrugs. "Not much. Some tools. A neat little gadget I bought that opens keycard doors, some surveillance gear. GPS and radio, as well as a cell phone."

The three would-be captors grow more and more agitated as he speaks.

Legion smiles at that, and smiles all the wider as he delivers the final blow. "Enough to know what you're doing here, and what's going on in the bunker. Meth, right?"

He has been staring at the woman as he speaks. She mutters a word he does not understand, then nods.

The man behind Legion is quick and silent. He barely hears him dismount, and only manages to turn halfway around before something hits him and a black hole opens in the center of his vision.

That's fine. He's been knocked out before. And being knocked out means they're not going to kill him – not right away. They'll take him with them, likely to exactly the place he is hoping to go.

He smiles, even as a second blow hits him and the black hole widens to take him away. It's all good.

He falls into darkness. And in the darkness he finds something *not* good. He finds, in fact, the one thing he still fears.

He finds Father.

11

Marcos stared at the remains of the man whose brains were splashed all over the wall and wondered if it was even *possible* to find really good help nowadays.

Not including Marcos, the lab had employed twenty-three people. Sixteen of them were in charge of production, doing the work necessary to pump out the meth that was Marcos' stepping stone to real power. Three more had consisted of Beaker, Heckle, and Jeckle, all of whom were tucked in drums in the back of the meth production facility.

The remaining four were on security. Today three of them were in charge of wandering the premises. They pretended to be offroaders, messing around on ATVs; or hikers who had strayed a bit from their intended path; or they just skulked around and kept a watch on things. It was potentially a bit of a giveaway for anyone who watched the area long-term, but Marcos had judged that an acceptable risk, banking on the fact that he would become aware of anyone surveilling him and the operation and could either draw back into complete hiding or simply lock up and abandon the place. The bunker was intended to be a fortress, and getting into it without knowing the place inside and out – and having the proper keys and passes – would be well-nigh impossible.

That left one more person. One more member of security. The one who was supposed to be manning the security station inside the bunker, watching for tripped alarms and keeping an eye on the monitors that showed camera feeds from the land outside the bunker.

The dead guy.

Earlier, when a motion sensor had been tripped, Marcos had taken the ever weirder-seeming Sheldon Steward to the security station to see what had happened. Yuri was manning the monitor – Mr. No Brains, as Marcos now thought of him, for a variety of reasons – but he had shrugged and said that sometimes deer or other animals tripped the sensors.

"You sure?" Marcos had said.

"This place is really nifty," whispered Sheldon behind him.

Yuri stared at Sheldon. He waited for Marcos' okay to start talking, which was probably the first, last, and only thing he had done with any competence.

"He's with me," said Marcos. "Don't worry about him."

Both statements were absolutely true. Marcos had known Sheldon all his life, and even though the guy got weirder every time Marcos saw him, he was still the best at what he did. Marcos suspected that sooner or later the guy's mental state would deteriorate to the point that he'd become a liability, but that was above Yuri's pay grade. Like all the others on the security detail, he was Marcos' man, bought and paid for. He knew the coup was already in motion, and had bet his life that Marcos could oust Demyan.

"You sure it's just deer?" asked Marcos, and Yuri said he was sure. Nothing but deer. Maybe a wolf. They were rare around here this time of year, but it did happen. That was what he said. "If it was anything else, security panel does not just beep, it *scream*," said the security guy and, like an idiot, Marcos believed him.

Marcos was a careful guy, as any good Dungeon Master should be. So when his phone buzzed at his side, off he went back to the security office at a quick but not panicked place. Inside, he found Yuri in a *definite* panic. The guy glanced at Sheldon only for a moment, then began babbling.

"Sir, I don't know how this happens, I just walk away for a sec to take a piss and when I come back Sergei is on radio telling me there is intruder and they are bringing him in and –"

"Where are they now?" Marcos interrupted. "The security detail and our guest?"

"Just coming in at west entrance," said Yuri. He looked like he wanted to continue babbling, but a single glance at Marcos' dark expression suddenly stopped him. He was, like most everyone here, a Russian, and suddenly seemed to remember that fact… along with the fact that Marcos was *not* Russian. His mouth firmed, and he looked disgusted – though whether at Marcos' lineage or at himself for being so afraid of a lesser human, Marcos did not know or care.

The guy was dead anyway. He had been from the moment Marcos realized how poorly Yuri had done his job.

"So Feodora, Sergei, and Mikhail are all bringing him in?" Marcos asked quietly. "They must be worried."

"Yes," said Mr. No Brains. His tone grew more surly as he added, "Sir," turning the honorific into an epithet that showed clearly his inner thoughts: he was following Marcos because that course led to greater money and power. But he didn't respect Marcos, and never would.

Marcos cursed the man silently, and cursed the moment in general. *Now,* of all things. The timing couldn't be worse. Everything had been going to plan, Demyan would be here imminently, and he just didn't have the time or interest to deal with other matters.

Still, Dungeon Masters were careful. They were thorough.

"Call them in. Have Fee report here," he said.

"And the intruder?"

"Tell Sergei and Mikhail to put him with the others."

Yuri eyed him skeptically. "Won't that mess things up with Demyan?"

Marcos didn't answer. He just waited until Yuri picked up a phone and dialed. "Feodora, have Mikhail and Sergei drop off our guest in holding room." He paused. "You come to security."

He hung up. They waited in silence. Sheldon started humming quietly. "Can you shut up?" said Marcos.

"Of course," said Sheldon. "I'm very good at being quiet."

So creepy. Marcos was definitely going to waste him soon. But not until the job was done. Sheldon was the best at grabbing people, making them suffer, and finally killing them. He'd done the grabbing Marcos needed, but the other two parts of the job were still to come.

And when it's done, Gandalf will pay a visit and boom.

The idea of his favorite gun doing its work was, as always, pleasant and calming, though less so than usual. Sheldon was standing there, and one night in a near-stupor of drunkenness Marcos had told Sheldon he named his guns. Stupid, but he did it. Sheldon had promised not to tell, but just knowing the guy knew that secret, and that he was right here, right now.

Damn, nothing *is going my way.*

For a moment Marcos wondered if Sheldon named *his* weapons. He didn't know why it occurred to him, but it did, and the possibility that he and Sheldon might share such a thing in common disquieted him. What would that say about *him,* if he turned out to be like Sheldon in that way?

Marcos thought he might have to quit naming his weapons if it turned out Sheldon did, too.

His irritation and concern over whether he'd be able to properly enjoy Gandalf's prowess and power was probably why Feodora was barely in the room, the door barely closed behind her, when Marcos pulled Gandalf from his holster and decorated one wall with the limited contents of Yuri's – Mr. No Brains' – skull.

Unlike Feodora, Sheldon didn't even flinch. He just smiled and said, "I wish Lucy could have seen that."

Creepier and creepier.

Feodora nudged Yuri's body. "You have a problem with that?" said Marcos, gesturing at the dead man.

"Yuri was idiot," she said. "He let someone in perimeter and if you had not killed him I would do it myself."

That was about the reaction Marcos had expected. Feodora was a warrior, an assassin – and sometimes served as Marcos' lover. She was the one person in here whose loyalty he most trusted. Even more so than the ever more unstable Sheldon.

"I need you to do a better job than he did," he said to Feodora.

She snorted. "A blind five-year-old can do this."

"A *much* better job, then."

She nodded and sat down at the security station. "Can you have Mikhail or Sergei come for body before too long?" she asked. She was already glued to the screens, not paying a bit of attention to Mr. No Brains, who lay cooling only a few feet away.

"I will do what I can, but…"

"But Demyan is first priority. Of course I understand this. I just do not wish to sit here with body. I worry his stupidity is maybe contagious even after death."

She still didn't look away, but she smiled and Marcos knew the smile was meant for him and him alone. Loyal, fierce – and something of a hellcat in the sack. He might actually keep her around for a while. Probably not – sooner or later he'd have to clean house and put in people who had never known the feel of Demyan's leadership – but maybe.

And until that day came, he'd use Feodora in any and every way possible. Sometimes she fought him, but that just made it more fun. And when he imagined she was a wood elf, it was even better.

"Any sign of Demyan when you came in?" he asked.

"No. I let you know when I see anything outside," said Feodora. Another tight smile. "Go find out who is our visitor. I call you when Demyan arrive."

"Go back through the guy's history as well. Backtrack the video to see where he came on the property and what else he was up to before Yuri –"

"– the idiot –"

"– spotted him."

Feodora nodded. "Of course, boss."

"But first priority is watching for Demyan. I want plenty of time to be ready for him."

"Yes, boss."

Unlike Yuri's "sir," her pronunciation of "boss" seemed both heartfelt and lacking in nationalist/racial superiority.

Yes, Marcos would definitely keep her around for a while. And after that? This world featured no sorcerers or dragons, but it *was* full of treasure and magic and beautiful possibilities.

That made him think of the woman Sheldon had brought in. She was a looker, too. He knew that Sheldon would do anything and everything to her that Marcos directed, but he rather hoped that wouldn't prove necessary. He would do whatever was necessary to destroy Demyan, but knew it wasn't likely that Demyan would be moved by her pain one way or another. If that was the case, then there was no reason to break the woman. Marcos could keep her whole and unmarked… at least long enough to allow *him* the fun of marking her up himself.

He smiled. There had been a complication. But he was handling it, the way a master strategizer and world class Dungeon Master would handle any complication. Plans changed, alliances shifted, fellow travelers died by the wayside. But at the end of the day he had created a game where he would level up to *pakhan* in the Odessa family. And after that… who knew? He was a Dungeon Master at heart, and that meant he was a man who created and controlled worlds. He was sure to come up with more treasure to find, more power to gain. Perhaps someday he would be a god.

12

Legion has been knocked out. But he does not float in blissful darkness. Instead he swims against a tide of memory; into pools of pain.

He is ten years old again. He lays in the bunk that he sleeps on one day out of every three. The other two of Him –

(they are my brothers even though we thought we were One we were always three how did I not see that?)

– sleep in the corners of the room.

There is a heavy thunk as the door swings open and Father enters the room. He ducks low as he always must to get through the door. Father is a big man, and even in the large spaces of the oversized place he has built and hidden away, he sometimes seems too large to be contained.

"Get up," says Father.

"Yes, sir."

Legion sees all this through the darkness of memory. But the memories are brightening; finally becoming clear. He sees himself sit up on the bed, and sees the other two he thought of himself as "Him" watching closely. Water and Fire, as they will one day call themselves after they die, wait in silence.

Father insists on seeing only one of them at a time. Legion, Water, and Fire become One under his eyes, his insistence. It is the only world they know, so it seems like the only world that is right. But Legion knows now, even tossed and turned in tides of memory, that such is madness.

I was insane.

We all were.

"It's Monday," says Father.

Legion knows that this means he will have combat training, which he likes. That is part of why he is sleeping here: so that he can be the first thing Father sees.

Father *does* see the other two of him, the three that make One and the One made of three. He is not blind, physically. But whenever his eyes rove over one of the brothers not playing the part of his "only son," his eyes glaze and he looks not at what *is* but rather what he wishes were so. Father never bumps into one of the other children he insists do not exist, he never trips over one… but he never acknowledges them, either.

Legion – unnamed at the time of this memory in the dark; just one of three nameless children who share one bed, one set of clothes, one of *everything* – quickly stands. Father does not like to be made to wait, so he tarries in the room only long enough to slip on jeans and a t-shirt. Water and Fire do the same.

Legion has only five shirts and five pairs of pants in his size, and Father will only do loads for himself and for a single son at a time. This means that the clothing Legion wears and shares with his brothers is often dirty: sticky with sweat, stiff with dirt. But dirty clothes are better than nothing.

Legion does not like to be naked. Neither do those who, in death, will become Fire and Water in his mind. Being naked in this place means that pain is soon to come.

Dressed, though still barefoot, Legion leaves the room. Water and Fire, dressed exactly the same in case Father should decide that one of *them* is his only child this day, follow at a discreet distance.

There are many rooms in the house of Legion's father. A few are for eating or sleeping. The rest are for learning the only thing that matters here: survival. Some rooms hold books on hunting and foraging, and hold all manner of seeds and supplies to begin farms. Some contain blueprints and drawings of buildings that Father uses to teach Legion the weak spots and pressure points of edifices great and small. Others spill over with computer parts and other electronics, and in these Father shows Legion and his oft-unseen brothers how to disrupt, destroy, or even – in extreme necessity – create communications and network infrastructure.

There is also a single room that Legion tries never to think about. It is the one room he never goes into willingly. He has to pass by it as he follows Father through the halls, and as always his buttocks clench and his insides feel strangely oily until he has passed that door.

But pass it he does. He does not look around to see if Water and Fire react as he does. He knows they do. Because in this place, in this time, he has already lived with Father's delusion so long that he shares it. In this time, in this place, he lives a life split in strange ways. A tiny part of him suspects he is a single person among several. A much larger part of him *knows* that he is One, because Father says so. And the smallest, most invisible part of him manages the delicate balance of preventing those other parts from meeting.

Past the room he does not like, the room he *fears,* stands the door to the largest room in his father's house. Legion and his brothers enter the room dedicated to combat. Father teaches Legion how to fight in this place, and even the fans that silently circulate air through the room cannot completely scrub the smells of oil and metal and sweat and blood that saturate everything.

Weaponry – everything from assault rifles that have been modified to fully automatic to small handguns to bows and crossbows to bladed weapons – hangs from racks that cover one long wall. Beside that: a workstation where Father has taught Legion and his brothers to strip and clean every one of the weapons. Fire is best at this, but any of them can disassemble and then reassemble any of the weapons at speeds that Legion knows few in the world could match.

Most of the rest of the room is taken up by a blue mat where most of the fighting – and the pain – take place.

Legion has barely entered the room when something grabs him from behind. Father's thick arm encircles his neck and Legion feels his air cut off immediately. He does not panic – this has happened before, and is mere routine even at this early age. But he does act quickly. He does not worry about lack of air. The immediate problem is the lack of blood as his father compresses the carotid arteries on either side of his neck. Legion has seconds before he blacks out.

This is one of the few tests he has never passed. Every time Father takes him like this, Legion passes into darkness. He awakes on the floor, or in his bed, or – sometimes – in Father's. But the darkness *always* takes him. He has never been able to peel away the thick arm at his neck before the world goes black and he wakes up with nothing but pain and his brothers' open-mouthed horror revealing that Father has done terrible things to the One.

Because he has never succeeded at peeling Father's arm away, this time he does not even try. Instead, he drives his elbow back and up, aiming for Father's groin. Father is waiting for this, and swivels his hips up and away.

And Legion is waiting for *that*. Father's movement shifts his center of balance backward, and he must brace his legs to avoid falling. Legion is already raising his leg and kicking down as Father plants his own feet. The kick takes Father in the side of the knee. He tries to dodge the attack, but the kick strikes true. Father grunts and slides to the side, but not before Legion kicks him again, in the same spot.

The knee pops. Father grunts again – the closest Legion has ever heard to a sound of pain. His grip loosens just enough that Legion can put his hands on Father's elbow and push up. He drops his own head down at the same time, his ears bending painfully as he yanks himself out of Father's headlock.

The rush of blood to his brain is almost as bad as was the compression of his carotids. He wavers, suddenly dizzy… but he *is free*.

He looks at Father, who is kneeling on the blue mat, staring up at Legion with an unreadable expression. "Go," the man finally says. "Get out of here. Go get yourself breakfast."

Legion does, his brothers close behind. He looks back as he crosses from the room into the hall, and though his father tries to cover it, Legion sees him reel to the side when he puts weight on the knee Legion attacked.

Legion turns away. Something inside him screams in terror, knowing that Father cannot allow his son(*s*) to see him as weak. But the weakness *was* there, and Legion *did* see it.

He has never seen Father show weakness before, and says as much to Himselfs. "I don't know what to feel about that."

"No, I don't," agrees one of then-Him, the one who will someday be burned alive in a house of sinners.

"But I *do* feel sad," says the other once-Him, the one who will someday drown.

"Yes, I suppose I do," says Legion.

He looks around. There is no sign of Father. That is good. That means that he can get the three helpings of food that he needs to feed the three bodies sharing his soul. When Father is in the room, he can only take one helping or Father gets mad.

When Father gets mad, pain is the best possible outcome. If not pain, then…

The room.

Legion shudders. He and his brothers eat. There are rations enough for decades – whole rooms piled to the ceilings with pallets of military-style Meals Ready to Eat. They bear such words as "stroganoff" and "soup" and "casserole." In reality, Legion thinks they all taste like clam chowder from which all the taste has been strained. All that remains is goo and salt.

Today, though, he and his brothers can feast on fresh meat. Fire and Father killed a deer three weeks ago, and the remains of that kill along with fresh vegetables from the hydroponics garden are an excellent alternative to MREs. Water seasons all their food with seeds from the mustard plants he found outside a few days before, and the brothers/one child enjoy/enjoys the tastes and the silence.

None of them talk. At the time of this memory, this *now,* Legion thinks of himself and his brothers as One, and the One rarely talks to Himself even when Father is absent. This is not because the brothers have nothing to say – Legion knows, with the hindsight that came with the deaths of Water and Fire – that they all had a great deal to say. He wished even then, in that small part of his mind that was not One but just him, that he could talk deep into the night with his brothers and discover what each of them thought of the things they saw that day.

But Father does not like to see the One speaking to Himselfs. What Father does not like, he judges as sin. And when Father finds sin, he *teaches* the sinner.

To Father, teaching is a many-splendored thing. It allows him to inculcate values, to discourage poor behavior, and to teach needed skills. The methods of instruction range from nights alone in the woods, to paddles and canes upon Legion's thighs and backs and buttocks, to knives and fire, and even to the darker and deeper horrors that come when Father's loneliness is too much for him to bear and he visits Legion in the night and takes whichever son he sees as real to his room.

So Legion does not speak as he eats. He eats in silence, and almost feels… happy. He is alone with his –

(brothers)

– thoughts, enjoying food and the memory of hurting Father.

Then he sees Water's eyes widen. Legion tries to turn, but before he can he feels Father's hand on his neck and feels that hand shove him down so hard he is bent over against the table. His knees, still bent over the chair, are forced against the underside of the table, pinning him in place.

Legion tries not to panic. Tries not to believe that Father will do the *thing*, that one thing that Legion hates and fears most of all.

But it is happening. It is happening *now*. Father yanks Legion's hands behind him. Something pops and pain scythes through his shoulder. In the next instant

Father grabs Legion's pants by the belt and suddenly he feels himself, his own self, his closest and truest –

(*single solitary,* one,)

– self, hoisted into the air. The tough material of his jeans bunches painfully against his groin as it bears his entire weight.

Legion tries not to scream. But scream he does. Long and loud and hard.

Father lets go of Legion's neck long enough to box his ears. A cupped hand sends an implosion of air that both rocks Legion to the side and makes him throw up as sudden dizziness tilts his universe.

He at least has the presence of mind not to throw up on the floor or – worst of all – on Father. He vomits, but clamps his jaw shut and manages to swallow it.

He barely notices that Father is speaking to him. He speaks softly, but intensely, whispering into Legion's still-ringing ear:

"You think you're tough, do you? Think that just because you ripped your mother to shreds coming out, killed her, maybe you can hurt your old man? Maybe you can *kill* your old man? Well that's good."

He has been carrying Legion as he speaks. Out of the room used for eating, into the hall. Toward the place Legion fears.

"No," he moans.

Father boxes his ears again. He tosses Legion on the floor. He strips Legion's clothes. "Can't have you cheating," he whispers. "Can't let you go in there with anything you weren't *born* with."

Legion hears the sound of cloth moving and knows that Fire and Water are disrobing as well. They are One. When one is naked, so must all be.

Father boxes Legion again, then flips him over once more. Legion is facedown on the metal floor, quivering and cold and in agony. He shrieks as Father takes his arms and yanks them behind his back. Legion feels cold metal and hears the ratcheting click of handcuffs locking around his thin wrists. "No!" he shrieks.

Father grunts. "Good to have the fire. Good to have the hate. The end of the world is coming, kid, it's coming soon and hard in a baptism of water and fire, and only the ones who are prepared will survive the light and the heat and then the cold and the dark."

As Father speaks the magic words of "cold and the dark," he throws his son into the room Legion fears above all others – even above Father's own room:

Father throws Legion into the Dark Place.

Legion tumbles forward. He hits his face on a hard metal floor, and cries out as his teeth grind against the insides of his lips. One tooth buries itself deep in the soft flesh there, and Legion screams.

He does not scream because of the pain, though it is tremendous. He does not even scream in this moment because he is in the Dark Place. He screams because he fears that one of his teeth may have punctured his lip. It may have gone right through and be jutting out the other side and if that happens he will not match the other Hims, his other Selfs, and then what will Father do? What will his own *Selfs* do?

Legion suspects that if he no longer matches, he will be killed. There is room only for one child in Father's heart, only a single soul in Father's mind, only one son in Father's eyes.

So if there is one Self who does not match…

In his pain and fear, Legion hears his brothers scramble forward. They hate and fear the Dark Place as much as he does. But at this time, in this place, they are still One. They are bound by Father's madness, stronger even than fear, and so when Legion goes into the Dark Place, Fire and Water enter as well.

Father, in one of the strange quirks of his insanity, steps aside to let them enter, though his eyes never waver from Legion's own. Then, once the three/One are inside, Father swings the door shut.

"If you get out of there," Father says on the other side of the door, "then you deserve to live. If you get out on your own, you may deserve my favor."

Legion screams, and his brothers scream as well. He feels wetness pour over his chin as he rolls onto his back, and feels the shattering pain in the shoulder Father popped.

In spite of the pain, he rolls around until he has gotten his handcuffs over his feet. His hands are in front of him now, and he frantically feels his lip and chin. Blood pours over his fingers from cuts in his mouth, but he does not see it. He sees nothing at all, because he is in the Dark

Place and even Father's soft, painful touches during his lonely nights do not frighten him as much as the blackness in this room.

Father's voice comes through the closed door. The words are frightening, but at least they give him a sense of direction. They tell him the way that leads out – and that is something.

"You think you're tough?" says Father. "Then get yourself out. Dig deep, and find the way inside yourself." Legion hears Father spit loudly. "The only people worthy in this world are the ones who can escape any cell – even the ones they make for themselves. The only people who can be called good are the ones who can survive the trials their teachers provide."

There is a deep, dry *thunk* as the unseen door is locked. Then nothing but Legion's own cries in the black.

A moment later, he hears the Self that will one day become Water say through tears, "Am I hurt?"

Fire, also crying, snaps, "Of course I am, dummy."

"Yes, I'm hurt," Legion moans between sobs. "I'm… hurt… so bad… so very very bad… bad… bad… bad."

The last word repeats over and over, first on his tongue and then in his mind. He knows he speaks not just of his injuries or his pain, but of his own Self. He has been proud. He has bitten the hand that feeds Him, as Father sometimes puts it. The One has hurt Father, and that means the One must be hurt in turn.

The One is bad, and the One deserves to be here, bound and injured, in the Dark Place. And if the One cannot find a way to escape, then perhaps He will die here as well. Father has taught an important lesson today: those who are true will survive. Those who escape deserve favor.

Legion lays in the darkness. After some time, Water says, "Do I still match?"

"I don't know," whispers Legion. "I can't see."

Hands feel him. The Him that will become Fire says, "My shoulder is weird."

"Father pulled my shoulder," says Water. "I saw him do it. It hurt. I saw myself scream."

"Feels like my shoulder is bent wrong," says Fire.

Legion feels cold. "I don't match," he says.

Something slaps him. "I *do* match," hisses Fire. "Or I will in a second."

Something flops down on Legion. It is Fire's hand. Legion holds it, knowing what must come next and dreading it all the same. He waits. "I have to do this," whispers Fire.

"Yes," says Legion. "I do." He twists Fire's shoulder (his Own shoulder) until he hears a *pop* like the one he has already heard. Fire screams.

"Now *I* have to match," says Water.

"Yes," says Legion. "I know. But…" He pants. "I don't know… I'm so tired…"

"I can make me match," says Fire. Legion hears another pop a moment later. Water does not scream, but sobs a single, wrenching cry.

"I match," whispers Legion. That is what passes for hope in the Dark Place.

Father told him to escape, just as he does every time. Father told him that survival is a measure of worthiness, just as he does every time.

Legion does not escape that day. Or the next. He cannot even get his handcuffs off, much less find the strength to pull open the heavy door that seals him in the Dark Place.

On the third day, Father opens the door. Legion cannot rise, and neither can his brothers. They are hungry and thirsty and near to death.

Father leaves a single cup of water. He leaves a single piece of bread. "Take. Eat," he says.

Legion cannot move. He is too weak, as is Water. Only Fire manages. He crawls – on only one hand, since his other arm dangles dislocated from the shoulder – to the bread and water Father has left behind. As he does, Legion sees in his brother's – in his Own – eyes a sudden desire to take and eat all of what Father has left. He sees Fire consider the possibility of surviving alone, and being one instead of One.

The moment passes. Fire sips only a small bit of water. He takes only a tiny morsel of bread. Then he pushes them toward Water, who partakes. Then Water pushes the offerings that remain to Legion.

Legion eats. Legion drinks.

And he hates Fire as he does. Because for one glorious moment he actually thought he might be allowed to die. But that moment was stolen from him. He is alive. He will remain here, and will remain One.

Father comes back later. He gathers up the cup and leaves. He returns and takes a shiny handcuff key from his pocket. He unlocks Legion's handcuffs. He wraps one hand around Legion's wrist and braces his other big palm on Legion's shoulder.

He pushes and pulls, and Legion screams as his shoulder rams back into its socket. "Get cleaned up and dressed, boy," says Father as he leaves. "You have a test on high value infrastructure targets in an hour."

Legion and his brothers are nearly late for the test. Cleanup takes less than five minutes, but figuring out how to pop Water's and Fire's shoulders back into place the way Father had done with Legion is a painful and grueling process.

Water is the One who takes the test. He passes – he is the best of the One at such things, though all the One are well-versed in the subject, of course.

Father rewards the One for passing the test. He gives another piece of bread and fifteen minutes of free time.

Legion tears off a piece of the bread and hands it to Water, then another and gives it to Fire. He chews the last piece and says, "He's going to put me back in again. The Dark Place."

"Probably," says Water. "Unless I do everything right, all the time."

"Which I won't," says Fire.

"So I have to be able to get myself free," says Legion.

"Yes. Or I won't ever *be* free," says Fire.

Legion says nothing. He understands what Fire is saying – though in this memory he is only understanding it as part of what He Himself says – and knows Water understands as well.

Someday, Father will kill Him. Or He will kill Father.

"I need to kill him now," says Fire.

Legion considers this. "I'm not ready yet. He's too strong."

"Then he will put me back in again and again," says Water.

"Then I need to figure out how to get out of the Dark Place," says Legion.

"Why?" says Water. "He always lets me out eventually."

"Because," says Fire, "one day he *won't* let me out."

"I know," says Legion. "He won't let me out and I will die and then I will have to die again and again so that I match."

"I don't want to die, or die again, *or* die again," says Water.

"So I have to figure out how to escape. Maybe that's what he wants. Maybe that's how I prove my worth." Legion deepens his voice in a passable impression of Father. "You think you're tough? Then get yourself out. Dig deep, and find the way inside yourself." Legion pretends to spit, just as Father did, before finishing, "The only people worthy in this world are the ones who can escape any cell – even the ones they make for themselves. The only people who can be called good are the ones who can survive the trials their teachers provide."

Water looks mournful. "But how can I survive?" he asks.

"I have to figure out a way to get the handcuffs off first," says Fire. "Father strips me before I go into the Dark Place, so how can I get the cuffs off with nothing to help me?"

Legion thinks of Father's shiny handcuff key. There are several of them secreted throughout the place.

The One is silent. Then Legion whispers, "Dig deep."

"What did I say?" says Fire.

Legion waits. He is thinking. He looks at his body, which shows many of the marks of Father's teaching. "Dig deep," he says, once again mimicking Father's voice. "Dig deep, and find the way inside yourself."

He laughs. Because he has perhaps found a way from the Dark Place. Perhaps then he will be worthy. And if not, the One will kill Father.

Legion tells the One what he has figured out. Fire and Water laugh also.

"Oh, I *am* clever," says Fire.

Father hears the laughter. He comes in the room and usually that would make all of them stop: Father does not like hearing three voices from his One. But this time is different. He has found a way out, and He is full of joy.

He will have to steal three handcuff keys, because that is how many He will need to make sure all of Him match.

It will take time.

But someday Legion will escape. He knows it now, and though it means Father will punish him in ways too old and terrifying for a boy to understand, the One laughs with three voices.

He is One.

And he *will* be free.

13

Danielle had tried several times to reach for Alex. She wasn't surprised that he didn't want to talk – she wouldn't have blamed him for being catatonic, given all that happened. But she *was* surprised when he not only pulled away, but actually growled at her. *Growled*. And in his eyes, just for a moment, Danielle thought she saw a look she'd seen in her mother's eyes.

Cancer was what did her mother in. It came quickly, a nodule in her breast that was too late a signal to stop the malignancy that had already spread to so much of her body. It almost felt to Danielle like her Mother's body, so beautiful and perfect even as she approached middle age, had finally realized what an ugly soul it held and had begun to change in order to match it.

Danielle remembered the aggressive chemotherapy and radiation therapy that had stolen first all of her mother's hair, then much of the woman's vitality. She remembered her mother, hunched over a toilet and vomiting so hard that one time she had to be rushed to the emergency room with what turned out to be a partially-fractured vertebra.

She remembered her mother's eyes, above everything else. As the cancer progressed they looked wounded, they looked pained. But most of all they looked angry. And somehow Danielle knew that the anger was not at the injustice of it, or the simple fact that she was going to die. It was rage at the fact that something – *anything* – had exercised power over Mother; that she herself was not strong enough to stop this thing from subjugating and then destroying her.

A cruel wake-up call, to be sure. And one of the things Danielle liked least about herself was the memory of how much she had savored that look. How much she had enjoyed the impotent rage she saw in her mother's eyes in the weeks, days, hours, and final moments before the woman's death.

Danielle's brother had deserved far better than he got. He received injustice, and pain, and death. But that same pain, that same burgeoning doom, was a fitting end for her mother. So Danielle, ugly though it was to admit, *enjoyed* it.

She went to the hospital every day – especially at the end, when the only sounds Mother could make alternated between whimpers and screams. The staff thought Danielle was a doting, loving daughter. She, in turn, tried not to show how much she enjoyed what was happening.

It was cruel, and ugly of her. She regretted it every day after her mother's death, and that, she supposed, was one more thing she tried to atone for by working so hard to see that justice *was* served – but only when tempered by mercy.

Yet no matter how hard she worked, still those eyes appeared to her in her dreams. And though that was bad enough, the worst part was how much the dreams of her mother's pained eyes ended with Danielle waking happy and refreshed.

But no happiness filled her when Alex turned that same look on her. Wounded, in agony… and, deep below that, she saw traces of rage. He growled at her, and turned on his side so he faced away from her. All she could see was his back and the mangled fingers dangling from the handcuff.

"Alex?" she said. "Honey?"

No answer. She let him sit there in silence – or in whimpering, wounded pain – for as long as she could. But a part of her knew she couldn't let this go on. Not just because it hurt her to hear this, and to see him turn his back on her, but because there were things that had to be said, now.

"What's going on?" she finally said. No answer, beyond a single, keening moan. "Alex, we have to get out of here, so anything you can –"

He turned toward her, and snarled, "How the hell should *I* know what's going on?" Again she saw a familiar flash of anger; rage at a world that had dared impose its will. It passed almost as fast as it came. "I'm sorry," he said. Tears shone in his eyes. "I didn't mean –"

"It's okay," she said. And she meant it. Could she blame him for his pain, and for his anger?

Can *I? Is this his fault?*

She didn't like that thought. And knew there was only one way to excise it. "What's happening?" she asked again.

"I told you: I don't know."

"Honey," she said, trying to sound soothing in spite of the terrified quaver that shook her voice. "I won't be angry, no matter what. But they want *you*. They hurt *you*. And it seemed like your pain mattered to the man who brought us in here."

Alex's shoulders shook as he visibly held back sobs. "I don't know why, I swear. Nothing like this has ever happened to me. Not like this. No one's even had the chance for years."

Something in that last phrase chilled her. "What do you mean, 'no one's even had the chance'?"

Alex eyed her. Silence but for his occasional sniffles and a *plip, plip* that she finally realized was drops of blood splashing from his ruined hand to the hard floor. The blood pooled and spread as they waited in silence.

Finally, Alex inhaled, blew out the air, inhaled again, and said, "I have a guardian angel."

Danielle blinked and shook her head. "I don't understand," she said.

Alex looked embarrassed, as though ashamed he had said anything about this subject. "It's nothing. Sorry." He looked around. "We need to figure out how to get out of here, in case…"

Danielle's brows bunched together. "In case what?"

"In case…" She sensed Alex was on the verge of telling her something important. But the instant before it happened – whatever *it* might have been – he shook his head. That rage so reminiscent of Danielle's mother flickered over him an instant before disappearing, and she wondered if it was the same way her mother's rage had disappeared when she wanted something. That was the woman's gift to herself: the ability to mimic human emotion when it served her needs.

That's ridiculous. Alex isn't like her. He couldn't be. He's too kind, too –

(Mother could be kind, too. When it served her.)

"We just need to get out of here," Danielle said. She looked around, as much to avoid thinking about the expression she had seen on Alex's face as from any hope of finding an escape. "Do you see anything helpful?"

"There has to be something," said Alex. He felt at his pockets. "Nothing in my pockets."

"Same here. They must have taken everything from us before we woke up. I don't have anything I can use."

Alex stared at the handcuffs that bound his one good hand to the ring in the wall. "Damn," he muttered.

"Is there at least anything we can do for your hand?"

His only answer was to clutch it closer to himself, as though trying to hide his injury from her.

Danielle didn't want to give up, but that moment almost broke her. She was stuck in this place for reasons she couldn't even begin to fathom, her new husband was caught up in it and either didn't know or didn't want to tell her why. Now he was visibly walling himself off from her. Part of that was the pain, no doubt – what he had suffered was horrific, what he now felt must be equally so;

and there was also the promise of more to come that she felt weighing down on both of them.

But that wasn't the only reason that he had turned away from her, or the reason he was hiding the injured part of himself from her eyes.

Do I know him? Do I really know him?

Of course I do. He's perfect. Life has been so good…

(Life could be good when Mother wanted it to be, too.)

She put that thought away as quickly as she could, but it still stung at the edges of her mind.

She looked away from Alex, because she couldn't stand to see him hiding from her. She turned instead to the room's only other occupant.

"Hey, Lucy," she said. She stared at it like it might hold the answer to all her problems. It didn't, of course. It was just a plant.

She straightened suddenly. Remembering something Sheldon had said.

Just as she had before, when trying to reach Alex's unconscious form, she slid forward on her hips and reached out with her toes. She hadn't been able to reach Alex, but maybe she *could* reach Lucy.

It took long, anxious minutes. Alex said nothing during that time, and Danielle tried not to think about what his silence might mean. Shouldn't he be asking her what she was doing, or if he could help, or… *something*?

What's wrong with him?

(Who is he?)

At first, the toes of her shoes just scrabbled along the edge of the small tree's pot. The pot turned and she stopped, worried she would push it completely out of reach if she kept going. She pulled her feet back, then untied her shoes one-handed and kicked them off.

She slid forward again, reaching now with her toes. And instead of going for the sides of the pot, this time she curled her toes over the top edge of it. She pulled. Her toes slipped off. She tried again. The pot tipped forward a bit before her toes slipped a second time. She pulled them back quickly, watching the pot slowly settle back to its base, wondering if she had just ruined the only plan she had before it began.

She reached out. The pot was still in reach, barely. She hooked her toes, pushing herself forward so far that her bottom felt like it was about to lift off the floor and her wrist ached from the pull of the handcuff.

She slipped her toes over the edge, insane thoughts –

(My toenails look awful! I need a pedicure!

"It takes a lot of work," that's what that nutjob said. "A lot *of work.")*

– percolating through her mind, jostling for attention she absolutely could not spare.

She pulled, slowly, agonizingly. The pot moved what seemed like a micrometer at a time, pulling closer, closer…

"Yes!"

Now she could reach it with both feet, putting the top of her right foot on one side, the heel of her left foot on the other and using them both to drag the pot closer.

As she did, she noticed that her feet were red. The blood from Alex's ruined hand, painted on the tree by Sheldon Steward, now stained her own feet and the bottom hems of her jeans. She shuddered, then pulled the tree the final few inches necessary before she could finally kneel down and reach it with her free hand.

It was beautiful, she had to admit. Blood notwithstanding, there was an artistry to it that she would have admired in another situation. Now, though, she was focused only on what she hoped to see *about* it.

She dug her fingers into the dirt at its base, examined every bit of the trunk. A moment later, she despaired. What she hoped to find wasn't there. It –

She froze as her questing fingers found something. She didn't move, didn't look at it, suddenly afraid that in doing so it would disappear like the end of a rainbow.

No. It's real.

She dared look. She teased what she had found into view.

"What are you doing?" asked Alex. "What's –"

The door clanked. The red-handled lever shifted slowly to the side.

Danielle realized that anyone entering the room would instantly see she had been up to something. She flipped on her back and pushed the tree as far away as she could, knowing her attempt at concealing her actions wouldn't make a difference. Sheldon was a madman, but he was attuned to the tree, tied to it by whatever weird fixation he held for it. *He* would notice. He would know – maybe not what she had done, but knowing *something*. She was blown.

She almost gave up. Then she saw her mother's eyes. Her mother's knowing smirk.

The look turned despair into anger, and Danielle cajoled that feeling into hope. She shoved the tree back into place as best she could, first with her hands then with her feet. She winced as the pot canted to one side and spilled a bit of soil before righting itself.

The lever finished clanking. The internal mechanism *thunked* and the door started to swing open, which was when she realized that her shoes were still off, sitting right out in the open. She barely had time to sweep them up and tuck both them and her bare feet below her before two men stepped into the room, holding a third man between them.

The man they held was limp, feet dragging behind him, blood streaming down his forehead. A stranger.

The two big men dropped the unconscious man to the floor, then handcuffed one of this hands to the ring on the room's third wall – the only one left that held neither prisoner nor door.

The two men, who both looked as though they had been blasted whole from matching chunks of granite, turned away –

(Please let them leave, please don't let them see –)

– then Danielle's heart leapt into her throat when one stopped at the potted plant. He scraped his shoe across the small pile of dirt that had tipped out. Danielle was certain he would ask what had happened, and that would be the end of any hope – maybe the beginning of something that would make Alex's crushed hand pale in comparison.

Instead, the guy snorted and, in a thickly-accented voice, said, "That man is weirdo," pronouncing the last word *veer-doe*.

The other man nodded at his companion and said, "I call killing him." Like the first man, his accent was Eastern European or Russian. A thick, rolling sound that made his deep voice somehow seem more menacing.

"What the hell that mean?"

The second man shrugged. "Something my woman's nephews say when they want to sit in front seat of minivan. 'I call front,' they say."

The first man rolled his eyes. "Your woman's nephews are idiots.'"

The second man laughed. "No, my *woman* is idiot, Mikhail. Her *nephews* are just pains in my ass."

"*All* of them idiots," insisted Mikhail. He looked at the dirt again, and again Danielle knew in her heart that he would find what she had done, and would hurt her or – worse – Alex. He did neither. Instead, he just said, "People here say 'shotgun.' Like, 'I call shotgun."

The other man shrugged. "I hear it both ways. But if it makes you feel better…" He looked at Alex, then at

Danielle. He smiled a cold, empty smile when his gaze fell upon her. "When time comes, I call shotgun."

Mikhail's lips curled as he laughed at that, the laugh just as cold and empty as his friend's smile. "Shotgun would be waste, Sergei." He leaned toward Danielle. "I have better plans for her. Slower. *Much* more fun than shotgun." Mikhail's eyes roved up and down the length of Danielle's body. It felt like she was being rolled around in the filthiest mud, and she acted without thinking.

Long nails were frowned on in her office. "They make you seem like you're going to a club instead of going to court," Danielle remembered hearing one of the senior attorneys say to her. So she kept them trimmed. But they were still long enough that when she clawed at Mikhail it raked a trio of red, seeping furrows across his cheek.

The big man reared back with a roar, one hand going to his cheek. Sergei laughed uproariously, as though Danielle wounding the other man was the funniest thing he had ever seen. He said something in Russian, and Mikhail snarled something back in the same language. Then he turned to Danielle again, one hand still at his cheek, the other drawing back in a huge fist that she knew would smash her face beyond recognition.

Danielle scrabbled backward, her body reflexively fleeing the danger. But there was nowhere to go. She was still handcuffed, so moving backward just gained her a few extra inches and a painful bruise as she smacked her head against the wall behind her.

Mikhail grinned tightly as she cried out, then that huge fist rocketed toward her… and was stopped only an inch away from her nose by his companion. Mikhail struggled against Sergei's hand wrapped around his forearm, but Sergei's eyes blazed as he snarled, "Boss wants her untouched." All humor gone from his eyes now, he turned to Danielle and added, "For now."

Mikhail's body still flexed, obviously wanting to smash Danielle into oblivion. A moment later he relaxed, almost drooping as he nodded. "That man is no boss. He's a dog," he said.

Sergei let go of his companion's arm and clapped him on the shoulder. "Maybe. But he's going to make us rich and powerful." He said something in Russian, and Mikhail's own smile returned.

Danielle shuddered at that smile. Cold seeped into her heart, her bones, her blood. When Sergei and Mikhail turned to go, that cold remained. And it intensified when she realized that Alex had witnessed the whole thing.

He had watched her strike Mikhil. He had witnessed the moment she was almost knocked into a smudge on the wall. He had heard the men threaten her with being shot and worse.

And he had said nothing to any of it. Nothing at all.

Danielle found herself in a room with four men. Two were obviously criminals, the third one an unconscious cipher. But one was her *husband.* So why was it that, even with him there, she felt so utterly surrounded by unfamiliar and threatening people?

A moment later she wished she *were* more alone, because the door opened. The room they were in was big, but with her, Alex, the huge Sergei and Mikhail, and the unknown newcomer, it was getting crowded.

More so as Sheldon and Marcos entered. They were both smiling strangely similar smiles, and the blood that had already chilled in Danielle's veins now seemed to freeze completely.

14

Legion is in the Dark Place. He is in pain. Hurt, gasping, terrified.

This time, though, is different than every other time Father has put him in here. This time, bright light flares. Legion gasps. He knows, somewhere deep inside, that this is still not real. That this has already happened and is but a memory. That is why it is so surprising when it plays out different than it did the first time.

(Do memories change? And if they change, does the truth of the past change with them?)

He does not know the answer to the near-silent question. He knows only that the light is new. Bright, and painful. It flickers and flutters, and a moment later Legion realizes it is flaring bright and then dimming again with the flutter of his lashes, the open-and-shutting of his eyes.

The wetness disappears from his chin. The torn flesh inside his lips suddenly mends. The pain falls away from his shoulder.

He is awake.

Father is gone. The Dark Place is empty, as it has been since that final day – the day he escaped. It took more than five years to carry out his plan; to find what he needed and to make new wounds and wait for the old ones to heal. But he finally did escape the Dark Place, and that same day taught *Father* for a change. Student became teacher, teacher became student, and Father learned a lesson of such delicious pain that it nearly made Legion grin as he floated to consciousness.

He is no longer in the Dark Place. But he is handcuffed as he was so many times in the past, and that is a surprise, though a comforting one in a way. The fact that he stares now at a tiny tree laying a few feet from his face is less comforting, because he has never awakened facing a tree before.

"Wake up!" someone shouts. The voice sounds far away, but the pain in his cheek is here and now. Someone is slapping him.

He blinks and rolls away from the pain, still pushing away memories of the Dark Place, and happiness of leaving it behind. He sees a woman looking at him. She is the one who was kidnapped. Without thinking, he says, "You seem like a nice girl. That's good. I don't know if I'll have anything to teach you."

The woman's eyes widen and her jaw drops as though this is the strangest thing she has ever heard, even though given what she has gone through of late this cannot possibly be true.

Legion is not here to make her uncomfortable. He does not believe that is ever necessary. Sometimes he must hurt people, sometimes he must bring pain to properly teach. But he sees no purpose in being rude.

He is saved from having to decide what to do next by another sharp pain on his cheek, and he finally realizes that he is being straddled by someone who has slapped him awake and now continues slapping him into wake*fulness*.

Legion does not flinch as the pain hits him. He simply looks at the man. It is the kidnapper. The one who grabbed the woman and the man and then also killed the family.

This is a man who must definitely be taught.

"He's awake," says the man. He looks over his shoulder. "Want me to keep going?"

Following the kidnapper's gaze, Legion quickly takes in the rest of the room. He sees the man who was kidnapped along with the woman. That man hunches in a corner of the room, one wrist handcuffed to a ring on the wall just as Legion's is, and just as Legion now realizes the woman is handcuffed.

The man in the corner stinks. That is not a mean appraisal, it is reality. He has fouled his clothes. Legion has seen and smelled things like this before – those whom he teaches sometimes do this, in the extremities of their instruction – and it does not particularly bother him. But he does not particularly *like* it, either.

"Just wait a sec," says another voice. It is a pleasant baritone, the voice of someone potentially trustworthy. But Legion is good at hearing things below reality, and can hear the snake writhing in the darkness below the voice. He turns to look at the man who said it. He is of medium build, with a dark complexion and dark hair that is receding a bit, and dark eyes that look strangely dead. He has a nose that is squat enough to speak of being broken more than once, and wears a blue track suit that seems strangely out of place, especially given the large gun hanging from a holster under his arm.

Flanking this man, obviously subordinates, are two more men. They are two of the three who caught Legion in the woods. He did not have much chance to study them before. Now he does. They are huge, wearing the kind of clothing that you might see on any hiker: jeans, flannel shirts, light jackets. The men are big enough that Legion suspects the jackets must be personally tailored to them. Expensive. Fitted to hide most of the bulges below their arms that speak to the fact that they are likely always armed.

One of them sports a trio of red lines on his face. They seep blood, and Legion suspects they were given him by the woman in the room.

Good for her.

The track-suited man speaks. "Who are you?" he asks.

Legion looks around. He wonders for a moment if he has been hit hard enough to knock some of the memories out of him. Because there is something missing. "Where…?"

His brothers step out from behind the large men. "We're here, bud," says Water. He shakes his head. "That was a rough dream, huh?"

"Shut up, dude," Fire barks at Water. Flame flares in his coal eyes, and Legion can tell he is so upset he is ready to burn the world. "Don't answer Water," he says to Legion. "They'll think you're nuts."

The man in the track suit repeats his question. "Who are you?" he says.

Legion does not speak.

The man nods to the kidnapper, who straddles Legion. The kidnapper smiles down at him. "You really should answer him," he says. "I don't want to hurt you."

He is lying. Unlike the man in the track suit, his eyes are not dead inside. They spark with need. He *does* want to hurt Legion. A lot.

Legion smiles. "What's up with the tree?" he says. "I've never had a student who carries around a tree before." Fire laughs his dry, crackling laugh. He laughs harder as Legion sees the kidnapper's eyes widen with upset surprise. Even more so as Legion adds, "Don't you think that's kind of weird?"

The kidnapper reigns in an impulse Legion knows and understands: the impulse to maim, to destroy, to kill. The kidnapper turns to the man in the corner.

As he does, one of the hulking men steps forward and speaks in Russian.

Legion speaks Russian. Not as well as he did when he was a child, when Father beat the language into him as the language of one of "the enemies most likely to destroy the world" (along with the Chinese; the Cubans: and sometimes, when Father was drunk, the zombies), but well enough to understand the hulk as he says, "You want me to make him talk, Marcos?"

Legion answers in Russian, "I talk well enough already, thank you."

The response seems to enrage Marcos. Speaking in Russian himself – though not well, Legion thinks; he has a terribly ugly accent – he screams, "Who are you? Did Demyan send you?"

Legion purses his lips. "No one sent me," he says, "but I *have* been led." He speaks quietly. Quiet tones in the face of rage have the effect of either quelling that rage or fanning it.

He can work with either extreme. After all, he has a permanently wet brother and one who forever burns. Legion understands extremes.

In this case, the response fans the track-suited man's rage. "Liar!" he screams. He pulls a gun from its holster – a very nice CZ 75 B 9mm, Legion notes – and screams, "Demyan sent you. He broke the rules! You'll pay! *He'll* pay!"

Again in Russian, again quietly, Legion says, "I don't know what rules you are talking about. But *you've* broken a great many rules, haven't you?" He sighs. "So much instruction, so many lessons unlearned."

In the corner, Water whispers, "Your accent is terrible, Legion."

Fire sighs. "Give him a break. He was always the worst at languages."

Legion hears them, but hears also the man in the track suit – clearly the one in charge – say, "Make him talk."

Another pain on his face. This time it is sharper, and Legion marvels at it. The man straddling him is fast – maybe faster than Legion, which is something he has never before come across. He is so fast that Legion never even saw him draw the knife, and had no chance to stop it as the man draws a red line across his cheek.

The cut is not deep, but it bleeds freely. Warmth washes down Legion's cheek and into his hair.

"Now I don't match for sure," he says.

"You already didn't," says Fire. He has no eyes, but Legion senses that if he *did* have them he would be rolling them in semi-disgust.

"What does *that* mean?" asks the man on top of Legion.

"What's your name?" says Legion.

The man again looks surprised at Legion's question – though not enraged, as he was when Legion commented on the guy's weird tree attachment. He shrugs. "I'm Sheldon Steward. With a *d*, not a *t*." He points with his red-edged knife at the tree. "That's Lucy," he says. "Isn't she beautiful?"

"Very," says Legion, because the tree *is* quite lovely, and he believes in being honest whenever possible.

"Enough!" says Marcos.

Sheldon Steward looks at him. "You want me to… *ask* him who he is again?" he says.

Marcos nods. "Definitely," he says, the grin on his face completely at odds with the snarl in his voice.

Sheldon leans in close to Legion. "I have to admit, I hope you don't tell me who you are. Not for a while, anyway."

He shifts a bit and eyes the hulk with the bleeding face. "Hold him still."

The hulk looks at Marcos, who nods. "Do what he says, Mikhail."

Something appears in Mikhail's eyes. It is just for an instant, but Legion's understanding of people's thoughts again serves him well. This man does not like Marcos. *Despises* him, in fact.

"*That's* interesting," says Fire.

"And probably useful," says Water. "Easier to teach when you know the students."

The big man grabs Legion's free hand. Legion does not struggle. It is not time for that. He knows pain is coming, but that is all right. Pain is an old friend.

The big man pulls Legion's hand until his body is a "T," one arm stretched out to full length by Mikhail and the other straining against the handcuff that binds him to the wall. "Good enough?" says Mikhail.

"Excellent," says Sheldon.

He uses the knife again, this time cutting Legion's shirt away.

Legion does *not* like this. He carries secrets on his body, and he worries that the madly smiling – and he is mad, Legion can see, totally insane – Sheldon Steward will see those secrets, and interpret them correctly.

"My, my," says Sheldon as he cuts away the shirt and sees at least some of what lays beneath.

"What the hell?" says Marcos.

Mikhail and the other big man curse – both in Russian.

"Well, at least we know he's not Odessa," says the other big man in Russian.

"Sergei's right," says Mikhail. "He's got no ink. Can't have come with Demyan."

"Maybe Demyan hired him. A freelancer."

Marcos shakes his head. "No. We didn't give him time for that." Switching to English he says, "So who *is* he? And what the hell happened to him?"

Legion does not have to look at himself to know what Marcos and the others have seen. There are long scars on his chest and belly, and a few rough patches here and there. Legion remembers well when he got them. Father gave each and every one of them as punishment. He used knives and canes and whips and – a few times – welding torches. Legion received each for not learning some lesson or other. For not doing chores, for failing to learn a skill fast enough, for screaming too loudly while in the Dark Place.

The worst part, though, wasn't the moment when Father beat or cut or burned him. The worst part was *after* he was done. That was when Legion and his brothers had to do the same thing to the two who remained unmarked.

They were One at the time. So they had to match.

Most of the lines of his body simply map the lessons he has learned. But a few – and one in particular – hide secrets that Legion worries will be seen; will be correctly interpreted and their secrets stripped from him.

But no one seems to understand the lines at all so Legion relaxes, even as Sheldon draws a new red line in his chest. This time Sheldon moves slowly, almost sensuously.

The knife bites deep, scraping the bone of Legion's sternum, then continues down to his belly. The man is careful – he cuts deep enough to grant pain, but not enough to permanently damage.

Though Legion knows that permanent damage will likely come next. Not that it matters. Pain is the best teacher, and damage a permanent reminder of lessons learned.

Fire nods. "True. But is it weird that it still kinda bugs me that we don't match?"

"We already didn't, so who cares if we don't match *more*?" answers Water.

Legion remains silent. Sheldon draws another line. Legion now carries a rough "X" across his body. It hurts, but he is relaxed. Pain, his old friend, ceased to worry Legion much a long time ago. Once Father took a lighter to the One's testicles. It wasn't Legion whom Father burned – he couldn't remember which it had been through the veil that marked the moment he and his brothers ceased to be *One* and became newly *three*. But he remembered the pain when his unmarked One-brother burned Legion that way. Then Legion, still trying desperately not to scream from the pain in his center, did the same to that brother-One. That was the day when his pain reached an apex. The pain of his body as he burned, the pain of his mind as he burned what he then perceived to be part of Himself.

So no, a bleeding "X" across his chest does not worry him. Legion just smiles and says, "X marks the spot," to Sheldon. "And my heart *is* where all the lessons live, so I suppose you've just made my body an accurate map of my truth."

For a moment, Sheldon worries. Legion sees it, and sees that this man does not know how to deal with someone who will not react properly to his ministrations. "I bet people always scream with you," Legion says quietly.

That worries Sheldon still further. He cuts another line in Legion's chest – this time deeper, spilling more blood. He watches Legion carefully as he does so.

Legion permits himself to scream. He does not *need* to scream. This pain is nothing. But he does want to escape, because escape will allow him to teach; and escape will be difficult if these men who believe themselves to be in charge are watching him. So he lets himself scream, knowing that eventually they will either believe he has told them what they want to know or he will reach a point where he can pretend to unconsciousness. Either way, some or all of the captors will leave. His job will be easier then.

Sheldon Steward smiles as Legion screams, the look in his eyes one of relief at a world which again makes sense to his warped mind.

"This dude's a nut," says Fire.

Legion agrees, but doesn't say so. He screams again through the next two cuts Sheldon makes.

"Who are you?" shouts Marcos. "Who are you?"

The other two occupants of the room – the woman and the man who were kidnapped – are mostly silent. The woman huddles in terror, and reaches for the man. The man only sinks into the wall, pushing himself further and further away.

"That's interesting," says Fire.

"He doesn't seem very nice," agrees Water. His nose wrinkles. "And you know I don't like to speak ill of others…"

"… but he stinks," Fire finishes. His nose does not wrinkle. There is only a charred hole where flesh used to be. For some reason, Legion thinks that look fits him.

Sheldon cuts Legion again. Again he screams.

Beside him, Mikhail sighs. "This takes too long," he says. "I can make him talk."

"No!" shouts Sheldon, but it is too late. Mikhail tightens his grip on Legion's hand, then yanks. With a pop, Legion's right shoulder dislocates, just as it did all those years ago when Father took him to the Dark Place.

The woman chained to the wall gives a sympathetic cry and reaches for Legion as though wishing to help him. Legion notes this, just as he notes the man who was kidnapped – whom he is starting to call Stinky Joe in his mind, for lack of a better name – draw farther away.

All this occurs as Legion screams. It is easy, because this is the injury Father gave him on that long-dead day when Legion decided how he would leave his father's house. It is the injury he gave Himselfs after all that happened, because *the One had to match*.

He is not a monster, not a machine. The pain is real, and he rides it into darkness. He does not fall unconscious but he allows that darkness to sweep over him, knowing it will make him look as though he has fainted because of the pain of the dislocation.

In the haze, he hears Sheldon scream, "Idiot!" and hears a gurgle.

Legion blinks. His eyes are fluttering – largely on purpose, to make it seem as though he is fighting to stay awake. Fighting to stay awake is what sells unconsciousness to those who watch. He knows this, because he has seen the look on many of his past students.

He has to sell it. This lesson has a time limit.

Through the fluttering, he sees Mikhail clap a huge hand to his neck. Blood spurts between his fingers, and there is no doubt where his wound came from, for Sheldon reverses his grip on his bloody knife, then plunges it sideways through the big man's neck. He twists and pushes at the same time, and Mikhail drops bonelessly as the knife exits the back of his neck, severing the huge man's spine so high up that the brain instantly stops working.

He is dead before he hits the floor.

Legion's eyes flutter a moment longer. He would like to see what happens next, but knows it will not look real so he closes his eyes and sags.

"What the hell did you do?" shrieks Marcos. "What the hell –"

Sheldon's scream is equally shrill. "He got in the way! You paid me to do a job, and I was doing this bit extra for no charge – that's just good business. But you don't pay me to let an idiot get in the way!"

"God help me, Sheldon," begins Marcos. "If you weren't –"

In a pouting tone, Sheldon cuts him off to say, "He almost kicked Lucy!"

Silence. Legion imagines that Marcos and Sergei must be digesting this; wondering how to take it. Perhaps more mayhem will ensue. That will not be a perfect scenario, but Legion knows he will be able to turn it to his advantage.

"Almost there," whispers Water right in his ear. "The lesson is about to begin." His wet voice sounds like a caress to Legion.

Marcos, Sergei, and Sheldon are silent, as are the man and the woman they hold captive. Legion imagines the three evildoers staring at each other. Imagines Marcos deciding whether to order Sergei to kill Sheldon. That would be bad, because Legion has now seen them all moving, and he believes it likely that Sheldon would kill both Sergei and Marcos should Marcos issue such an order. That in turn would mean he had nothing to keep him from attending to Legion, as well as the man and the woman chained to the walls.

Legion is not sure he can take Sheldon like this, chained to the wall with one hand and the opposite arm useless at the end of its dislocated shoulder.

And maybe not at all. He was so *fast.*

"You can take him," Fire whispers in his ear.

"For sure," whispers Water in his other ear.

But neither sound sure. Legion wonders if, just as Father did all those years ago, the time has come for him to lose *his* place as teacher. To die.

Marcos is the first to speak. “Get that out of here.”

Legion hears the sound of someone inhaling as though to speak. But whoever it is says nothing. He sighs. Then Sergei says, “Where should I put him?”

“Wherever. Put him in Beaker’s room.”

Who is Beaker?

Legion hears a grunt, then a raspy sound, and knows that Sergei is dragging the body of his dead coworker Mikhail out of the room.

Silence reigns. He hears only muted sounds of pain that he knows belong to the man and the woman who were kidnapped by Sheldon.

Heavy footfalls announce Sergei’s return. “Done,” he says sullenly.

“Good,” says Marcos. “And Sergei, we’ll make things ri –” A phone ringtone sounds, interrupting Marcos. A moment later he hears Marcos snarl, “*What*?”

Legion strains to hear whoever is on the other end of this new phone conversation.

“Some woman’s talking to him,” says Water. “I can’t hear what she’s saying, but my guess is it’s the woman who nabbed you outside. So it’s the one big guy still alive, Sheldon, Marcos, and her.”

“He knows all that,” hisses Fire. “You should say useful things if you’re going to talk.”

Water’s voice bristles. “I *do* say –”

He cuts off as a beep announces the end of the phone call and Legion hears Marcos say, "He's here."

Sheldon says, "Do you want me to wake this guy up?"

"No," says Marcos. "We'll ask Demyan about him."

"Ask?" says Sheldon.

"Nicely. Very nicely."

The two men laugh. Then Sheldon says, "And your man?" He sighs. "I'm sorry, but he really was a moron."

Marcos sighs as well. "We'll figure that out later."

Legion has to concentrate on *not* smiling. He can tell a few things from Marcos' voice. The first is that the man is trying very hard to sound like he's okay with the death of his employee. The second is that he is most definitely *not* okay with it, and he is going to kill Sheldon eventually – or at least, he's going to try.

"This gets better and better," says Fire.

Legion agrees in silence. He suspects Sheldon hears the lie in Marcos' voice as well. Sheldon is obviously crazy as a loon, but he deals in pain and death. The fact that Sheldon lives in that twilight world, that gloaming when the light of life fades away and the darkness beyond encroaches, means Sheldon understands at least some truth. Because only those who see extreme pain followed by blissful death – and who see both brought at their own hands – can ever *really* understand what truth looks like.

That is why they can be such excellent teachers. Because the greatest truths only fully reveal themselves through pain. Pain bares itself in the moments Legion has handed someone their own glistening entrails, or their still-beating heart. The moment when someone sees death, and cannot help but reveal to him the hidden corners of their soul.

So yes, Sheldon definitely hears the lie in Marcos' voice. The kidnapper-torturer-killer knows Marcos will come for him, sooner or later, and so will act to preserve himself.

The two men are supposed to be on the same side. But Marcos and Sheldon, similar though Legion senses them to be in many ways, are enemies to each other in their hearts.

And Sergei, Legion suspects, loathes them both. That man is Russian, he has lost a friend. He will be bound by a twisted sense of pride and honor to kill the man responsible for that loss, as well as the man who openly acquiesced to it, whether sincerely or not.

Yes, all three hate each other.

That is good.

That is useful.

"Come on," says Marcos.

Sheldon stands. He whispers something nearby – so close that he must have his face near the floor. "Almost time, Lucy," he whispers. "I will paint you in my love, then destroy you and you will finally truly grow into yourself."

"Come *on*," says Marcos.

Legion hears three sets of feet leave the room. He hears the door close. He hears the lever shut.

He knows these sounds. He is again in a Dark Place.

Only this time it is different. This time he is the teacher.

And he will begin his lesson soon.

15

After leaving the room with Danielle, Alex, and the unknown newcomer, Sheldon turned to Marcos and said, "Do you want me to get my equipment?" He did not look at Sergei, whom Sheldon had decided was every bit the moron the un-dearly departed Mikhail had been.

Marcos raised an eyebrow. "There much to get?"

"The usual. It's in the car."

The car still sat in the underground parking area where Sheldon had driven it upon arriving at the bunker. Sheldon had really enjoyed the moment the crack opened in seemingly-unbroken ground of a small clearing, revealing a ramp that he drove down while humming the theme from the old Batman TV show.

He liked that show much more than Batman movies directed by Christopher Nolan. Nolan was a genius – everyone said so, both on Twitter *and* Facebook, which meant it was definitely true – but his visions of the Caped Crusader had been too violent for Sheldon's liking. *Children* watched those movies, for goodness' sake, and the headline of an online article from *Elite Daily* very clearly spoke against such things.

Marcos shrugged. "Later. First I wanna see exactly where Demyan is and what he's doing." He turned to Sergei. "You go make sure everything in the production room is still going."

"You should not have killed Doctor Schmidt," said Sergei with a frown.

"Who?" says Marcos.

The big man sighed. "Beaker."

Marcos waved. "I've already got a replacement in mind. But that guy'll have more trouble if you don't make sure the equipment is ready for him when things start up here again."

Sheldon could see that Marcos was angry at Sergei for rebuking him. Sheldon approved of Marcos' righteous rage, but he knew voicing his approval would have made Marcos blush with pleasure so he said nothing of it. He didn't want to make Marcos have an orgasm or something under the ecstacy of Sheldon's praise – that would be embarrassing for Marcos, and Sheldon was far too kind to embarrass people.

Sergei lumbered away, muttering as he disappeared down a side corridor. "How big *is* this place?" said Sheldon, genuinely curious.

Marcos puffed out his chest. "Big," he said proudly.

Marcos turned and began walking down another hall, toward the security room that Sheldon had passed on the way in. "Who's Beaker?" Sheldon hurried after him. They passed openings with barracks-style rooms, a kitchen big enough to cook and serve food for all those beds' occupants, and several other rooms Sheldon noted automatically.

This place is cool.

As cool as the Batcave?

Maybe not. But definitely cool.

"Beaker's the science guy who used to work here." Marcos grimaced and pointed at his outfit. "He gave me this thing."

"Not pretty," said Sheldon agreeably. "What's Sergei doing then?"

"You ask a lot of questions, Shel. Always have. And I've never liked it."

Sheldon was spared having to figure out a polite way to answer such rudeness without killing someone he had known for so long and who was paying him a lot of money right now. They reached the open doorway to the security room and Marcos stepped through. Sheldon followed.

Feodora was still waiting where they had left her. So was the body of the man Marcos had killed earlier, though Sheldon could tell from the smears of blood on the floor that Feodora had scooted the body as far away from her as she could without leaving the room. She probably didn't like to look at the mostly headless corpse; women, he knew, could be squeamish about things like that.

Sheldon Steward looked at the monitors as well. He hoped they would show that the man he had been paid to destroy was indeed here. He was good at so many things it was almost impossible to count them. But being *good* at things wasn't necessarily the same as *enjoying* them. So though he was excellent at waiting, he did not particularly like the experience.

Especially when there was Lucy to see to. Waiting for her final adornments, and pining – if that was the right word for a tree that was not a pine tree at all – away for him in the other room.

Sheldon delighted to see that the center security monitor showed a sedan winding along a small dirt road. It was different than the one Sheldon had taken when he approached the bunker, and he idly wondered how many other ins and outs there were in this place. Maybe he would get one of these for himself someday. Mother might enjoy living in a place like this.

The car stopped. "Is he at the right place?" asked Sheldon.

Marcos nodded. "Yeah. There's a hidden entrance right near there."

Sheldon had to concentrate to keep himself from jumping in the air and clicking his heels together. But he did not manage to keep down a heartfelt, "Woohoo!"

"We'll let him stew out there for a minute," said Marcos, looking at him oddly.

Meaning *we* have to wait, thought Sheldon. He managed not to sigh, cheering himself with thoughts of killing everyone down here as soon as possible.

He did not see this as a violation of his contract. Everyone down here was rather unappreciative, and he thought he could convince Mother that such a move had been necessary. Besides, he would finish the contract first, so would as always have acted with the highest level of ethical behavior.

Yes, Mother will be fine with that. She might be sad at the killing, but she understands that rudeness is rudeness.

Marcos leaned in close to the monitors. "Anyone else out there?" he said. "Demyan bring any other cars?"

Feodora was already cycling through the images on the monitors. "*Nyet.* No one is on the property."

"And outside the property?" said Marcos sharply. "I'd rather not have anyone *else* join the party." Sheldon, because he was extraordinarily perceptive, heard the unspoken, *"Like the guy who's unconscious with a dislocated shoulder in the other room."*

"Nothing anywhere I see from here," said Feodora. "Though we should increase coverage."

"What do you mean?" asked Marcos.

"We've been so busy down here that no one noticed blind spots."

"What blind spots?" said Marcos, worry in his voice.

"I go back and review video of when intruder arrives, like you tell me earlier," said Feodora.

Her English is appalling.

"And…"

"And I find this." The image of the car – Demyan's car, if Marcos was right – remained in the center, largest security monitor, but one of the others flashed and showed a van drive up to a gate Sheldon recognized as the one he himself had driven through.

For a moment he wondered if he *had* been followed here after all. He discarded the thought a moment later. No one was that good. So this was something else.

On the monitor, the van sat for a while. The image was grainy, but good enough to show the single person inside it: the unknown man with all the scars chained to the wall beside Alex and Danielle Anton. Then Feodora fast-forwarded the feed until the van turned and drove off the screen.

"Where'd he go?" asked Marcos.

"I don't know. That is why I say we should increase coverage."

"*Shit!*" Marcos shouted. "Yuri didn't mention any of this."

Feodora glanced at the nearby corpse, which Sheldon's excellent analytical facilities instantly determined to be the aforementioned Yuri.

"Yuri does not have chance to say it, I guess," said Feodora. Sheldon was pleased to know his mind was, as ever, bright and quick to figure things out at the speed of light.

"Okay, okay," said Marcos, dismissing both the body and his role in the security lapse with one quick wave of his hand. "But dammit, what if this new guy *is* with Demyan?"

Sheldon spoke up. He had spotted something the others had missed. "I don't think so," he said. "Your detail picked him up outside."

"So?"

"So if he were with Demyan, wouldn't he have just walked in?"

"Maybe he wanted to get caught," said Marcos with a shrug.

Feodora shook her head. "No. I think he wanted to get caught, yes. But he does not know where entrance is when we pick him up. Too far from right place."

"And you didn't give Demyan much time to get here, right?" added Sheldon. "Not enough to get a third party to come scope the place out for him – and even if he did, would your Demyan guy risk that, given what was on the line?"

"No," said Marcos. He chewed his lower lip, deep in thought for a moment. "No, probably not. He would have called Chernov."

"Boss...?" Feodora glanced now at Sheldon. "Do you really think –"

From Feodora's expression Sheldon could tell that Marcos had just named someone high in the organization, and that she was rightly concerned about security. But Marcos clapped his hand on Sheldon's shoulder and said, "Don't worry about him. He's discreet as a cat at a dog show."

Sheldon saw differently in the man's eyes. Marcos was planning to kill him when this was over. That surprised him. Not only was it rude, but Sheldon knew his dear Mother would be far too angry for the universe to allow such a cruel thing to happen.

He decided then that Marcos' end would have to be a painful one. Bad enough that there wouldn't even be enough left over to paint a single tiny leaf on a bonsai tree.

He was good at hiding feelings, though. Excellent at it. So he smiled one of his practiced smiles – Sincere Smile No. 6, an especially good one – and said, "Thanks, Marcos. That means a lot."

"There," said Marcos, as though the matter was settled even though he was obviously planning Sheldon's own death. He smiled insincerely at Feodora. "See?"

"Sure, *lyubimaya,*" said Feodora. She glanced momentarily at the monitor that was showing the van drive up and then away in a loop. "If he is not with Demyan, then what is he doing?"

"Okay, we'll figure that out. You did good, Fee," Marcos said. He reached down and squeezed her breast, which Sheldon thought was both rude and disgusting.

Feodora smiled and made a small pleasure-moan.

Yuck.

Sheldon decided then that he would have to let Feodora see what a real, manly man could do before she died. That would be nice of him, and she would no doubt keep smiling even after he skinned her and made Marcos eat the skin.

That's what I'll do. Skin all of them, make him eat it, and then he'll *get something* really *nasty. Maybe I'll make Mother a blanket or a table out of them so she can think fondly of them when they're gone.*

Marcos looked back at the center screen where Demyan's car sat. "What you want me to do with him?" asked Feodora.

"Well, we've changed all the entry codes, so he can't get in," said Marcos. "He'll just have to sit on his ass and wait on *me* for a change." He smiled.

Sheldon was *not* smiling, either on the inside or the outside.

More waiting.

And wait they did. Marcos groped Feodora a few more times, which made Sheldon's gorge rise. He was a very open-minded guy, but the man's behavior was disgusting. He was obviously some kind of psycho-pervert, which Sheldon had long suspected but which always made him sad. How could Marcos have gone so wrong when Sheldon himself had turned out so superbly? Life was such an unfair thing sometimes.

Sheldon shrugged internally. He was antsy, but he would wait, because he was supremely patient and had a wealth of educational opportunities with him at every moment – necessary for a prodigious intellect like his (Dwayne "The Rock" Johnson once used the word "prodigious" on an Instagram post, and after looking it up Sheldon knew it applied especially to him).

He pulled out his phone and opened his ereader app. He had all the classics downloaded – everything from Milton to Shakespeare and beyond. He had culled the "top ten classics" lists from numerous websites – Buzzfeed, Nicky Swift, and Zergnet among them – and made sure to download all the books he found listed. He opened one at random, something called *Anna Karenina* by Leo Tolstoy, but grew bored and switched to his Angry Birds game instead. He didn't like wasting time on a video game when there was work waiting in the air, but that was life sometimes.

When even Angry Birds grew tiresome, he looked up and said, "Maybe I should get to work on the new guy. That intruder. You said you don't know who he is, so –"

"He's probably still out cold," Marcos interrupted.

"Thanks to your man," said Sheldon. Marcos looked irritated at that, but Sheldon believed in being truthful. "I could bring him around. I'm good at that."

Marcos stared at him. "You're good at a lot of things."

Sheldon knew he was sincere – he had to be, since everyone invariably noticed that Sheldon was, indeed, good at a lot of things – but still couldn't help feeling like he was being mocked. Just a bit, but even just a bit was far too much. Respect was a requirement.

Yes, he was definitely going to waste Marcos. The man was making him wait, and now seemed like he was making fun of Sheldon, which was impossible given that there was so little to make fun of *about* Sheldon. But still, the man had to die.

"Soon," Sheldon whispered.

Marcos frowned. "You talking to yourself?"

Sheldon grinned. "I'm the best conversationalist around, so it makes sense I'd want to talk to me whenever possible, doesn't it?"

Marcos was obviously awed by the logic of that statement. His mouth opened slackly and he laughed. "You're such a weird bird, Shel."

Sheldon did *not* like that.

Yep. You're dead, buddy. Prodigiously *dead.*

Sheldon actually felt himself start to slip into a mental state that could only be assuaged by blood. That had not happened for a long time. It was, truth be told, one of the reasons he preferred to have as little interaction with most clients as possible. It wasn't that he was impatient or easily irritated – he was blessed with extreme tolerance, which he knew was important in today's social climate – but rather that the world was so full of stupid people it was reasonable for someone as brilliant and well-rounded as Sheldon Steward to take a few of them out of the gene pool.

Soon. I'll just have to convince Mother it was the right choice.

Sheldon did not say this. He merely smiled and said, "A bird in the bush is worth two in the hand, right?"

Marcos looked nonplussed – no doubt surprised at Sheldon's wisdom in all situations – and then nodded. "Sure. Yeah, whatever." He squeezed Feodora's boob again and said, "We've waited long enough. Time to bring the bastard inside."

"And then?" Sheldon asked, trying hard to keep the excitement out of his voice. Professionalism was important. Tom Cruise said that once, he was pretty sure.

"And then you go to work."

Sheldon could not help but clap his hands in excitement. Lucy would be so happy!

16

Alex waited and waited. He knew in his heart that his angel would come. His angel had *always* come, and certainly there was no better time – and no greater need – than now.

He tried not to cry. He mostly succeeded.

Making matters worse, Danielle was being a pain. When she wasn't whimpering, she was asking him how he was, which Alex found to be a deeply stupid question given that he had been kidnapped and chained to a wall, an unconscious stranger to one side and a naggy woman on the other.

How had he never noticed this side of her before? Her whining, incessant, cringey *neediness?*

This had happened to him with Brenda, too. Like Danielle, his first wife had appeared perfect at first, but somehow became whiny and naggy within the first few months of their marriage.

Alex had been willing to let it slide with his first wife, at least for a while, because Brenda was pretty great in a lot of other ways, and he figured she'd change when she realized it bothered him. Eventually, though, he had regretted being so subtle with her. She had kept asking him what he was thinking, what he was feeling, where he was going at night. Danielle at least hadn't asked him about his nights – she'd absolutely believed he just worked late a lot – but she was making up for it in the nagging department. "How are you?" "You okay?" "Why won't you talk to me?"

Neither Brenda then nor apparently Danielle now understood that sometimes a man needed his space.

It's okay. The angel will fix it all.

He knew it was true in his heart: the mysterious personage who had paved the way to his security and success would be here at any moment, and would make every single person involved in all this pay. He believed, too, that if Danielle didn't go back to the way she had been before this – so calm, so kind, so willing to listen to him and be swayed by his every desire – she herself might be escorted out of his life. He wouldn't do it with her like he had with Brenda, but sooner or later, she *would* be gone. Because that was what Alex was coming to wish more and more, and the angel was always there for him.

He really thought he got it right with Danielle. She *had* been more willful than he really liked, but he thought he could put up with it long enough to break her of that bad habit. He could teach her. He could help her be her best self, and in so doing they would both be fully and finally happy together.

He had tried so hard. Had put up with little things – like her mocking him about his Dr. Pepper preferences – and with big things – like her insistence on doing client work during their *honeymoon*. But now, in this place where he was captive for reasons he could not possibly understand, he was finally coming to know that he would never be able to cure her of her bad habits.

"Honey," she was whispering now. "Alex, I –"

"Can't you be quiet?" he spat. "Can't you let me *think*?"

He didn't have to look to see the hurt on her face. But look he did… and was shocked to see not only hurt but surprise. He was acting totally reasonably, so why would she look *surprised*?

It just made him angrier. Angry enough, in fact, that he said, "This is all your fault."

It was a mistake. Not the fact of it – he knew it had to be her fault, no matter what anyone else might say. There was no way *he* could be at fault for something like this. But he shouldn't have said it out loud. What would it help right now? He'd probably just end up in a tiresome argument, just like with Brenda.

He was spared the need to think of something new to say by the door opening. He perked up inside. This was it. It *had* to be it.

And it was.

The door opened, and *he* was there. The *angel* was there!

He was older than Alex remembered. Alex last saw his angel watching him ten years ago. He had just moved into a new, bigger office at the company he worked with, after his superior in the company had inexplicably packed up his things and quit, leaving a vacancy that only Alex could really fill.

Of course, he knew that this was just one more of the ministrations of his angel. He would have known even without hearing the office rumor that the old supervisor's wife was laid up in the hospital. So when he saw his angel across the street on the day Alex started his new job, just watching quietly, Alex felt a quickening of excitement but no real surprise.

He ran across the street, but a few cars passed between him and his angel and when they finished crossing, his angel had – as always – just disappeared.

But now… he was here. More gray in his hair and more lines in his face than Alex remembered. He could even be called *old,* and that was a surprise given that he had really come to believe his angel was just that. God or the universe or whoever was really in charge behind the scenes had sent a celestial being to watch over Alex.

But should an angel age?

It doesn't matter. He's here and I'll be saved. I'll get out of here, and I'll find someone better to share myself with, and I'll be happy again.

That was when he realized that, though he was going to be just fine, Danielle wouldn't be coming home with him. He didn't feel bad about it, either. They'd had a good run, and Alex was sure the angel had paved the way for most of Danielle's success – surely no one her age and with so little experience could have done as much as she did without help from Alex's angel. But there was also no doubt in his mind that the angel would sense that Alex didn't like her anymore and would take care of things.

"You're here," he breathed.

For the first time in many, many years, the angel spoke to him. And it was nothing that Alex expected to hear. The angel's voice quavered, and a tear shone in his eye. "Oh, Sasha," he whispered.

Then something shoved him – shoved *Alex's angel* – from behind.

"What's going on?" said Alex. His mind felt like it was short-circuiting. The angel was here for him, here to *save* him. So why was this powerful creature allowing himself to be shoved forward?

The angel stumbled into the room as he was shoved again. To his horror, Alex saw the man who had kidnapped him was the one doing it, followed by Marcos and the man's flunkie, Sergei.

And the angel was *crying*.

What is happening? How can this be happening to me?

The kidnapper, Sheldon, shoved the angel again. "There, Sergei," said Marcos, and pointed at the center of the room. The big guy stepped forward and Alex realized he was holding a metal chair. He put the chair where Marcos had shown him, then gestured almost apologetically for the angel to sit.

"Don't do this, Sergei," said the angel – the *man*, Alex now knew, for no angel would weep and beg the way the old man was now doing.

"Don't embarrass yourself, Demyan," Marcos said.

The old man –

(*Demyan? Is the angel's name Demyan? How? Do angels* have *names?)*

– looked at Marcos, and Alex felt a flare of hope that matched the flare of rage in the other man's eyes. "Do you call me by my first name now, Marcos?" All trace of tears disappeared as he shifted his eyes to Sergei. "And you allow this dog to speak to me like this?"

Sergei shrugged. "He offers better deal than you ever do."

The old man spat something in Russian. No one else seemed to care.

Alex looked around, trying in vain to find something that would give him hope. There was a body on the floor – the man Sheldon had killed earlier. There was the still-unconscious form of the newcomer who'd been cut and then had his shoulder nearly yanked out of its socket. There was Danielle, mouthing something that looked like, "It will be all right," over and over. He winced.

Stupid. How is it going to be all right? Doesn't she see? *Doesn't she see what's happening to me?*

There was no hope in this room.

He looked back at Demyan. "Can't you do anything?" he said.

Demyan said nothing. He cast down his eyes. "I never wanted this to happen." He glared again at Marcos. "Chernov will never let this stand."

Marcos had pulled out his phone and was dialing or texting. "So you didn't call him?" He shook his head. "I owe Fee twenty bucks." The phone beeped, then Marcos held it up, face outward. The screen showed a video call starring a cruel-faced man with a low brow and a long scar that twisted his mouth toward his ear.

"But I *will* let it stand, Demyan," said the man on the phone.

Demyan's face shifted from rage to a pale, empty expression. "How can you let this *sukin syn* do this?"

"You broke the rules, Demyan," said the man on the screen.

Demyan said something harsh in Russian. He continued spitting out angry words for a long time, then the man on the phone shouted, "Enough!" followed by a harsh barking of his own.

"Do not pretend this is because I broke rules, Nikolai," said Demyan.

The man on the phone shrugged. "The forms must be kept, no? So you know what comes next." His eyes flicked to the side, and he said, "Marcos?"

Marcos shifted the phone so he was looking at it. *"Da?"*

"You are willing to serve as my right hand?" said Nikolai Chernov.

"Da," said Marcos.

"You are willing to obey the rules of the family, to live them –" and Chernov's eyes flicked toward Demyan as he added, " – and to die for the breaking of them?"

Marcos said something in Russian. Chernov nodded, and the phone went dark.

Demyan had grown ever-more stonefaced during all this. Now he sat down. He never took his eyes away from Alex. "Sasha, I'm so sorry," he said.

Alex went cold inside. This man wasn't an angel, he knew that now. But if not an angel then how did he –

Marcos laughed, the first sincerely joyful noise Alex had heard since this began. "You didn't know?" he said to Alex. Another laugh, then, "I thought you might not, but… oh, this is delicious!" He turned to the old man in the seat. "Tell him, Demyan."

Demyan was silent. Marcos nodded at Sheldon, who stepped forward. The man produced a knife from a pocket and slowly pushed it into Demyan's shoulder. The old man gasped.

"Easy," said Marcos. "We don't want him dead."

He nodded at Sergei, who left the room for a moment, returning with a camera on a tripod. He set it on a corner of the room where it could take in all the captives: Demyan, the stranger, Danielle, and Alex himself. He pressed a button. "Recording."

Marcos returned his attention to Demyan. "You going to tell him?"

Sheldon twisted the knife. Demyan didn't even groan during any of it. His face twisted in a wry smile and he spat to the side. "You think this will hurt me? I suffered worse than this before I was ten. And worse when I joined Odessa, showing I would be true to the family." Again he spat, this time toward Marcos, who danced back to avoid the liquid. "I am no cur, to be savaged and to cry out."

"I thought you might say that." Marcos shifted his attention to Sheldon, then jerked his head toward Alex. "Cut off his toes."

Danielle, the dumb bitch –

(oh how I was wrong about her how I misjudged her she would have said something would have done *something if she was any good)*

– finally made a sound. "Don't!" she screamed.

Sheldon was already moving toward Alex, his step not stuttering in the least with the sound of Danielle's shriek. But Marcos turned a sad look at her and said, "Sorry, my dear. You picked the wrong person for a partner."

Alex kicked at Sheldon, but the man just caught his foot and twisted it and pain blossomed as his ankle cracked. Alex screamed, and could do no more than kick weakly as the psychopath tore off his shoe.

The knife flashed, and suddenly Alex felt a strange fire, then a nothing, at the end of his foot as his pinky toe was severed. Sheldon held it up, though Alex could not tell whether he was showing it to Demyan or to the silently-recording camera. Alex was far too busy screaming, thrashing.

Sheldon loosed his foot – not because Alex had been successful in kicking away, he was sure, but because the man was grandstanding in a sick way. Regardless, Alex's frantic thrashing rolled him onto his stomach and he came face to face with the stranger. The man who had been brought in after everyone else was laying there, eyes still shut, nearly *peaceful*.

Damn him. Damn all *of them!*

Sheldon caught Alex's foot in the same easy, perfectly controlled movement as before. Another flash, and another toe was in Sheldon's hands.

Alex's screams wound down for a second. He stared at the toe – not him, not him, it *couldn't be happening to him* – in the man's hand. He stared at the thing that would never again serve him.

He started to cry. He switched his gaze to Demyan. "Can't you do something?" he cried.

The man's face softened. Sheldon grabbed Alex's foot again, and Demyan said, "Enough." The word was soft, but carried authority. He looked at Marcos. "You're just going to kill us all anyway."

"Yes," said Marcos simply. "But as you know, Demyan, there's dying, and there's *dying*." He flicked a glance in Alex's direction. "Tell him. He still has fingers, sort of; his toes, most of them. But he's still got his tongue, ears, eyes. Testicles, penis. Give him a man's death, at least."

Demyan looked down, and in a broken voice said, "Your name."

Alex felt a thrill of fear roll through him. Was Demyan about to tell everyone about the name he'd given Alex? About *why* he gave him the new name? Looking at Danielle he said, "I don't know what you're talking about."

"*No*." Demyan's eyes locked onto his. "Do not lie, boy!"

"I don't understand!" Alex's voice was rising toward a panicked pitch. "You know my name. It's Alex! Why does that matter? It's Alex An –"

"No!" The old man cut him off. "That is the second name I gave you. Tell him the name you were born with. Your *true* name."

Alex looked at Danielle. Her gaze was switching from him to the old man in the chair, to Marcos, to Sheldon, to Sergei – then began its rounds again. The only person she wasn't staring at like a rabbit in a cage was the unconscious stranger in the corner of the room.

Everything seemed to swim in unreality before Alex. "The second name?" was all he could think to say.

Marcos laughed. "Oh, this is good. This is *too damn good*." He nodded at Sheldon, who flicked his knife. He didn't bother catching the third toe to show to the camera or to Demyan. It just rolled away, hitting the unconscious stranger in the face. The man did not flinch. Out.

Sheldon walked to the stranger and picked up the toe. Then he did the thing that was, for some reason, the worst thing so far: he pushed all three of the toes – *Alex's* toes – into the dirt at the base of the damn tree that had watched all this happen.

It was the worst, because that was good-bye. Could a doctor reattach toes that had been ground into the dirt at the base of a tree? He didn't think so.

They were gone. Truly, *finally* gone. Part of him was forever changed, forever stolen away from him.

For a moment, Sheldon looked confused. "Lucy?" he said. "What happened?"

"What the hell are you talking about, Shel?" demanded Marcos.

"I don't know. She seems… different. Did someone move her?" He glared around the room.

"Oh, geez, Shel, give it a rest." Marcos turned to look at Alex. "Don't think about refusing to answer any questions asked from here on out, *Alex*," said Marcos, all laughter gone from his voice. "You're mine. You're all mine, and the only thing you can buy from this point out is your own pain. So what name were you *born with?*"

"Aleksandr," said Alex. "I was born Aleksandr." He glared at Demyan before adding, "But I have no idea who this *Sasha* is or what she has to do with me." He switched his gaze to Marcos, his gaze softening as he said, "You have the wrong guy. Please. Please just let me go."

A gasp came from somewhere, and Alex was so focused on the man who held his life in his hands he didn't for a moment understand where it had come from. Then the small part of him not completely zeroed in on Marcos realized: it was Danielle. It took him a moment more to figure out why. He glanced at her, and sure enough, she was looking at him with hurt and pain and it was all he could do not to laugh.

You're upset I said let me *go instead of let* us *go. You dumb, heartless cow. Worried about yourself instead of me!*

Marcos laughed again. "You don't know who Sasha is?" He turned again to Demyan. "And you thought of *me* as the cur? As the half-breed? At least I know that Sasha is the nickname for that good, solid Russian name, *Aleksandr*." He turned to Alex –

(Not Aleksandr, I'm not him I'm Alex Anton, Aleksandr died a long time ago.)

– and added, "But that's not your whole name, is it?"

Again Alex hesitated. Again Sheldon took a step toward him, and again he relented.

Out loud, he said, "It's Antonovich."

"So it is," said Marcos. "Aleksandr Antonovich."

I'll make you pay, you bastard. Make you all *pay. You, Marcos, this Demyan dipshit… even Danielle. Why isn't she doing something? Offering herself?*

At the same time, Danielle gasped, and Alex added another item to the list of reasons why she would have to die:

She knows.

17

"Aleksandr Antonovich."

The two simple words rang through Danielle, converting her skull to a bell with a spiked clapper inside. She actually, *literally* put her free hand to her head, as though trying to stop the bell from ringing, the words from stinging.

It worked. A little. She felt her mother's eyes on her, strangely – and even more strangely, it gave her strength. Once Mother was gone, Danielle had vowed to never again let someone make her cringe like that, to cringe like she was doing *now*.

She straightened. But it was hard, so hard. Even harder when Marcos said in a strangely sad voice, "Sorry, my dear. Truly sorry that you were unlucky enough to get dragged into this. But I needed Demyan to see what he had done, and what I would do to those who dared love him."

Aleksandr Antonovich.

She knew who it was. Every defense attorney knew. It was a cautionary tale of what could go wrong when a kid was left in the system. When *justice* wasn't done. Aleksandr Antonovich had grown up in foster care, bounced from one place to another… until the day he tortured and killed his foster parents and took everything of value from their house. He disappeared without a trace. And even – what was it, fifteen years ago? – it was hard enough to do that in the world of near-constant surveillance and *totally* constant digital footprints that already existed that everyone more or less assumed he had died.

But he wasn't dead. He was *here*.

But it can't be. Not him. Not Alex.

Only…

Only he's the right age.

Only…

Only he could *be him, couldn't he? Same eye color, same hair color I remember from the grainy pictures in law school.*

Only…

Only there was the way he looked *at me.*

That last thing cinched it. That last thing made her sure.

It *was* him. It was the little boy who had grown up everywhere and nowhere as the system passed him from place to place until he murdered two people, then fell off the edge of the world and apparently ended up nowhere at all. She remembered it well because it was a tale that reminded her so much of her brother in so many ways – a different tragic end, but all the same reasons. Just a poor kid with no luck, who ended suddenly and cruelly at the hands of a world that didn't care.

She cared. She always had. And, she found, she still did. She felt an ache in her gut that came of betrayal, of fear. But she found, to her surprise, that that didn't matter. What mattered most was the simple fact that what was happening wasn't *just*. It wasn't the way things should be.

And most surprising of all, she found that mattered so much that she looked at Marcos, the man in charge, and said, "Even if he killed your friends or family, you don't have to do this. You don't have to punish Alex – Aleksandr. He'll serve time. He'll go to jail."

Again Marcos turned genuinely mournful-seeming eyes on her. "Shhh, my dear. So sorry, but this isn't about them at all. This is about the fact of his existence. That can't stand, and it has to be rectified. Besides, even if I just handed him over to cops…" and he spread his hands wide before continuing, "… what if he has a defense attorney as good as you?"

"It won't matter. He'll still serve. I'll *see* to it. But this… whatever it is, it won't solve what you're trying to solve."

She glanced at Alex as she said this, and somehow wasn't surprised at all to see the hate rippling over his features. Not just at Marcos, not just at the situation. At *her*. Maybe because she dared to speak of him in jail, maybe because of the situation in general.

Again that cold went through her. Alex, the man she had fallen for so quickly and completely, was suddenly revealed. Not just as Aleksandr Antonovich, but as a true sociopath.

She didn't want it to be. But she knew it was. She knew what evil looked like, just as she knew that sociopaths could hide in plain sight. They'd be charming and pleasant, smiling and loving you in a way that seemed like you meant the world to them. Then times got hard, or they became disenchanted with their situation for some selfish reason or other and they were willing to hurt anyone physically, mentally, or emotionally to get what they wanted. It wasn't even a matter of survival, just one of control and convenience.

Danielle hadn't even registered this as a possibility in her time with Alex. Sure, it had been fast. But usually sociopaths didn't hold positions of responsibility and authority like Alex did. Not the worst cases, as he evidently was. Usually they self-destructed, their own need for short-term gratification overwhelming their pittance of self-control.

Usually. But not always.

Mom didn't self-destruct.

But she had help. She had money, and Dad covered for her for years, so she had help and…

… and so did Alex.

Marcos leaned toward Alex and said, "Do you even know where you're from, boy?" He looked at Demyan. "Tell him why he's here."

"You're…" Demyan shook his head as he looked away. "You're my son."

Alex looked from Marcos to Demyan. "I… I don't even know him," he said in a shocked, pathetic whisper. To Marcos specifically, he said, "I don't know what you have against him but you don't need to involve me. I haven't done anything to –"

Marcos cut him off with a curt shake of the head. "Oh, but you have. You're his son, Ale*ksandr*." He jerked a thumb at the man on the chair. "You're the son of Demyan Antonovich, a member of the Odessa family."

"I don't understand what that means," sobbed Alex.

Danielle did. "He's his *son*? And you're all Odessa?" she blurted.

Danielle suddenly understood, just as she suddenly understood Alex's true nature, and with this last information knew also why Alex was here. And what would happen to him and to her both because of it.

Marcos looked at her with irritation. That expression softened to amusement. "*You* know? You know but your husband doesn't?" He laughed. "Will wonders never cease? Why don't *you* tell him, then?"

"Tell me what?" Alex's panicked eyes settled on Danielle. "Tell me what, sweetie? Who's Odessa?"

Danielle's skin prickled at his suddenly affectionate tone, at the word *sweetie*. He didn't mean it. He only wanted what she was good for.

But that didn't matter. Not now. What mattered was not pissing this volatile Marcos guy off. "Odessa is the name of the biggest Russian mob family in the United States."

Marcos nodded. "Correct. Though I'm surprised that even a criminal defense attorney would know what I think you do. You must be a great lawyer." He leaned toward her. "You're the kind of person that we'd try to hire."

Danielle couldn't help her expression. It curdled as she said, "There's not enough money in the world."

"Oh, now, honey… there's *always* enough money in the world to buy someone. Sooner or later, people bend."

"I want justice for people," she said, shaking her head. "That's the only reason I'm in this field, and from what I understand, Odessa wants anything *but* justice happening to them."

Marcos' eyes flashed, and for a moment Danielle wondered if she had gone too far; if her clearly insulting tone had inflamed him to a dangerous point. But he snorted and said, "An attorney with ethics? How rare." He smiled. "But you *do* know Odessa. So do you know why Sasha is doomed?" Danielle didn't answer, but Marcos' smile widened as he said, "Ah, you do. I can see it. Would you like to tell him?"

Danielle considered refusing to answer. But what would it gain? They would just hurt her, and someone – be it her or someone else – would tell Alex. Would it matter who the information came from?

No.

"He's Odessa, you said," she said, looking at Demyan.

It hadn't really been a question, but Marcos nodded and his reptilian grin widened, his eyes grew colder. "He is."

"People who swear themselves to the highest levels of Odessa also swear not to have anything more important in their lives."

"Like…" prompted Marcos.

"Like families. Like children."

"So you see why I have to kill you both, don't you?" asked Marcos. "The father and the son. To make things right. And you," he added to Danielle, "to tie off loose ends."

"And him," said Sheldon, his voice dreamy, the voice of someone high on some unknown and perhaps unknowable drug. He gestured at the unconscious man. "To make things *fun*."

"And him," said Marcos, though disgust was clear in his expression. "But first the boy. First the son."

"No, please!" shouted Demyan.

"And why not?" screamed Marcos. Now it was his turn to spit, right into the old man's face. "How *stupid* of you. You left him at an orphanage with *your name pinned to his shirt.* You followed him, you watched him. Do you think I would have found him if you didn't do such stupid, egotistical things? You covered up seven *murders* for him, for God's sake."

Danielle again felt cold. *Seven* murders? She already knew of the two foster parents, but who were the other five? Who else had Alex put permanently away when they grew inconvenient?

She tried not to let it happen, but the thought came all the same: *And how long before I became number eight?*

Demyan lunged upward, hands grasping at Marcos. Sergei moved toward him, but Sheldon was faster – *much* faster. He was a blur as he swept forward. His knife flashed, and suddenly Demyan was falling, both his Achilles tendons cut, his feet suddenly useless appendages.

Sheldon caught him and grinned at Marcos as he lowered the old man to the floor. Demyan tried to crawl forward, but a couple of quick stomps on his arms and the old man could only thrash like a dying fish. In that same loopy voice as before, Sheldon said to Marcos, "Don't worry, none of this is life threatening. You'll have plenty of time with him."

"Good," said Marcos. "But first he has to see what he's done." He nodded at Alex.

Alex began shrieking, driving his feet – one still in a shoe, the other naked to the world and blood streaming from the stumps of three toes – against the floor. Danielle had heard Sheldon break his ankle, too, but Alex didn't seem even to notice the injuries. His legs fluttered, pushing him against the wall. Sheldon was on him in a flash, stretching him out and then kneeling on Alex's left upper leg. There was another crack and Alex's screams rose to a truly terrifying pitch as his femur broke under Sheldon's weight.

"I have found," said Sheldon pleasantly, "that the whole thing lasts much longer when the person is strong and full of hate." He cocked his head. "I can tell you have one of those, but are you *strong?* I hope so." He looked at Marcos. "How long do you want this to last?" he asked.

"As long as you can," said Marcos.

"For all of them?"

Marcos nodded at Demyan and Alex. "For them, as long as possible. For the other two?" He shrugged. "Depends on how long you drag it out for the first ones."

He stared at Danielle, and the point of his tongue ran along his lips. "And how much I feel like participating."

Sheldon shrugged. "I'll need my bag. To do a really *good* job."

"Then get it," Marcos said.

Sheldon sauntered to Lucy, and Danielle heard him whisper something. Marcos and Sergei looked on, obviously disgusted by the man's weirdness. Demyan and Alex just thrashed – Demyan soundlessly, Alex with screams and tears of self-pity, snot running down his nose and lip.

Sheldon stood and left the room. Long seconds ticked by. Marcos finally moved to Demyan, leaning down and obviously intending to say something. Demyan didn't let him. "Who is that madman?" the old man said, voice surprisingly strong and steady despite his injuries. "I do not know him."

"That's because I'm better at keeping secrets than you, old man." Marcos sighed. "I really wish I was better at pain. I'd do more of you myself, but…" He shrugged. "Shel always had the skill in that department."

Demyan coughed out a laugh. "Always been a pain to *me*."

Marcos almost kicked him, halting his attack only inches from the old man's face. "Not true. I made you more money than you ever dreamed possible. I was your real son, your *true* son."

Demyan thrashed until he was looking at Sergei. "And you just let him do this? You stand for it?"

Sergei stared straight ahead, expression so blank it was practically inert.

Danielle didn't know what to do. She had something in her hands that *might* help her – something she had guarded and, she thought, successfully kept secret, though Sheldon had given her a heart attack when he looked at his plant.

And it was a totally academic secret now. She couldn't use what she held, so what *could* she do?

Her eye fell on the stranger. "You could at least let him go." Marcos turned to her. To her own surprise, she didn't flinch. "That guy isn't connected to us, is he?"

"I don't know," said Marcos. "Is he?" he said to Demyan.

The old man said something angry in Russian. Marcos laughed and responded in kind before turning back to Danielle. "I honestly don't think he is. Which is something of a surprise, I must admit." Turning to Demyan once more, he said, "I didn't expect you'd really come alone. You were losing your touch, your nerve, well before this happened, old man."

More angry cursing from Demyan. Marcos sighed. He said something in Russian to Sergei, which only amplified Demyan's cursing. Sergei continued to say nothing.

Marcos straightened and went to Danielle. Kneeling before her, he said, "You seem like a good person. Always makes me sad when I have to do bad things to good people." He shrugged. "But I gotta break the old man. It's the price of admission, you know? And that means I gotta break everything that matters to him first." He thought for a moment. "I think that means I should change my plans. I should probably torture *you* first, to hurt his son – which will hurt the old man. Then I torture the son to death, and Demyan last of all."

He was ruminating, not really talking to her. But Danielle answered him. "You don't *have* to do any of it."

Marcos turned the single most frightening gaze she had ever seen on her. "Oh, but I do. And more than that, I *want* to." He looked her up and down, his gaze making her feel as though snails were trailing over her entire body. "With you, I know just how to start."

This was it, she knew. Even if he hadn't already been pulling at his belt, even then – she knew what was coming. She opened her mouth to scream.

And the lights went out.

Almost instantly, dim red lights glowed at the corners of the room, providing more shadow than light. They were enough to show Marcos leaping to his feet, though. "What the –" he shouted, turning to Sergei as the big man headed to the door. "Where the hell do you think you're going?" shouted Marcos. Sergei said something to him in Russian. Marcos stood and buckled his belt as he said, "No, *I'll* check the security station. You stay here. Or should we leave them unguarded, you think?"

Sergei went stone-faced, clearly angry but trying to hide it. He returned to his spot by the door as Marcos ran out of the room.

Danielle waited until she was sure Marcos was gone, then said, "Please let us go." She didn't really expect an answer. She got one.

Not from Sergei, though. Instead, the stranger in the corner groaned. Then he screamed, a strange, high-pitched scream. "What did you do?" he shouted. "What did you do to me?" The red light in the room was bright enough – barely – that Danielle could see a dark spot spread across the crotch of the man's jeans as he thrashed about in purest terror.

"Shut up," said Sergei.

The stranger turned horrified eyes on the man. He screamed again, even louder. "Don't come near me! Don't touch me, Father!"

"Shut up," Sergei said again. "Or I shut you up."

"Don't you dare! You'd never dare!" screamed the stranger, his voice now completely hysterical. "No one –"

He cut off, shrinking against the wall, as Sergei stomped toward him, leaning over to grab him. "I said, shut *up* or –"

Danielle never got to hear what the "or" might have led to. The stranger's shoulder was dislocated, the wrist on that side anchoring him to the steel ring in the wall. That left only one hand.

And that was enough.

The stranger's hand darted out, withdrew, then darted out again. The first time, his finger speared right into Sergei's eye. The man bellowed, his hands clapping to his ruined eye reflexively. He opened his mouth to scream, but the stranger's second strike jammed the ridge of his hand into Sergei's throat.

The big man's voice disintegrated to a horrid gurgle and he fell back, hands clawing at his crushed windpipe. Between his clawing motions, Danielle could see that the man's throat was grossly misshapen, a huge divot where his Adam's apple should have been jutting out.

She looked at the stranger. He was no longer shouting. Just watching quietly, his eyes transformed from terror and panic to something serene. Patient.

Sergei gurgled once more. Then he fell. Then he twitched.

Then he was silent.

The stranger turned to Danielle. In a voice every bit as calm as his eyes, he said, "I can't quite reach him. Can you?"

Danielle, utterly shocked by this sudden turn, couldn't quite understand what he meant. "Just breathe," said the stranger.

She understood then: Sergei. Maybe he had a key. Maybe he had a phone.

Just as she had before, first with Alex, then trying to reach Sheldon's plant, she reached out with her feet. She pushed herself even farther than before, even though it hurt her wrist where the handcuff dug into her. She felt blood pouring down her arm, but no matter how hard she tried…

"I can't," she panted, pain rendering her breathless.

The stranger sighed. "Okay. It's probably for the best."

He turned to the wall. Again, utter uncertainty overwhelmed Danielle. What was happening? What was he going to do?

The stranger twisted at the waist, then slammed his bad shoulder into the wall. There was a loud, almost bright-sounding *pop,* and his shoulder shifted. He never made a sound, and as he turned back to her she saw not the barest trace of pain in his gaze, even though popping his shoulder back into place had to be agonizing.

The stranger knelt down. He felt across the new cuts on his chest, inflicted after he was brought in here. His fingers moved across them, then traced some of the older marks on his body. One on his side in particular.

The stranger's fingers seemed to glow bright pink in the red emergency lighting as he pressed into his side. Then Danielle cried out in sympathetic pain as that glow was swallowed by a burst of crimson as the stranger dug his fingers into his own flesh. Questing, probing, they disappeared up to the first knuckle.

His eyes never changed. They never so much as flickered. "Dig deep," he said to her. "That's what Father always said." Before Danielle could figure out how to respond to that, the stranger looked to his side and, speaking to someone Danielle could not see, said, "I agree. They shouldn't have left me alive." Then his head swiveled to his other side. "No, we don't know for sure. So we'll leave it for now."

"What are you..." Danielle's voice trailed off. She tried again, for a different question. "*Who* are you?"

The stranger smiled. His fingers still questing below his skin, he said, "I was just One. For a long time. Now I'm three. Now..." He twisted his fingers, prompting another gout of blood, but did not look away from her as he said, "I am Legion."

18

"Aren't *we* the smart one?" says Water, the words almost lost in burbling laughter.

Fire's body crackles as he turns on Water, and flame literally spits from his eye sockets as he snarls, "We're not *one* at all." In a softer voice he adds, "Not anymore. And that's a good thing. Right?"

That last word sounds almost desperate to Legion, and he wonders if he might break down here. Or perhaps even worse, what if he loses his brothers, or they become part of him – become somehow *One* – again?

That, he knows, would make him insane. Because how can he be One when his brothers are dead? To think of that is to think of madness.

"It's just the pain," says Water soothingly.

"Just the pain," echoes Fire. The flames in his eyes dim. They are not frightening, but warm, just as the moisture on Water is cool. Together, they have blended to create something perfect.

Legion knows this, and it is a comfort as he digs into his side a few inches above his waist. He knows that his face betrays no pain – Father never approved of such, and Legion has learned over the years to dull any expression of agony. But that is different than actually *feeling* no pain.

But what he is doing now hurts, it most definitely does.

He starts humming the song "3" by Britney Spears. The music is soothing, and he feels better. He tries to ignore a new flicker behind Fire and Water both. A shadow.

"Father?" he says.

The flicker dies. But both Fire and Water swing around in terror.

"No," Fire says in a shaky, dry, brittle voice. "Father's dead."

"We killed him," says Water.

"But then… *we* died –" says Fire.

"– and *we're* still here," finishes Water.

The shadow flickers, and Legion can almost see the man's face. The face of Father. Legion's first and hopefully last teacher.

I am the teacher now.

The shadow flickers and disappears.

"Are you… are you okay?" says Danielle.

Legion looks at her. "Is she someone worthy? Does she need instruction?" asks Water, just as he did a moment ago.

Legion can only give the same answer: "I don't know. We'll have to wait and see."

His fingers, which have not stopped moving all this time, finally find what they are looking for: the thing Legion worried might be discovered if Sheldon kept digging with that sharp knife of his.

"Don't do that," says Danielle. She holds out her free hand. It is clenched tightly. "Don't hurt yourself, it's not as bad as that, we can get out of here. Look." She opens her fist, showing what lays on her palm.

Legion looks at what she holds. For a moment he hears Father's voice.

"The measure of a man is what he can do. The worth of a man is what he can survive. So survive this, get yourself out."

Legion smiles at Danielle. "You're very kind to worry, but I won't need that." He pulls his fingers free. They pop out with a wet sucking noise, holding tight to the thing he buried so many years before. As he does, he whispers, "Dig deep, and find the way inside yourself."

He remembers again Father putting him – the One him – in the Dark Place. Saying the words that taught Legion how to escape.

"Dig deep, and find the way inside yourself. The only people worthy in this world are the ones who can escape any cell *– even the ones they make for themselves. The only people who can be called good are the ones who can survive the trials their teachers provide."*

And Legion had decided to be a good man. He waited until there was a time between Dark Place times. He took three keys. Each time one disappeared, Father raged and searched all of the One – rare instances where he seemed to notice and interact with all three bodies that were One in his mind as they had so long been One in Legion's own.

But the One was clever. The One waited each time to steal a key only after Father had cut Him. The One would make sure all three of Him matched, cutting the same marks in the unmarked skin of those Father had not seen.

Then, before He could heal, the One would bury the key He had stolen in one of His bodies. Legion recognized now that he could have escaped his father much earlier, but back then he had still been One. So he had to wait until he had stolen three keys over a period of nearly six years – long enough that Father would rage each time, but not connect the thefts. Legion hoarded his treasures carefully, moving them often so Father would never find them again. And when he had three – the magic number, just enough and not too many or too few – the One buried the three keys in the three bodies He shared.

He had to wait until he had all three keys. Because the One had to match.

Then, finally prepared, he failed a lesson. Father stripped him and handcuffed him to the wall as he always did. He closed the door on Legion as he always did.

Only this time Legion had a key, hidden in plain sight among the map of scars and cuts that were his first birthright. Only one key was needed, but all of the One pulled their keys from the healed wounds in their bodies, tearing their own flesh to find them. Because even in this moment of freedom and ascension, the One had to match, or it could not be the One.

The One did not leave the room. He counted seconds, one at a time, until it was the middle of the night. The Dark Place was not locked – Father counted on the handcuffs to contain the One. Still nude, the One went to Father's room and strangled him in his sleep. All of Him did it, three sets of teenage hands gripping Father's throat and squeezing so hard the man's neck snapped.

Legion had left the Dark Place that night – for the last time, he had thought. But now he is in another Dark Place, and to his surprise he finds that he is afraid not at all. He feels at home.

"That's what Father gave us," says Water.

"Old bastard," whispers Fire.

"That's not very nice," says Water.

"Not nice at all," agrees Legion. "But true."

He wipes the key he has taken across his pants, being careful to avoid the urine he coaxed from his bladder to lull Sergei into carelessness. He will put the key back in him later – it has proven useful there, and he would not like to give it up – and though he knows urine is sterile, still he does not want any on the key, even though he knows he will have to disinfect it before it goes back in. You don't put a piece of metal in you without disinfecting it first. Doing such a thing would be crazy.

"What about us?" demands the man who had had his toes popped off – Legion had risked a glance through slitted eyes off and on during the man's ordeal – in a whiny voice.

Legion squints at him, then looks at Demyan. The man just lays there. He is down for the count, unless he gets carried out on a stretcher or wheeled out on a gurney. He doesn't say anything, and Legion can respect that, just as he respects the cunning and danger in the man's eyes.

Legion sighs. He looks at Demyan, then Alex, then Danielle. "I haven't made up my mind about all of you yet. So I don't know what lessons to teach you."

He turns to leave. Alex starts to shout behind him, but someone – Danielle, no doubt – *shushes*, and he is quiet again.

Legion smiles. "Good girl," he says.

"Maybe," says Fire noncommitally. Ash falls from his shoulders as he shrugs.

"I think so," says Water.

"You always do. You're too warmhearted, which is ironic given the two of us." Fire laughs. Flame belches out of his open mouth.

"And you're too coldhearted. Also ironic," says Water. He does *not* laugh.

"Come on," says Legion. "We haven't decided about all of them, but we have work to do."

"Lots of students in need of teaching,"' agrees Fire.

Legion debates what to do first – to attend to those in this room, or to move out into the wider place beyond. He decides to come back in a bit, when he has finished what he must do in the rest of the bunker. He goes to the body of the big man he has killed. Sergei's bladder and bowels loosened in the last moments of his life. Unlike when Legion did it, it was not a purposeful action done to lull an attacker into a feeling of confidence. It was just meat, letting go of itself in the instant of death.

Legion is not disgusted by it. He has seen it many times. He does not even wrinkle his nose as he leans in close and pats the man down.

"Let us go! Help me!" shouts Alex, already forgetting Danielle's urging that he be silent. Legion ignores him. He pulls Sergei's gun free from its holster under the man's jacket. He also finds a push dagger – a small, double-sided blade with a handle that extends like a "t" in the back, perfect for tucking in a person's hand with the blade sticking out between the index and middle finger – in a small sleeve at the back of the man's belt. He takes it and sees even in the dim red light how the blade reflects. A honed edge that would give any razor a run for its money.

Alex is still shouting. Danielle relents a bit, adding her voice to the mix. "Help us, please."

It is not lost on Legion the difference in their pleas: "help us" versus "help *me*." And while Alex sounds panicked and whiny, Danielle is calm. She is afraid, but she is not begging or losing her cool.

"A point in her favor," says Water. He smiles and water bubbles from watery lungs.

"A point against *him*," says Fire. He smiles, too, though his smile is of a different breed – tight and sparkling with hints of rage.

"But do we act on either?" says Legion.

Demyan speaks at last. "Who the hell are you talking to?"

Legion laughs quietly. "Not myself, that I can promise you."

He turns to leave the room. "At least leave us the gun!" shouts Alex.

Legion looks at the unmourned Sergei. Certainly a beast of a man who delighted in others' pain – the gun and the push dagger would attest to that even if he hadn't so obviously enjoyed dislocating Legion's shoulder.

"At least Father left us that little skill," says Fire.

Legion winces, but does not answer. He still is not sure what was worse: when his brothers – the One of so long ago – popped his shoulder back in its socket, or when he was forced to dislocate *their* shoulders.

They had to match – and match they did. They could even dislocate them at will after that, which, though painful, Legion had used to good effect earlier. He doubted Sergei really would have dislocated his shoulder with that quick jerk he gave, but letting it pop loose allowed Legion to pretend to pain so massive that it made him pass out. Handy.

He looks at Sergei's gun. It is a Beretta. Newer than the ones Father had made him endlessly drill on, but still a familiar weapon.

"Give it here! Leave it!" shouts Alex. "Let me have it!"

Legion looks coldly at him. He almost hears Father's own voice speaking as he says to Alex, "The only people worthy in this world are the ones who can escape any cell – even the ones they make for themselves. The only people who can be called good are the ones who can survive the trials their teachers provide."

He breaks down Sergei's gun. He rarely uses guns in his lessons – too impersonal, too much like assassination rather than instruction. But he knows them well, and in seconds he is scattering the pieces across the floor. He pockets the magazine with the bullets.

"Are you mad?" says Demyan. Legion looks at him and sees that the man is pale and has started to gasp. Apparently Sheldon's assessment of his injuries was off by quite a bit. Or no…

"Did you do something to yourself?" he says.

Demyan looks surprised for a moment. He shrugs. "I knew, one way or another, I would not leave here. Either I would come and he would let Sasha go and kill me, or he would kill us both. I figured Sasha would be gone in an hour or two at most, if he *was* going to leave, so I took something. I can stand torture, but do not like it."

"Everyone's crazy," whispers Alex. "You're all –"

"Alex," begins Danielle.

"Shut *UP!*" Alex shrieks, and she falls silent.

Legion looks back at Demyan. "To answer your question: no, I'm not mad. But there is so much to teach here. And I will admit, I *am* angry."

"Niiiice line, bro," says Fire. He laughs a gout of coal ash that brightens the air around him while somehow not adding a bit of light to the room.

Legion nods a *thank you* to his brother then steps out of the room.

Alex starts screaming the instant Legion leaves.

"We need to stop that," says Water quietly.

"That moron's going to make this harder than it has to be," agrees Fire.

Legion sticks his head in the room he just left and says, "Do you really think it's a good idea to scream like that? Most people in here aren't your friend, so I'd stay quiet and do my best to get out of this."

"How are we supposed to do that?" pleads Alex.

"Can't you help us?" says Danielle. Again her voice holds no trace of begging. Just a sincere entreaty.

"I hope you can help yourself," Legion says to her, and means it. "That's one of the great measures of a person."

Then he turns and leaves the room again.

Legion is in a new Dark Place.

He is home.

And now… it is time to teach the ignorant.

It is time to hunt.

19

Marcos looked over Feodora's shoulder as she banged away at the keyboard in front of the security monitors. It didn't help. No matter what she did, the screens remained blank.

"What the hell's going on?" he demanded.

"I don't know," she snapped. "I only know that lights go out, then monitors go off."

"How is that even possible?" said Marcos, thinking already how he would punish her for speaking to him in that tone. Maybe in bed? Hurt her so much she didn't like it anymore?

It didn't matter now, he decided. Now he had to figure out who had cut the power to the bunker, and how come they were completely blind in here.

"It makes no sense," said Feodora.

"What if someone cut the lines?" said Marcos. "Would that sever the feeds?"

"*Are* no lines," said Feodora. "All wireless. No one can sever them unless they set up jammer."

"Is that even possible?" Marcos said, a hole opening in the pit of his stomach. Demyan *must* be doing this, he knew. The old man must have brought some people after all.

"They would have to have either jammer that hits narrow band of our wireless cameras or wide enough band cameras are useless."

"How hard is that?" asked Marcos, wondering if it was the kind of thing Demyan could have set up. Maybe *that* was why none of this had happened before a few moments ago: maybe Demyan's people simply hadn't had enough time until now.

"Pretty hard," said a voice behind them, "but I'm *really* good with electronics."

Marcos turned, but not fast enough. Something hit him from behind and he tumbled forward. Feodora was already turning, drawing a gun from under her clothing, but Marcos fell against her, jamming her own arm between her and his bulk.

Marcos slipped. Not a graceful or calculated move, but it saved his life as a knife plunged into the place where the back of his neck had just been. At the same time Feodora, her arm suddenly loosed, raised her gun and fired. Then she made a strange noise and Marcos, now on his hands and knees in front of her, felt something warm and sticky splash over the back of his head and neck.

He looked up long enough to see a knife he recognized as Sergei's push dagger jutting out of the bottom of Feodora's chin. She tried to say something but evidently the knife had stapled her lower jaw and tongue to the roof of her mouth, and all that came out was a burbling "*nnnnng*" and more blood.

She fired again. Not at anything in particular, just panic-twitches making her fist clench and release. Marcos rolled to the side, hearing the bullet ricochet off the floor, feeling a red gash of pain open on his side. He felt there automatically and found blood, even as he looked up to see just what the hell was happening.

It was the *stranger*. The one Feodora had found outside the bunker, in the woods.

The stranger yanked the push dagger out of Feodora's mouth. The lower jaw jerked down with his motion, the mouth hanging open wide enough that Marcos had a single instant in which he could tell the stranger must have twisted as he pulled, jerking Feodora's lower jaw half off her head in the process.

The stranger punched out again. The knife – hideously sharp, Marcos knew – flashed, and blood sprayed. Crimson sluiced down Feodora's arms in sheets so thick and pulsing that Marcos knew the stranger had expertly, *perfectly* slashed her brachial arteries.

She had only seconds left.

Marcos did not spend them mourning her. He ran.

All thoughts of making this place into the premier, most high-security meth-lab in the world, of climbing the ranks of Odessa, of making all those who had mocked him grovel and lick the dust at his feet – it was all gone. He only thought of survival. Of escape.

He got out of the room. He took three steps into the hall beyond.

Then he felt something – strong, so hideously, shockingly strong – grab him and yank him once more into the security room.

He fell once more, this time not as an accident, but because the stranger had tripped him. The man looked down at Marcos. He cocked his head strangely, and Marcos saw that the man was bleeding. Not the wounds he'd gotten when that nut Sheldon carved on him: one of Feodora's wild shots had found a home in his side, which bled freely.

Marcos smiled at that. The smile fell away as the stranger reached for him. "Don't!" he shouted. "Do you know who I am? What's going to happen if you touch me?"

The stranger smiled. "Yes to both. You're a man in desperate need of instruction." His smile widened. "And hopefully when I touch you, you'll *learn*."

20

Sheldon was in the underground garage when the lights popped off and were replaced by the blood-red illumination of emergency lighting.

He had gotten his bag from the trunk, spending a few minutes to make sure everything was there. He was a very careful person, and didn't like having to walk back for a forgotten instrument. So he checked, double-checked, then *triple*-checked the contents of his bag of tricks and tools.

Satisfied, he closed the trunk and walked away. Then, halfway out of the garage, he knocked his forehead with his hand. "Almost forgot the big reveal," he said to himself.

He went back to the car. Not to the trunk this time, but the back seat. He leaned into the car, feeling for what he had left there. For a moment he worried they had somehow escaped. Then he found them. They had rolled under the front seat. He wrinkled his nose as he pulled them out from under the seat, one at a time, and transferred them to his bag. He didn't like them being in there with all his wonderful instruments of pain and death, but the Cadbury Eggs would definitely play a part, however crude, in what was to come.

He closed his bag, closed the back door to the car, and started walking out again. He had a spring in his step and a song in his heart. He did a little soft-shoe dance as he walked, and it was right in the middle of his elegant stylings that the bright lights that were ever-present in this place snapped off. Darkness, heavy and complete, fell for a moment. Another snap, and red emergency lighting took over.

"Isn't this interesting," he said aloud, and wondered what could be happening. He ticked off the possibilities, and quickly discarded the idea that this was some kind of cost-saving measure while the majority of the production staff was offsite. That would seem ridiculous in the extreme, especially given that Marcos had told him on the way in that this whole facility was solar-powered. So unless the sun had gone away, this was not a lack of power – and likely not any automatic process, since Sheldon was very good at figuring things out and if even *he* could not think of an automatic process that would explain this situation then there must not be one.

That left human causes.

Sheldon, on the whole, loved people. One of his sterling qualities was a deep, almost spiritual appreciation for those around him. One time he met a young woman in a bus station during a job, and she was so full of life and love and beauty that he wept as he killed her, knowing that she was too good for a world so full of sadness and danger. So yes, he loved people.

But he also knew that the vast majority of them were often deeply troubled, boring, stupid, or a combination of the three. And all other things being equal, stupidity was almost always the main reason anything went wrong. Not *his,* of course, but others'. Human stupidity, as his beloved mother was so fond of saying, was like a tidal wave of fecal matter: get in its path – even accidentally – and you were likely to be bowled over by it and *certain* to end up inconvenienced, if only by the necessity of cleaning yourself up at the end.

So yes, this was likely someone stupid doing something that came naturally to them.

Who was in the facility?

Marcos? Sheldon discarded this option almost immediately. The man was weird and rather rude, and had been as long as Sheldon could remember, and Sheldon had decided he would have to die at some point, but he didn't think the man was so stupid as to cause an outage in the place.

What about Feodora? She let Marcos feel her up, which was yucky and showed she had poor taste in men. On the other hand, she *had* made eyes at Sheldon when she thought Marcos wasn't looking, so that meant at least she had *some* class and a modicum of intelligence.

So it probably wasn't her, he decided.

That left Sergei. Sheldon sensed that the man was cut from the same cloth as the moronic (and thankfully dead) Mikhail: about as bright as a block of wood painted black and sitting in a forest during a cloudy midnight.

Sheldon had read that insult in a thread on a 4chan chat board, and decided it perfectly fit Sergei.

He would have to talk to Marcos about his human resources policies; obviously the screening process to get into this outfit was abysmal.

All this went through his mind in the first few moments after the lights went out. Sheldon was very smart, so thinking deep and Sherlock Holmes-like thoughts on this level came as second nature to him.

He knew what Sherlock Holmes thought like because he had watched an episode of the show starring that one guy who looked like a ferret. He hadn't figured out the mystery at the end, but he knew that Sherlock wasn't smarter – the writers had just cheated, so after breaking his TV in little pieces Sheldon realized it would be hard for someone as smart as him to think *down* to Sherlock's level. He bought another TV and all was well.

But what if things are not well here*? What if something has gone wrong? Not human error but something else? What if one of the three prisoners caused this? Or Demyan?*

Sheldon discarded this thought. Demyan had been effectively hobbled by Sheldon himself. Not even a Navy SEAL high on PCP could have done anything after Sheldon broke his arms and severed the tendons of his feet. Even the greatest strength of will would not countermand the simply physical requirement that muscles be able to pull on tendons which in turn would have to pull on bones to move the body properly. Sheldon had himself severed the right tendons and broken the right bones, so there was nothing more for him to do there.

What about the three others?

Chained. Not a threat.

Yes, this was definitely Sergei.

What a bore.

All this stupendously incisive thinking only took the time for him to walk a few steps toward the door that would take him from the garage to the rest of the compound. There were several other cars in this place but he had no trouble negotiating them given the red emergency lighting that had come on when the main lights snapped off.

At least the people who built all this had accounted for the possibility of stupid human error, which he applauded. The red lights were quite beautiful, actually. He suspected that, could he see Lucy right now, she would be absolutely radiant.

Still holding his bag, which contained all the tools and medical supplies he would need to cause maximum pain for maximum time, he walked from the garage into the rest of the installation.

He heard gunshots.

The structure of this place made it impossible to tell if the shots came from close by or far away. The shots were muted, the thick walls and hatches between rooms both muffling and warping the sounds. The person or persons who had discharged a weapon could be nearby, or could be laying in wait at the other end of the underground compound.

Sheldon stood still. He listened. He knew he would have to move forward, but he also knew he didn't want to rush into danger. He was brave, he was strong, he was smart. But he was also properly cautious, and aware of how poorly the world would get along without him adding his unique talents to it.

He heard nothing.

When he stepped into the hall beyond the garage, he smelled a subtle undercurrent in the previously-fresh air. Something tangy. Something familiar.

He smelled blood.

Everything in his mind shifted. Perhaps it *was* still human stupidity that had caused the lights to go out, and perhaps that same stupidity had even caused a gun discharge – yes, it had to be, given that he had already decided such to be the case, and Sheldon was so very rarely wrong – but it was stupidity to a dangerous degree. Someone had shed blood here, or had their own shed by others.

That meant Sheldon, who was good-looking, quick-thinking, *and* prepared, should take the appropriate precautionary measures.

He put down his bag and opened it. It was a big one, full of compartments and smaller bags inside it, but he easily found what he needed. He was always armed, but he thought it wise in the present uncertainty to add to the weapons he already had at the ready. He withdrew from the bag a pair of scalpel-thin blades in a sheath that he tucked into his jacket pocket. He had named the knives Mother One and Mother Two because they were so sharp and bright they reminded him of her. They would join the two knives (Kipling and good old Hemingway, whom he had used to hobble Demyan) he already wore at his sides; and the 9mm gun (Thompson) he held under his arm.

Yes, he was ready for whatever might occur.

Pallets of supplies lined this hall. Some were marked "MRE," obviously holdovers from when this place had been an actual shelter in case of nuclear war or zombie apocalypse. Others were laden down by piles of supplies that Sheldon assumed went into the meth production process.

Whatever they were, a gap between two of the pallets provided a perfect space for Sheldon to secrete his bag with the rest of its contents. He didn't want anyone finding and opening it. Coca-Cola had protected the secret recipe for its sodas for many years, and Sheldon viewed his own methods as even greater secrets. He was an artist, a scientist, and verged on being a miracle worker of pain – so taking care of the tools of his trade was of utmost importance.

Once his bag had been hidden away from prying eyes, Sheldon continued down the hall. He heard a series of grunts from somewhere beyond him, then something fell. A moment later, and another *thud* announced gravity hurling something large and solid against something larger and even more solid.

Sheldon's aspect changed. He had been reasonably alert, but also fairly at ease. Now any sense of relaxation disappeared. He lowered his body slightly, rising up on his toes at the same time. Shifting his balance to allow for maximum speed and maximum power.

Not stupidity after all. His verdict that this could not be the prisoners in their cell had not changed – they were secured, disabled, or both, and nothing could change that – but he wondered if Sergei or Feodora had perhaps decided they would be better off as the person in charge than Marcos. Probably Sergei. Feodora not only permitted herself to be felt up in a way that showed her to be in thrall to Marcos, but she was a woman, after all – notoriously incapable of things like trying to take over a crime ring. Sheldon's mother might have managed such a feat, perhaps, but other than someone who had won the genetic lottery the way she had, he could not think of a single other woman he'd ever met with the drive or competence to do... whatever it was that was being done now.

He moved toward the noise he had heard. Shadows pooled around him, but they were not the thick, inky shadows Sheldon preferred to utilize when stalking someone. It *was* red, which was a lovely color and went so well with green leaves that had been cut and trimmed and wired, but in this case it gave enough light to make him quite visible but not enough to allow him a perfect idea of his environment. A bloody twilight that was the worst of all possible worlds.

He passed several doorways as he walked down the hall. They went to other rooms in the place, and he was acutely conscious of the fact that this place was an interlocking grid of rooms, most of which had at least two doors leading in and out. That made it tough to properly clear the place as he went, since any room he verified as empty could just be used via another entrance.

"Ah, well. We persevere."

He said it quietly, knowing he shouldn't make any noise at all but also knowing he was more than the equal of any problems that might arise. He would be cautious, but if he couldn't take care of a Russian mafia security guard – perhaps even a *female* one, to boot – well… he would never again be able to look Mother or any other member of his family in the eye.

He moved on. The first rooms to his right and his left were the sleeping quarters for the people who worked the production line. Steel frame bunks that looked like dead animals filled the red-lit room, all skeletal limbs and thin chests. Nowhere to hide.

The next doors led to a kitchen on one side and another, smaller sleeping quarters on the other. This one was devoted to the security staff. The kitchen was clean and tidy, obviously well-maintained, probably by the people who worked in the meth production line. Sheldon couldn't really see Marcos or any of the security folks doing things as menial as washing dishes and cleaning floors.

He had to force himself to look into the security sleeping quarters, trying not to think of the icky cooties in there. He had no doubt that Feodora had done it with everyone – if she'd let someone like Marcos feel her up, she probably had the promiscuous nature of a horse in heat – and on every available surface. Thankfully, the bunks here were the same as in the previous rooms; again the bare frames and thin mattresses left nowhere to hide.

The same problem was in evidence here as in all the other rooms, however: they all had at least one more door other than the one that led to the central corridor through which Sheldon was passing. Each room had another door leading to at least one other room beside it. Many had doors that were closed, but he knew that none of them had locks. He had noted this issue to Marcos, but the man had shrugged and said, "No one could get into here in the first place, so what do we need locks on the inside for?"

Sheldon successfully managed not to voice the response, which was the obvious, "To keep people like *you* from taking over, I would think." He was very proud of his restraint in not saying it, though he would probably point it out to Marcos when he killed him. People should know things like that.

The room he came to next was the security station, and Sheldon felt a surge of pleasure that he had correctly assessed Feodora after all: she was *not* the one behind the problems. She could not be, because Feodora was dead.

She lay on the floor beside the man Marcos had killed earlier, her eyes staring sightlessly at the ceiling, her mouth, jaw, and throat twisted into masses of gore and hanging tissue, and her arms sheathed in blood. If Sheldon had not possessed amazing strength of will, he might have been sick. He had never seen such violence visited on a person, other than when he himself did it, and found he was not at all happy seeing this. He didn't mind that it had happened, but minded very much that someone *else* had done it.

Not very well, though. Whoever did it was just a brute, not an artist *like you, Sheldon.*

Sheldon smiled. He was right, of course. That made him feel much better.

The monitors were blank. Sheldon could not see anything outside this small world. He did not like this fact any more than he liked knowing there was some predator nearby.

He would have to fix these problems, toot-sweet, quick as a bunny. Kill everyone in here, just to be sure. Sergei, then Marcos. Sergei probably caused all this inconvenience, and no matter how close Marcos and Sheldon were, there was still no mistaking that Marcos had gotten too big for his britches.

Sheldon *would* still torture and kill the prisoners – he had been paid to do so, and Sheldon did his best to complete every job – but first he would hunt down and destroy every other living creature in the bunker.

He left the security station. He passed a locker room and a shower room, both of which were empty, both of which had closed doors leading to adjoining rooms.

No good. None of this is any good.

He was supremely brave. But the hairs were standing straight up on the back of his neck, and nervousness seemed to send static charges all over his skin. He had drawn his 9mm, Thompson, at some point, as well as his favorite blade, Hemingway, and realized he was holding them so tightly that his palms ached. He loosened his grip, but it had tightened again only a moment later.

No good for sure.

He kept walking. He passed a bathroom. There were stalls inside, and he weighed the idea of looking in each of them. If he did that, he would certainly find anyone who might be hiding in there, but he would also be out of sight of the central corridor and so anyone hiding in this place – Sergei and Marcos were still unaccounted for – and waiting to do damage to Sheldon would be able to just slink by in the hall and Sheldon would have to start this whole tedious process over again.

He decided against looking into the bathroom. Not an optimal result, but he was excellent at weighing the relative merits of any decision that presented itself, so he felt confident that he had made the right choice. Just like always.

The next moment brought some real problems. The corridor had reached an intersection. If he kept going straight he would reach the room the prisoners were in. It had been a media room, but Marcos had changed it to its current "holding cell from a torture porn movie" look.

To the right side was a corridor that led to the production area of the bunker. Marcos had told him it originally held a bowling alley with two full-size lanes and a resting area, presumably for the people the original owner intended to bring to be able to sit and play while everyone on the surface was melted by radiation, frozen by a nuclear winter, or sucked dry by mutant vampire zombie hillbillies.

To the other side lay the private quarters of Marcos and the unseen Beaker, as well as the office Marcos used as his HQ.

"Which to do, which to do," Sheldon mused. He heard a thud down the right-hand passage: the direction of the production facility. "So we go that way," he said. That was the way he would have chosen regardless, because he suspected the production facility would have far more weaknesses and far more places to hide. Anyone trying to make mischief would likely head there.

He turned down the passage.

21

Marcos woke to see the stranger leaning over him, but other than that he couldn't tell where he was. Someplace dark. Someplace red.

"It's pretty here," he said.

"No," said the stranger.

Marcos felt something. A strange coldness where he wasn't used to it being cold. He looked down. "Hey, are my pants off?"

"Yes," said the stranger.

"How come?"

"Do you know where you are?"

Marcos looked around. The world had gone somehow both fuzzy and in sharp relief. Everything was bright, but everything somehow *hid* from him. He blinked and blinked, but it was hard for him to figure out…

"Hey," he said. His voice sounded funny and he laughed. "Am I in the place?"

"We all are in *a* place," said the stranger. "The question is whether it's a good place or a bad one. And the place you are is a *very* bad one."

Marcos opened his mouth to say something, laughed, and said, "Why are my pants off?"

"Because you were unconscious and I thought it would be easier this way."

The stranger leaned down. Marcos cringed away. "What're you doing? I'm no faggot!"

The stranger looked at him, and the darkness in his eyes managed to drive away some of the euphoria that had gripped him. "I'm not trying to have a sexual relationship with you, Marcos. And I don't really approve of the crude insult."

"Then what are you doing? Answer me, dammit!" The stranger reached down again. Marcos felt something pry open his butt cheeks. Something slid inside him. "You sure you're not gay?" he said, which struck him as a strange, wrong, and yet perfectly right question.

The hell's going on with me?

"That's the wrong question, Marcos."

"What's… what's the right one?" The euphoria was back. He was drifting. He felt something moving in his rectum, but the feeling got farther and farther away.

"Normally I would take my time, you know. I'd watch and watch, and when I knew you were in error, when I knew beyond doubt that you were in need of education, then I'd move. Normally I'd also watch to see if you *could* be taught. Confession, contrition, payment for your wrongs. But you're a lost cause, so the best I can do is provide a graduation ceremony of sorts."

Something else slithered inside Marcos. "Why are my pants off?" he asked. Everything was bright, everything was dark. He felt like laughing, he felt like screaming.

"Because the drugs you make can be snorted, taken orally, taken intravenously, or taken anally. I thought it unlikely that you would snort or eat them while unconscious, and couldn't find the tools for intravenous introduction. So…"

The stranger held up a hand full of sparkling diamonds.

No, not diamonds. What… what are those things? So pretty. So… pretty…

"So I decided to give you the drugs anally."

Drugs. That word penetrated the giddy fog that was rapidly closing around Marcos. He asked, "How much drugs? How many much much much-much-much?" At the end of the sentence he wasn't even sure what he was saying, or what the sentence had started out as in the beginning.

The stranger smiled. "I found a lot. Normally they wouldn't have hit you so fast, I think. But I also have this." He produced a knife –

(Doesn't that belong to Sergei or Fee or my mom or something?)

– and held it in front of Marcos' eyes.

"Pretty," said Marcos.

"Do you have anything you want to say? Any confessions you want to make?"

Marcos laughed. The stranger nodded. "So far gone," he said. He looked to the side. "Is he gone too far?"

"Who you talking to?"

The stranger looked to his other side. "And you agree?" He nodded. "Good. Me, too." He turned to look at Marcos again. "You are someone who can never be taught.

We all agree. And when Fire and Water both agree, you know it's got to be true."

Marcos looked around. "All? Who are you –"

He didn't finish the sentence. The stranger leaned down again and Marcos felt a new sensation at his rectum. Not a pushing, but a pulling. The stranger shifted, and Marcos saw the knife he had been holding, still red. He felt pain, terrible pain. He tried to scream as the remaining rational part of his mind told him that the stranger must have cut him in a place Marcos had never pictured himself being violated. But the scream never came. He giggled.

The stranger stood. He still held the knife in one hand, jeweled rocks in the other. The knife was soaked in blood, as was the stranger's arm past the wrist.

The rocks he had been holding – meth crystals – were mostly gone from his hand. And those that remained now looked more like rubies than diamonds – they were covered in dark fluid that looked red even in the already-red light of the room.

"Wha –"

Again, the stranger's motions quieted Marcos. Marcos felt something tug at his abdomen. The stranger leaned down slightly and pushed, and when he stood straight again his arm was red to the elbow and the hand that had held the diamonds/rubies was completely empty.

"I know you'll bleed out before the drugs *really* hit, but I thought it fitting that you have half of what I found shoved up your ass and the other half pushed into your stomach."

Marcos opened his mouth. He felt something spill out, something sticky and warm and red. The spilling continued, and he realized then that his center was covered in the same warm stuff, as were the backs of his legs and buttocks.

He felt his pulse bouncing hard in his neck. Then softer and softer. He felt something let go inside him.

"Interesting," said the stranger. "I think your intestines just spilled out of your slit rectum," he said. "Which is definitely an appropriate note for someone like you to go out on."

Marcos tried to reach for the stranger. He thought about killing the man, about grabbing his throat and squeezing. But his hands wouldn't work. He couldn't even lift his arms.

He looked around and suddenly realized that he was in the production room. The noisy sound of fans and filters and machinery was quiet.

Damn him, I told Sergei to check that.

Wait, the guy musta done it.

Who is this guy?

How'd he wreck everything so fast?

I'll kill him. KILL HIM.

The thoughts came hard and fast, though each fled as fast as it came. By the end, he barely heard himself screaming, "*KILLLLLLLL HIIMMMMMMMMM!*" as he rode the thought into red-tinged silence, wondering how this could possibly have happened to the world's greatest Dungeon Master.

22

Danielle waited only seconds after the stranger named Legion departed before she finally looked at the precious item she had been holding since she took it from Sheldon's pet tree.

"It's quite an accomplishment to create a thing of beauty like that. I have to pinch the leaves, cut and prune them, use wire to train them…"

Sheldon's words, and the only thing that had given her an ember of hope, which blossomed into a flame – small, but a full flame nonetheless – when she reached for Lucy and found the bit of wire that she had hoped to find.

Now she shifted it in her palm until she could fit it in the small keyhole of the handcuff that locked her to the wall.

"What are you doing?" said Alex.

Aleksandr? Do I call him that now?

Disgust rippled through her at the sound of his voice. She wasn't sure if it was more at him for being who he was, or at herself for not spotting it in time. He was a sociopath, he was a liar, he was a *murderer*.

But she answered him just the same. Because that was what she had trained herself to do: to give everyone a chance. She had meant what she told Legion: there was a process, there was *law*, and she intended to have Alex brought to a police station – hobbling in on his broken leg and ankle and dripping blood from his toe stumps if necessary – and then she would testify in court about the things he had said and the things she now knew about him.

But that was different than just ignoring him; than turning her back on him. That was not what she did. Not what she had promised Jakey every day since he died.

So she said, "I'm trying to get us out of here," even though part of her wanted to ignore him – or better still, to scream and fling herself at Aleksandr and claw his lying tongue out. But she refused to give in to either hate or the need to control others that had defined her mother or, it turned out, her husband.

She would be better. She would make Jakey proud, and maybe he wouldn't stare at her in despair. Maybe if she did this he would finally close his eyes and find peace.

Aleksandr snorted. "What, you an expert in picking locks?" he said.

She stared at him. "I've been talking about this for months. My current client was accused of what I'm trying to do, and I've had to learn about it in order to represent him."

Another snort, this time from Demyan. She looked at him. The old man was glassy-eyed. Blood – which had streamed down his ankles when Sheldon first sliced him – had slowed to a trickle, but either the trauma or whatever he had taken to keep from suffering was rapidly overcoming him. Even if he received immediate medical attention Danielle didn't know if he would have pulled through.

Still, as weak as he was he managed to summon scorn – and the derisive sound that came from him was so exactly like the noise Aleksandr had made only a moment before that she would have known they were family even without having already been told.

"Studying something is different than actually doing it," said the old man. He mumbled in Russian and went limp for a moment and she would have thought he was dead if he hadn't shuddered and added, "Good luck picking your lock, little girl."

"Thanks," she said, sarcasm twisting the word in her mouth. Or maybe it was the fact that he was right: she wasn't getting anywhere with the handcuff lock.

She hadn't been lying: she really did study about the process while she prepared to defend Antoine Lewis, but Demyan was very right about the difference between studying a thing and actually doing it. She kept twisting the wire in the keyhole, but after a few minutes – each of which felt like a thousand lifetimes – she had to admit she wasn't going to be able to get the cuffs off.

It was about that time when the gunshots sounded. The door to the room was closed, so the sounds were muffled. But there was little doubt in Danielle's mind of what she heard.

She looked at Aleksandr. He flicked his eyes to her hand, still holding the wire. He laughed nervously. "Knew you wouldn't be able to."

"How stupid are you?" she demanded. "Would you prefer that I just give up?"

His face went from sarcastic to sullen in an instant. "Doesn't matter. You're dead no matter what."

"You mean *we* are," she said. "At least, if we don't get out of here." She almost couldn't believe his choice of words. Maybe it was just self-centered wishful thinking on his part, but she didn't think so. Aleksandr truly believed on some deep level that no matter what, he was going to come through this, just as her mother had believed to the very end that not even cancer would beat her. Like Danielle's mother, Aleksandr just couldn't believe in a universe that did not revolve around him, and so also believed the universe must and *would* fix this somehow. For him at least, though whether Danielle made it out would be largely irrelevant. Probably *worse* if she did, because then he'd have to worry about her knowing who he was.

How did I not see him for what he was?

Get mad at yourself later. For now, figure out how to get out of here.

She returned her attention to the handcuffs, going over what she had learned from Antoine as she prepared his defense. The lockpicking was out, sure, but that wasn't the only way to open a handcuff. The other way she knew wouldn't feel good, which was the reason she hadn't tried it first, but it was now the only option.

"Give it here," said Aleksandr. "Gimme the wire."

"Do you know what to do with it?" she said.

"Yeah," he said.

She saw the lie flash in his face as he said it. She turned away from him and geared up for what came next.

"Give it to me!" shouted Aleksandr. "I –"

"Shut up," said Demyan. Danielle looked at the old man again. He was staring at Aleksandr with an expression she couldn't understand. "You have always been stupid. Just like me, for loving your mother, and stupider still for loving you. But this woman here is not stupid, so *let her work*. Have dignity, if you can't have sense."

"I…" Aleksandr, clearly shocked at this display of anger, didn't know what to say for a moment. Finally he managed, "How can you say that to me?"

"Is truth," said Demyan. "And it is also true that this woman can save you if anyone can. So shut up and let her work."

Danielle nodded a quick thanks at Demyan, and somehow wasn't at all surprised that he looked only irritated; perhaps even angry. He had said that she was the best hope for his son, but that did not mean he liked her.

She examined the handcuff for a moment. She rolled the length of wire in her hand, wondering if she would be able to do what she had to. Antoine had been clear that doing it hurt, and if you did it wrong you could lose a hand.

You'll lose a lot worse – and for sure – if you don't get out of this.

Just about every handcuff in the world had a few similarities. Almost all of them used the same basic design, which was why the stranger had been able to use a key he pulled from inside himself –

(And who the hell is *he?)*

– to unlock the cuff from his own wrist. Modern handcuffs consisted of two rings typically connected by a short chain. Each ring was in two parts, one composed of a single arc of metal with teeth at the free end, the other of a double length that housed a ratchet mechanism. The ratchet mechanism was just a locking bar that a spring held in place against the toothed edge of the other half of the handcuff ring, and all a handcuff key did was push the locking bar away from the handcuff arm.

"Easy to shove it away with a bobby pin or even just a piece of thick wire," Antoine had constantly said during her interviews with him.

"Any other way out?" she had asked. "Since you didn't have any wire?"

"Sure. In a car you can maybe work the tongue of the seatbelt into the sleeve and try to pry it apart far enough the lock fails."

"Then the handcuff would show the damage. And it didn't have any, so is there any other way?"

Antoine had shrugged. "If you're willing to risk loss of blood, maybe nerve or muscle damage. But you still need wire or something to do it."

The last method Antoine had detailed was what she was trying now, since "easy to shove it away" hadn't proved that easy at all. This final way featured sliding something – in this case, the wire from Lucy's pot – between the teeth of the lock bar and the notched arm of the handcuff. Theoretically, as soon as the wire got between them, it would hold the grooves apart and would allow the handcuff to slide open.

The dangerous part was that to work the wire in she had to tighten the handcuff more than it already was, working the wire between the grooves a little more with every click of the ratchet mechanism. If a person slipped or did it wrong, they could be left with a handcuff that was so tight it cut off blood supply, pinched nerves, and – if left tight enough – could cause permanent damage.

Danielle didn't know if anyone was coming back for them. Things had changed too suddenly and strangely to know, so she hadn't opted for this latter means of getting out of her cuffs first. Now, however, with the "artful" way of opening them shut off to her, she found herself having to do it the "crude, boring way," as Antoine had put it.

She thought about trying to unlock the cuff on the ring, but could tell instantly that wouldn't work. She didn't have room to move the wire, push the cuff, and keep it steady as it flopped around on the ring. She would have to clamp the other cuff against her breast, trapping it there with her wrist while she worked on it with the other hand.

She did it, and pushed the wire into the small clearance space between the toothed arm of the handcuff and the sleeve of the other half. It barely went in at all before finding the obstacle created by the lock bar and the teeth on the other half of the handcuff ring. Gritting her teeth, Danielle pushed on the handcuff. It clicked, and tightened a bit.

The wire didn't go in at all.

All she had done was tighten the handcuff. It wasn't painful, but it was already uncomfortable, for sure. How long before it hurt too much to continue?

And how long before you're straight up killed *if you don't just suck it up and do this?*

She pushed the handcuff again. Again it clicked, again the wire didn't move in at all: proof she wasn't doing this right, since working the wire deeper was the key to it all.

"Try rotating… the wire… slightly… as you push," wheezed Demyan.

Danielle looked at him, a bit surprised he was still able to talk at all. He was clearly in a bad way, pale and starting to wheeze as his body coped with blood loss, broken bones, and poison. Still, his eyes were bright and fixed on what she was doing. For all his negative points, the guy was tough.

Danielle did as he said. She spun the wire slightly between her thumb and forefinger as she pushed this time. The wire sliced the pad of her thumb painfully and she almost let go, but thought of hugging Jakey and flipping off her mother and found the strength to hold on, to push harder… and was rewarded by the wire spinning deeper into the mechanism the next time she pushed.

Click.

The handcuff was tighter, but at least she was getting somewhere. She thought. Still, she didn't have a lot of wire to work with, and the handcuff now felt like it was compressing her bones. It hurt, and she didn't know how much tighter she could force it.

Click.

She pushed again, and again the wire followed the mechanism a bit deeper.

Mother's eyes frowned at her in her mind, as though to say, *"How dare you?"*

"Good. Good, that's it," said Demyan.

Aleksandr did not speak, but he looked at Danielle with something other than disdain for the first time, and she was surprised at the sudden reaction she felt:

He does *love me. He was just stressed. Just afraid.*

She knew it was a lie even as she thought it. Aleksandr *was* stressed, he *was* afraid. But the way he had reacted to those feelings had shown her his true colors. She had thought their lives suddenly blessed, and it had seemed like a dream, an omen. But wasn't that the reason so many of her clients made bad choices? Because they were trying to secure a life like that, a dreamlife that held no pain or struggle?

She had been swept off her feet into a fairy tale, a world with no dragons to be slain beyond the actions of unethical opposing counsel. But now she recognized the horror of a life without pain or difficulty. The struggles were what showed her true character, and the character of people around her. Those people could stand and fight with you, they could abandon you, or they could try and throw you to the dragon themselves in the hope that the dragon would be too busy eating you to focus on them.

Aleksandr was this last. And she hadn't known it because, quite simply, their lives had been too easy for her to realize such a thing was possible. He hadn't thrown her to the dragons before… but only because there hadn't been any dragons to run from.

The handcuff slid in another notch. It ate a bit more wire. *Click*. She pulled on the handcuff, thinking to release it. "Don't let go of the wire," whispered Demyan, in almost the same moment. "You'll have no chance if the wire slips to the side and jams. You have to hold it right in the middle, hold it in place until the cuff opens."

Danielle nodded. She twisted and pushed, twisted and pushed. Her wrist caught fire as the nerves in them ground between metal and bone. She gritted her teeth. Kept pushing, twisting, pushing, twisting. *Click, click, click*. The skin of her wrists striated into bands of bright white, bright red, and dull gray. The wire sliced her thumb until blood soaked her shirt and sleeve.

No more clicks. The wire wouldn't go in any farther.

She strained against the metal, gritting her teeth to keep from screaming as the band dug into her flesh. Her hand was numb, dead. She couldn't feel anything there.

How long does it take a hand to die?

Less time than you in this situation. PUSH!

It didn't help. Nothing did.

*"**Just a little harder.**"*

She jumped, startled at the voice. She saw Demyan, whose eyes had finally drifted completely shut. She saw Aleksandr, staring at her with a mix of rage and despair.

She didn't see the person who had spoken. She didn't see Jakey. But she had heard him. She knew she had.

"You're almost there," he said. Not here after all, but she was hearing the words, just as she saw his eyes the day he died, the day of his funeral, and every day after that as she tried to live life for two. Jakey was gone, but he also remained. He lived in her, and though that was a strange sort of afterlife, it was enough.

"Just a bit more," he urged.

Danielle dug inside her, past her mother's frown, into the place in her heart where she guarded Jakey's memory and the goodness she hoped to do in his name. She saw his eyes, his smile. She saw the sadness when he talked to her the last time, and for a moment she faltered. Then she remembered before that. The good times, the reasons – so many, many of them – that she loved her brother. She remembered stealing candy from the pantry and eating it together, hunched under a blanket they made into an impromptu tent. She remembered him teaching her to dance the waltz, and introducing her to his favorite video games.

She remembered his smile, and that smile another drop of strength into the hand that was pressing the handcuff. She pushed, and felt her grip slip against the metal. Blood slicked her fingers and –

Danielle had been half slumped against the wall, her body so focused on her hand and fingers, on the process of trying to loose herself, that the rest of her was nearly limp. Now she jerked fully upright as she realized:

she hadn't felt her fingers slipping over the metal of the handcuffs after all. She had felt the handcuff *itself* moving, the arm, sliding inward a millimeter more, *but no click.*

The wire had finally reached the point where the lock plate and the grooved teeth of the handcuff arm came together. The slim length of metal –

(Thank you, Lucy!)

– created a toothless buffer, allowing the arm to slip forward that last bit… then allowing it to slide back.

The hinge that connected the two halves of the handcuff bracelet swiveled. Her wrist caught fire again as blood trapped in her hand flowed at last up her arm, and as blood in her arm flooded into her hand. She almost screamed in pain.

"Good job," said Jakey.

Even though she knew he was dead, and the voice in her brain was really her own voice speaking in a pale imitation of his, she smiled and said, "Thanks, Jakey." Then the smile drifted away. She was free of the handcuffs. Now she just had to get free of this *place.*

"Hey! Get me out of here! Get us out of here, babe!" shouted Aleksandr. She looked at him. At his handsome face, twisted to such cruel expressions only moments before. He was smiling again, and she saw how real-looking it was and understood how easy it would be for anyone to fall into such a smile. Even now, knowing what she did, nearly everything in her screamed that this was his real face; that this was the *real* man.

She thought again of her mother. Of how she was the nicest, kindest person around… so long as she *wanted* to be that person. So long as being that person was the best, quickest way to get what she wanted. Then, when thwarted, she became a stone-cold killer.

Aleksandr is like her.

He's killed people.

He would have killed me.

She stared at the wire she had kept a grip on as her handcuff slipped free. She looked at Aleksandr's cuffs.

"Babe?" he said. Again she looked at him, at the expression he wore: deep, sincere, loving. "Sorry I snapped." He grimaced. "I was just scared."

Another moment passed. Danielle knew she should get out of here. She knew she should run. That would be the pragmatic thing, the *safe* thing to do.

Aleksandr screamed, his kind expression crumbling once more, leaving behind a ruin of selfish rage. *"Get me the hell outta here!"*

Danielle walked out of the room.

23

Legion watches Marcos fall to pieces – literally.

When he first came down here, he was worried. He didn't usually do things this way. He had braced many ignorant evildoers in their most secure places, but usually it was after weeks or even months of study and surveillance. He wondered if he was doing the right thing.

But watching Marcos and his crew had convinced Legion that he was on the right path. Watching Marcos slip into a final coma induced by the powerful combination of illegal drugs and loss of blood was a fitting way to show Marcos the error of his ways, and now Legion knows beyond a shadow of doubt that he is meant to be here.

He remembers feeling like he was led to this place, and though he still does not know *what* led him here, he knows now that that feeling was real.

Legion lost his brothers during their last attempt to educate and refine other lives. But even death has not stilled Fire and Water, not really. They continue to live in him, and as Marcos slides into a messy, ignominious death they both laugh as one.

"This is *fun!*" shouts Fire as the pool of red around Marcos spreads out. The blood touches Fire's ever-burning feet, sending puffs of steam upward. Legion knows this is not real, that it is only in his mind, but he likes the effect. Just as he likes the sound of Water sliding his own waterlogged shoes forward as he dances in the blood of the dead man and sings Blue Öyster Cult's "Don't Fear The Reaper."

Legion smiles at them both.

"Are you done?" he says a moment later, and can't help but laugh a bit as Fire sticks out the blackened, curl twig of his tongue and says, "Buzzkill."

Water chuckles at them both, water droplets spraying all around – wetting nothing beyond Water himself – as he shakes his head ruefully. "He's right, we probably should get going." Then he grows suddenly serious. "It's different, isn't it?"

Legion knows what he is saying – of course he does. This is a different way of doing things. The One did the same things the same way for so long. The One watched, and instructed in the most dire and eternal ways. Now Legion is alone – in reality if not in his mind – and things are changing.

"Yes," he says. "Everything is different."

In a low, almost haunted tone very different from the bluster he usually evinces, Fire says, "But is that a bad thing?"

Legion does not know. Bad or not, there is work to be done. There is evil to find, and evildoers to teach.

He hears something behind him. A small sound no louder than the sound of a hummingbird's wing slashing the air, but it alerts Legion just in time. He spins and as he does something inside him screams that he must fall back. He allows the instinct to take control of him, and that saves his life. The knife aimed at his carotid artery instead draws only a thin gash across the base of his neck. He feels blood well out and knows he will have one more scar to add to the well-traveled pain mapped over the whole of his body.

Legion reacts automatically. The man – Sheldon, he sees now – brings up a gun, and Legion knocks it away from him. The gun clatters into the room, disappearing into the bloody gloom.

Sheldon barely pauses. He switches his grip, reversing the arc of the knife so that it flashes in the red light. Again Legion falls back, stumbling a bit this time, realizing that he lost Sergei's push dagger at some point. Sheldon presses his momentary opening, thrusting again and again with his knife. Legion dances away each time, but each time the blade nips him and draws blood.

When at last he fully regains his footing, he takes a huge leap back and stands, panting.

The other man smiles brightly, a sincere grin that echoes the glee in his eyes. "You're fast," he says. "Most people aren't fast enough to get away from me even for a moment."

Unlike Legion, he breathes easily. He passes his knife from hand to hand, flicking it and flipping it end over end like a juggler at a circus. Then he pulls another blade from somewhere at his back. Things have just gone from bad to worse.

"You're… fast as well," Legion wheezes.

"Don't let him think he's better than you," says Fire. The embers that burn within him flash brightly.

"Shut… up," Legion barks, looking at his brother.

Sheldon looks surprised. "Who are you talking to?" he asks. Without warning, he lunges with his blade and Legion barely manages to avoid being cut. "Fast," says Sheldon. He looks at the – to him – empty air that Legion spoke into. "Crazy as a loon, though."

"You… should talk," gasps Legion. He has cuts at his chest, both arms, and one leg. He has been shot in the side. Blood runs down his body in rivulets that may tear open and become rivers at any moment. "Totally… bonkers," he manages.

Sheldon reacts unexpectedly. He laughs. "So many people think that," he says between hoots of mirth. "But you know what I think? I think they just say that to keep from being angry."

"About… what?"

Sheldon opens his mouth to speak. Then seems to realize for the first time that Marcos lays slumped on the floor nearby. He gasps. "What did you do?" he says.

"He wasn't a very good man," says Legion.

Sheldon turns on him. "Not a good *man*?" he says incredulously. "Do you know how mad this is going to make our mother?"

Legion blinks; it is his turn to be surprised. "You're his –"

He doesn't have time to finish. Sheldon roars and rushes Legion. And as fast as he was already, rage seems to have fueled him to even greater speed and strength. Legion twists and turns, but feels three more gashes open on his body.

When he at last puts some distance between himself and Sheldon, he eyes the man. Legion is wheezing hard, and can see that his gasps are not lost on his enemy. Sheldon grins at him, but now the grin is an angry one.

"I was always going to kill you," says Sheldon. "But now I'm going to do it so it really hurts."

"Wasn't that… the plan anyway?" Legion manages. He takes a step back, wincing as he puts weight on the leg that is now a criss-cross of bloody gashes.

Sheldon's gaze flickers, going somewhere only half seen. "Yeah," he admits. "But I'm really going to try my hardest to make it last days. Weeks."

Legion steps back, nearly slipping on something soft and squishy that he suspects is a part of Marcos' small intestine. "You're good… at your job, huh?" he manages. A random sentence he knows Sheldon will see as a desperate ploy for time.

Sheldon shrugs. "I'm good at most things I do. It's kind of a curse." He looks sadly at his brother. "Poor guy. He was a weirdo, and I was probably going to kill him, too, but –"

"Then why do you care if *I* do it?" says Legion. He glances around. Fire and Water are standing at right angles to Sheldon. It would be a perfect flanking maneuver – if only they were still here, still flesh as Legion is flesh.

"Because you're not family," says Sheldon. He sighs. "Look, I don't really want to get into this with you. I doubt you'd understand it anyway."

"Watch out," says Water. He holds out a hand, water spraying off his skin in droplets that hang like rubies in the red light, then fall and twinkle out of existence before touching the floor.

Legion does not need the warning. He sees the subtle shift in Sheldon's posture, the sudden tightening of his grip on his knives.

Sheldon springs forward. He is the fastest man Legion has ever met. Legion twists, but knows the motion will be too slow to avoid Sheldon's final, fatal cut.

"This is it," breathe both Fire and Water in one voice, knowing as Legion does that this is the end.

24

Alex Anton – Aleksandr Antonovich, to those who knew him as a child, before the old man he thought was his guardian angel gave him a new and better name – watched Danielle loose herself, and felt a certain satisfaction. He could have gotten himself loose, he had no doubt, but this way was easier.

Maybe I really did *pick someone worth having as a wife. Not* forever, *of course, but she certainly panned out for now.*

Of course, that was before the bitch walked out on him. He stared after her as she left, then looked at the empty hole of the open doorway in this bizarro place. It seemed to mock him somehow, like an eye widened by surprise that someone as mousy and vanilla as Danielle had been the one to leave in the relationship.

Alex knew he would kill her. He would get out of his handcuffs somehow, because the universe always bent itself to him.

That was when you had a guardian angel, though. What about now?

He tried to silence that voice inside him that warned that perhaps – just perhaps – everything had changed. He looked at the old man on the floor, the one whom Alex had thought had devoted celestial attention to making his life go smoothly, easily, *perfectly*.

"Not an angel after all."

The old man, who had been so silent and still for the last few seconds that Alex had thought he must be dead –

cracked an eye. He found the energy to smile thinly. "Is that what you thought I was?" he snorted, though the effort of even such a small motion seemed to cost him enormously. "Such a disappointment."

Alex almost said, "Yes, you are," then realized that the man wasn't talking about himself. He was talking about *Alex*. But that was impossible, wasn't it?

"How can you say that?" he said.

The man's eyes closed. Again Alex thought the man must have died. Again he was proven wrong as the man answered, "How can you not *understand* the reason I would say it?"

Alex felt like crying. Not because the Demyan had actually hurt him – the old fart couldn't hurt a dying worm at this point. But the words were *unfair*. They weren't *true*. Alex wasn't a disappointment at all; the universe loved him. The universe had always provided for him, and always would.

And that was why it was no surprise at all when he glanced up and saw that Danielle had come back into the room. A bleeding heart that was here to "save him." Which he would let her do. He would smile and whisper sweet nothings and she would release him. The lovestruck moron would probably smile as he strangled her.

"Hey, babe," he said, and rattled his cuffed hand against the ring. "Come to rescue me?"

He had no guardian angel. But he had the universe. And he supposed that, at least for now, that would do.

25

Sheldon loved moments like these: the instant when his victims saw the end. They might see it minutes or hours or days or sometimes even weeks before they actually *died,* but at some point he always saw the flicker of realization when they realized they were outclassed, outsmarted. The revelation that came to all of them when they looked into their futures and saw nothing but Sheldon's smile followed by total and eternal darkness.

That was what Sheldon knew he would see now. The loon who killed Marcos had gotten out of his bonds somehow, and that was troubling. More troubling was the fact that he somehow killed every one of Marcos' people, then Marcos himself.

But it would all be worth it. Sheldon would cut the man, he would bleed him dry and make him pay for daring to stand against Sheldon's plans, however ineffectually. The stranger was gasping, bleeding, slipping on legs made weak under Sheldon's relentless, expert attack. And now, lunging across the final centimeters before his blade punched a hole in this troublesome stranger, Sheldon searched the other man's eyes for that all-powerful *moment…*

… and did not see it.

He expected to see the realization of doom. He expected to see pain and fear.

Instead he got something he had never seen before in any of the men and women he had tortured and killed and disposed of through the years: glee.

The stranger had been moving fast, but not fast enough to completely avoid Sheldon's cuts. He had been winded and wounded and on the edge of collapse. But as Sheldon slashed at him for the final time, the pain and weariness suddenly disappeared from his eyes, his gasping breathing mellowed to something Sheldon would have expected to see in an athlete during the first moments of a long-awaited game.

The man was excited. He was happy. He was *not* afraid or tired; hell, Sheldon didn't even think the guy looked *inconvenienced.*

Oh sh –

Sheldon didn't even have time to finish the thought as the stranger turned to the side, effortlessly allowing Sheldon's knives to skate past him and wound nothing more substantial than air. Then, moving so fast that even Sheldon's better-than-perfect vision could not follow, the stranger stepped inside the arc of Sheldon's attack.

Sheldon couldn't believe how fast the guy was. Faster than anything he'd ever seen. Still, coming to him like that had been a mistake. He was inside Sheldon's reach, so close it almost looked like the guy was trying to hug Sheldon. Sheldon reversed his grip on one of his knives and drove it down hard. The knife blade pierced the stranger's back, cutting through his torso and ending in his heart. The stranger stiffened and then fell.

Sheldon saw it all the way it had to happen.

So why… why was the stranger still standing there? Why was he smiling? Why was he… he…

Sheldon looked down. Saw *both* of his own knives punched through the right side of his chest. He suddenly felt like an elephant was stepping on his sternum, bearing down on him. He tried to suck in air, but only a strange bubbling came out.

"You sound like my brother," said the stranger. "He's dead, but he's always bubbling."

"What the… hell… does…" The words dissolved in Sheldon's throat, turning to a red sludge that curled over his lips and drenched his shirt.

The stranger reached out and, almost delicately, twisted one of the knives –

(Hemingway! How could you do this to me?)

– embedded in Sheldon's lung. Sheldon tried to scream, but the attempt made him feel like drowning.

"Your lung's filling up with blood," said the stranger. "Which I know is a particularly unpleasant way to go." He twisted the other knife. "At least, given the time constraints we're working with."

Sheldon tried to say something. He couldn't. The blood filling his lungs had pressed out the air he needed. He couldn't talk, couldn't even breathe.

But I'm so good *at breathing. Better than most, I'd say.*

The thought was strange – maybe even crazy. But it kept coming back, repeating over and over.

The stranger yanked both knives out of him. Blood gouted, then just frothed at the ragged edges of the wounds.

"You're a kidnapper, a murderer, and a torturer. Normally I'd spend more time thinking of a really *fitting* way to teach you some important life lessons, but time is short." Then he looked to the side again and frowned before saying, "I *know* we don't have much time. You don't have to keep reminding me."

Sheldon looked at the empty space into which the stranger was speaking. He didn't understand. His wounds hurt and he desperately wanted to see Lucy and his mother. He was her favorite – Marcos never talked to her, refused even to visit her. But Sheldon did. All the time. He visited her and Mother loved him and she would make things all better. She always did. She was the best and most beautiful and most wonderful thing he knew.

The thought spiraled down a dark red river. Sheldon's mouth opened wide and he felt like the blood came so fast and thick it must have left him hollow inside. It washed down his chest, soaked his waist. He fell, and now the knees of his pants saturated and grew sticky as he knelt in the pool of his own rapidly-exiting lifesblood.

The stranger put a finger to his lips. "Don't try to talk," he said. "There's nothing you could say that would change how much you deserve this."

Sheldon slid into nothing, wondering to the last if he would be very good at dying.

Probably better than most people. After all, I'm very good at most th –

26

Legion stares down at the man who is dying. His lungs bubble with blood.

"Yuck," says Fire.

"Don't like it?" says Water. "I find the sound soothing."

"Of course you do. It sounds like big wet farts," says Fire. Turning to Legion he says, "Can we burn the next one alive?"

Legion does not answer. He stares at Sheldon, watching him go from darkness to darkness. He knows that the man was evil – not just in what he has *done* to this point, but in the very things he *feels*. Legion has sensed from the beginning that Sheldon believed himself better than everyone, and that is both his greatest sin, and the source of his downfall. It was easy for Legion to fool him, to pretend to greater pain and exhaustion than he actually felt, to supply the pretense that this man was on top of the situation.

Perhaps this man *was* formidable, in a way. To the average person, he no doubt has been able to bring a pain that debilitates their minds, that wears down their emotions.

But what is a knife cut – or even six or eight or ten or a *hundred* – to a man like Legion? Such things pale when compared to a life that began in death, that continued in pain and Dark Places; and not for minutes or hours, but for long years?

Legion is a good fighter. When he grimaces in pain, it is to draw in the proud. When he slips on blood, it is a purposeful action that brings out the merciless. Both pride and vindictiveness are malevolent tumors of the soul, and Legion adds them to the already enormous blotches on Sheldon's soul.

Sometimes Legion lets his students live. Sometimes he permits them a chance at redemption, and a few – a very few – avail themselves of this chance. And there are many people whom he feels no compunction to punish at all.

The world is full of good people, and that gives him hope. But Sheldon is definitely *not* good. He is, in fact, beyond any chance of redemption. So Legion watches the man struggle for breath. Watches him gasp as he drowns himself – fitting, to die in a way that forces his own body to betray him, just as his own soul has betrayed so many others.

"*Can* we burn the next one?" asks Fire again.

Legion holds up a hand for silence. Another moment, one last bubbling inhalation, one last exhale of red froth… then nothing. Sheldon is dead.

The world is a better place for it.

"Let's go," he says, and turns back into the tunnels of the place. Time is short, but there are still people down here, they still require his attention, and he has less and less time left to properly see to what must be done.

27

Danielle only got a few feet down the hall before stopping. She didn't know which way to go. Not just in the sense that she wasn't sure which direction would take her out of here, but also because she sensed she was at a crossroads.

She saw her brother – wrongfully imprisoned, dead before his time. He looked at her as he always did, with a woeful kind of resignation. He had sounded happy and proud when she got herself loose of the handcuffs; had given her the strength to do it, in fact. But now, in her mind she saw him sad again.

She saw her mother. Cold, sharp. Mother's eyes were the eyes of someone who had beaten justice time after time. She had money, she had power. She had everything she needed to live the most selfish of lives, and never to be harmed by any force less powerful than nature itself.

Danielle didn't know why she stopped. She didn't know why those twin sets of eyes that always haunted her now seemed to do far more. They had overtaken her, and for a moment she wondered if they had *become* her. Was she to become a victim, or a selfish sociopath?

For a moment, those were the only two choices. The bunker, the halls, the rooms… it all disappeared. All that remained was her in an empty void with only the ghosts of her past – and possibly her future – to keep her company.

A long moment. An eternity of reviewing all she knew of her mother, all she knew of her brother. She looked at them both, and looked inside herself to see which she would be.

And decided she would be neither.

That was why she turned around and went back to the place from which she had just escaped. She stepped back into the room where Alex – *Aleksandr* – remained chained. Where her husband's father lay in a pool of his own blood on the floor.

"Hey, babe," said Aleksandr. He bounced his wrist, making his handcuff tinkle. The sound rang almost obscene in this blood-colored place. "Come to rescue me?"

"No," she answered. "To rescue myself."

Aleksandr's face went blank, and Danielle could see that he didn't understand – just as she could see that he decided to discard it. The sentence didn't make sense to him, ergo it didn't *matter* to him, ergo it couldn't possibly have any importance at all. "Cool," he said. "So…" He rattled his handcuff again.

"You deserve to go to jail," she said to him.

"Fine, fine," he said. "But that's something we can't do down here, right?"

"Lay on the ground," she said.

Aleksandr opened his mouth, and she saw his intent to complain, to wheedle, to whine. It was a look she had seen in her job a hundred times… but had missed the one time it mattered most. She had been blind, but now she saw clearly.

"Shut your mouth and do it."

Aleksandr's eyes flashed with rage, but he forced the rest of his face to soften. "Sure, babe," he said. "Whatever you say. Just get me out of here and we'll make everything right."

Again she saw what lay behind his eyes, his smile. She saw the intent to get out of here, and the further intent to kill her as well. She had become a liability, but she knew that was not what doomed her in his sight. No, that had come earlier – the moment she became an *inconvenience*.

Aleksandr shifted so that he was laying on the ground, the hand with the mangled fingers hanging off the cuff and the ring.

"On your stomach," she said.

"Babe, what –"

"*Now*." She spoke in a low tone, but one that brooked no argument. "We can argue until they come back, or you can do what I say and we get out of here."

"Sure. Whatever you say."

He flipped over, groaning as his cracked leg and ankle scraped the floor, as the toe stumps at the end of his bare foot leaked more blood.

"Grab the ring," said Danielle.

"I can't – my hand."

"You still have one good one," she said, her tones clipped. "Use it."

He sighed – all the burdens of the world on him, and now *this*, she could practically hear him thinking – and then scooched back so that he was laying at a perpendicular to the wall, his good fingers grasping the ring as tightly as possible. His knees and thighs lay on the floor, his hips pressed into the cold surface.

Danielle waited. "Move back as far as you can."

For once, Aleksandr didn't fight the order. He just moved back farther so that he was stretched out to full length. "Now what?" he said through gritted teeth.

"Now I get your cuff off you and we get out of here."

"Then why the hell do I have to –"

He cut off as Danielle edged toward him. He tensed, and she could see he was getting ready to throw himself at her the moment he could. "You so much as twitch, or if I see a single finger come off the ring, then I run. You could maybe catch me, but I doubt it. And if that happens, then I leave you here to rot. Good luck getting out with a busted ankle, busted leg, and one good hand."

"Could *you* get out of here without *me*?" he asked, as though the answer was a self-evident negative. But his fingers stayed clamped on the ring in the wall.

Danielle still saw death in his eyes. He would wait until he was free, then would throw himself upon her and either maim her and leave her for dead in this place or just kill her outright.

"Don't even think about it."

"I wouldn't dream – *AUGH*!"

Aleksandr screamed as Danielle kicked out, hard and fast. She wanted to take him by surprise, but part of her speed was simply that she did not want to give herself a chance to think about what she had to do. There was a brittle, rustling crackle as her heel smashed down on his remaining good fingers. The ring he held served as a fulcrum, bending the fingers hard over it and smashing the bones to kindling.

Aleksandr continued screaming, screaming.

"Shut up," she said. She jerked her head toward the door. "Unless you want anyone out there to hear you and hurry back."

"Why?" he managed. The clinking of his handcuff chain did not quite mask the raw sound as he prised his fingers away from the ring to which they had been pressure molded.

"Because she is not stupid," said a weak voice. Danielle glanced behind her. Demyan smiled at her from his place on the floor. "Because she sees you at last."

Danielle turned away, trying to think of what to do about the old man.

"I don't under… under…" Aleksandr's voice broke.

"You're wrong," she said. The weariness in her voice did not surprise her, but the fact that there was nothing of betrayal or hurt there did, at least a little. "I'm very stupid. But that's life, right? We're stupid so much of the time, and that's what makes us people. But we try to do better, and that's what makes us *good* people." She shook her head, watching with disgust as Aleksandr wept. "Most of us, anyway." She stepped closer. "So I'm trying to do better here. I'm not going to leave you down here to die, but I don't want to let you go to kill me, either. You've only got one leg, so you'll have to hop out of here. But I figure with all your fingers hashed you won't be able to choke me or hit me with something before I get you out of here and then take you to a police station where I sincerely hope you get a *fair* trial."

At that moment, the hairs on the back of Danielle's neck raised. She turned, but even before she had completed the movement she knew what she would see. Maybe it was the way he had ignored having a knife drawn over his chest, or the way he had so easily killed the giant Sergei even with his shoulder dislocated… and then so casually and quietly knocked that shoulder back into place by bashing it against the wall.

Mostly, though, it was his eyes. Somewhere inside her, she had known that he would be the one to return. No one else.

Just the stranger. Legion.

He gazed at her now, eyes going from Danielle to Aleksandr to Demyan. Blood dripped from numerous wounds on his arms and legs, and Danielle could see that some of them were severe enough to require stitches if not outright hospitalization. But as bad as they were, they weren't enough to account for all the blood on his clothes and skin. He looked like he had been dipped in crimson paint. It pooled at his feet, dripped from his clothes. Streams of it ran down the blade of the knife he held easily in one hand.

As when she had returned to the room, Danielle acted instinctively. She moved to stand between the stranger and Aleksandr. In that moment she could not have told anyone *why*. The man was scum.

But it didn't matter. Scum did not deserve whatever the stranger had planned for him, or for anyone else.

"Don't do it," she said.

"What am I going to do?" asked the stranger. Before she could answer he turned slightly and spoke to the empty air. "Of course *I* know what I'm going to do." Then he turned to the other side. "Because she said not to do it, and that means she thinks she knows what I'm going to do, and I want to see if she actually knows." He turned back to her. "So?" he said.

The moment was so strange, so surreal, that Danielle's words utterly failed her. She tried to say something, but nothing came out. She just opened and closed her mouth, repeated the motion, then settled in open-mouthed confusion.

The stranger nodded. "I thought not." He glanced at Aleksandr. Then back at her. "I think –" He broke off as Demyan moaned. The old man was, somehow, still alive.

The stranger grimaced. "Sorry," he said to Danielle. He turned to Demyan, then almost jauntily reached down, grabbed the man's hair, and lifted him so high his shoulders left the floor.

"No!" Danielle shouted.

She was too late. The stranger drew his knife across Demyan's throat. It wasn't the blade he'd taken from Sergei, but a much longer knife she recognized as Sheldon's.

A red line appeared on Demyan's neck. For a moment it appeared too thin for such a large blade to have drawn, then the slit gaped like a hungry maw. Blood surged out. Pumped twice in arcs that splashed halfway across the room. Demyan shuddered and sagged. With an oddly gentle motion, the stranger lowered Demyan to the floor and watched as the last bits of life leaked from the old man's body.

"Who – *what* – are you?" said Danielle quietly.

"I'm Legion," said the stranger, just as quietly. He cocked his head. "Didn't I already tell you that?" He turned his head side to side, staring at the same empty spots he had spoken to a moment before. "Well, it seems like we can't agree. Water thinks I did tell you, but Fire isn't so sure." He shrugged. "Whether I did or not, here it is again: my name is Legion. Which is a strange name, I know, but I like it and it makes sense if you know me. Besides, it's only a few days old and I figure I'll grow into it."

He nudged Demyan's body with his toe. "But you didn't ask who I was, I suppose; you asked me *what* I was. And I have to confess, I'm not really sure. Not anymore. I used to match, and it was all so simple. Now…"

Danielle said nothing. She didn't understand much of what he had said – the words were English, but strung together in ways that just didn't register. "What are you going to do?" she asked. She tried not to look at Demyan's still form, but averting her eyes just brought her to Sergei's body. Death everywhere.

"I'm not one hundred percent sure just yet. But I do know this," Legion said, his voice drawing her gaze back to him. "I was led to this place. I am here for a purpose."

"Killing people?" she said, looking at Demyan.

Legion again nudged the dead man with his toe. "The ones who deserve it. Who won't learn."

"We don't deserve it! We can learn!" said Aleksandr loudly. He had been silent this whole time, waiting no doubt to see which way the wind blew during this strange tableau. "Let us go!" He shook his still-cuffed arm, then cried out as the motion sent shockwaves through the fingers Sheldon had crushed. "At least let *me* go."

"Why just you?" said Legion.

"Why me?" Aleksandr. His mouth gaped. "What have I ever done to you? I've been kidnapped, knocked out, chained up –" He rattled his cuffed hand again, and again drew a cry of pain with the motion. "And this crazy *bitch* just crushed what's left of my hand!"

"That's not very nice," said Legion. "But then, I listened to everything that everyone said while I was in here, and you don't seem very nice, yourself, so I guess I can't expect you to say nice things."

Danielle said nothing, but couldn't help shrink back as he stared at her. "Why did you hurt his hand?" said Legion. He looked to the side – that empty space – and said, "I *know*. Give me a sec! Sheesh." Legion looked back at her, crossed his arms, and said, "Well?"

"Because she's *crazy*," said Aleksandr. "She –"

Legion turned lifeless eyes on him. "If you talk again before I ask you to I'll cut out your tongue."

Aleksandr shut his mouth so hard Danielle thought he probably cracked a tooth or two. Legion nodded, waiting a moment before turning back to Danielle and saying, "Well?"

"Because I wanted to keep him from hurting me," she said.

Legion shrugged. "Then just leave him here." She shook her head. He squinted. "No? Why not?"

Danielle couldn't answer. She didn't know what to say, and even if she had thought of something that might make sense to this madman, she doubted she could have put it into words.

Just the same, Legion nodded as though she had answered. He looked to his left. Cocked an eyebrow. "You think?" He waited, nodded, then turned to his right. "What about you?" Another nod. He leaned over and began picking up the bits of Sergei's gun from where he had dropped them on the floor. He pushed the pieces back together, his hands moving so fast they were a blur.

"What are –" began Aleksandr. He clapped his jaw shut again as Legion turned halfway around, and this time he *did* crack a tooth. He groaned and spat and Danielle heard the *tic-tic-tic* of something hard bouncing across the floor.

Legion sighed. Then, still moving with that preternatural speed, he pulled the magazine from his pocket and slapped it home. "I think I'm going to take one of you out of here," he said. "But which one?"

He looked at Danielle. "You aren't very good at hurting people."

"I –"

"No, no, don't say anything. It's a good thing. But Aleksandr's fingers aren't as bad as you think they are, and certainly not as bad as he's pretending."

With that, he tossed the gun on the floor. It clattered into the space between Aleksandr and Danielle.

She moved as fast as she could. Aleksandr was on the move, too, lurching toward the gun. Legion was right: Aleksandr's fingers were sprained, bruised, but they were flexing as he reached for the gun. His cuff stopped him only an inch shy of reaching it.

Danielle swept her foot across the floor, shoving the gun away from them both. It ricocheted off the wall and fetched up against Demyan's body.

Legion sighed. "Really?" he said. Staring at Danielle, he said, "Fine, if you don't like the gun, then choose who dies."

"Why don't I get to –" began Aleksandr.

"CHOOSE!"

Legion's shout was deafeningly loud. For a moment Danielle saw a madness beyond anything she had ever known, fighting to free itself from whatever shackles held it imperfectly in abeyance.

"NO!" she shouted back, just as loud and almost as fierce. She wouldn't play his game. Even if it meant she forfeited, she wasn't going to participate in whatever twisted version of justice Legion was acting out.

He smiled tightly. "Fine. But someone has to. You don't want to, so I guess I'll let *him* decide."

He threw the gun to Aleksandr, who caught it and without hesitation aimed it at Danielle. "You'll let me out if I decide?" he asked.

"Free as a bird," said Legion.

Aleksandr smiled. He shrugged at Danielle. "Sorry, babe," he said. "It was fun while it lasted."

He pulled the trigger. Danielle felt something punch into her, and darkness fell instantly over her. She felt herself hit the floor, and after that she rode a dark wave into emptiness, watched over by the eyes of her brother and bearing a single thought in her head: if she had to die, she hoped there was something *after*, because it would be nice to see Jakey again.

28

Danielle had never thought much about what Heaven might be like. She was sure, however, that it shouldn't involve a painfully throbbing headache.

She tried to open her eyes, and was possessed of a strange sense of *déjà vu.* She was seatbelted into the front seat of a car she knew: the car of a madman. She looked down and there was Lucy, his tree, sitting on the floor by her feet.

But when she shifted her eyes a bit more, she did not see Sheldon. She saw Legion.

He was not watching her. He was staring at the road ahead, tension visible in the way he hunched his shoulders and the hard lines of his clenched jaw.

She fumbled at the latch on her door, thoughts ajumble but still clear enough to know that she had to get out of this place and get away from this man.

Whump.

A dull pounding throbbed through her body. She wondered if she was having a stroke; if this was the last moment before Aleksandr's gunshot killed her.

WHUMP.

This time the feeling was different. Louder. It almost felt like…

WHUMP.

The third explosion she heard bucked the entire car forward.

She slammed against the seatbelt.

Darkness returned.

29

"Oh, good, you're up."

Danielle flinched. She wasn't in Sheldon's car anymore. She was in a van. It was dark outside.

Beside her, the stranger drove.

"What… I thought… I thought I was dead."

"Not you, Danielle. You're too tough for that."

She frowned. The flexing of even the minute muscles in her forehead caused her head to throb, and that pain led automatically to remembering the pain when Aleksandr had shot her. She gasped and clutched at the back of her head. "I was shot. I was –"

Legion reached out and patted her on the shoulder. The move was so odd, so out of place, and yet so obviously heartfelt that it stopped her panic dead. "No one shot you. I did have to knock you down, though."

"Knock me down?" Danielle shook her head. "Why… why do that?"

"Well, you were in the way." Legion's eyes went to the rearview mirror. "I know, but I also didn't want her fighting me on the way out. There wasn't time for that," he said.

Danielle didn't bother turning to see who he was speaking to. She knew she wouldn't see anyone there.

She felt the back of her head. An egg-sized lump was growing there. "Not shot," she said. Her tongue felt thick and the road ahead of them kept swaying back and forth like a child's swing. "You did it."

"Yes," said Legion. "I had things to do, and I had to do them quickly." He looked at her with a strangely regretful expression. "I didn't think you'd just sit there and let me do them in the time I had, so…" He mimed hitting the back of his head and grinned.

"I heard something."

"Oh, that would be the explosions." Legion correctly interpreted her look of confusion and explained: "You were in a meth lab. I set up some plastique on a timer near the solar cells I found – they really weren't hidden *that* well, all things considered – and knocked out the power. That was when it got dark. You follow me?"

She nodded, as much by rote as anything – she wasn't at all sure she followed *anything* this man said.

"So the power was out, and the place we were in, well… Meth labs have a tendency to explode if not watched over very carefully. Especially when you've also set up explosives that shut down all venting systems." A smile of the sort you might see on a child shyly proud of a school science project crept across his face. He laughed, flicking his eyes at the rearview mirror again. "Yes, Water, you were always much better than me about the technical stuff." A shrug. "But we do the best we can with what we have, right?"

"All gone…" She said the words quietly, already knowing the answer to her next question. "And the people?"

He shrugged. "I imagine they are in a bunch of very small pieces." He looked suddenly concerned. "But don't worry! Most of them were already dead, so it's all right that they blew up."

The road had stopped bobbing about quite so much, but Danielle still felt like she was in the grips of a bad dream. And just as in a bad dream, she felt powerless over herself and couldn't have stopped the next words even had she desired to do so. "Most of them?"

He looked at her. "Most of them," he repeated. He didn't elaborate, and she could tell by the hard cast of his face that he wasn't going to.

She looked away. The darkness outside was complete. There was no way to know where they were, or where they were going. For some reason that didn't bother her as much as she thought it should.

Concussion.

"And Alex?"

"Alek*sandr*," Legion corrected. "He was going to try to kill you, you know. I could tell. Nothing to teach you at all, but he was going to kill you just the same which is pretty rotten."

The dream sensation changed. Horror and shock mixed with a level of anger that she recognized might get her killed if she wasn't careful. But she couldn't help it, the words just spilled out. "*Rotten*? You *killed* that old man –"

"– a Russian mobster, also rotten –"

"– and you gave the gun to Alex –"

"– Aleksandr –"

"– in the first place, so what did you expect him to do?"

Legion shrugged. "Pretty much exactly what he did. But don't worry, he wouldn't have killed you. He couldn't have. Not with an unloaded gun."

Danielle remembered Legion putting the pieces of Sergei's gun together. Remembered him pulling the magazine from his pocket and slapping it home.

But did I see that? Or was he moving so fast I couldn't tell the difference between him putting in a magazine and just miming *doing it?*

"Why do all that?"

Legion sighed. When he spoke, he didn't exactly sound exasperated, but more resigned to not being understood. "Because normally I have more time to watch and wait and figure out what people need. Who needs education, and how much pain they require to learn. But I didn't have the time." He cast a sidelong glance at her. "I thought you were a good person. I wasn't *sure* at first, but when the chips were down you came back to get Aleksandr and even stood up for him – even though he didn't deserve it. Aleksandr, on the other hand, struck me as the kind of person you definitely wouldn't want to continue on his ignorant, destructive path. But I wanted to have a final quick test. An unloaded gun. You passed."

"And Aleksandr? What happened to him?" asked Danielle.

"He didn't pass," said Legion. "He was not a good person, Danielle. Not like you are. You stuck to your guns, you made choices that helped others."

"I broke his fingers."

Shut up*, Danielle. Are you so much of a lawyer you have to argue no matter what? Are you trying to talk this maniac into killing you?*

Legion chuckled. "Not very well. Besides, I was listening outside and I know it was a good call. You did it to protect yourself, but – and this is an important *but* – you didn't abandon anyone. You're a good person. You don't deserve my attention."

He said "attention" with a totally normal inflection. And that totally normal word, spoken in a totally normal tone, made Danielle's skin feel like it was trying to crawl into her bones.

"What… what are you going to do now?" she said.

Again Legion glanced in his rearview mirror. "Either of you have any answers to that one?" He waited, nodded, then looked back at Danielle and said, "Just more of the same." He smiled, then added, "Here's your stop."

He pulled over to the side of the road, coming to a dead stop, though he kept the engine running. Danielle waited, afraid to move.

"You can go," he said.

"Go?"

"You're something of a parrot, aren't you?" He laughed and pointed out her window. She followed the gesture and saw a smaller road butting up against the one they had been traveling. "Follow that road for five miles and you'll get to the entrance to a state park. TripAdvisor says it costs ten bucks to get in, so there should be a ranger's station or something. Someone will show up tomorrow morning and you can get them to drive you wherever you need to go."

"You're letting me go?" she said again, not believing it could possibly be that easy.

"Yup."

He leaned over her, pulling the door latch and then shoving the passenger side open. "Sorry I'm not driving you all the way, but I could use the extra time to get to wherever I'm led to next."

She put a foot down, standing half in the road while still remaining partially seated in the van. For some reason she said, "You know I'm going to tell them what happened, right?"

He shrugged. "Sure. Like I said, you're a good person. You proved it with the way you acted, and you escaped your own cell. You freed yourself before I freed you. The only people who can be called truly good are the ones who can survive the trials they are given."

"And you? Do you think you're a good person?" she said.

She wasn't sure why she said that, and immediately worried she had just killed herself, because Legion's gaze darkened. "Not the same way you are," he said.

"Then… then what?" she asked, her voice quiet.

He hesitated, thinking. "I'm the thing that came from the Dark Place," he said.

She didn't ask anything further. She got out of the van, still expecting him to lunge out, grab her, and whisk her away to someplace she could be painfully disposed of. None of that happened. She stood in the gravel at the side of the road. Legion leaned over and pulled the door shut. He waited until she began walking down the long road.

He pulled away, the back of the van knocking slightly as something shifted there – though what cargo he held she did not care to think about – and the vehicle disappeared in the night.

She walked to the ranger station. The road was dark, but she felt like she had company. Eyes watched her. Jakey. His eyes were no longer sad, no longer resigned. They felt like the eyes of someone truly alive, and Danielle felt strength surge in her. He wasn't at rest after all – he never would be, because she couldn't rest. She had to be…

"Good," she said, though using the word Legion had described her with felt strange. She said it again. "Good." It felt less strange this time.

Legion was as good as his word. He did not follow her. He did not try to steal her away. She found the ranger's station and waited. A few hours after the sun rose, a kid who looked barely out of high school, with large ears that stuck out from under his ill-fitting park ranger cap, pulled a car into a parking spot near the station.

An hour after *that,* Danielle was sitting in the back of an ambulance, having her blood pressure checked for what felt like the thousandth time, fielding questions from a dozen detectives who asked the same things over and over again.

"What happened?"

"Where did it happen?"

"Where did this guy go?"

And, as often as any other question: "Did he hurt you?"

Danielle had been hurt. She had been kidnapped, bruised, beaten, drugged. She had been threatened with torture and worse.

But had *he* hurt her?

He was crazy.

But he got me out of there.

He killed all those people.

But not me.

He killed Aleksandr.

And Aleksandr would have killed me *eventually.*

"Did he hurt you?"

"No," she finally said. "I don't think he did."

EPILOGUE

Legion watches the woman disappear from his rearview mirror as he pulls away and she walks down the street he showed her. He drives on for a while, until the thumping that has grown louder and louder starts to bother him. He pulls over.

"We don't have time for this," says Fire. He has been amped all evening, the fires that burn forever in his core bright enough that he shines like a newly lit coal. "We gotta go, gotta move, gotta *do*."

"You know that doesn't matter," sniffs Water – a sound that Legion guesses is meant to be dismissive, though the effect is marred by the water in his dead brother's nostrils. What should have been derision sounds more like tar bubbling or –

"Wet farts," says Fire.

"Hey!" shouts Water. "Would you stop saying that?"

Legion smiles. Both his brothers are at each other – they have grown more apart in nature as this particular lesson wore on, and he wonders if they will continue to do so. But whether similar or different, they are still brothers, they still love each other. That is the way of family.

Another thud from behind him reminds Legion why he stopped the car. Before Fire can could say anything snarky, he says, "I *did* promise him."

Fire sighs. Embers spat from his mouth. "Fine," he says.

Legion gets out of the van. He takes the tree with him. He will find a nice spot to plant it at some point. For now, he walks around to the back and opens up the double doors and places the tree next to the large box where the noise is coming from. He pops the latches on the box – an old-fashioned steamer trunk that he picked up years ago – and flips open the lid. He stares down at Aleksandr Antonovich, son of a Russian mobster, and a murderer and sociopath in his own right.

Aleksandr has awakened faster than Legion expected, given how many bones he had already broken, and how many more *Legion* broke in the process of stripping the man of an empty gun. The stump where his hand had been is no longer bleeding, and that is good. After breaking both Aleksandr's arms when he took the unloaded gun away from him, Legion had opted not to use a key on the man's cuffs, but had instead used Sheldon's knife – a very nice one, which had the word "Hemingway" engraved on the handle for some reason – to just cut Aleksandr's hand off. He had used the belt of the dead Sergei to fashion a tourniquet, then hit Aleksandr hard enough in the head that Legion had figured he would be out for at least two days.

"Nope," says Fire. "Two days was *way* off."

"Be nice," says Water. "You were always the one who was good at guessing things like that."

"I suppose," says Fire. Legion can see his brightly burning brother is secretly pleased at the offhanded compliment. Legion winks at Water, who winks back, his eye flushing a half-cup or more of water down his cheek as he does so.

Aleksandr groans. Legion looks at him. "Sorry about the gag," he says.

He loosens the gag and Aleksandr starts screaming. Not in pain, but in rage. "Let me out of here, you mother – "

Legion grabs the stump at the end of Alex's arm and squeezes. Alex gasps. "Do you remember what I said back there?" asks Legion.

"I don't think he can answer," says Water. "He can barely breathe."

"But he *does* remember," says Fire. "You can see it in his eyes."

That is true. Aleksandr's eyes are wide, and he starts shaking his head. Or trying to – he whips once to the side and then Legion slams his head against the inside of the trunk.

"You are the worst kind of person, you know that?" he says, even as he pulls the Hemingway knife out of his pocket. "You don't just kill people or hurt them. No. You have to keep *secrets*." He leans in close. "I *hate* people who keep secrets. I *hate* hypocrites. Saying one thing, doing another." He switches his grip. Reaches down. "So even if I hadn't told you I was going to cut out your tongue if you spoke again – which you definitely did, and which was quite stupid of you under the circumstances – even if you *hadn't* shot off your mouth… I think I'd cut out your lying tongue just the same."

The knife flashes. Aleksandr tries to scream. It comes out strange, mangled by the absence of a tongue.

"I always keep my promises, Aleksandr," he says. "Unlike you, I always do what I say I'll do. You might remember that while we have some quality alone time." He smiles. "I have some very special lessons in mind that I want you to learn."

Legion shuts the trunk. It muffles the screams enough that they won't be bothersome, but not so much that he can't hear and enjoy them.

Legion tosses the tongue into some scrub on the side of the road. Animals will eat it, and that is appropriate, too.

He gets back in the van. Fire and Water wait for him.

"Where now?" asks Water.

"Someplace quiet," says Legion.

"Fun time with Aleksandr. Lots of bad in that man. Lots of lessons to be learned," says Fire. He rubs his hands together and Legion hears the sound of logs crackling in flame.

"Definitely," he says.

"But what about after?" says Water.

Legion shrugs. "More of what we do."

"But… you know it's changing. We've changed – *you've* changed," says Water.

Legion looks at Water. He looks at Fire. He nods at them both. "Yes, things have changed. But whether you're alive or dead, we're together. And I have to admit that I liked what we did."

"Punishing," says Fire.

Legion shakes his head. "Not just that." He cocks his head to the side, trying to think how to express what he feels. "I liked the part where we rescued Danielle."

"She was nice," agrees Water.

"And good," says Fire. "Though she rescued herself, too."

"That was part of what made her worth it," Legion agrees.

"Yes," says Water. "For sure."

"Maybe we'll find someone else nice and good – someone being bothered by someone not so nice, and not so good," Legion says after a moment.

"And…" says Water.

Legion grins at his brothers. "And we'll see what happens next."

His brothers smile back.

Legion puts the van into gear and pulls back into the road and sings the very funny "3-Way" by the gag band The Lonely Hearts. Fire and Water join in, singing the parts of Justin Timberlake and Lady Gaga respectively, and Legion harmonizes and laughs with his two dead brothers as they drive.

Legion does not know where he is going, but he does not mind. He feels once more as though he is being *led* toward some specific place, some specific person. By whom, he still does not know. He knows only this: he is with his brothers; he is happy; and wherever he is going, it will be someplace dark and new and so very *full* of promise.

Because he is a teacher, and there are so many people with sins to destroy, secrets to reveal, and lessons to learn.

A REQUEST FROM THE AUTHOR:

If you loved this book, **I would really appreciate a short review on Amazon (or anywhere else you'd like to post it).** Just click the book's product page, then go to where it says, "Write a review" and let others know what you thought of the book.

Ebook retailers factor reviews into account when deciding which books to push, so a review by you will ABSOLUTELY make a difference to this book, and help other people find it.

And that matters, since that's how I keep writing and (more important) take care of my family. So please drop a quick review – even "Book good. Me like words in book. More words!" is fine and dandy, if that's what's in your heart.

And thanks again!

Author's Note

Stranger Still, for those of you who don't know, is a sequel to my novel *Strangers*. I hate sequels that leave new readers in the dark, so hopefully I've written a self-contained story that is understandable, thrilling, and fun to readers who have never met Legion or his brothers. But if you *do* want to find out more about him, and see how two of "him" died, then please check out *Strangers,* enjoy the stories… and maybe Legion will show up again soon to teach a few more lessons to people who deserve them.

- Michaelbrent Collings

HOW TO GET YOUR FREE BOOK:

As promised, here's a goodie for you: sign up for Michaelbrent's newsletter and you'll get a free book (or maybe more!) with nothing ever to do or buy. Just go to http://writteninsomnia.com/michaelbrents-minions to sign up for your freebie, and you're good to go!

*

FOR WRITERS:

Michaelbrent has helped hundreds of people write, publish, and market their books through articles, audio, video, and online courses. For his online courses, check out http://michaelbrentcollings.thinkific.com

*

ABOUT THE AUTHOR

Michaelbrent is an internationally-bestselling author, produced screenwriter, and member of the Writers Guild of America, but his greatest jobs are being a husband and father. See a complete list of Michaelbrent's books at writteninsomnia.com.

*

FOLLOW MICHAELBRENT

Twitter: twitter.com/mbcollings

Facebook: facebook.com/MichaelbrentCollings

ACKNOWLEDGMENTS

This one was a tough one to write. I'd done a few series before, but they were limited in scope – they were books connected by a single through-line, with a definite end. *Stranger Still* was my first plain ol' sequel, an episode in a life full of (grim) adventures. And I found it to be surprisingly tough, so I have to thank my wife and kids for putting up with me as I came home convinced that this story had beaten me, and who yelled, "CONGRATULATIONS!" as I came home on the night I finally finished it.

Second thanks goes to the Collings Cult. My Street Team deserves so much credit for helping make my book launches fun and rewarding, and for keeping me from letting mistakes and typos run amok in my work and in the wide world. In particular, a big hug and thank you to (in alphabetical order because they are all so amazing I couldn't figure out a "top billing" kind of thing) Chevy Allen, Julie Balla, Shelley Butchert, Julie Castle-Smith, Shannon Coleman, Bonnie Coponen, Doreen, Amanda Dunsdon, Heather Escobedo, Lyn Eubanks, Chris Forbes, Elizabeth Frenette, Hjordis Eythorsdottir, Debra Hartman, Christine Huff, Denise Oien-Italiano, Kellie Purcill, Mary Jude Schmitz, Cherie Spradin, Barb Stoner, Nicole Toscano, and others who found so many errors I am consistently both grateful and embarrassed.

And to my fans and readers, to those who write kind emails and notes about my work, and who review it online and generally spread the word… thank you. I write because I must, but I make a living writing because you permit it.

NOVELS BY MICHAELBRENT COLLINGS

SCAVENGER HUNT
TERMINAL
DARKLING SMILES
PREDATORS
THE DARKLIGHTS
THE LONGEST CON
THE HOUSE THAT DEATH BUILT
THE DEEP
TWISTED
THIS DARKNESS LIGHT
CRIME SEEN
STRANGERS
DARKBOUND
BLOOD RELATIONS:
A GOOD MORMON GIRL MYSTERY
THE HAUNTED
APPARITION
THE LOON
MR. GRAY (aka THE MERIDIANS)
RUN
RISING FEARS

THE COLONY SAGA:
THE COLONY: GENESIS (THE COLONY, Vol. 1)
THE COLONY: RENEGADES (THE COLONY, Vol. 2)
THE COLONY: DESCENT (THE COLONY, VOL. 3)
THE COLONY: VELOCITY (THE COLONY, VOL. 4)
THE COLONY: SHIFT (THE COLONY, VOL. 5)
THE COLONY: BURIED (THE COLONY, VOL. 6)
THE COLONY: RECKONING (THE COLONY, VOL. 7)
THE COLONY OMNIBUS

THE COLONY OMNIBUS II
THE COMPLETE COLONY SAGA BOX SET

YOUNG ADULT AND MIDDLE GRADE FICTION:

THE SWORD CHRONICLES
THE SWORD CHRONICLES: CHILD OF THE EMPIRE
THE SWORD CHRONICLES: CHILD OF SORROWS
THE SWORD CHRONICLES: CHILD OF ASH

THE RIDEALONG
PETER & WENDY: A TALE OF THE LOST
(aka HOOKED: A TRUE FAERIE TALE)
KILLING TIME

THE BILLY SAGA:
BILLY: MESSENGER OF POWERS (BOOK 1)
BILLY: SEEKER OF POWERS (BOOK 2)
BILLY: DESTROYER OF POWERS (BOOK 3)
THE COMPLETE BILLY SAGA (BOOKS 1-3)

Cover image elements by chaiyapruek from Depositphotos.com
cover design by Michaelbrent Collings

website: http://www.michaelbrentcollings.com
email: info@michaelbrentcollings.com

For more information on Michaelbrent's books, including specials and sales; and for info about signings, appearances, and media,
check out his webpage,
Like his Facebook fanpage
or
Follow him on Twitter.

Made in United States
North Haven, CT
19 November 2023

44268778R00245